Duchesses in Disguise

GRACE BURROWES
SUSANNA IVES
EMILY GREENWOOD

Published as a three-novella compilation, Duchesses In Disguise, by Grace Burrowes Publishing, 21 Summit Avenue, Hagerstown, MD 21740.

Cover design by Wax Creative, Inc.

ISBN: 194141947X
ISBN-13: 978-1941419472

TABLE OF CONTENTS

DUCHESS IN THE WILD

GRACE BURROWES

PROLOGUE

"Avoid the London Season, you said. Enjoy the peace and quiet of the beautiful dales." Sir Greyville Trenton fell silent as his gelding slipped, then righted itself—again.

"The dales are beautiful," Colonel Nathaniel Stratton replied over the huffing of the horses and *slip-slop* of hooves on the wet road.

"If you like varying degrees of wet as far as the eye can see," Kit Stirling added. "Or if you've a penchant for cold. I haven't felt my toes since the first mile out of Lesser Puddlebury."

Grey brought Zeus to a halt as they crested yet another rise and were smacked in the face with yet another wet, frigid breeze. Early spring in Yorkshire left much to be desired.

"What the devil is that?"

"It's a coach wheel," Stratton said, extracting a flask from the folds of his greatcoat.

Twenty yards ahead, the wheel protruded above the grassy swale at the side of the road like a dark flag of surrender. The ruts gouged in the roadway indicated a recent accident.

"Save your brandy, Nathaniel," Stirling suggested. "The survivors might need it."

The coach lay on its side, an enormous traveling vehicle that had apparently taken a curve too hastily. The mud-spattered horses were held by a young groom at the head of the leaders. The lad was soaked to the skin, and looked as if the next gust of wind might blow him down the lane.

The door popped open, and a head swathed in a scarf emerged.

"Halloo!" Stratton called. "Have you need of assistance?"

"Ever the gallant soldier," Grey muttered. "At least we'll die of exposure in company."

"Your sunny nature will prevent that tragedy," Stirling replied.

A long-barreled horse pistol appeared in the hand of the person trapped in the coach. "Stay back."

"*Women*," Grey said. "Worse, we've found a damsel in distress—an armed damsel." The lady had a slight accent, something Continental.

"My favorite kind," Stirling replied, riding forward. "Madam!" he called. "If you're in difficulties, we'd like to render aid."

The lady's head disappeared like a hedgehog popping down into its burrow. She emerged a moment later, still brandishing her pistol.

"Come no closer."

"Female logic at its finest," Grey said. "We're to render gentlemanly aid by freezing our arses off at gunpoint. This damsel has no notion how to be properly in distress."

"Who are they?" the lady asked, wiggling her pistol in the direction of Grey and Stirling.

"Those good fellows are my guests at Rose Heath manor, my home."

"Perhaps the introductions might wait," Stirling suggested. "We're two miles from safety, the rain shows no signs of letting up, and it's getting colder by the moment."

The lady once again dodged down into her coach-burrow, then emerged *sans* pistol, a second scarved head beside her.

"Our coachman should return at any moment," the second lady said. She spoke with great—utterly irrational—certainty regarding the prodigal coachman's impending arrival.

"That is at least a baroness," Grey observed. "A woman who expects a man in service to defy the very gods of weather when her comfort is at issue was to the manor born."

"Then let's get her and her friend to the manor posthaste," Stirling said, "before we all freeze for want of somebody to make proper introductions."

I miss the jungle, where welcome was either an honest threat of death or immediate and genuine hospitality.

The thought went wafting away on a sideways gust of rain. Or possibly sleet.

Stratton rode forth and touched a gloved finger to his hat brim. "Ladies, pleased to meet you. We three gentlemen are at your service. Your good coachman might well return, but that he'd leave you here while a storm howls down from Scotland, does not speak well for his judgment. We offer you a cozy hearth not two miles away and assurances of our gentlemanly conduct."

Exactly what a trio of highwaymen would say. Grey rode forward to join his friends at the lip of the ditch. "Ladies, we'll all soon succumb to the elements, making your understandable caution an exercise in futility. Take your chances in the ditch or with us. In the ditch you will drown. With us, you will merely endure bad company, but do so in the midst of adequate creature comforts."

"He makes sense," said a third woman.

Good God, how many of them were in there?

Grey nodded. "Thank you for that observation." He wasn't about to take off his hat in this weather. "Perhaps you'd allow us to make haste as well as sense?"

Some sort of silent conference ensued, with the ladies exchanging glances among themselves. The first one, the pistol-wielding woman, hoisted herself from the vehicle with a nimbleness that surprised, given her voluminous cloak and skirts.

"You," she said, gesturing at Grey. "I'll ride with you."

"If you can contain your enthusiasm for my company," Grey said, riding as close to the coach as he could, "I shall endeavor to do likewise regarding your own. Sir Greyville Trenton, at your service."

She was a youngish woman, and yet, her posture as she stood on her upturned coach was regal, despite the dirty weather pouring down around her. Grey waited—patience was another of his few gifts—until he realized the lady was trying not to smile.

At him.

"Madam, you are welcome to enjoy the invigorating weather at your leisure once my horse is safely ensconced in his stall. That objective remains two miles distant, so I must ask you, for the sake of all concerned, to consider getting into this saddle with all due haste."

She put a hand on his shoulder, adopted an approximate side-saddle perch before him, and tucked her skirts about her.

"You may proceed, sir, and please inform this good beast that one ditch per day is my limit."

That was an Italian accent. An *imperious* Italian accent, something of an oxymoron in Grey's experience.

"Of course, madam. Zeus, take heed."

Grey's mount shuffled back onto the muddy road, while Grey—for the first time since returning to England—also tried not to smile.

CHAPTER ONE

Francesca Maria Lucia Theresa Amadora Heppledorn Pomponio Pergolesi, dowager Duchess of San Mercato, sat as properly as she could, given that she was in the wrong kind of saddle, on the wrong sort of horse, in the wrong country, in the wrong season.

Also with the wrong man, but the concept of a *right* man defied definition in any of the languages with which she was familiar.

Her English was in good repair, but she'd forgotten so much about the land of her parents' birth. The cold, of course, but also how bleak the light was, what little light England had in early spring. How relentless the wind, how cheerless the landscape.

She missed Italy, where being a widow of rank was a fine status; where sunlight, hearty food, excellent wine, and warmth had been hers in abundance.

"Madam will please remain awake," the gentleman sharing the saddle said. "If you fall asleep, the cold can steal over you and create injuries you'll never recall receiving. The ensuing infections can end your life."

His voice would give her a permanent chill before the elements did. "I'm not likely to fall asleep in such charming company, Sir Greyville."

"I beg your pardon?"

He was a big man, and he moved with his horse easily. When Francesca had spoken, he'd tipped his head down to put his ear nearer her mouth. The fool hadn't even a scarf to protect those ears.

"I'm awake," she said more loudly. If nothing else, proximity to Sir Greyville would ensure she remained conscious. With a hand on each rein, he was all but embracing her, and because of the motion of the horse's walk, she was hard put not to bump against him.

"You will have a more secure seat if you permit yourself to lean against me, and you'll make Zeus's job easier as well."

"You're very solicitous of your—"

The dratted animal chose that moment to put a foot wrong and slip in the mud. The jostling tossed Francesca against Sir Greyville, who remained relaxed, steady, and calm behind her.

The horse plodded on, and Francesca gave up the battle for dignity in favor of greater safety.

"Take my scarf," she said. "If I turn up my collar, I'll stay warm enough."

"Take the reins."

Very odd, to converse with a man in imperatives, but for the present situation, expedient. Sir Greyville soon had her scarf wrapped about his neck and ears, while Francesca bundled into his chest and missed Italy.

"What brings three women out to the dales at this time of year?" Sir Greyville asked.

Well, perdition. Englishmen ruled the world—the parts they wanted to plunder—and thus the world was supposed to answer to them.

"A coach, Sir Greyville. A coach brought us out to the dales."

"If we're both to impose on Colonel Stratton's hospitality for the foreseeable future, I had best warn you now. I am a scientist, madam. I study flora and fauna in exotic locations when funds permit. My mind is prone to questioning, to assembling cause and effect from observed data, the way some men must wager or ride to hounds."

He used the word *scientist* as if it were a lofty title—cherubim, seraphim, archduke, scientist. Francesca had agreed with Olivia and Mary Alice that none of the ladies should disclose her true identity for the duration of this holiday— the roads were doubly unsafe for women of wealth—and yet, she had the sense Sir Greyville wouldn't care that he rode with a duchess.

He wasn't a fortune hunter then. Thank God for small mercies.

"I see neither flora nor fauna to speak of," Francesca replied. She saw green and wet, wet and green, with a topping of slate-gray clouds. Perhaps the epithet Merry Olde England was intended to be ironic.

"In this environment, my objective is to organize and edit the notes gathered from more than three years' investigation into the Amazonian jungles. A lack of biological distractions serves that goal. You have yet to explain what brings you to this corner of Yorkshire."

Weariness brought her here, along with despair, boredom, and—Pietro would laugh heartily at the notion—even some lingering grief, five years after losing her husband.

"Like you, I seek peace and quiet. London at this time of year becomes crowded and pestilentially social."

Widowhood had allowed Francesca to retreat from the worst of the entertainments for a few years, but she was in England now, where the London Season was an orgy of matchmaking in the guise of a social whirl.

Execrable English cuisine didn't help one bit, and the chilly reserve of the typical Englishman tempted a sane woman to leave the realm. The impecunious English bachelor, by contrast, was the social equivalent of a barnacle.

The horse started up another incline, leaning into the wind, and the weariness that Sir Greyville had warned Francesca of threatened to overtake her. This was her life now, varying degrees of uphill, bad footing, and bleak terrain.

How had this happened? How had a lively, good-humored, young girl, appreciative of all the privileges of her station, become a creature to whom a muddy ditch did not look nearly as perilous as it should?

"That's our destination," Sir Greyville said as they topped the rise some moments later. "We'll be at the gates within a mile, and the going will be easier after that."

Across the dreary landscape, nestled at the foot of a great hill, sat a manor house. From this distance, details were obscured by rain and mist. Lamps lit on the front terrace and along the drive gave the edifice a fairy-tale quality in the afternoon's deepening gloom.

"I have it on the best authority that we admire the view at the risk of imperiling your dear horse," she said. "Onward, Sir Greyville."

He sent the horse forward without comment. Perhaps Sir Greyville was the kind of man who made a mistress of his work. The Italians understood passion, whether aimed at a vocation, a pastime, or another person. No cold reserve for them.

Sometimes not much sense either, though.

Francesca had plenty of sense, which was why, purely for the sake of conserving warmth, she tucked nearer to Sir Greyville and closed her eyes.

* * *

What sort of woman brought the scent of jasmine with her even in the midst of a pounding deluge?

The lady's hair tickled Grey's chin, the same way her scent tickled his awareness. Pleasing, soothing, enticing—jasmine had a mischief all its own when a man had lived in the tropics for years at a time.

The lady nestled closer, and purely to secure her more safely in the saddle, Grey switched his reins to one hand and wrapped an arm about her middle.

Somewhere in the jungles, he'd been freed of the bothersome longing for female company. Other biologists on the expedition had taken pleasure with the local women, but how was a fellow to explain that the relationship was one of mutual convenience rather than something more permanent when that fellow spoke very little of the lady's language?

And then there was the matter of children. A man who'd leave his own progeny behind was no sort of gentleman, in Grey's opinion, and thus he'd earned all manner of nicknames.

Saint Greyville.

His Holiness.

Sir Monk.

Deprivation had come to his rescue just as the taunts, in combination with the heat, bugs, poisonous plants, jungle predators, and bickering biologists, had plucked his last nerve. Somebody had made off with all of the expedition's rations and two of their boats. The simple challenge of preserving his life had taken precedence over the urge to procreate, an observation Grey would document for the greater scientific community, just as soon as he could deposit—

Who the devil was this woman, anyhow?

"I don't know your name, madam."

"Francesca… Heppledorn… Pomponio."

She spoke as if selecting names from a list, and it occurred to Grey he might have a courtesan in his arms, or a thief, or one of those Italian wives given to poisoning inconvenient husbands.

He took another surreptitious whiff of jasmine before launching his investigation. "My guess is Amalfi Coast, or thereabouts, but you're either not native to Italy, or you were educated at a very young age by people not native to Italy."

She lifted her head from his shoulder. "You can tell that simply by listening to me?"

"I am a scientist and well-traveled, and have met many of your countrymen in pursuit of my investigations." Intrepid lot, the Italians, if prone to contention.

"My father was an English diplomat in an Italian court. I was born and raised in Italy, and Papa thought it prudent to educate me in keeping with the local culture. My mother demanded that I have some exposure to England, so I was sent here occasionally for summers with my grandparents and for a year of finishing school where I met the other ladies in our party. What's your excuse?"

Her story was plausible. Italy was a collection of courts, states, duchies, and shifting alliances—enough to provide employment for an army of Englishmen who preferred good wine and ample sunshine with their diplomatic intrigue and exotic mistresses.

"My excuse?"

"For abandoning the shores of Merry Olde England? You are not a Captain Sir Greyville, or a Colonel Sir Greyville, so you chose to turn your back on your homeland and go larking about in the tropics."

"I wanted to explore the world beyond Kent and Mayfair, of which there is more than most English boys can dream."

Not the whole truth—he'd wanted to get free of his father's expectations and get on with the thankless business of being an earl's spare.

"You don't think English *girls* dream, Sir Greyville?"

Contentious, indeed, though she wasn't strictly Italian. "It's adequately documented that female children of many nationalities dream, but in the normal course, one expects they dream of a home of their own, some babies, a good tisane for a megrim, or a safe lying in. I haven't gathered data on the subject of an English girl's dreams, so I ought not to speculate."

"Perhaps you have noted in your vast observations that the *normal course* is typically the course that benefits men."

"Benefits men? If it does, that's because to the male falls the duty of providing and protecting," Grey countered. "Without his good efforts, which society justifiably supports, the female, given her weaker physical attributes and burdened by the duty to produce young, would soon find herself at the mercy of predators and unkind elements."

Let her argue with that from the comfort of his saddle.

"If the blighted male could keep his breeches buttoned, the burden of producing young would not become one of the most regular threats to the lady's life. Moreover, the reckless incompetence of a male coachman must be considered when assigning responsibility for my current predicament. Then too, I have yet to see women take up arms for twenty years and leave a continent in ruins."

Her arguments were not without a scintilla of logic, but that was the trouble with amateurs playing at science. They could concoct fancies from anecdotes, casual reasoning, and passionate convictions that bore only a passing relation to logical discourse.

The gates of Rose Heath manor house came into view, and because Stratton ran a proper establishment, the gatehouse was occupied, and a welcome light shone from its windows. As the horses descended the final declivity, a signal light also appeared on the roof of the gatehouse.

"Well?" the lady demanded. "Do you admit that ordering the universe to suit the whims of men rests not on a scientific foundation but a selfish one?"

"Mrs. Pomponio, a gentleman does not argue with a lady."

"He who refuses to fight cannot lose the battle, though he can lose the war." In perfect Latin. "Who said that?"

"*I did*, and I can say it in six other languages."

She had Grey by two languages, and that included the native dialect he'd picked up in the jungle.

He would not ask her how many of her instructors had been men. "The manor house has been alerted to our arrival. You'll have a hot bath, sustenance, and a warm bed within the hour."

The household would not know to heat enough water for six baths, so the gentlemen—coach-wrecking, rutting, war-mongering incompetents though they might be—would have to wait for their comforts until the ladies had been accommodated.

"I am not normally so combative," Mrs. Pomponio said. "I apologize for my lack of graciousness. You are being most gallant."

"Gallant? That's doing it a bit brown, don't you think? It wasn't my decision to rescue you, but rather our mutual host's, and we haven't gone so much as ten yards out of our way to bring you to safety."

Though Stratton and his lady had turned off at some point. Stirling was bringing up the rear with his sodden damsel, who looked none too pleased to be in the company of a notorious London rakehell.

Mrs. Pomponio shifted, tucking her scarf more securely about Grey's neck. This inflicted another whiff of jasmine on him, as well as the novel experience of being *fussed*.

"I would rather you were full of manly drivel and flirtation, Sir Greyville. If you continue being so blunt and honest, I might begin to like you."

"Can't have that, can we?" For then Grey might find himself liking her, with her odd notions, lively mind, imperious speech, and sweet scents.

"I am a Continental widow of comfortable means, Sir Greyville. For the most part, I can *have* whoever and whatever I please. Consider yourself warned." Mrs. Pomponio settled into his arms and closed her eyes, as if napping the last few hundred yards was what she pleased at that moment, and bedamned to sleet, logic, cold, and Grey himself.

Grey let her have the last word, despite all temptation to the contrary.

He hadn't held a woman in years, and her last assertion—that a Continental widow of means was free to dally at will—was true enough, provided the parties were discreet. Fortunately, his own inclination to dally—his potential, possible, *hypothetical* inclination to dally after three endless years of abstinence—would be entirely subsumed by the burning need to get his notes into publishable form.

Thank the everlasting powers for science, yet again.

* * *

To be held in a masculine embrace that sought nothing other than to provide security was lovely.

Also bothersome.

Francesca resented Sir Greyville's gallantry even as she admitted she was starved for proof that *homo gentlemanliness* was not an extinct species. The men who fared best at the ducal court in San Mercato were handsome, flattering, utterly selfish, and as randy as boar hogs in spring. Her father had fit right in, as had her husband.

Francesca had no reason to believe Englishmen were any different, and yet, Sir Greyville's hands hadn't once wandered where they ought not, his conversation had borne no sly innuendos, and his smiles…

He hadn't smiled. Not once. *How dare he be so genuine?*

Very likely he'd thought Francesca's warning about dallying where she pleased a sophisticated jest. In fact, she hadn't had the nerve to dally anywhere, not with half the court plotting her demise and the other half trying to propose to her.

Sir Greyville smelled good, of fine wool, cedar soap, leather. Masculine, English scents that put Francesca in mind of girlhood summers in Dorset.

Worse, Sir Greyville Trenton *felt* good. He was solid and warm, a bulwark of masculine confidence and competence. In bed, he'd know what he was about—provided he didn't lapse into biology lectures between rounds of frolic.

As the horse slogged up the drive, the manor house loomed larger and larger. This was not a quaint country cottage, but rather, a substantial and well-maintained dwelling.

A fountain in the middle of the circular drive boasted a sculpture of three swans that would have been a convincing addition to the Palazzo Ducale in Venice. Numerous windows marched along the building's front.

Wealth—old, understated wealth—stood before Francesca, and she respected that. A man who commanded resources of this magnitude could have ridden past a toppled coach without a backward glance.

She shivered, despite Sir Greyville's sheltering presence at her back.

"Almost there," he said. "You will be cosseted and pampered within an inch of your reason. Only by virtue of unrelenting self-discipline do I make any progress with my work at all."

"Couldn't you be self-disciplined later?" Francesca asked. "You've endured privations without number, for years. A little cosseting might put you to rights."

"I assure you, madam, I am as much to rights as I care to be put. Science is a competitive undertaking, and findings that remain unpublished do nothing to fund future expeditions. Time waits for no man, particularly not the man of science."

Francesca was growing to hate the word *science*.

"Well, I hope a hot bath waits for this woman of limited patience and frozen toes. I could eat a banquet about now as well, provided the menu included something other than boiled beef, boiled cabbage, and brown bread. If the English could devise a way to boil bread, they'd probably do that as well."

The horse came to a halt beside the mounting block without any apparent guidance from his owner.

"I believe you describe the dumpling, more or less. Feel free to argue with me, however, for the dumpling has no leavening and you seem to enjoy airing your opinions. Lean forward, that I might dismount."

Francesca complied, though she was impressed that Sir Greyville knew how to make dumplings, and would admit as much.

He got off the horse and immediately the cold was worse. The wind cut like so many blades of stiff grass, the sleet came down with more force. Grooms had come out to take the horses, and Francesca had to consciously review the process for getting out of the saddle.

Sir Greyville put his hands at her waist. Francesca braced her hands against his shoulders and prepared for a graceful descent to *terra firma.*

Her boots hit the ground, pain shot up both legs, and the *terra* refused to hold *firma.* She slipped, slid, sloshed, and would have gone down into the mud except for Sir Greyville's steadying hold.

"It's the damned cold," he said. "It steals into the limbs like a fever, but worse. I spent three years longing for the English countryside. I must have been demented to miss this place."

He scooped Francesca up against his chest and strode toward the house. A footman scampered beside them, an enormous umbrella doing nothing to hold the elements at bay.

"I am capable of walking," Francesca said, though her dratted teeth chattered.

"I am *not* capable of providing a decorous escort when the sooner we're out of this blighted weather, the less likely we'll be to die from exposure. If your extremities are numb, you are already at risk of harm."

He could lecture while he hauled her about, though Francesca stifled further protest when being hauled about was such a lovely experience. Whatever else might be true about men of science, their expeditions made them fit and surefooted.

When Sir Greyville got to the front door, Francesca expected him to set her down, but he simply kept moving past the liveried footman, pausing only long enough for the aging butler to whisk off his hat.

Francesca had a vague impression of soaring ceilings, acres of oak paneling, and sparkling pier glasses before Sir Greyville carried her into what looked like a small library.

He deposited her on a sofa before a roaring fire, then tossed two bricks of peat on the flames.

"This is the estate office, and the fire is always kept blazing in here at my request. My notes are arrayed about. Don't touch them. I have a system. Disturb it at your mortal peril."

"You rescue me from the elements only to threaten me with your wrath?" The heat was heavenly, the scent of peat delightful.

"You're a quick study." He went down on one knee and began fussing with the laces of Francesca's boot. "I like that in a woman. So many ladies feign a lack of wits, thinking it attractive. It's not. Nothing could be more uninteresting to the typical Englishman than dull-wittedness in a lady."

"You've courted many Englishmen that you've gathered data regarding their preferences?"

Sir Greyville paused between boots. "Have you courted many Englishmen?"

The scarf lay loosely about his shoulders, and Francesca got her first good look at him. His hair would probably be auburn when dry, possibly Titian. His nose belonged on an emperor, and the rest of his features lived up to that nose.

Strong, masculine, by no means pretty, but hopelessly attractive.

He was a man in his prime, his complexion darker than most Englishmen's, and he'd age wonderfully.

Unless one of those tropical fevers carried him off prematurely, or some woman delivered him a mortal blow he'd never see coming.

"What are you doing with my boots, sir?"

"Getting them off of you. I assume your fingers are stiff with cold, and the last thing Stratton needs is a sick woman malingering under his roof or passing along an ague to his small daughter. Do you drink tea, coffee, or chocolate? Perhaps you'd rather a toddy or a medicinal glass of brandy?"

"I am perfectly capable of removing my own footwear." Francesca ran her fingers through his hair, flicking the dampness from it. "Your gallantry is appreciated, but unnecessary. Perhaps you'd best get your own boots off, lest the colonel have a sick Englishman under his roof, hmm?"

Sir Greyville's hair was marvelously soft. For a moment, they remained in a tableau, with Francesca engaging in some retaliatory cosseting—he'd presumed to unlace her boots—and Sir Greyville oddly docile on his knees before her, his lashes lowered.

He rose in one motion. "I'll send a maid to you. Don't touch my notes."

Francesca let him have the last word.

Why on earth would she bother touching his notes when touching him was so much more interesting?

CHAPTER TWO

Because Grey had misrepresented his publication schedule as pressing to both Stratton and Stirling, he was not expected to take meals with the rest of the household. He was permitted as eccentric a routine as he pleased, which was very eccentric indeed.

And yet, nothing much was getting accomplished. A lassitude had afflicted Grey ever since arriving here at Rose Heath, and while his mind toyed with ideas—and worries—his work did not progress.

That relative inactivity might explain why he'd taken such notice of Mrs. Pomponio's boots when he'd unlaced them for her two hours ago. Her footwear was beautiful, if impractical. Soft, tooled leather with a ridiculous number of hooks and buttons. Restoring those boots would cost some servant a significant effort.

"You there," Grey said to a maid passing by as he emerged from his bedchamber. "If you'd please fetch a substantial tray to the estate office, I'll take my evening meal while I work."

The maid looked like she wanted to say something, or ask him something, but she merely bobbed a curtsey and scurried off. The help at Rose Heath manor was blessedly well trained, and thus Grey had enjoyed a hot bath despite the presence of the stranded ladies.

He'd enjoyed carrying Mrs. Pomponio inside from the drive too, male brute that he was. He'd claimed to her that his show of strength had been for pragmatic reasons, but in fact, he'd simply wanted to be a gentleman—a useful, helpful creature worthy of a lady's notice.

Elsewhere in the house, Stratton was probably presiding over a delightful meal with the three lady guests and the flirtatious Stirling. The witticisms would flow along with the wine, and the company would be as merry as it was tedious.

"Everything bores me of late," he muttered, sailing into the estate office.

The heat hit him with a welcome impact, as did the sight of his notes, all exactly where he'd left them.

Mrs. Pomponio was where he'd left her too, though she was wrapped in a man's night robe and a small hot air balloon's worth of silk nightgown. She looked quintessentially English, with golden hair cascading over her shoulder in a thick plait and the elegant height of the Saxon aristocrat.

At present, that height was curled on the sofa before the fire, and the lady was softly snoring. Completing this picture of feminine contentment were thick wool stockings on her feet—men's stockings, if Grey weren't mistaken.

"Madam."

Her breathing continued in the slow, relaxed rhythm of restful sleep.

She was a widow, and she'd had a trying day. Grey decided to leave her to her slumbers, rather than rouse her. Not strictly proper, but then, neither was ending up in a muddy ditch at the mercy of the elements.

He sat at the desk and resumed transcribing where he'd left off. If he contemplated the magnitude of his task, he'd never complete it. The sheer variety of life in the Amazon jungle was staggering, as was the quantity of rain, the mass of insects, and the array of potentially fatal mistakes a biologist might make.

How long he sat scribbling away, he did not know, but he eventually became aware of Mrs. Pomponio staring at him.

"Madam is awake."

"My eyes are open," she said. "Not quite the same thing. What time is it?"

"Going on nine."

She rose and stretched with her back to Grey, and damned if he didn't find her unselfconscious maneuver attractive. Cats stretched with that thorough, unapologetic sensuality. She put him in mind not of the nimble little ocelot, but of the sleek jaguar—the cat that kills with one leap, according to the guides.

"I'm sorry I fell asleep in your sanctum sanctorum," she said, rustling over to the desk, "but for the first time in ages, I'm not cold. You have an interesting collection of notes."

Grey rose, torn between outrage that she'd trespass on his notes and the temptation to invite her to stay warm as long as she pleased.

"I asked you not to disturb my documentation. Was my request in any way unclear?"

She patted his cravat. "You didn't ask. You ordered me not to touch your notes. More than once. A man giving me orders is novel enough in my life that I remark such occasions. Because you have all these papers arranged in piles by date, I didn't need to touch them to read those pages plainly on display. Have you considered arranging them by topic instead of date? I assume that's what the symbols in the right-hand corner are for."

"They are."

She'd bathed, and the scent of dear old English lavender soap clung to her person along with a hint of that damnable jasmine. The nerve of the woman, smelling so luscious.

Her eyes were gray—he'd wondered—and without boots she was a good six inches shorter than he. In bed, the fit would be exquisite.

Grey was wondering if she might caress his hair again—because he was daft, of course—when a knock sounded on the door.

"Come in," he yelled.

A footman and a maid brought substantial trays into the room and set them on the low table before the hearth. The maid built up the fire, the footman lit an extra sconce, and the pair of them withdrew with a murmured, "G'night, ma'am. Sir."

"Did you order dinner for me?" Mrs. Pomponio asked, taking a seat before the tray. "Most considerate of you. I hadn't anything suitable to put on after my bath and couldn't possibly dine in company as I'm presently attired. Doubtless, our trunks should be here sometime tomorrow, but until then, I'm a monument to purloined clothing."

That was *his dinner* she was about to consume. Grey sat beside her, prepared to tell her as much, but she picked up a roll and tore it open with her fingers.

"Is there anything on earth more delightful than fresh bread?" she murmured.

"I can think of a few things."

She gave him a look, steam wafting from the roll along with the fragrance of yeasty sustenance. "Such as?"

Thick wool stockings on a pair of slim, feminine feet. Delicate, contented snoring from the couch while Grey finally made some progress on the section of his treatise that dealt with plant poisons.

"Sunshine, in moderation," Grey said. "Healthy children and how they can laugh at almost anything. Old women telling stories around the fire at night. A sharp razor against the whiskers, safe passage home. Shall I butter that roll for you?"

"I can't possibly eat all of this by myself. You must join me, or I'll earn the enmity of the cook. Never a good idea, to disappoint the cook."

She passed him a butter knife, and Grey nearly forgave her for reading his notes. Her diplomatic upbringing had given her the gift of convivial conversation, and before Grey knew it, he'd eaten two sandwiches, finished a bowl of soup she'd claimed was too bland for her palate, and consumed a sizable plum tart.

The soup *was* bland, though it was hot and hearty, and the conversation was charming. Mrs. Pomponio told him of spilling punch on her own bodice to get away from a presuming ambassador, "pulling a swoon" to earn freedom from another state dinner, and pretending an ignorance of French to avoid the flirtatious advances of a young colonel.

The food disappeared, the fire burned down, and half the bottle of merlot was consumed as well. Despite her outlandish attire, Mrs. Pomponio had shared a meal with Grey as graciously as any grand hostess, and she'd eased some of his restlessness too.

"May I assume your French is as facile as your English and your Italian?" he asked, topping up her wine glass.

"French isn't difficult if your Latin and Italian are on firm footing, and in Italy, we heard French all the time. Why?"

Grey ranged an arm along the back of the sofa and prepared to humble himself—or give the lady something to do besides snoop through his notes.

"One of the pressing tasks before me is to solicit funds from those who support the sciences and have the means to finance expeditions. As much as I must organize my notes and publish my findings, I must also attract the support of a worthy sponsor for my next venture."

"Always, we must be practical," she said. "I take it you have potential sponsors in France?"

"One can't know until one asks, as difficult as it is to request anything of anybody. My family would offer some support for my endeavors, but they tend to confuse support and control."

At every turn.

She took a considering sip of wine. "How can they control you when you're thousands of miles away, beyond the reach of civilization?"

Insightful question. "They will offer funds, provided I marry the bride of their choice. I'll capitulate to that scheme, thinking that one must marry, and if doing so enlarges society's grasp of the known world, it's an acceptable compromise."

"One wonders why the lady would find it acceptable, for she'd be essentially widowed for years at a time while you were off doing all of this commendable enlarging, and she wouldn't be able to remarry or even frolic."

That had troubled Grey as well. What sort of woman married with the expectation that her husband would cheerfully abandon her for the company of insects, poisonous plants, and deadly snakes?

"The scheme had many flaws."

"I gather you are as yet unmarried."

"With the assurances of the young lady involved, I was willing, but my brother took me aside weeks before the nuptials and informed me that, well, yes, the funds were promised, though not at the level initially proffered. The settlements had been drafted, all was in readiness, but a man new to the institution of holy matrimony would be better off exploring, say, the standing stones no farther away than Orkney, preferably in summer. I was to content myself with the study of rocks, for God's sake. Rocks that had been sitting plainly in evidence when Gilgamesh was a lad. No wonder the young lady had had no qualms."

"You were to study rocks indefinitely?"

"Until two male children were thriving in my nursery, and I know what would have come next."

She set the wine glass down. "You would be exhorted not to leave your children without a father figure, or to deny their grandmother's fondest wish for a granddaughter, and of course the granddaughter would desperately need her papa and at least one sister. Family can be most vexing. What did you do?"

"Wrote the young lady an apology, marshaled what private resources I had on hand, and took off for South America. That was nearly four years ago. The young lady married another and has two sons. My brother apologized and said the entire situation was all Mama's fault. She is a countess. If you've not met many titled women, they are a species unto themselves."

She curled her feet up onto the cushions. "Oh?"

"I admire my mother without limit, but I draw the line at studying damned rocks for years on end. In any case, my French is good, not perfect. If I'm to correspond with potential funding sources in France, a review of my prose would be appreciated."

He was asking for Mrs. Pomponio's help, but resorting to that handy fig leaf of English syntax, passive voice.

She bounced about on the cushion, tucking her hems over her toes, her braid inadvertently brushing against Grey's arm.

"I will edit your French," Mrs. Pomponio said. "You have shared your cozy office with me, though I do think your work would be easier if you let me organize your notes by subject."

He liked looking at her, he liked talking with her, he liked arguing with her. Some part of his rational mind was strongly admonishing him that this way lay much trouble, but the wanderer who'd finally come home—to a cold, dreary welcome—ignored the warning.

"You might be departing on the morrow," he said. "You'd get partway through the job and leave all in disarray. I have little tolerance for disarray, else I'd never survive my explorations."

"We'll work on your tolerance," she said, patting his hand. "Surely Colonel Stratton would not begrudge three ladies a few days to recover from an accident and repair our coach?"

Why hadn't Grey done a more thorough inspection of the vehicle when he'd had the chance?

Because he'd been too preoccupied with the lady atop it.

"I'll draft my correspondence this evening, and in the morning you can start with my French letters—"

Oh God. He hadn't said that, had he? Yes, he had. He'd referred to contraceptive sheaths by their most common vernacular appellation and set the lady's eyes to dancing.

"I'm sure your French letters will be all that a lady could wish for," she replied, rising. "The meal and your good company have made me quite relaxed. I can hope my bedroom has been adequately warmed by now, and I'll see you— and your letters—in the morning."

"Shall I light you up?"

"Please. I am certain I know where my bedroom is—the Peacock Room, if I recall—but I was certain I'd arrive safely to my destination when I set out this morning."

Grey took a taper from the mantel and used it to light the carrying candle on the sideboard. "Had your expectations been met, my evening would have been impoverished."

That specimen of gentlemanly drivel happened to be the truth, which might be why Mrs. Pomponio merely smiled and took his arm.

She was not a giggling girl, or a countess who regarded her family as so many chess pieces.

And she'd not touched his notes, not in the strictest sense of the words.

Grey led her upstairs in silence, their footsteps muffled by thick carpets. The house was too big to be anything but frigid in the midst of an early spring storm, and yet, for Grey, a little warmth lingered. He'd spent an enjoyable evening with a lady who didn't expect brilliant wit or boring small talk from him, and she'd agreed to read his French letters.

He almost burst out laughing halfway up the steps, but instead settled for kissing Mrs. Pomponio's cheek when he bid her good night.

If she was to read his letters, he'd best spend the rest of the evening writing the damned things, hadn't he?

* * *

How could a man who was so clearly brilliant at his calling be an utter dunderhead about asking for funds?

Francesca sat at Sir Greyville's desk, reading letters that swung from abject pleading, to exhortation, to flights of biological hypothesis, to claims of grand medical contributions (and profits), back to scolding.

As a professor, Sir Greyville would be magnificent. His ability to advocate on behalf of science was touchingly inept.

"Ah, Mrs. Pomponio, you are an early riser."

The great scientist stood in the doorway to the estate office, a cup of something steaming in one hand, a slice of buttered toast in the other.

"Good morning, Sir Greyville. I trust you slept well?"

He closed the door with his foot. "You may trust no such thing. I have yet to acclimate to this dreary latitude, and everything from the quality of the daylight, to the cold, to the texture of the sheets against my skin, conspires to keep me from the arms of Morpheus."

Even in a royal pet he exuded energy and rationality.

"I slept wonderfully, thank you," Francesca said. "To be safe and warm and in the company of good people with hot chocolate and shortbread to break my fast was a much rosier fate than I courted yesterday."

He wrinkled his lordly proboscis. "Quite. How bad are the letters?"

So that's what had him worried?

"Awful. Your French is good, with just enough minor imperfections that the recipient can feel superior to yet another hopeless Englishman, but your technique is sadly wanting."

He slouched into a chair on the other side of the desk. "I know. I haven't the knack of cajoling, which puts me at a sore disadvantage. I had a devil of a time at public school. Can't say the young ladies thought much of me either. No charm."

On that signal understatement, he bit off a corner of his toast with good, straight, white teeth.

"You have integrity and brains," Francesca said, passing over the first of the letters. "I took a few liberties with your prose."

He set aside his coffee—the scent was wonderful—but not his toast and munched his way through the letter.

Francesca enjoyed watching him, enjoyed watching his gaze move across the page as he demolished his toast slice. That he would approve of her efforts mattered more than it should.

"You're a damned genius," he said, springing to his feet. "This is brilliant. A touch of flattery, a bit of regret for the loss to the world should its wonders remain needlessly unexplored, a casual disparaging of those squandering means on idle pleasures… You're very, very good, Mrs. Pomponio."

His praise was precious, not only for its sincerity, but also for its uniqueness. Men complimented duchesses incessantly. Francesca had endured odes to her eyes, her hair, her wit, her hands, her grace, her eyebrows, for God's sake.

The men offering all of this praise did not bother to ascertain whether the compliment bore any relation to the woman at whom the words were flung.

"I'm glad the letter meets with your approval. I was raised by diplomats, and delicacy of expression was served at every meal. I was also my father's secretary and amanuensis after my mother died. I revised a few more of your letters, but have several yet to read."

Francesca had been eager for something useful to do, something interesting. After peeking at Sir Greyville's notes yesterday—but not touching them—she'd gained an impression of a restless mind as insightful as it was observant as it was imaginative.

God forbid this man should be shackled to some dreary old ring of stones for the rest of his days.

He peered down at her, his expression quite severe. "Madam, I do not approve of this letter, I damn near venerate it. Show me the others."

Another order. A woman whose letters were worthy of veneration could make a few rules.

"Say please."

He aimed another glower at her over the last of his toast. "Everlasting goddamned please, I beg you, won't you please, I entreat you, may it please madam to look favorably upon my humble treaty—and for good measure, because I am a man smitten by the talent I see on this page—if you'd be so endlessly kind, may I *please* see the other letters?"

Francesca handed over two more letters. "Smitten lacks credibility coming from you, but you did say please."

Smitten was lovely, as was the ferocity in his dark eyes. They were brown, with agate rims that put Francesca in mind of winter seas.

"I am as smite-able as the next man, and I tell you sincerely…"

He trailed off, the second letter in his hand. He wasn't like some Englishmen who had to move his lips to read French. He could drink coffee and read at the same time, unerringly grasping the cup, bringing it to his mouth, and setting it down without taking his gaze from the page.

"Shall I do the rest of them?"

"A moment."

His concentration was absolute. What would it be like to have that concentration turned on *her*? And did the texture of English sheets offend his skin because he slept without benefit of a nightshirt?

Francesca hoped so.

"This one is as magnificent as the last," he said, setting the second letter down. "Your penmanship, your turn of phrase, your salutation—every detail— is rendered to encourage a favorable reply. I am in your debt."

His penmanship was legible, but like him. No soft curves, no graceful details. Communication in its most utilitarian form.

"Nonsense. You pulled me from a muddy ditch, Sir Greyville, and lectured me to safety, then fed me dinner and kissed me good night. I will have to write many letters to repay your kindness."

"I did kiss you good night," he said, peering down at his mug of coffee. "I hope you took no offense."

She'd been surprised, pleased, and slightly disconcerted.

Duchesses were not allowed to be disconcerted, poor dears.

Though scientists were apparently allowed to be shy.

"My name is Francesca," she said. "You have my leave to use it."

"My friends call me Grey."

A nice moment blossomed, with morning sun streaming in the windows, the peat fire blazing in the hearth, and Sir Greyville smiling at his coffee cup.

His smile was sweet, devilish, subtle, and unexpected. Francesca was surprised to discover that the man was gorgeous, but for the toast crumbs on his cravat.

"Do you need to work at this desk?" she asked. "I can manage at the table."

"That would suit. Shall I ring for a tray?"

"Nothing for me, thank you." She rose, pleased to have more work to occupy her. All of her personal effects—her embroidery hoop, her flute, her lap desk—was lashed to the boot of the upended coach. This situation had proven something of a challenge when it came time to dress.

The Rose Heath attics had been raided though, and Francesca was attired in a marvelously warm wool day dress ten years out of date.

She organized herself at the worktable, Sir Greyville settled in at the desk, and soon the sound of two pens scratching across foolscap joined the ticking of the clock and soft roar of the fire.

"I'm happy."

Sir Greyville looked up. "Beg pardon?"

"I didn't mean to say that aloud, but it's true. I'm happy. I have nothing of my own with me, I'm far from home, in very unexpected surroundings, but I'm happy."

"Then you're on a successful expedition. Study the terrain, weather, flora, and fauna well and take copious notes."

He went back to his transcribing, and Francesca to her letters. One went to a lady, a French comtesse who was visiting friends in York. Currying her favor required a slightly different approach. Francesca took a break between letters to look in on Mary Alice, who'd suffered a few injuries when the coach had overturned.

When Francesca returned to the estate office, she finished the letters and stacked them on the sideboard. She then indulged in the temptation to study the fauna sitting behind the massive desk.

Sir Greyville had hooked a pair of wire-rimmed spectacles about his ears and propped his boots on a corner of the desk. Very likely, he'd forgotten Francesca was in the room, much less in the same country. From time to time, he'd mutter something in Latin, or brush the quill feather with the fingertips of his right hand.

"You're left-handed," Francesca said. "That explains part of your difficulty drafting pretty correspondence."

"So it does, but not all. I simply haven't your gift."

She brought the letters over to the desk, and he stood, as if realizing that a gentleman doesn't prop his boots on the furniture in a lady's presence.

He took the letters and set them aside. "I will read them word for word, not to assure myself that you accurately conveyed my sentiments, but rather, to learn from your example."

"If one of the Frenchmen funds your next expedition, you must write to me. I would be pleased to know I was of aid to modern science."

She brushed the crumbs from his cravat and kept smoothing her hand over the froth of lace and linen when not a single crumb remained.

"Madam?"

"You asked me a question earlier."

"I am a font of curiosity. You'll have to be more specific."

He smelled good, he looked good, and Francesca abruptly felt both bold and vulnerable. "You didn't ask, exactly. You said, 'I hope you took no offense.'"

He caught her hand in his. "Because I kissed you. On the cheek."

"I took no offense. I haven't been kissed, on the cheek or anywhere, for a very long time."

Then she kissed him. Not on the cheek.

CHAPTER THREE

The last person to kiss Sir Greyville Trenton had been Professor Hiram Angelo van Ostermann, a Belgian with a passion for orchids. Grey had brought him several intact, healthy specimens from Mexico and had been treated to that Continental effusion, the triple kiss—left cheek, right cheek, and left cheek again. They'd been parting after a long evening of wine and science, and the professor was the sentimental sort when it came to orchids.

Sentiment was too tame a word for the response Mrs. Pomponio—Francesca—evoked with her kiss. She was no blushing girl to ambush a fellow then go giggling on her way. She remained in the vicinity, her lips moving on his, tenderly, sweetly, intimately.

Not a good-night buss, not thanks for orchids safely delivered. She offered a kiss as lovely, intriguing, and varied as the densest forests and loftiest mountain peaks, and *by God*, every sense Grey possessed begged her to continue her explorations with him.

As her arms stole around his waist, and the soft, full female shape of her swamped his awareness, he could admit that he'd been starving for human touch and parched for sexual joy.

Not mere erotic pleasure—pleasure was as close as his left hand. *Joy*. The delight of reveling in animal spirits with another, the glory of being a human creature in the full flood of shared biological imperatives.

Grey took Francesca in his arms and settled her on the desk. A pile of notes went cascading to the floor, and he jolly damned didn't care.

She broke the kiss and rested her forehead against his shoulder. "Mother of God, Sir Greyville."

He stroked her hair and marveled at the arousal coursing through him. "Was that a happy Mother of God or a dismayed one?"

She lifted her head enough to meet his gaze. "Both, or more accurately, impressed. Have you made a study of kisses, gathered data on many continents, compared findings?"

Grey rummaged about for the pretty way to say what he felt, then gave up, because if he bungled his answer, this would be their first and last passionate kiss.

"If I were to undertake such a study of kisses, I'd have to start in Italy, among the daughters of English diplomats." He was distracted for a moment by the scent of Francesca's hair, which bore the fragrances of lavender and jasmine.

"To narrow the sample population further," he went on, "I'd focus on the blond ladies with fine gray eyes, who have put the foolishness of youth behind them and yet gained impressive skill with the kiss. Ideally, my investigation would be limited to those subjects named Francesca Pomponio. If the subject were willing, I'd make a very thorough study of the topic."

She gave him her weight. "You are a very silly man."

"Yes."

Silly and, to use her word, happy. At that moment, with his notes littered across the carpet and Francesca in his arms, he was happy.

He and she remained thus, arms entwined, while Grey wallowed in the pleasure of holding a willing woman, one who returned his embrace and enjoyed his kisses.

"I'm distracting you from your work," Francesca said.

She was asking a question, exercising the delicacy of expression that preserved Grey from being the one to inquire.

"You have distracted me from everything. I think perhaps I needed a distraction. What news do we have of your coach?"

She eased away, and Grey let her go, only because he could console himself with the sight of her. Her lips were a touch rosier, and a single pearl-tipped hairpin was dangling from her chignon.

"Our host says that righting the coach will take some effort, and then at least two wheels will require repair, and he suspects an axle has been cracked as well. He predicts, between spring storms, the Yorkshire roads, and the extent of the damage, we will be cast on his hospitality for at least two weeks."

Thank God for Yorkshire mud. "Are you disappointed?"

She went to her knees and began picking up Grey's notes. He assisted, passing them to her so she could restore them to order.

"You will think me one of those forward, pathetic, Continental widows, but no, I am not disappointed. I am *interested*, Sir Greyville, in making a study of you."

They were on the rug, both of them kneeling, several pages still lying about.

Her admission troubled her, while it delighted Grey. "I would like to be studied. I have so little to offer any woman, that my opportunities for... What I mean to say is, that in so many words, I rarely find myself... Bloody hell. I want to kiss you for the next two weeks straight."

She regarded him as if he'd lapsed into the native dialect of the upper Amazon basin.

"I gather you neglected your kissing while you were so attentive to your science."

"I neglect everything when I'm absorbed with a project. I get crumbs on my cravat, forget where I put the glasses sitting on my very nose, and have been known to write on my cuffs rather than go in search of more paper, but for the next two weeks, I would very much enjoy getting to know you better."

That was as delicate as he could be, and damn anybody who intimated that a short mutual indulgence in pleasurable intimacies with Francesca Pomponio would put him behind on his work.

Further behind.

"You are bound to return to your jungles?" she asked.

The jungle belonged to the Almighty or to the Fiend, depending on the day. Grey couldn't tell whether Francesca wanted reassurances that he wouldn't plague her with expectations, or wished he had more to offer her.

So he gave her the facts. "I doubt I'll return to the Amazon, but I will return to the field. I'm suited to investigation, and it makes me feel alive."

So did her kisses. Interesting coincidence.

She cupped his cheek with her palm, soft female warmth to freshly shaven male angles. "I have been a widow for five years, and I do not undertake an intimate friendship with you lightly. I barely know you, and you know even less of me. Maybe that is what allows us to wander into this jungle together, the knowledge that we'll part, and fondly, but we will part."

Englishwomen didn't make speeches like that. They also didn't seem a very happy lot.

"We'll part very fondly if our first kiss is any indication."

"That was our second."

Grey crawled to her side of the rug. "This will be our third."

* * *

Francesca had watched all of the intrigue, drama, and influence-trading in the Italian courts with a certain dispassion. When affairs of the heart had entangled with political machinations, as they often did, she'd been honestly baffled.

What could possibly be worth enduring such a *mess*? Such inconvenience and potential loss of dignity? Horrendously public marital discord, needless violence, lavish gestures, and plots behind every marble column had seemed like so much farce to her, much to her father's amusement.

"Someday, you'll understand," he'd said.

Pietro, nearly twenty years her senior, had said much the same thing.

Well, the great insight was at last befalling her. As Sir Greyville Trenton prowled on all fours across the carpet, Francesca gloried in the sense that nothing, not his science, not a servant banging on the door, not a promise of funds for his next expedition, would have stopped him from initiating their third kiss.

Better still, he wasn't embarking on this frolic in the dales because he wanted political favor, or access to the family wing of the palace, or the cachet of having had intimate favors from the ducal widow.

Sir Greyville wanted *her*.

In her plain, borrowed dress, with her hair in a bun worthy of a retired governess, and not a jewel in sight, Sir Greyville wanted her.

He touched her hair and leaned very close. "I need to lock the damned door." He kissed her nose and got up in one lithe move, then locked the door.

Francesca remained on the carpet, not trusting her knees to support her should she stand.

"Madam, if you continue to gaze up at me like that… On second thought, I wish you'd always look at me like that." He extended a hand down to her and pulled her to her feet. "When you regard me thus, I feel like one of those sinfully delectable cream cakes devised by the Italian chefs. All I desire is for you to consume me, and you are happily intent on that very goal. I have never been anybody's cream cake. The sensation is rather like being addled by fever."

He was fearless, if a bit eccentric in his choice of comparisons.

"When you look at me," Francesca said, "I want to kiss you. I can't believe I said that. I'm not normally… That is… The Italian court culture is interesting. The men can be hounds, but then, with whom are they hounds, if not with the women? Some men prefer the company of other men, of course, but on the whole, between wives, mistresses, ladies of easy virtue, and affairs, a great deal of…"

In no language could Francesca finish the thought she'd been bumbling toward.

"A great deal of mating behavior takes place?" Sir Greyville suggested, kneeling to pick up the last of the papers.

"Yes, exactly. Mating behavior. I did not participate in it. I didn't want to compromise my privacy, or allow anybody undue influence over me."

"You flatter me," he said, rising, "though I gather flattery is not your intent. I've been similarly unwilling to embroil myself in any situation that could prove inconvenient when it came time to embark on another expedition. One must avoid creating expectations, on the one hand, and subjecting oneself to the risk of disease, on the other. One must be prudent, and that is a bloody nuisance I am happy to temporarily depart from."

He stacked the papers, tapping the edges of the pages against the desk until the lot was tidy, if no longer in exact date order.

"We must exercise discretion," Francesca said. "My friends are ladies, as am I."

"And you are in the company of gentlemen. Have no fear that what transpires between us will become grist for the London gossip mill. I can't stand Town, myself, and if I didn't have to periodically give papers or meet with potential sponsors, I'd never set foot south of Oxford."

Well, thank heavens. Francesca was in the wilds of Yorkshire precisely because she too had no use for the London Season. A wealthy widow with a title was bachelor-bait, and she'd had enough of that in Rome, Paris, Milan, and Berlin.

"How do we do this?" she asked.

"You aren't asking for a biology lecture, I trust?"

He'd launch into one if she were. And if he did, she'd find it arousing. Ye gods and little fishes.

"I was married for five years," Francesca said. "My husband was thirty-six when we married and assured me he was quite competent in the bedroom. He was considerate and... considerate."

With his mistresses, he'd doubtless been passionate, but with a wife, his attentions had become downright boring. That hypocrisy was an aspect of Italy that Francesca didn't miss at all.

"Then he was a dunderhead," Sir Greyville said, shaking a drop of coffee from his empty cup into his open mouth. "Meaning no disrespect to the departed, but he ought to have been passionate, wild, demanding, playful, inventive, tender, adventurous, accommodating, and—why are you looking at me like that?"

"You are an authority on marital intimacies?" Pietro had accounted himself such, though Francesca had had her doubts. What woman would tell a ducal lover that he lacked playfulness?

Though he certainly had.

Sir Greyville set down his mug. "The institution of marriage is a uniquely human invention. In the wild, animals mate at will and, in many species, un-mate at will. In varying degrees, they cooperate to raise the young, but just as often, the union is based on mutual protection or passing whim. One cannot escape biology, and if the male of the species doesn't want his mate growing bored, uninterested, or quarrelsome, he'd damned well better show some willingness to contribute to her contentment."

"I'm in the presence of a radical," Francesca said, but then, Sir Greyville was likely passionate in all his opinions.

"Marriage," he said, "has no counterpart in nature, unless you allow for a few species that pair for life to raise young, though their sexual fidelity is far from assured. The human parties, by contrast, speak their vows and are stuck with one another. If the lady plays a man false, he is compelled by law to support the resulting offspring. What is radical about taking steps to ensure those offspring are his? If he is the most attractive source of intimate pleasures, those odds increase. I'm considering writing a paper along these lines, but Stratton says he'll disown me if I publish it."

Sir Greyville had taken to pacing, as if his mental energy was so abundant, it even moved his body.

"I suspect the Church of England would ex-communicate me," he went on, "which means my mother would have an apoplexy. Over a simple theory supported by common sense and abundant observation. You see the frustrations a man of science endures on every hand?"

His friends probably told him he'd been in the jungle too long and had no idea how their teasing bewildered him.

"Galileo was threatened with death for propounding a theory," Francesca said, "one that has been proved true."

If she'd kissed him, he could not have looked more pleased. He took her by the wrist and led her to the sofa.

"You asked a question earlier," he said, waiting for her to be seated, "about how we go on with this intimate friendship. How would you like to go on with it?"

Ten minutes ago, with kiss number three a heartbeat away—kisses to the nose didn't count—Francesca would have said she wanted to *go on* immediately, on any handy surface that wasn't too far from the fire.

"May I have a day to think about that?" she asked, feeling very bold—also stupid. What woman delays eating a cream cake after five years of going without?

"That is an excellent notion," he replied. "My best experiments have all been the result of focused contemplation. If I might make a suggestion, though, I'd like our first encounter to be in a bed."

Good heavens. "Not too much to ask."

"I am easily chilled in this climate and in this house, and cold is not conducive to optimal reproductive functioning for the human male. Beds are not cold when occupied by an enthusiastic couple."

Sir Greyville Trenton was not cold either. He was brilliant, unusual, fearless, and unique, and even before Francesca had become his lover, she knew one other thing about him: When she climbed into the repaired coach with her friends and left the Yorkshire Dales behind her, she'd miss Sir Greyville Trenton for the rest of her life.

"Beds are cozy," she said. "I will look forward to embarking on this adventure with you in a warm, cozy bed. Shall we get back to work now? I'll start on that stack of notes that was knocked asunder by our... that was knocked asunder."

By their mating behavior.

"A fine plan, though given your skill with a pen, I might have word of funding in less than our allotted two weeks."

He didn't seem entirely pleased with that prospect, and Francesca took what comfort she could from the briskness of his observation.

* * *

Contrary to common perception, the scientific mind was driven as much by imagination as by ratiocination, at least Grey's was. The prospect of an intimate liaison with an intelligent, lovely, learned, and discerning lady—and no messy entanglement to follow—ought to have distracted him from his work.

To his surprise, the opposite was true.

With Francesca rustling about in the office, Grey could finally settle to his writing. He could let his mind roam over hypotheses, data, and conclusions, over descriptions of specimens he'd not seen for more than two years, but must bring to life on the page for his scientific brethren.

And sisters. The occasional woman plied her hand at science, usually side by side with a spouse, father, brother, or uncle. Intrepid lot, though none of them had ever stirred Grey's mating fancies.

"Your lunch," Francesca said, causing him nearly to jump from his chair. "Which you will please eat."

She stood beside Grey's desk, arms crossed, looking like a delectable governess—a contradiction in terms, based on his childhood acquaintance with the species.

"Is it noon already?"

"One of the clock. You ordered a tea tray at ten and then didn't touch a thing on it. I was compelled to help myself lest the staff be offended."

"What is this staff you speak of?" Grey lifted the lid from a bowl of soup. The scent of beef and potatoes alerted him to the fact that he was hungry—famished, in fact. "I don't recall seeing evidence of any staff."

"I refer to the footmen who came in twice to build up the fire, once to deliver the tea tray, and once more to inquire regarding our wishes for the midday repast. I'm off to assure my friends I yet draw breath, while you, I suspect, must remain in the wilds of Peru."

"Brazil, actually. I won't reach Peru for a week at least." Grey's desk was littered with paper, most of it covered with writing and sketches, a few pages bearing a single heading.

The tray at his elbow included sandwiches and a bowl of stewed apples. He adored stewed apples, had dreamed of them in the jungle, which was probably a sign of mental imbalance.

"Sir Greyville." Francesca leaned closer. "Eat. Put the pen down. Pick up the spoon, or the butter knife, or a sandwich, but eat. You'll be nodding off over your notes an hour from now if you don't take sustenance."

He did that—fell asleep at his desk.

"You and my mother would get on famously," he said, buttering a roll and dipping one corner in the soup. "She is a formidable woman, and I respect her greatly. None can stand before her version of hospitality. At the conclusion of her house parties, guests are rolled out to their coaches in wheelbarrows, felled by an excess of Mama's hospitality. Have you grown weary of my scintillating company already that you must flee our literary laboratory?"

Francesca wandered off to toss more peat onto the fire. "Some of us must get up and move occasionally. I'll take a turn in the garden while the sun is out. I suggest you leave the room as well. Inspect the fountains, visit your horse, lose a game of billiards to yourself. Get out of that chair."

Grey considered lifting the bowl of soup to slurp the contents jungle-style—he was that hungry and the soup that good—but he was in the presence of a lady, one spouting daft notions.

"If I leave my desk, the work, which is going well for once, ceases to progress."

"If you fall asleep over your soup," she retorted, "the work ceases to progress, and your linen is the worse for your lack of moderation. I should be back in an hour or two."

"Francesca." He didn't want her to leave, which was silly. Perhaps he was a very silly man, after all.

"Sir Greyville?"

"Grey will do. Thank you for your company this morning."

He'd flustered her. He rose, because a little flustering was good for the soul. Possibly. The hypothesis wanted testing.

"My father was much like you," she said, rearranging the peat over the coals. "When he had a pen in his hand, all else ceased to have meaning for him. He wrote books on diplomacy, memoirs, travel guides. He loved to write, to listen to other people's stories, to document his observations. He had a marvelous wit, which was half the key to his diplomatic success."

Had that worthy diplomat ever listened to his own daughter?

Grey took the wrought-iron poker from Francesca's hand, set it aside, and wrapped his arms around her. "I will miss you." He referred to the general case, commencing two weeks hence, but when Francesca said nothing, he retrenched. "I made great progress this morning. If you tarry among your friends, I will pine for your quiet presence. How are the notes coming?"

She'd begun the reorganization of his notes, from chronological order to grouped by subject. The task was tedious, thankless, and detailed. Grey would have put it off for years, but Francesca was not only plowing through it, she was making cross indexes, so any topic or date could be found easily.

"My greatest difficulty," she said, reciprocating his embrace, "is that I start to read what's on the pages. You have a gift for accurate description, for connecting stray bits into a coherent whole. I'm learning a lot."

She was probably learning a lot about the man who'd written the notes, which bothered Grey not at all.

He held her for a moment, gathering her warmth. Lions sat close to one another while watching the moonrise, and Grey understood a little better why. In Francesca's embrace, he found peace, and also sadness. They'd part as she'd reminded him.

Fondly, but they would part.

"Off to lunch with you," he said, easing away. "The jungle calls me."

She kissed his cheek and was gone on a soft click of the door latch.

In fact, the jungle no longer called to Grey. He'd been so bloody sick of the place after the first year, he'd known he'd never return. With that conclusion in mind, he'd made his one expedition count, staying until the last possible month. He respected the jungle, appreciated its beauty and its great variety, but he'd not make a career of braving its dangers.

He'd earned the right to describe himself as "an explorer of the Amazonian jungles," a coveted credential, but at present, he was more interested in exploring his friendship with Francesca Pomponio.

They had only the next two weeks for that adventure, after all.

CHAPTER FOUR

Francesca had spent the morning peeking inside the mind of a man who was part poet, part artist, part logician, and part healthy male animal. Sir Greyville had delighted in exertion of the body as well as of the mind and had covered thousands of miles in the time some of his colleagues could barely cover hundreds.

He noticed everything, from insects, to rock formations, to tiny blooms, to wildcats that outweighed most grown men. His sketches included smiling native women—not a stitch of clothing to be seen—and a fearsome fellow who had worn a necklace of enormous teeth and little else.

Francesca had told her friends that she was delighted to assist Sir Greyville with his work—which she was—and that she'd be equally delighted to depart when the coach was repaired.

Which she would not be.

Oddly enough, she suspected her friends might also be reluctant to resume the journey, which made no sense, for they had to be bored. If they'd sought boredom, they would have endured yet another London Season.

Francesca detoured to her room to fetch a shawl, for even on a sunny day, a turn in the garden had left her slightly chilled.

The lunch tray sat outside the estate office door, not a morsel of food remaining. She opened the door without knocking, lest she disturb Sir Greyville's concentration.

At first, she didn't see him, but a soft snore alerted her to his presence on the sofa. He didn't fit, so one knee was bent, and the other foot was on the floor. His arms were crossed, and his neck was at an awkward angle against the armrest. His battered tall boots stood side by side at the end of the sofa, like a pair of grizzled, loyal hounds waiting for the return of their master.

In sleep, Sir Greyville looked younger, also more tired. His English complexion had been darkened by the sun, and even in repose, he had crow's feet at the corners of his eyes. Francesca eased the earpieces of his spectacles free and draped her shawl over him.

He craned his neck and muttered something, possibly the Latin words for cooked apples.

Francesca lifted his head, tucked a pillow against the armrest, and left him to his slumbers—despite the temptation to run her fingers through his hair a few more times. She'd been back working at the notes for some time, developing an index of maps and sketches, when the sofa creaked.

"I am brought low by beef stew," came from the sofa. "Why doesn't anybody make a damned sofa sufficiently commodious that a short respite after the midday meal need not occasion a crick in the neck and cramp in the shoulders?"

"Why doesn't anybody think to leave the office and use a bed for such a respite?" Francesca replied.

He sat up abruptly, a crease bisecting his left cheek. "You have finished your luncheon. What time is it?"

"Going on three. The mail has arrived and is sitting on your desk."

He rose, folded the shawl over his arm, picked up his boots, and came to the table to lean over Francesca's shoulder.

"I dreamed of you. You were swimming in some damned grotto, attired as nature made you. Shall I come to you tonight, Francesca?"

In his notes, he'd referred to a jungle cat that killed with a single leap. Francesca felt the opposite, as if she'd been quickened, brought to life, by that one question. Sir Greyville's breath fanned across her neck, followed by a sensation so tender, so warm and unexpected, she closed her eyes the better to withstand it.

His fingers pushed aside the fabric of Francesca's dress, followed by his lips, right at the join of her neck and shoulder. He cradled her jaw against his palm, traced her ear with gentle touches, and in the space of a minute melted every coherent thought from her mind.

"This will not do," he said, resting his forehead against her shoulder. "I grow aroused simply touching you. Tell me to sit at my desk, Francesca, and say it as if you mean it."

"Grey."

His lips again, so soft, and the barest scrape of his teeth. "Hmm."

"Yes. Now go sit at your desk. This instant."

He tarried another moment, then straightened and ever-so-cherishingly draped the shawl around her shoulders. Francesca nearly asked him to do it again, so precious was his casual consideration.

"Yes, I should come to you tonight?"

"Must I draw you a diagram?" Francesca took up a penknife and pared a finer point onto her goose quill. "You asked a question, and I answered it. Now answer your mail, or grouse about your neck, or put your boots back on. Your spectacles are in your pocket."

He sauntered off. "I hope you're as assertive in bed as you are in the office, for I am not shy when it comes to carnal joys—as best I recall. I like to approach such occasions with an agenda, a list, if you will, of activities and the order in which I'll undertake them."

"The mail, Sir Greyville. Correspondence. Sci-ence."

"In our case," he said, settling into the chair, "my agenda will be succinct." He pulled on both boots and sat back. "*Make Francesca scream with pleasure.* Best to stick to simple imperatives when a situation is likely to become fraught, don't you agree?"

"Heartily. Shut your naughty mouth, or I will revise my agenda for the evening."

He donned his glasses and shut his naughty mouth, and Francesca did not revise her agenda.

She hoped he wouldn't either.

CHAPTER FIVE

As the afternoon wore on, the weather continued unabatingly English, which was to say, cold, wet, windy, and disobliging for two minutes, then achingly lovely for five. If Grey had been able to take a turn in the garden with Francesca, he might have abandoned his increasingly discommodious chair. If he'd been able to go for a hack and put her up on a guest horse beside him, he might have even left the estate grounds.

Perhaps tomorrow, after they'd become lovers in fact.

He set aside a page full of detailed observations and never-before-published theories to take a moment to behold Francesca Pomponio. Surely the mating urge was affecting his brain, for the picture she made tempted him toward maudlin phrases and impossible hopes.

Firelight gilded her hair.

The curve of her jaw begged to be cradled against his palm.

That sort of maudlin tripe.

Grey consoled himself with the knowledge that maudlin tripe contributed substantially to perpetuation of the species. He'd simply never been afflicted with such a bad case of the mating urge before, and that had to be a consequence of prolonged deprivation.

A good scientist put his faith in the simplest hypothesis that explained all the data.

He did not "tear his gaze" from the sight of Francesca brushing the quill feather across her lips, but rather, resumed reading his correspondence.

Scientists did their part to keep the royal mail in business, and Grey was no exception. He debated theories and experimental design with dozens of colleagues, congratulated them on their triumphs, and commiserated with their frustrations.

The third letter had him out of his chair. "May the Fiend seize that rabid, two-faced weaseling disgrace of a poseur and inflict on him a lifelong case of the quartan ague."

Francesca put down her pen. "I beg your pardon?"

Grey waved the letter at her. "Harford, the ruddy bastard. He stole my idea."

"How can one steal an idea?"

"He assured me at great length that he was done with fieldwork, had had enough of its savagery and deprivations. He vowed he was ready for a professor's chair, pipe, and slippers. Too many damned biologists, he said, as if the botanists aren't overrunning the jungles at a great rate. I maundered on about the vanilla orchid and the insect that must be responsible for its pollination."

Francesca rose and took the letter from him, scanning its contents. "He's off to search for this moth or bee or whatever, and thanks you heartily for encouraging him to pursue the idea."

"I never encouraged him, not in the least, and I should have known he was inviting me to unburden myself of a lucrative theory. Harford is by no means a pure scientist, but then, neither am I."

She folded the letter and set it aside. To Grey, the correspondence should have come banded in black, so bitter was his sense of betrayal. He'd liked Harford, had enjoyed arguing plant morphology with him, and had considered collaborating with him on some future expedition.

"What is a pure scientist?" Francesca asked, leaning back against the desk. "You make it sound as if there's some sort of chastity at stake."

"Not chastity, but nobility of purpose." She'd moved enough stacks of Grey's notes that he had room to sit on the desk, so he perched beside her. "One can pursue new knowledge for its own sake, because knowledge in itself has virtue, or one can take a more applied approach."

She took off her shawl and folded it over her arm. "You refer to money, though you resort to typical English roundaboutation to do it. A pure scientist has a rich papa or wife. The fellow who takes a more applied approach might turn his discoveries into coin."

Grey would forever associate the scent of jasmine with the soothing balm of honest, common sense.

"More or less, but even among the more pragmatic men of science, we don't steal each other's ideas."

"*You* don't steal other people's ideas, Sir Greyville. Of that, I am convinced. Moreover, your close associates well know where this theory originated, because they know you. If this Harford person goes off on his bee quest, your colleagues will all know where he got his inspiration. I cannot but think that a profession dedicated to accurate observation and clear understanding will ostracize such a charlatan."

Grey took off his glasses, folded them into a pocket, and kissed Francesca's cheek. "Thank you. I would have taken two weeks to talk myself around to such wisdom. You're right, of course, and my colleagues will all be very circumspect in their discourse with Harford henceforth. The problem is, this was one of my ideas most likely to attract a wealthy sponsor. Vanilla is valuable, but hard to propagate outside its native environment. The issue is pollination, which refers to that process by which, from season to season, the plant propagates—"

"Copulation, you mean, for the vanilla plant."

"It's an orchid, technically. I do seem fixated on certain activities, don't I?"

She leaned into him and slipped an arm about his waist. "You're a biologist. Of course you're fascinated with propagation. You'd be reduced to studying rocks, otherwise. Rocks needn't propagate, poor darlings."

They remained for a moment in that half-embrace, for Grey's arm had found its way about Francesca's shoulders.

"When I was nine," he said, "my older brother decided he preferred my pony to his. He'd got a pony a year before I had, being the elder and the heir, and thus my pony was a particular joy to me. I'd trained the little beast in all manner of tricks and told him all my sorrows. His name was Tiger. I was informed by my father that one pony was as good as another, and I was to surrender my mount out of filial loyalty. My brother was taller than me and thus deserved the larger equine."

"I hope Tiger tossed your brother into the ditch on his spoiled little head."

"Tiger was a perfect gentleman, and so was I, but I've taken a dim view of thievery and dishonesty ever since—a dimmer view. My brother was not taller than me. I'd already gained nearly an inch on him, though my father had failed to notice. I take infantile delight in the fact that I'm two inches taller than his lordship now."

"Good. Did your brother ever apologize? Stealing a horse is a grave offense under English law."

A capital crime, as a matter of fact. The realization gave Grey's childhood memory of betrayal a better sense of proportion.

"I'm not sure he knows an apology is necessary. I yielded what was mine and pretended I'd rather enjoy the countryside on foot anyway. Thus was a biologist born, at least in part."

Francesca shifted so she stood between Grey's knees, her arms about his waist. "I pretended I didn't mind my husband's endless procession of mistresses. I yielded what was mine too."

* * *

A small boy's pony was of great importance to that boy, whether he was English, Italian, or Persian. Francesca stood in the circle of Grey's embrace and admitted that at least Pietro had not set his sons against each other intentionally.

Just the opposite. With the children of his first marriage, he'd been generous, but fair and even-handed. He'd also been a model duke—and a disappointing spouse.

"If your husband was variously unfaithful, he was an ass," Grey said. "I hope you told him as much. Men are not beasts, entirely at the mercy of their procreative urges."

Was a duke more or less of a beast than other men? "The wealthy, well-born Italian male is a privileged creature from the moment of his birth, rather like your brother. Pietro was simply an exponent of his upbringing."

Grey rested his cheek against the slope of her breast. "I don't believe that, else my brother should have turned out to be a tyrannical, selfish, philandering terror. Sebastian is actually a decent fellow. Your husband made choices, and one of them was to wed you and recite public vows of fidelity. I gather he was somewhat older than you?"

To hold on to Grey, and to be held, fortified Francesca. She did not normally dwell on her marriage, but Grey saw the situation with a logical mind and, apparently, no particular loyalty to his gender.

Refreshing, that.

"I was eighteen, he was thirty-six and so very dashing. He flattered, he flirted, he charmed as only an Italian man at the height of his powers can charm. My father encouraged the match for diplomatic reasons, and I was desperate for a household of my own. The wedding night was sweet, magical, enchanting, and I convinced myself I'd found a fairy-tale prince."

Why did the grand old fairy tales never feature dukes as their heroes?

Grey sat back and brushed his thumbs over Francesca's cheeks. "Francesca, I'm sorry. If a man will break his vows to his God, his community, and his wife, he has no honor. I realize my views are quaint, laughable even, but I cannot abide a hypocrite."

Francesca turned so she could lean into Grey's embrace. She'd rather be closeted in a dreary office with this quaint man than share the splendor of a ducal court with her late husband. She hadn't realized she'd needed a man—a man whom she esteemed—to confirm her instincts, but Grey's apology helped ease a grief that had started within two weeks of her wedding.

"To appearances, Pietro was attentive, and that was the extent of the fidelity he believed was required. He found my histrionics juvenile and even touching, but really, what was the problem? He'd always be available to *accommodate me* when I had need of him. His mistresses in no way diminished his regard for me, or his willingness to tend to me in bed. I simply made no sense to him. I was a toy he could not figure out, though a pretty enough toy."

Grey stood, which put the length of him smack up against Francesca. He was quite tall up close, a good six inches taller than Pietro had been.

And yet, to an eighteen-year-old bride, Pietro had been imposing indeed.

"If that was your husband's view of his marital obligations," Grey said, "then he was nothing more than an orangutan with powers of speech, meaning no disrespect to the orangutan. I have argued this point with many a colleague.

We cannot as a species claim the Almighty awarded us dominion over the earth and then act among ourselves with no more civility than stray dogs. Even in the most remote wilderness, predator and prey manage to share the water holes without descending into outright interspecies warfare."

Francesca kissed him. "And at that point in the discussion, somebody changes the subject, for your logic is irrefutable while their arguments rely on an interpretation of Scripture uniquely supportive of their vices."

"They change the subject or mutter about how poor Sir Greyville was in the tropics for too long. Kiss me again, please."

Francesca obliged Grey with a spree of kissing that banished the miseries of the past and reassured her that he desired her honestly and for herself.

"Promise me something," she said, stepping back. "Promise me you won't accommodate me tonight."

Grey took out a prodigiously wrinkled handkerchief. "You will please explain yourself."

The handkerchief was for polishing his spectacles, which Grey held up to the light coming in the window. He might have been asking Francesca to explain her mama's recipe for syllabub, and yet, Francesca knew she had his attention, despite the call of the jungle.

"Don't insinuate yourself beneath the covers without uttering a word," Francesca said. "Don't kiss me on the cheek, climb aboard, and start thumping at me until you collapse two minutes later as if you're Pheidippides after running from Marathon to Athens. One wants some communication about the business, a certain mutuality of participation, not… not thumping."

She could never have said that to her husband, because after the first two weeks of marriage, she'd mostly wanted his thumping over with. From his mistresses, the duke had expected passion; from his duchess, duty was all he'd sought.

The rotter.

Grey stuffed his handkerchief back into his pocket, all willy-nilly. "Francesca, if I begin to thump, however you define the term, you tell me to stop, describe how you'd like us to proceed, and I'll make appropriate adjustments. You are not the subordinate on this expedition, and I have no more of a map or compass than you do. That said, my bed is the larger, so I'd rather you insinuated yourself beneath my covers than the other way around."

"That makes sense." And also allowed her to arrive and depart as she pleased. "Are we expected to join the others for dinner?"

"I am forgiven my eccentricities when it comes to attending meals, in the interests of science, or perhaps because my dearest friends need only a little of my company to remind them why they allow me to disappear into the jungle for years at a time. It's threatening rain again."

The office had become cooler as the afternoon had progressed. For a man acclimated to the tropics, the chill would be significant.

Francesca wrapped her shawl about Grey's shoulders and returned to the table, which was closer to the fire. "I'll order us trays, and the others will have to manage without us."

Grey resumed his place at the desk, her cream wool shawl about his shoulders like an ermine cape. He made an eccentric picture, but as he read, he occasionally paused, sniffed at the wool, and smiled.

Francesca got back to work—the ocelot was an interesting creature—but her view of the upcoming days and nights had changed. She wasn't merely addressing lingering disappointment over her marriage, or taking advantage of an opportunity for some discreet pleasure.

She was falling in love, and with a man who longed to disappear into the jungle once again.

* * *

Grey's pride had not let him share with Francesca the full brunt of his dismay at Harford's betrayal.

Dismay being a euphemism for utter, roaring, wall-kicking, head-banging rage with generous helpings of profanity in at least three languages.

Harford had not only charmed Grey's theories about the vanilla orchid from him, he'd spent an entire bottle of wine listening to Grey debate which widowed countess, beer baron, or coal nabob would likely support an expedition to test that theory.

And one of Grey's carefully cultivated wealthy contacts had apparently decided to fund Harford's expedition.

"Damn and blast." Sebastian had introduced Grey to most of those wealthy contacts, and this turn of events would disappoint the earl mightily.

"Did you say something?" Francesca asked.

"The time has got away from me," Grey said, rising stiffly. Good God, his arse hurt. "One would think I had nothing to look forward to this evening, when in fact my anticipation knows no bounds."

So his acquaintance with Harford was a failed experiment in resisting the lure of professional charm. Francesca's hand in marriage had been surrendered on the strength of some randy Italian's charm, and that loss had been far greater.

And yet, she had arrived to widowhood with dignity, humor, and self-respect intact.

"I wanted to get through an entire year of your notes," she replied—*primly*. "You've been in that chair for the past ten hours, more or less. I don't know how you endure it."

Grey had taken a short break when the call of nature had become imperative, as best he recalled. "I'm the determined type, though my detractors call me stubborn. Shall you seek your bed now?"

The clock had chimed eleven, and the house had acquired the quiet stillness of nighttime deep in the country.

"I will seek *your* bed," she said. "Do we go up together, or exercise some discretion?"

"We go up together, and I bid you good night at your door, so you might enjoy some privacy as you prepare for your slumbers. You dismiss the maid and then come to me."

She peered at him over his glasses, which she'd purloined after they'd eaten supper. "You've thought about this."

"I've thought about little else." And yet, Grey had been productive. Not only in the sense of having scrawled words onto pages, but also on a deeper level. Francesca's occasional questions, her counterexamples, and pragmatic retorts were his guides in a jungle of words and theories, did she but know it. As the afternoon had worn on, Grey had grasped theoretical interrelationships, sequences of ideas, and narrative connections that would make his summary both lucid and interesting to average readers.

"You've thought about little else?" she asked, taking her shawl from his shoulders. "Then what were you writing about the livelong day?"

Without her shawl, the room was colder, though Grey could ignore cold. He'd liked having the scent of jasmine all around him and knowing he wore something of hers.

Perhaps he truly had been in the tropics too long.

"I was writing about adventures," he said, plucking his glasses from her nose. "And now, instead of writing about adventures, I'd like to embark on one. With you."

She sailed out the door ahead of him, but he suspected he'd pleased her. Grey snatched up a candle from the mantel and followed her into the frigid dark of the corridor.

"Where exactly will your next expedition take you?" she asked.

"India, I hope." Provided somebody put a small fortune at his disposal.

"To do what?"

He took her hand as they gained the stairs. "Set up a tea plantation, if I'm lucky. Before I went to South America, I had a chance to tour parts of China in the company of some Dutchmen. When I left China, I found that somebody had used my luggage to smuggle a quantity of tea seeds and slips out of the country."

"Another one of your high-minded men of science at work?"

"Not bloody likely. The Chinese guard their tea more closely than we do the crown jewels, and with good reason. But for tea, in my opinion, we'd still be a nation of gin sots. Had the contraband been discovered before I left China, I'd be the late, disgraced Sir Greyville Trenton. I'm hopeful the plants can thrive in parts of India, but must undertake further experimentation."

"You've waited four years to make these experiments?"

"For the past four years, while I've been bumbling about in the jungle, those plants have been carefully propagated by a trusted friend in the far western reaches of India. I hope that habitat closely approximates the growing conditions in China. Ceylon might do as well and is more accessible by sea. I simply have more investigation to do."

To talk with Francesca about his dreams was precious, just as watching her spin his notes from straw to gold was precious, just as seeing her bustling about with his glasses on her nose was precious.

If this was a manifestation of the mating urge, Grey had never seen or heard the symptom described by any biologist. Poets had probably maundered on about such sentiments, but little poetry had found its way into Grey's hands.

"India is very, very far away," Francesca said, pausing outside her door. "I'm glad, for the present, that our bedrooms are only across the corridor."

"So am I."

Grey was also glad that the windfall of tea had shown up in his baggage, though doubtless, somebody else had been very un-glad not to recover their stolen goods, and yet, Francesca was right. India was so very, very far away.

"Take your time," he said, bowing over her hand. "Take as long as you need, and join me if, and only if, you truly wish to do so."

She went up on her toes and kissed his cheek. "I won't be long."

And then she was gone.

* * *

India was not darkest Peru, but it was still half a world away, and as Francesca took down her hair and tended to her ablutions, she hated India.

For good measure, she hated China too, and ocelots, and those larger exotic cats with the name she wasn't sure how to pronounce. She hated biology, and botany, and that Harford weasel—she hoped the Mexican jungles gave him a bad rash in an inconvenient location or two—and she hated desperately that coach wheels and axles could be repaired in a mere fortnight.

"I have landed in a very muddy ditch, indeed," she informed her bedroom. The maid had built up the fire, bid Francesca pleasant dreams, and quietly withdrawn.

If the staff or any of the other residents of Rose Heath suspected that Francesca and Sir Greyville were embarking on a liaison, they'd given no indication, and yet, Francesca hesitated.

She'd never done this sort of thing before—of all the pathetic clichés—though she'd also never encountered a man like Sir Greyville Trenton, and probably never would again. On that thought, she charged across the corridor and entered Grey's room without knocking.

"I'm nervous," she said, remaining by the door.

The room at first appeared empty, then Grey's head appeared over the top of a privacy screen in the corner. Half his face was covered with lather, and he had a razor in his hand.

"I am unsettled as well," he said, scraping lather from one cheek. "This is not my typical excursion into uncharted territory. Do I shave, or will that make me too much the fussy Englishman? Italian males tend to be hirsute. Perhaps the lady likes a fellow sporting some evening plumage. Will my English pallor and relatively light hair coat be unappealing to her? Do I turn the covers down, or is that presumptuous? Cold sheets are damned unromantic, if you take my meaning. You will note I've turned down the quilts and built up the fire. Give me a moment, and I'll pour you a glass of wine."

He could shave himself and prattle at the same time. Francesca had never seen her husband shaving—being shaven, rather. Dukes did not tend to their own whiskers.

Francesca came around behind the privacy screen and treated herself to a view of a long, trim back, shoulders and arms wrapped with muscle, and damp hair curling at Grey's nape. Even at twenty years old, Pietro would not have exuded this much fitness and vitality.

Watching Grey complete his toilette, his movements unselfconscious even when half-naked, Francesca was abruptly angry all over again.

Two weeks? All she was allotted with this considerate, handsome, brilliant, plain-spoken, hardworking man was *two weeks?*

Then she'd damned well make them count.

"Take as long as you need," she said, going to the bed, "and join me if, and only if, you truly wish to do so."

She was unbelting her robe when Grey embraced her from behind. "Don't be nervous, Francesca. Be honest, and for the next little while, be mine."

His words gave her a bad moment, because she hadn't been entirely honest. To him, she was merely Francesca Pomponio, widow of some wealthy Italian. Would Grey, who was English to his bones despite his world travels, be upset to learn she was a dowager duchess, and not simply well-off, but disgracefully rich?

Francesca decided to ponder that issue later, when Grey's lips weren't tracing the line of her shoulder and his arousal wasn't increasingly evident at her back. She turned, wrapped her arms around him, and kissed him as if he were departing for India in the morning.

And merciful angels, did he ever kiss her back.

He could have plundered her mouth, but instead he investigated. His kisses were by turns stealthy, sweet, tender, and devious. He sipped, tasted, teased, and all the while, his hands wandered over Francesca's nightclothes. He shaped her hips, then her waist, then cupped her derriere and urged her closer.

"Bed," she muttered against his mouth. "We embark on this adventure in a bed. Now."

"That's honest. Also an excellent suggestion." He stepped out of his trousers and tossed them in the direction of the privacy screen. "If you need assistance disrobing, I'm happy to oblige."

Happy, was he? His *felicity* was magnificent, and he was utterly unselfconscious about that too. More Englishmen should spend time exploring the jungle, if Sir Greyville Trenton was any example.

"What is the scientific term for that particular variety of happiness?" Francesca asked, handing him her robe.

He sent it sailing to the privacy screen as well.

"The *membrum virile*, aroused," he said. "Erect, rampant, engorged. Happy applies as well, while you are shy."

Duchesses were modest, at least in Italy, but Grey had not only seen all manner of women unclothed, he'd sketched them.

In detail.

"I need assistance." And time. Francesca wanted years and eternities with Grey, and not two dreary little weeks in the Yorkshire Dales.

He started at the top of her nightgown, untying bow after bow with deft, competent fingers. With each bow, Francesca felt her past and all its disappointments and frustrations falling away. She wasn't a dewy, innocent bride and was glad, for once, that inexperience and ignorance no longer plagued her.

Grey stepped back when all the bows had been undone and nakedness was a single gesture away.

"Only if you want to, Francesca."

He meant that. He would take nothing from her as a matter of right or assumption—not her time, not her trust, not her body.

She drew back the sides of the nightgown, let it fall from her shoulders, and handed it to him. "Tell me what you see."

He folded her nightgown and tucked it under the pillows, then walked a slow circle around her.

"Female," he said. "Age between twenty-five and thirty. Caucasian, blond hair, gray eyes, heritage likely Saxon, possibly by way of the Danes or the Norsemen. Height about five and a half feet. No obvious deformities or significant scars. In good weight, with good muscle tone. No evidence of parturition."

He was asking a question. They'd avoided the topic of children until now.

"Two miscarriages," Francesca said. "One somewhat bruised heart, though time has mended most of the damage." Then she was back in his arms, skin to skin, the scent of cedar blending with his body heat.

"Francesca, when I look at you, I see heaven. I see every good thing. Every human, wonderful, pleasurable joy, and I want to share them with you, right now."

He scooped her off her feet and laid her on the bed.

* * *

Someday, Grey wanted to ask Francesca about the miscarriages, about how she came to be widowed, about any family she still had in Italy. He wanted to know about growing up at an Italian court and if her heart would again be bruised when they parted.

He wanted to know everything about her, and not as a scientist examines a specimen.

"I promise not to thump," he said, which caused Francesca to smile against his shoulder. He'd come down over her when he should have taken a moment to admire the picture she made naked on his bed. She was the mature female goddess, rounded in ways the typical Englishwoman was not—thanks be to Italy—and both sturdier and more feminine as a result.

"Aren't you cold?" Francesca asked.

Grey had neglected to draw the covers up, and yes, his backside was cold. She was warm, though, and soft, and fragrant, and naked.

"How am I to think of covers when your abundant charms are resplendent in my very bed?" he groused, sitting back to yank the quilts up. He took the place beside her on the mattress and drew her into his arms.

Now that the moment was upon them, any pretense of finesse had deserted him. "You mentioned communication and mutuality of participation. This would be an ideal time to elucidate your meaning."

She sighed and snuggled closer, and Grey relaxed. They were to talk, apparently, and of all people, Francesca was the person with whom he'd never wanted for conversation.

"Tell me about your home," Francesca said. "About your dragon of a mama and your decent brother. I was an only child, and both of my parents are dead. I have two aunts, whom I dutifully visited in Sussex before coming north."

His home? A fine place to start. "I haven't a home, exactly. I have some means thanks to one of my grandmothers, and I own a lovely estate in Kent, which I rent out. Property close to London is in demand, and I'm seldom in England for long periods."

"Do you want a home?"

She asked the most peculiar questions, but they bore the insight of a colleague at a distance from the subject.

"I haven't given it much thought." *Until now.* "There are nomadic peoples who thrive, but their wanderings are driven by the need for food, fresh grazing, fuel, or other necessities. As an Englishman, I was raised with an attachment to the land—king and country, et cetera—but my livelihood and my contribution have rested on exploring wildernesses. What about you?"

He'd dodged the question. Spouted off knowledgeably on irrelevant tangents in the best scientific tradition. Though how was a man to ponder imponderables when delicate female fingers were stroking over his chest and belly?

"I own property in Italy and England," Francesca said, "also lands in France, though I'm thinking of deeding the French land to my tenants. It's difficult to manage an agricultural holding at a distance, and the wars left so many in France with so little."

"Keep a portion of that land," Grey said. "French vineyards are a lucrative proposition, though they take time to become profitable. I have an associate who can advise you in detail. The man is mad about grapes."

Francesca's caresses were driving Grey mad, and she still hadn't ventured below his waist.

Time to do some exploring of the treasures at hand. Grey drew Francesca close, close enough that he could stroke her neck and shoulders.

"I would not have thought you'd be mad about tea," she said, leaning over to kiss his chest. "I've become fascinated with the scent you're wearing."

"A colleague sent it to me. It's made from a bunchgrass native to India. *Khus* is drought resistant, and can also withstand submersion for weeks if the root system is developed. Generally noninvasive—God in heaven, Francesca."

She'd scraped her teeth across his nipple. "Perhaps you can grow this grass in your tea garden."

Grey endured in silence while she explored his chest, his ribs, and eventually—three eternities and four ground molars later—the contours of his arousal. Her touch was more curious than bold, suggesting her late husband had failed utterly to indulge his lady's scientific inclinations.

"You desire me," she said.

"Madam has a talent for understatement. One hopes my sentiment is reciprocated."

She arranged herself over him and pinned him at the wrists as the end of her braid hit his chest. Her next experiment involved letting just the tips of her breasts touch him as she fit herself over his arousal.

Grey tried to catalog impressions, but got no further than *heat, dampness,* and *madness* as Francesca began to rock.

"I have investigations to make too," she said, "and experiments I've longed to perform, but I was never in the right company, never properly provisioned. Move with me, please."

He became her private wilderness as she kissed, tasted, caressed, and undulated. By the time Francesca took Grey into her body, he was a welter of need and delight, longing and jubilation. This was erotic intimacy in the ideal, a joining so profound it eclipsed awareness of any other reality. Grey might have been back in Brazil or on a ship to India, for all his surroundings had fallen from his notice.

There was only Francesca, pleasure, and wonder.

"Up," he said, patting her bum. "I want to touch you." Needed to, and not only for his own satisfaction. He was in bed with a woman glorying in the wonders of her body, and he was determined no pleasure should be denied her.

"You are touching me," she retorted, complying nonetheless. "You are most assuredly… I like that."

He'd covered each full, rosy breast with a hand and counterpointed thrusts and caresses. Francesca's nipples were wonderfully sensitive, and when her head fell back, and she surrendered to sensation, Grey made a vow to get her damned braid undone before the next time they coupled.

Because there would be a next time, and as many times as he could manage between now and when she left him.

Francesca's breathing quickened, and she pitched forward, her movements becoming greedy.

Grey held her, and held on to his self-restraint, while she thrashed her way to completion on a soft, sweet murmur of his name. For long moments, she remained panting in his arms, and his own satisfaction surprised him.

He hadn't spent, and didn't intend to when it would risk conception, and yet, he was happy, proud, and content, despite the clamoring of desire.

Francesca's breathing slowed. She kissed Grey's cheek and whispered in his ear. "I bring news from Marathon. The Persian invaders have been routed by our brave forces. Let the celebration begin."

CHAPTER SIX

Reason, the enemy of passion and adventure, tried to dim Francesca's joy not three hours after she'd left Sir Greyville's bed, and bedeviled her over the next sennight.

She was not a giddy girl, to be falling in love after five years of widowhood. In one week, she'd be leaving, and then this interlude on the stormy dales would be nothing but a memory. She had been overdue for some pleasure, long, long overdue, and Sir Greyville Trenton had happened into her life at the right time under the right circumstances.

"Balderdash," she muttered.

Grey peered at her from the chair behind the desk. "Beg pardon?"

He looked delectable, with his spare pair of spectacles perched on his nose, his cuffs turned back, and his jacket hung on the back of the chair. His eyebrows would grow more fierce as he aged, but Francesca couldn't imagine his heart growing any more fierce than it already was.

Perhaps Pietro had been a selfish dullard, but Francesca suspected the boot was on the other foot: Sir Greyville Trenton was a force of nature in bed, on the page, and everywhere in between.

"Creating these indexes will be my undoing," she said. "You refer to the same plant or insect by its English name, its local name, and its Latin name, if it has one. I often don't grasp that you're referring to the same bug or flower until the tenth time I see it. You're just as bad with landmarks, and that's before Spanish and Portuguese get involved."

"I hadn't realized I'd created such a muddle."

He'd created the muddle to end all muddles, and not only in his notes.

"I've decided to use English as the unifying reference," Francesca said. "The glossary will be in English, with all foreign language terms listed after the English definition. If that doesn't suit, you can devise some other system on the voyage to India."

He rose and came around the desk. "If I get to India. I've had nothing but rejections and silence in response to my letters."

They'd developed a system in this regard as well. The mail came in, Grey opened it, and he stacked the rejections on the corner of the desk. When Francesca wanted a break from ocelots, jaguars, and indexes, she wrote a gracious response to the rejection. She begged leave to keep the esteemed party informed regarding future developments and thanked them for their continued interest, with all good wishes, et cetera and so forth.

Grey signed the letters and off to the post they went, to be replaced by more disappointment the next day.

Each night, Grey made love with her more passionately and tenderly. Each afternoon, he opened the mail and became quieter and more pensive.

"Your friends seem well-off," Francesca said. "Colonel Stratton and Mr. Stirling, I mean. I realize asking for their support might be awkward, but needs must."

Grey drew her to her feet and wrapped his arms around her. "They both supported the last expedition generously. I have hopes that some of the samples I brought back can be developed for medical or horticultural purposes, but so far, it seems I've discovered more poisons, of which the world already has enough. My memoirs will bring in some revenue, and I did find four new species of orchid that will catch the interest of the bromeliad enthusiasts. Even so, I can't ask for more money without showing a return on the investments already made."

He would not accept support without giving something in return, damn him.

"What about your brother?" Francesca asked. "You gave him your pony. If he's an earl, surely he has some coin to spare."

Grey drew away, went to the sofa, and patted the place beside him. "I'll tell you a secret, one unknown even to my friends."

Francesca knew much about Sir Greyville Trenton that she suspected nobody else knew: what a mare's nest he made of the covers when he was dreaming, that he missed England for all his talk of thriving on exploration, that he was an accomplished artist with an eye for natural beauty, that he was both affectionate and playful.

And that she would miss him for the rest of her days.

"As a diplomat's daughter, I learned to be wary of secrets," she said, coming down beside him. "They can be more trouble than they're worth."

He wrapped an arm around her shoulders, and Francesca cuddled close. They'd taken to working like this in the evenings, she reading over his writing for the day, and he reviewing her work. The closer the time to part came, the more constantly Francesca craved Grey's touch.

"Here's the Trenton family secret: Earldoms cost a bloody lot of money. If anybody ever offers you one, politely decline, lest you end up bankrupt. I suspect this is why peers cannot be jailed for debt, because a need for coin goes with the lofty title."

Francesca's late husband would not have argued. On the rare occasions when Pietro lost his temper, it was in response to one of his sons overspending, or one of his ministers failing to manage within the budgetary means allotted.

"Your brother is pockets to let," Francesca said. "That's why you rent out your estate in Kent, because your family needs the money."

Grey let his head fall back against the cushions. "I made the suggestion that Sebastian and my mother use my estate as their residence and rent out the family seat. This is done, though I know it causes talk. The scheme was eminently sensible, the family seat being huge, commodious, and well maintained. Mama threatened to disown me. Sebastian's wife would rather plague visit the house than become an object of pity."

Francesca scooted about, wiggling down to rest her head against Grey's thigh. "They refuse to practice economies, so you go hat in hand to strangers, hoping to find a means of supporting your family while risking your life, braving all manner of hardship, and having no home of your own."

His hand paused mid-stroke over her hair. "You sound like Stratton and Stirling, though they aren't half so blunt and at least wait until we've done some justice to the brandy."

"I loved my husband, Grey. He was a good man, though far from perfect. When he became ill, and his mistresses took up with his wealthy friends, he apologized to me. He began to make promises, all of which began with, 'When I'm back in good health…' He never regained his health, and our marriage never blossomed into what it might have been. I want you to blossom."

She used the edge of her sleeve to wipe at her eyes. "Two years in China, four years in the jungle, you mentioned a voyage to Greenland when you were twenty. Is that what you want for the rest of your life? Do you really owe your family that much risk and deprivation, year after year?"

He lifted her into his lap, when Francesca had feared he might leave the room.

"I cannot abide your tears," he said, mopping at her face with a wrinkled handkerchief. "Francesca, you must not cry. Please stop."

"I c-can't," she wailed. "I don't want you to go. I know you love the adventure, and I know you make a great contribution, but I want you to be safe and happy, and I want—"

He kissed her, which was fortunate, because she'd been about to confess to wanting to sleep beside him every night, whether in a bed, a hammock, or on the bare, hard earth.

"This is why I must go to India," he said. "Because there, if I can learn to cultivate tea, I will have a commodity of great value, and I'll be able to produce it within the British empire. I can also teach others how to grow it and use my plantation to start more tea gardens. The venture could be enormously lucrative, and while India is exotic, it's not the Amazon jungle. I can see no other way to justify the faith my friends and the scientific community have shown me, Francesca. Fortune for once smiled upon me, and I owe it to my country and my family to seize the opportunity with both hands."

Grey grabbed the afghan from the back of the couch and wrapped her in it. Francesca closed her eyes and reveled in his embrace, even as she resented his devotion to honor.

All too soon, one of those dratted wealthy sponsors would realize what an opportunity Grey's next adventure posed, and he'd be away again, for years, possibly for the rest of his life.

And yet, she found a reason to be comforted too.

He was no longer spouting lofty platitudes about science, knowledge, and the betterment of mankind. He'd admitted to a very human ambition to look after his family. Francesca had been unable and unwilling to compete with science as Grey's first passion, but she understood the need to care for loved ones.

She understood that need very well and fell asleep pondering how she might assist him to reach his goal, because she cared very much for him indeed.

* * *

"Another one," Grey said, putting the letter on the stack for the day. "The comtesse has developed a passion for mummies. I had high hopes for her, but even your skill was insufficient to interest her in my next expedition."

Grey was losing interest in his next expedition. India had seemed perfect—exotic but not a series of unrelenting perils. He'd visited a few of the Indian ports on the voyage to China and liked what he'd seen. In India, he could find a balance between a need for scientific stimulation and a need for goddamned coin.

He'd lost his balance the moment Francesca Pomponio had joined him in Zeus's saddle. What he needed more than anything was time with her.

Francesca rose from the table and came over to perch in Grey's lap, which she'd occupied for some agreeable time the evening before.

"I'm sorry the comtesse disappointed you. Are there more potential sponsors you'd like me to write to?"

He drew her close, the feel of her in his arms a comfort against all miseries. "I've gone through my old journals, asked my colleagues, and importuned my brother. My resources are exhausted. I will be reduced to taking a professorial chair at Cambridge, while better connected, more charming fellows are getting back out into the field."

He was whining, and Grey detested whiners.

"You're tired," Francesca said. "You haven't taken a break yet today, and the sun is even shining, or it was."

Some considerate soul named Francesca had put a cushion in Grey's chair, and thus his ability to remain seated had improved. His ability to remain optimistic had deserted him utterly.

"Francesca, I am not very good company right now. Perhaps you should dine with your friends."

She rose, when he wanted to cling to her and bury his nose in her hair.

"I will order us trays," she said, "because the dinner hour approaches. I suspect my friends are finding the company of *your* friends very agreeable, though one wonders where Mr. Stirling has got off to. Are you fretting over money?"

"Yes." No money meant no travels to India. No travels to India meant no hope of repairing the family fortunes. No hope of repairing the family fortunes, much less fortifying his own, meant no hope of taking a wife.

Grey had admitted that to himself in the small hours of the morning, as he'd carried a sleeping Francesca back to her bed.

Because Francesca was regarding him with that level, patient look, he told her the rest of it.

"I'm also increasingly resentful of my brother's unwillingness to take what steps he could to put us back on solid footing. It's not as if I'm inviting him to move into a crofter's hut."

"You've made do with much less than that on many occasions."

"I've slept in my canoe and been grateful. Slept in trees, subsisted on coconuts, fished with a knife lashed to a stick, and damned near watched my toes rot off, but my brother cannot make do with a mere three thousand acres of some of the best farmland in the home counties."

"You put me in mind of a duchess I once knew," Francesca said, picking up the letter from the comtesse. "Her life looked like one grand soiree, all jewels and pretty clothes, lavish meals and handsome courtiers. She was terribly lonely, often exhausted, criticized for what she did and for what she failed to do. Court intrigues ranged from affairs with her husband, to plots on her life, to attempted poisonings. I would not wish that life on anybody."

She spoke with quiet vehemence, perhaps about a friend she'd known in Italy.

"In every fairy tale, there's a wolf," Grey said. "In every garden, a serpent or a poison frog. Do you miss Italy?"

He was changing the subject, or trying to.

"I have money, Grey. I have pots and buckets of it, and it's my money, earned enduring years of marriage. I will sponsor your expedition to India."

She flung the offer at him as if she knew he'd refuse it, for he must.

He rose and took the letter from her. "I am more grateful to you than I can say, Francesca, but you are a widow, alone in the world but for two aunts whom I suspect you support. I see how you attire yourself here—no jewels, no costly silks, no ostentation whatsoever. Even your nightgown bespeaks a woman of modest means. You're young, and what funds you have must last the rest of your life. I cannot allow you to do this."

She whirled away. "*Allow?* You cannot *allow?* Who are you to allow me anything, Greyville Trenton?"

He was an idiot. "I misspoke. I cannot ask you to do this. An expedition is exorbitantly costly. Stock all the machetes you please, and if nobody lays in a supply of whetstones to keep them sharp, you're doomed by the fifth day in the jungle. If some idiot accepts a block of sugar instead of salt, more doom. The contingencies and precautions all cost money, and I cannot safeguard my future at the expense of your own."

Francesca was standing before the fire, her arms crossed, and Grey felt as if he were bludgeoning her with a poker.

"You were willing to accept money from the comtesse."

"She is a noblewoman," Grey said. "She has an obligation to do what she can for the greater good with the means entrusted to her. She has taken such risks before and has extensive family to care for her if an expedition comes to naught."

The argument had the barest pretension to logic, but Francesca could not possibly grasp the sums at issue and that the money—an entire fortune—could simply disappear. All Grey had to show for his trip to Greenland was a few papers in scholarly journals and memoirs purchased mostly by his friends.

Also a lung fever that had nearly killed him.

"That's your justification for rejecting my help?" Francesca said. "I'm not a noblewoman?"

"You're oversimplifying. I cannot be responsible for squandering your widow's mite, Francesca. I'll sell my estate in Kent before I'll allow you to put your future at risk for me."

"Don't do that," she said, marching up to him. "Don't part with the only asset you have of your own, the one place you might call home, in a desperate gamble to bring the family finances right. Don't do it, Grey."

Her previous display had been pique, annoyance, or mere anger. This was rage.

"People sell estates all the time, Francesca, and the more London sprawls into the countryside, the more the estate is worth. I will provision a modest expedition, let my brother manage the remaining proceeds in the funds, and content myself with a succession of projects that allow me to do what I do best."

He'd never planned on selling his only property, and the idea made him bilious now.

"Englishmen go home, Grey," Francesca said. "My father told me this, and he was right. An Englishman might spend twenty years in India, Canada, or Cape Town, but he'll come home. If you suffer an injury in the field, where will you retire for the rest of your life? If the title needs an heir, where will that future earl be raised? Under your brother's roof? In a canoe? And you'll entrust your money—the last of your private funds—to a man who can't understand a basic budget?"

She was magnificent in her ire, and her litany was nothing more than Grey's own list of anxieties, though there was plenty of time for Sebastian and Annabelle to have a son.

"I mention selling the estate as a last resort," Grey said. "I can always sell a farm or two first."

"No, you cannot," Francesca said, pacing before the fire. "You sell a farm or two, and your income from rent drops, and the value of your estate falls too, because you sell off the best tenancies first. You have a bit of cash, but that cash always seems to disappear into necessary repairs, pensions for the elderly retainers, or emergencies. Do not sell your land."

Her husband had been wealthy, and she spoke with the conviction of one who knew her subject well. Still, she wasn't merely lecturing, she was quietly ranting.

"Why are you so upset, Francesca?" She hadn't been this emotional discussing her husband's infidelities or his death.

"Because you are an idiot, Greyville Trenton. You are the most intelligent, dear, principled, hardworking idiot I've ever met. Your brother is the earl, your mother is a countess. They are relying on you to *risk your life*, over and over, to keep them in pearl necklaces, matched teams, and Bond Street tailoring. Forget an obligation to do what they can for the greater good. Where is their obligation to do what they can for *you*?"

She asked a question that Grey had not permitted himself to pose.

"You make a valid point." More than that, Grey could not say. His family had no idea the dangers he'd faced, and he'd left them to their ignorance rather than risk them meddling. They likely pictured the Amazon forest as a dampish place populated with spotted house cats, pond frogs, and the occasional parrot to add a dash of color.

"You mean I'm right," Francesca said. "You're right about something too."

"An increasingly rare occurrence."

"You said you were poor company and advised me to take myself off. I'll oblige you. Leave the letter from the comtesse on the desk. I'll answer her in the morning."

She left without a hug, a kiss, or a touch of the hand, and she didn't even have the decency to slam the door.

* * *

As Pietro lay dying, he'd stopped referring to the time when he'd regain his health and instead resorted to a series of warnings. Each of them had begun with, *You must listen to me, Francesca.*

The man who'd seldom listened to his wife demanded that she listen to him, and Francesca had tried her best to oblige.

He'd told her widows were vulnerable, and she might find pleasure where she chose, but to guard her heart. Always end an affair too soon, he'd said, end it with a smile and fond kiss. Let no man develop assumptions where her future was concerned—or her money.

Sir Greyville would have failed spectacularly at Italian court intrigue. He refused to develop designs on a fortune laid at his booted feet.

"He'd make a study of an intrigue," Francesca muttered. "Sketch its parts in the wild."

The maid looked up from banking the fire, but said nothing, for Francesca had spoken in Italian. Working with Grey's notes, calling upon Latin, French, Spanish, Portuguese, and even the occasional reference to Dutch, had revitalized her linguistic facility.

Also her body and, damn the man, her heart.

"Will that be all, ma'am?" the maid asked. Ma'am, not Your Grace, not even *signora.*

"Yes, thank you."

The maid curtseyed and departed on a soft click of the door latch, and then Francesca was alone. She had no intention of wasting a night in solitude when she might spend it with Grey, even though he was a stubborn, pig-headed, arrogant...

No, not arrogant. Protective, but also presuming.

Francesca could not afford to indulge his gentlemanly sensibilities. She gathered the candles from the mantel, sat down at the escritoire, and took out paper, ink, sand, and pen. She was halfway through a letter to her banker in York when the door opened.

"I apologize," Grey said, closing the door. "I'm not very good at it, and not sure it will do any good when I cannot accept your money, but I upset you and must make what amends I can."

He was attired in a worn blue velvet dressing gown and his black cotton pajama pants, though his feet were bare.

"You'll catch your death without slippers," Francesca said. "Give me a moment to finish this letter, and you can make another try at soothing my ruffled feathers, though you're right. It won't do any good."

While she signed and sanded her letter, Grey wandered the room like a wild creature in a menagerie—restless, exuding unhappiness, in want of activity. He opened the wardrobe, where pressed gowns hung and slippers were lined up by color. His next investigation led him to the cedar-lined trunk at the foot of the bed, where Francesca kept shawls, pelisses, cloaks, and boots.

He closed the trunk and sat on it. "I must get to India, Francesca, but I'll not bankrupt you to do it."

"You wouldn't bankrupt me." She hadn't the means to prove that to him, though, not here in England, and he'd demand proof.

"You can't know that. The optimal approach is to outfit an entire vessel, hand-choose my subordinates, bring all manner of botanical equipment with me and enough of my personal effects that if I never return to England, I can establish a household, conservatory, and laboratory of my own. The effort is comparable to moving a small, highly specialized army."

And one stubborn Englishman.

"I have resources you do not," she said, capping the ink bottle and pouring the sand back into its container. "By way of compromise, please allow me to contact them on your behalf. You'd be surprised how many princesses and dowager duchesses a diplomat's daughter befriends at an Italian court. Don't let your pride get in the way of your reason."

Grey had great pride, but was also eminently rational.

"You think *women* will fund my next investigation?" He hadn't dismissed the idea out of hand, which was encouraging. "I had considered the comtesse an anomaly, an eccentric."

Whose coin he'd been willing to take.

"You drink tea in England largely because Catherine of Braganza made it a popular court drink, else you men would have hoarded it in your coffee shops. Think of the last time you took tea, Grey, and the time before that. A lady presided, and she doesn't go through her day without drinking tea several times."

He was on his feet again, poking his nose into Francesca's effects. He lifted the lid of her jewelry box, which held only the few decorative pieces Francesca traveled with.

"I will concede that tea is a lady's drink. What would you say to these women?"

"That I've learned of an investment opportunity full of both risk and potential reward." *He has dark eyes, dark hair, a brilliant mind, and a good heart, for all he's sometimes dunderheaded.*

Grey examined a strand of pink pearls that had been Francesca's first gift to herself as a widow. "All investment opportunities present those factors. What else?"

"That if this investigation goes well, greater society could benefit as much as the investors do, eventually, but that scientific snobbery means this project will likely not receive the attention it deserves from other sources."

He threaded the pearls through his fingers and sat cross-legged on the bed. "That's very good, and you're right. Haring about India in search of optimal conditions for a tea farm is hardly glamorous, not when compared with orchids in Mexican jungles or emeralds from darkest Africa. I also can't disclose exactly why I'm looking now, lest I put my own fledging operation at risk."

He toyed with the pearls, luminous beads among candlelit shadows. "Send a half-dozen letters, no more. I can't have it said that Sir Greyville is growing desperate, though I am."

He'd apologized, he'd listened to her, he'd made concessions. Francesca had by no means made her last argument, but the time had come for her to compromise as well.

"You're desperate to find funding?" she asked.

He regarded her across the room, his expression unreadable. "Very nearly. I'm also desperate to see you wearing these pearls and nothing else."

They had so little time. "If I asked you to leave, would you?"

He was off the bed, the pearls put back where they belonged. "Of course. I'll bid you pleasant dreams and hope to see you in the morning."

Another man would have tried to change her mind, flirt her past her frustrations, or explain to her that his stubbornness was an effort to put her best interests above his own. With Grey, Francesca didn't need to protect her privacy, and maybe because of that, she couldn't protect her heart.

"Stay with me," she said. "For the time we have left, please stay with me."

* * *

Lady Hester Stanhope was said to be leading an excavation of the ancient city of Ashkelon—leading it, not tagging along after her father, brother, or husband.

After serving as hostess for no less person than the British prime minster, she'd collected a companion, a personal physician, and such other retainers and supplies as she'd needed, before embarking on an adventure that was the envy of half the British scientific community.

Where it would lead, nobody quite knew. The scientific establishment seemed torn between discrediting her as an eccentric and admitting grudging envy for her pluck. Nothing—not shipwreck, not cultural prohibitions against women, not privation or hardship—had deterred her from her objective.

Caroline Herschel, sister to the recently knighted William Herschel, had been his salaried assistant when he'd served as royal astronomer. The woman had discovered no less than eight comets, among her other contributions.

How many anomalous data points could one man's theory of himself as scientist withstand?

Grey set aside the question as imponderable, for science was useful only in situations lending themselves to measurement by the five senses. More complicated questions, such as how to put matters right with Francesca, required tools Grey did not command.

Last night, he'd apologized, but he hadn't agreed to take her money. For the first time, they'd made love silently, no lover's talk, no whispered confidences or spirited arguments. The aftermath had left him wrung out and, in some way, unsatisfied.

He missed Francesca already, though she sat at her customary place across the office, her pen moving steadily. She'd sealed up her letter to the countess before Grey had come down, and now she was occupied writing to her "resources."

"Francesca, might you attend me for a moment?"

"I'll be through here in two minutes."

He took out a clean sheet of paper and let his pencil flow over the blank space. When she'd stormed off last night, he'd sat in his pillowed chair and tried to sketch her. Without a live model, he'd made a bad job of it.

"That's done," she said, setting her correspondence aside. "What would you like to discuss?"

"Join me on the sofa, please."

Francesca took off his best glasses—maybe they were hers by now—folded her arms, and remained in her chair.

He still hadn't the goddamned knack of phrasing his needs as requests. "I meant, would you please join me on the sofa?" Grey said, depositing his own aching backside in the middle of the cushions. She'd have to sit next to him, one way or the other.

"For a brilliant man, you are difficult to educate," she said, taking the place to his right. "But I do see progress."

Grey took her hand, knowing full well she was still unhappy with him. They'd made love, they'd not made peace.

"Stratton informs me that your coach should be repaired by week's end. You'll be free to resume your journey by Monday at the latest. Will you allow me to write to you?"

She stared into the fire rather than at him. "Why?"

Because he'd go mad without knowing how she fared, because his theories would not be as well-reasoned without her questions to test them, because nobody would celebrate with him as sincerely when he'd finished a publishable version of his accounts.

"Because there might be a child."

She withdrew her hand. "But you…"

"I have taken precautions, but conception can occur nonetheless. I have at least two godsons whose existence attests to this fact." Darling little fellows he didn't get to see often enough.

"And if I've conceived?"

What was the right answer, assuming there was one? "I will, of course, take responsibility for the consequences of my actions." Not an outright proposal, which Francesca might well fling in his face, but not a wrong answer, Grey hoped.

And why hadn't he proposed when they'd first become lovers?

Because he had so little to give her. No real home, no income other than what little he set aside from the revenue his estate generated, no solid prospects of a professional nature—*none*. A time of shared pleasure was all he could honestly offer.

That answer didn't satisfy him. He doubted it would satisfy her.

"You are a good man," she said, "and in the grip of circumstances not entirely of your own making. I have ample means to raise a child, Grey, and you needn't fear I'd foster out my own progeny. After two miscarriages, if I have a chance to be a mother, then propriety can go hang, and a loving, joyously devoted mother I shall be."

He should not have been surprised, at either the ferocity of her maternal instinct, or his reaction to her assurances that means were the essence of the discussion. He'd seen many families in far-flung locations whose means would be pitiful by British standards, and yet, their children had been happy and thriving.

"I cannot make demands of you," Grey said, "but I can ask that you inform me if such developments are in the offing."

"I'll think about it."

He also could not insist that he had a right to know. Not even that monument to patriarchal arrogance, the British legal system, gave a man the right to supervise the upbringing of his children unless that man was married to their mother.

Grey rose and for once could not make himself return to the damned chair behind the desk. "Please know that your joy in and devotion to the child would be matched only by my own. If you'll excuse me, I'll catch a breath of fresh air while the sun yet shines."

* * *

In the few days remaining, Francesca developed a routine with Grey that ensured they'd not have any more difficult discussions. He took to riding out in the morning, while she worked diligently on the indexes and glossary. In the afternoons, while Grey focused on his manuscript, Francesca napped or tended to correspondence she'd neglected the previous week. A duchess had every bit as much correspondence as a biologist, after all.

What time they spent together was taken up with discussion of poison plants, poison fish, and poison frogs, that being the topic of Grey's current chapter. He did not seem to be making much progress on it, though Francesca suspected she knew why.

To use Grey's terminology, their experiment had yielded unexpected results.

In plain English, they'd surprised each other. A short, spontaneous liaison undertaken in the interests of pleasure and affection had become something altogether different. Friday arrived without Francesca having replied to Grey's request to stay in touch by letter.

Grey had said he'd treasure a child of theirs, and yet, he still waited anxiously for word regarding funding for his expedition to India.

What was she to make of that?

"You have an avalanche of mail today," she said as a footman put the stack on his desk. "If I can work without interruption for the rest of the afternoon, I can finish up your glossary, and you'll have your notes arranged by subject and cross-referenced by date."

The footman—his name really was John—bowed and withdrew, while Grey wrinkled his nose at the mail. "I almost dread reading my correspondence anymore. Do you depart tomorrow, Francesca?"

Their nights had been spent in a silent frenzy of tenderness, and then they'd fall asleep, too exhausted to do more than hold each other in the darkness.

"Monday," she said. "I'll part from my friends in York."

"You'll not spend a holiday with them?" Grey's question was oblique, but at least he was admitting interest in her future.

"My friends appear to be making plans at variance with our original intentions. I have business in York, and it's a lovely city." If one enjoyed a crumbling Roman wall and a minster so old its stone roots sank into antiquity.

Though an Italian duchess had no need of more antiquity.

Rather than inquire directly of her itinerary, or bring up again the fraught notion of a child, Grey went back to his correspondence. He had the ability to soldier on, despite reluctance or difficulties. That came through in his notes and in Francesca's observations of him.

He was a good, honorable man, and she was so frustrated with him that when he opened her door that night, she nearly tackled him.

"I take it today's correspondence held nothing of importance?" she asked.

He closed the door and locked it. "No rejections. I will count that as progress. I finally get a glimpse of you with your hair down."

"My hair? What has hair to do with—?"

He stalked across the room, his dressing gown flapping about his knees. "Your hair is beautiful, and I want to sketch you with it down. We're almost out of time, Francesca. Let me have at least a likeness to recall you by."

Not too much to ask, and yet, Francesca hadn't counted on the fact that when she sat for him, she had nothing to do but watch him sketch her. Grey's focus was singular as his hand moved across a blank page. The gap in his dressing gown, the lock of hair that refused to stay behind his left ear, he took no notice of either, while Francesca was forced to stare at both.

"Will you let me see the finished result?"

"Will you let me write to you?"

His question gratified her on a purely selfish level. "I'll leave you the direction for my aunts in Sussex. They always know how to reach me."

"Thank you."

For another half hour Grey was silent, the only sounds his pencil scratching across the page and the fire burning down. Francesca's shoulders were growing chilled when he finally set his pencil and paper aside.

"Shall I braid my hair now?"

"No," he said, rising and shrugging out of his dressing gown. "You shall not. Do you know I made more progress with my infernal manuscript when you were on hand to distract me in person? This business of disappearing for naps... I'm aware that I deprive you of sleep, Francesca, but I've missed you these past few days."

She would miss him forever, if he had his way. "Grey..."

His trousers went next, tossed over the back of the chair at the escritoire. To her surprise, he was fully aroused.

Simply from looking at her?

"Now," he said, stalking to the bed, "you distract me from within my own mind. I see you on the banks of the Amazon, in the high Andes, in the blinding sunshine on the waves of the Atlantic. I hear you scolding me for inconsistent terminology, and I listen to the soft rustling as you shuffle stacks of chaos into a tidy, rational order."

Some fever had seized him, an anger and a determination Francesca couldn't fathom. "If I don't braid my hair, come morning—"

"Come morning, we will be that much closer to your departure," he said, untying the bows of her nightgown. "Come morning, I will bury myself once more in plants that yield a paralyzing toxin, twenty-foot-long alligators that can swallow a man whole, and schools of pretty fish that make a plundering army seem tame. Right now, I'd like to bury myself in you."

All over again, she was swamped with terror at the risks he'd taken, month after month, and the risks he'd take again.

"No more jungles, Grey, please. Find places to explore that won't try to kill you twice a day."

His answer was an openmouthed kiss, one that sent her sprawling onto her back across the bed. He kept coming, wrapping his hands in her hair, crouching over her as if he were a wild beast let loose from the pages of his journal.

He was no longer the man of science, confident of his powers, observing and analyzing from the safe distance of intellect and reason. He was the storm in Francesca's heart and the fire in her body. He was hope, misery, rage, and longing, and at least until Monday, he was hers.

Grey had shown her any number of ways to make love—side by side, back to front, on her knees, her back to the wall, and her favorite, him on his back beneath her. For this coupling, Grey remained for once above her, his weight anchoring her to the mattress.

"I have nothing to offer you but this," he said, joining them on one hard thrust.

The words were jarring and the sensation overwhelming. Too soon, Francesca was spiraling upward, desire besieging her from within.

"You have so much—" she managed, before Grey was kissing her again, his passion nearly savage. She went over the edge, bucking against him until she could see, hear, touch, and taste only a pleasure so intense it left her in tears.

CHAPTER SEVEN

The staff apparently knew not to disturb Mrs. Pomponio of a morning until she was stirring behind her door. In any case, Grey recalled locking Francesca's door the previous evening. In the cool light of approaching dawn, he studied his sketch where it sat on her escritoire, a good effort, if a bit too...

Too passionate, too wishful, and too wistful.

"Grey?"

He tended the fire and climbed back under the covers. "I should have left you two hours ago."

Francesca moved into his embrace easily, for they'd acquired the knack of sleeping together the first night. "It's hard to get back to sleep in a cold bed, isn't it?"

Impossible. "I suppose if one is tired enough, sleep comes eventually. Francesca, will you be all right?"

She turned to her side, so Grey was spooned around her. "I will miss you and be upset with you for some time. Rub my back, please."

He'd learned to do this and wished he could ask her for return of the same favor. He had much to learn about asking for kindnesses and had a sinking suspicion that if he couldn't learn those lessons from Francesca, he'd never master them.

Her back was a wonder of feminine grace, but sturdy too. He'd studied anatomy—what biologist hadn't?—but in the past week, he'd studied her. Her right shoulder was a fraction of an inch higher than her left, and that asymmetry was repeated in her hips. The hair at the juncture of her thighs bore a reddish tinge, and her second toe was longer than the first.

She liked chocolate—vanilla was bland by comparison—and a German fruit brandy made from cherries. She sometimes dreamed in Italian, sometimes English, and had a collection of cream cake recipes inherited from her late mother-in-law that she considered a dear treasure.

"You do that so well," she murmured. "Your greatest talents lie in the bedroom, Grey, not the jungle. Will you be all right?"

No, he would not. In the past two weeks, his concepts of family, science, himself, and his place in the world had been upended, thanks to one forthright, passionate widow.

"One expects challenges."

Francesca rolled over and peered at him in the gloom. Her hair was a glorious mess, and desire rose as the covers dipped low across her bosom.

"I meant what I said, Greyville. Please do not consign yourself to the most dangerous, difficult, disease-ridden corners of the earth in an effort to prove you don't want your pony back. You've racketed about for ten years and made both your point and your contribution."

He pushed her hair away from her brow and arranged himself over her. "I adore you when you lecture me." He adored her every waking moment and in half of his dreams.

She ran a toe up the side of his calf. "Somebody needs to lecture you. I will worry about you."

"India is civilized enough." In places. At times.

"India is too bloody far away, and so are you." She urged him closer by virtue of clutching his backside.

Grey retaliated by getting his mouth on her nipple, and for long, lovely moments, they teased each other into a fever of desire. He managed not to hurry the joining or the lovemaking, because he needed to hoard impressions against the coming separation.

That effort was hopeless. Memories were not objects, to be cataloged and preserved, and no memory would lessen the pain of sending Francesca on her way Monday morning.

Her breathing took on the rhythm of escalating desire, and Grey needed all of his focus to restrain his own pleasure. He dared not open his eyes to watch as passion claimed her, and he dared not close his eyes lest sensation claim him. He settled for fixing his gaze on the spill of Francesca's hair across the sheets, gold on ivory, silk on cotton.

She shuddered beneath him, and when he was sure she could bear the sensation, he withdrew and spent on her belly.

"I wish…" she said, stroking his hair. "I wish, and wish, and wish, Greyville."

He wished, he dreamed, he racked his brain, and second-guessed himself. "I know, my love. I know."

He held her while she dozed off, and wishes lay in silent disarray in his mind, like so much leaf litter on the forest floor after a terrible storm. He could not leave her, he could not offer for her, he could not take her money and risk it all in India, but to India he must go.

Grey awoke to the scents of jasmine and peat—a distinctive combination—and the warmth of the sun on his shoulder. He got out of bed, dressed, and kissed a sleeping Francesca farewell.

How he hated himself for keeping the truth from her.

He'd said the mail contained no more rejections, which was true but not honest. A titled acquaintance of the comtesse had caught wind of his project and made so bold as to express an enthusiasm for his proposal and a desire to invest in it.

Funding had been very nearly promised, and all Grey could think was that he didn't want to leave Francesca, not for all the tea in… not for all the tea, anywhere.

* * *

Francesca had found the Sabbath observation in England a form of purgatory. Nobody undertook travel unless from most dire necessity, industry of any kind was frowned upon, and even Sir Greyville Trenton limited his activities to reading.

While Francesca packed up her belongings and worried. Grey was keeping something from her, though she wasn't sure what. He'd had no correspondence from family that she'd seen, but then, she didn't go through his correspondence like a snooping wife.

"Have you left already, Francesca, that you disdain to join me in the office this afternoon?" Grey stood in her bedroom doorway, and despite the late hour, he was still dressed.

Just as well.

"I am, as your powers of observation confirm, very much still here. I did not want to burden the maids with tending to my belongings, so I've packed my trunk and will be ready for an early departure tomorrow."

"Damn it, Francesca, I don't know whether to bow and wish you safe journey, or make passionate love to you for the next ten hours."

For all but the last few months of her marriage, Pietro would never have thought to consider Francesca's wishes in either regard. He'd come and gone as he pleased, in her life and in her bedroom. What a miserable lot a duchess endured, if Pietro's example held true across the ducal species.

"Greyville." She stood immediately before him. "You should do what makes you happy, but I cannot… That is…"

He closed the door and took her in his arms. "Tell me, Francesca."

The lump in her throat had grown to the size of an Italian duchy. She shook her head and clung to him. "I'm being silly."

He carried her to the bed—how she would miss his masculine displays of consideration—and sat with her in his lap.

"Do you know," he said, "I have spent more time talking with you than with any other adult woman, save perhaps my mother? One doesn't exactly talk with

Mama though. One accepts orders. In all the times we've spoken, Francesca, I've never heard you refer to any friends, save your traveling companions."

What blasted observation was he going on about now? "Olivia and Mary Alice are friends of long standing. Good friends."

He scooted back so he was supported by the headboard. "And did these good friends, in all the years since your come out, ever visit you?"

"My acquaintance with Olivia doesn't go back that far. Mary Alice wrote."

"Twice a year?"

"What is your point, Grey?"

"You have made me ponder my situation, Francesca, and it seems in some ways similar to your own."

She doubted very much he'd been married to a self-important Italian duke. "Explain yourself."

Grey kissed her temple. "There are wildernesses, and wildernesses. Some pose a danger to the body, and some pose a danger to the spirit. I was nearly dragged overboard at one point early in my last exploration by a great, black creature similar in nature to an alligator, but twice as long."

"The caiman. You drew pictures of them."

"Sketches made from a great distance, I can assure you. I think your husband's infidelity nearly dragged you overboard. You mention no friends in Italy, no in-laws with whom you still correspond. I suspect you came to England because your aunts are here and because it holds at least memories of friendship."

Francesca had made that discovery in the past two weeks herself, but memories of friendship were not the same as the living, breathing article.

"Do you have friends, Greyville?"

"I have colleagues and, like you, close associations left over from my youth. I account Stratton and Stirling true friends, and I hope they would say the same of me. Friends tell each other what's amiss, Francesca, and though we part tomorrow, I am your friend."

She snuggled closer and considered his hypothesis. "Do friends typically make passionate love with each other at every opportunity?"

"Friends are kind and honest with each other. They are tolerant of one another's foibles. They offer acceptance, commiseration, and companionship. They share joys and sorrows and often hold each other in great affection. You will have to explain to me how that definition precludes shared intimacies."

It didn't, and worse, Francesca had hoped her marriage would have all of those qualities. In the end, it had, but only in the end.

"There's no baby, Greyville. My courses started this afternoon."

His hand on her back slowed. "And how does this development find you?"

Weepy, angry, bewildered. "It's for the best."

He gathered her close. "That's not your heart talking. What is convenient is not always for the best. Your news leaves me feeling sad, thoughtful, disappointed—also relieved that association with me has not unduly burdened your future."

They remained on the bed while Francesca considered his list. If she'd been carrying his child, he would have married her, and all manner of complications involving money, science, and friendship would have ensued.

She hoped there was another way. "I wish you weren't so noble."

"Noble, I am not. That burden at least remains my brother's. Would you like me to sleep in my own bed tonight, Francesca?"

She sat up enough to peer at him. "What are you asking?"

"You needn't look at me like that. I would not impose on you when you're indisposed, but I would like to stay with you."

Grey so rarely asked for anything for himself, and Francesca very much wanted his arms about her, more than ever.

"Please stay." She couldn't have asked that of any friend, nor did she think it a typical request between lovers, considering her indisposition.

Only a husband would be allowed such intimacy. Before the tears could claim Francesca again, she helped Grey out of his clothes and climbed beneath the covers with him one last time.

* * *

Saying good-bye to Francesca was hell.

Grey insisted on walking her to the coach wherein her friend Mary Alice waited. All the way, Francesca lectured him, about indexes, subheadings, and lists of sketches and figures. Was this how his family had felt when he'd maundered on about curare and caimans as his departure date had approached?

"Francesca, you will please recall that I am acquainted with the notion of an index and that the figures you mention were drawn by my own hand. I might have some insight into their organization."

The Yorkshire breeze blew nearly constantly, and already a strand of her hair was whipping across her lips.

"Insight and action are two different things, Greyville. If you don't start listing the figures separately from the sketches now, you will never do it. Several years of illustrations is an enormous body of work, and unless it's well organized, none of it will be of use to anybody."

One of the coach horses stomped, causing the harness to jingle. Other farewells were in progress several yards away, between Stratton and the woman Mary Alice. Stratton's small daughter looked as woebegone as Grey felt.

"I will be no use to anybody for at least a month after you get into the coach, Francesca."

She glanced back at the house, where at least six dozen servants were doubtless watching from the windows.

"Then I'd best be on my way, hadn't I? Thank you, Grey, for everything, and please be safe."

She kissed him, and not some tame peck on the cheek. She kissed him as if her kiss would have to last him the whole distance to India and beyond. He kissed her back as if, more than funding, science, honor, or reason, she was all that would sustain him for the journey.

If he made the journey.

His arms stole around her, and she leaned on him, and to perdition with whoever might be watching.

She was about to climb into that coach and leave him, as if he were a wilderness that had been adequately explored and documented, and he could in good conscience do nothing to stop her.

"Francesca, will you write to me?"

"I need your handkerchief. This shouldn't be so difficult."

He produced the requested item. "I've been considering some options and will write to you, even if you don't write to me. Your welfare will always concern me, and my work matters, but depending on variables outside my control, at some—"

She put two gloved fingers to his lips.

"I love you, Sir Greyville Trenton. Wherever you go, whatever endeavor you undertake, however your fortunes wax and wane, I love you."

Before Grey could respond, before he could form a single word, he had to stand back so Francesca's traveling companions could join her inside.

Then some idiot—Stratton perhaps?—had slammed the coach door closed, and the team trotted off.

Grey raised his hand in farewell and stood in the drive apart from the others long after the coach had disappeared, staring at the drifting plume of dust, waving at nothing.

"Your expression suggests that woman just departed for darkest Peru and will never return."

Stratton walked over to Grey, and from the look in his eyes, the past two weeks hadn't exactly been his idea of a springtime frolic. He'd appeared quite fond of Francesca's friend, and she of him. The child had apparently returned indoors.

"Francesca is bound for York," Grey said.

"And you'll shut yourself up in the damned office and pretend your heart isn't breaking?"

The last of the dust had dissipated, leaving only the wind and the high green hills on all sides. "Two weeks ago, I would have told you that the heart cannot break," Grey said. "The organ can cease to function, but it's not a watch, to stop running as a result of an imagined impact on the emotions."

"That does sound like your typical pontifications, but it's not two weeks ago. What do you say now?"

Grey started marching for the house, his host in step beside him. "Now, I want my pony back. Sebastian has been riding my Tiger long enough."

"Greyville, I have endless respect for your brilliance, but perhaps it's time you took a repairing lease. A short respite never hurt—"

"Don't lecture," Grey said, "or I shall have to strike you. Manifestation of the frustrated mating urge perhaps, or a simple reaction to a surfeit of nonsense."

"My dear friend, I suspect you've been in the tropics too long, and now you're determined to hare off to India, of all the bug-ridden, fever-infested, pestilential purgatories. Stirling and I have often discussed the benefits of an academic—"

"The problem isn't the jungle," Grey said, striding into the manor. "I am the problem."

"Was there ever any doubt of that?"

"Some friend you are. I need to think. Be off with you."

"You've said farewell to the first woman you've noticed as anything other than a specimen in years. I will make allowances, but you're being an idiot. How will you get her back?"

And there was the problem, now that Grey had let her go. "I don't know, but I am the determined sort, and I'm well aware that a machete has little value in the jungle without a whetstone."

"Greyville, I do believe the bonds of friendship require that I get you drunk."

"A reciprocal burden falls upon me, given the mournful expression with which you watched that coach depart. Let's be about it, shall we?"

* * *

Italian women often wore black quite well, while Englishwomen, especially blond, blue-eyed Englishwomen, seldom did.

"Blond, gray-eyed Englishwomen," Francesca corrected herself, pulling off her gloves.

Despite how black washed out her complexion, Francesca had found that traveling in widow's weeds made sense. She need not attire herself as a duchess, and her privacy was respected more than it would have been had she not been heavily veiled in black.

"Good day, Your Grace. I hope your walk was enjoyable?"

MacDuie, her butler, had conveyed with the leased house, like the furnishings and cook. Francesca liked to hear him speak, for his Scottish accent was as unrelenting as his good cheer.

"My walk was peaceful, thank you."

"You have a caller, Your Grace. A gentleman."

She paused, her bonnet ribbons half untied. She'd worn her favorite mourning bonnet, the one with thick black netting that preserved her from prying eyes but still let her see and breathe.

"Has Mr. Arnold come over from the bank?"

"The gentleman's card is on the sideboard, Your Grace. A Sir Greyville Trenton. Quiet fellow, and he has some sort of letter for you. He said he wanted to deliver it in person."

Oh heavens. Oh gracious.

After nearly two weeks of waiting, hoping, and wishing for even a note, Francesca had all but given up. She was certain he'd have written, but being Grey, of course he had not. He was here, in person, ready to observe, collect data, and draw his own conclusions.

She draped her veil over her face. "No tea tray, MacDuie. I don't think the gentleman will be staying long."

Perhaps he wanted to thank her in person. She stopped halfway up the winding front stair, nearly felled by the notion that he'd already made plans to depart for India.

She entered the formal parlor very much on her dignity.

"Your Grace." Grey stood, his bow most proper. He was exquisitely attired for a morning call, not a wrinkle to be seen, and the sight of him left Francesca's knees wobbly. "Thank you for seeing me."

She gestured to the chairs arranged before the hearth. "Please have a seat, Sir Greyville."

His brows knit at the sound of her voice. "Now that is most odd. I am here because your handwriting bore a striking resemblance to that of another, a lady I esteem most highly. Perhaps an Italian education accounts for such a similarity, but you even sound like her. In any case, an offer as generous as yours deserves the courtesy of a reply in person."

Of course he'd recognize her penmanship and voice. Francesca had an Italian accent, but she usually worked to keep it behind her teeth.

"You received my letter?" she asked, putting a hint of Tuscany in the question.

"I did, two weeks ago, and I must thank you from the depths of my being for your proffered generosity."

"Shall we sit, Sir Greyville?"

He was studying her with *that look*, the one that said a quizzing glass was unnecessary, because Sir Greyville Trenton was examining the specimen, and no instrument or measuring device could improve upon his powers of observation.

He waited for Francesca to choose one of the velvet-cushioned seats, flipped out his tails, and settled near enough that she caught a hint of his exotic fragrance—the one from dratted India.

"I have penned my reply to your offer," he said, passing over a letter. "My abilities with spontaneous social discourse are wanting. Perhaps you'll read my letter now?"

Francesca broke the seal and recognized the tidiest sample of Grey's penmanship she'd ever seen. He must have copied the letter several times. And yet, as legible as the words were, Francesca could not make sense of them.

He was *rejecting* her offer. Throwing it aside when she'd delivered his heart's desire on a silver platter. Bewilderment, rage, and a curious frisson of hope had her reading his words three times.

"I don't understand, Sir Greyville. In the space of two weeks, you've decided your passions lie in another direction? I was given to understand that your dedication to science is second to none and your interest in this Indian venture considerable."

He rose and prowled the room, which was about as nondescript as elegant furnishings and good housekeeping could be. The oil painting over the mantel was of some red-coated stag posed just so in an alpine meadow, and the sideboard, chairs, and sofa were all of matched blond oak.

England at its genteel finest, and but for his sense of energy, Grey belonged in this room.

"My interest in the Indian venture will continue unabated, Your Grace, but I find for the present that more pressing concerns keep me in England."

Whatever did that mean? "Should one be concerned for your family, Sir Greyville?"

He left off admiring the stag and looked at her as if he could see right through her veil. He couldn't. Francesca had seen her reflection in enough mirrors to know the veil shielded her from observation.

"My family will be making a remove from our seat in the Midlands to a more modest property in Kent."

"*What?* I mean, I beg your pardon?"

He made a circuit of the room, pausing to study an etching of some flower or other. "The time has come for me to explore a wilderness closer to home. The matter involves a lady, Your Grace, so I will keep my comments oblique, but my mind is made up. I'll not be leaving for India in the immediate future."

He looked very severe, very resolute, also tired and dear.

Francesca folded her veil back and pinned it to her bonnet. "Grey, what on earth are you going on about? India is your heart's desire, your dream. I can make that happen for you."

He was across the parlor in two strides. "I knew it was you! By damn, Francesca, what are you about? You leave me, and now you're a duchess, and possibly not even English. I can make no sense of this."

She saw in his eyes the same emotions roiling through her—bewilderment, anger, and a small gleam of hope.

"I am the dowager duchess of the Italian duchy of San Mercato, also Francesca Pomponio Pergolesi, widowed these past five years. One travels more safely without a title, and my friends and I had a significant need for privacy."

"You haven't been sleeping," he said, scowling down at her. "And you stole my glasses."

"You stole my heart."

"One can't—you stole mine first."

They stared at each other for a fraught moment, then they were kissing, wrapped in an embrace that brought back memory upon memory, all of them happy.

Francesca broke the kiss, feeling as if she'd taken her first decent breath in days. "Are you traveling to India or not?"

"Not… without you," Grey said. "Black does not become you, Francesca. The weeds threw me off, which you probably intended. *Camouflage*, as the French would say."

"If you start spouting science now, Greyville, I will put you on a boat for India myself."

"You'd save me the trouble of getting you to the docks, for I won't leave without you, Francesca. I've had a brisk exchange of letters with my brother."

"Come," she said, taking his hand and leading him to the sofa. "Tell me."

It wasn't their sofa, but sitting beside Grey anywhere soothed an ache in Francesca that had been building for two weeks.

"I told Sebastian I wanted my pony back. He was the earl, not I, and responsibility for the family finances rested on his shoulders, not mine. My family is welcome to reside with me in Kent, but I'll no longer spend years hacking my way through insects, snakes, and mud to keep him in matched teams."

"You quoted me?"

"You have the better command of persuasive prose, Francesca. We needn't belabor the obvious."

She took his hand, drew off his glove, and laced her fingers through his. "So you'll live in Kent, cheek by jowl with your family? What about your science? What about your tea plantation?"

What about us?

"Francesca, I have more specimens, journals, and drawings than I can organize in a lifetime. I've sent plants to Kew, to the family seat, to my own conservatory, to Cambridge, and to colleagues. I can busy myself with that inventory for the next six decades. I don't need to single-handedly establish the tea industry in India. I need you. Only you."

He kissed her knuckles, while Francesca looked for holes in his theory.

"You were concerned that you'd deplete my means if I financed your voyage to India. I am scandalously wealthy, Grey. My banker will happily meet with you and describe the extent of my holdings. I'll give it all away in a moment if penury is necessary to merit your continued notice."

His arm came around her shoulders. "When I watched your coach roll away, I realized something."

Francesca had realized a few things too. "Tell me."

"Family should look after one another. Sheep know this, dogs know this. My impulse to aid my relations was not wrong, but I domesticated my family instead of allowing them to develop their natural abilities. Sebastian has composed heaps of music he hasn't published because an earl should give away his talent. That's balderdash, to use your term. Mama has jewels she never wears and doesn't even like. She should sell them and invest the proceeds. I could go on."

"You're very good at going on, among other things." Mostly, he was good at being Sir Greyville Trenton, scientist at large and the man Francesca loved.

"Well, my dear family can either accept my hospitality or fend for themselves. A little time in the wilderness is good for us all. Having discovered the obvious, I am now intent on offering you marriage."

"Don't you dare go down on one knee," Francesca said, rising. "Pietro did that, in the greatest display of hypocrisy I've ever endured. I don't want to live in Kent with your dragon of a mother and your spoiled sister-in-law."

He rose and took out his handkerchief, and even that had been neatly folded into his pocket. He produced a pair of spectacles from an inside pocket—the second-best pair.

"Francesca, I would like to support my wife, assuming you'll have me. We can reach an accommodation—my manor house has thirty-six rooms—but you will have to elucidate your reservations."

Thirty-six rooms was nearly the size of the ducal villa Francesca had called home for five years.

"I understand that you want to support your wife and children, Grey, but I want to support science. As it happens, I meant what I said in my letter to you. Establishing a tea industry in India strikes me as a brilliant investment opportunity and a way to contribute significantly to the realm."

If he polished his spectacles any more vigorously, he'd part the lens from the frames. "You *want* me to go to India? Francesca, the voyage can take months, and my destination is the western region of the subcontinent. I could easily be gone for five years."

"We could be gone."

He dropped his spectacles on the carpet and made no move to pick them up. "I'm not sure I heard you correctly."

The handkerchief in his hand shook minutely, as if a small tempest beset it.

"We could be gone. Officer's wives go out to India all the time, Grey. My plan was to follow you out and capture you in the wild. I never anticipated that you'd pounce upon a widowed Italian duchess right here in England."

"You were prepared...? You were prepared to *follow me to India?* Francesca, I hardly know what to say."

She picked up his glasses and handed them to him. "Say what's in your heart. I love you, and I want you to be happy. I want you to make the contributions only you, Sir Greyville Trenton, can make. If that means I sleep with you in a hammock, then I'll sleep with you in hammock. It's as you said, Grey. Loneliness stalks us, bitterness, regret. Against those predators, the only haven is love. For two weeks with you, I was content, complete, and full of dreams. I want that back. If I have to go to India to get it, that's a small price to pay for a lifetime of happiness."

His arms came around her. "You deliver a very convincing lecture, Francesca, and I cannot hope to equal its eloquence."

She kissed his cheek. "Try."

"Yes, love." He fell silent for a moment, then spoke very softly, right near her ear. "I enjoy science."

"And you are very good at it." Brilliant, in fact.

"And I am very good at it. I love you. I would like to become the best in the world at that undertaking. I would like my expertise in this regard to eclipse all known records and become a species of love unto itself. I can pursue my objective in India, in Kent, and anywhere in between, but only if you are by my side, as my wife, my companion, my lover, and my guide."

"Your skill with a lecture is improving."

"I'm the determined sort. Say yes, Francesca. Please, or I'll make an idiot of myself and start begging."

"Yes, Grey. Yes, I will be your wife, and all those other things, in India, Kent, and everywhere in between. Do you suppose we might remark the occasion by exploring my private apartment in the next ten minutes?"

He resorted to a manly display of consideration and swept her up into his arms. "A logical place to start the expedition, though you will have to give me directions."

"It will be my pleasure."

Francesca directed him up to her bedroom, and from there through the weeks of preparation for their next adventure.

On the way to India—they named the vessel *Tiger*—she frequently directed him in their private cabin, and as the wildly lucrative Trenton tea garden became productive, she remained an invaluable source of guidance.

By the time Francesca, Grey, and their two sons sailed back to England some five years later, the family finances had come gloriously right. When His Lordship—Grey was raised to a barony—wanted a taste of the wild, he had to look no farther than the other side of the bed, where his duchess in disguise was always ready to pounce and, in a single leap, love him as wildly as ever his heart desired.

—THE END—

To my dear Readers,

I hope you enjoyed Francesca and Grey's happily-ever-after. My family includes many scientists, and every one of them contributed to Grey's charming character (I mean that in the nicest possible way). Of the nine people in my immediate family, I'm the only one still living east of the Mississippi River, though I grew up in Pennsylvania. Two of my brothers own ranches, another works in the Utah mountains, and yet another is raising a family in Montana's Big Sky country.

Maybe that's why I had so much fun writing my April 2017 release, **Tartan Two-Step**, which I'm publishing in a two-novel bundle with contemporary romance author M.L. Buchman. In my contribution to the **Big Sky Ever After** duet, Scottish distiller Magnus Brodie needs an expert to rescue his signature batch of whisky, while Montana native Bridget MacDeever needs a miracle to outwit an old enemy. Even so, Bridget refuses to sell her distillery to the Scotsman who's stolen her heart. Big fun under a Big Sky! You can read an excerpt below, and look for the sequel, **Elias in Love**, in May 2017. Find more information on both titles at:
graceburrowes.com/bookshelf/

And of course, I'm writing more Regencies! I hope to have my next **True Gentleman** out in May 2017, and my second Windham Bride, **Too Scot To Handle**, hits the shelves in July 2017. Find more information here: graceburrowes.com/bookshelf/handle/.

To keep up with all of my releases, signings, and sales, sign up for my newsletter at the link below.

Happy reading!
Grace Burrowes

Sign up for my newsletter:
graceburrowes.com/contact/
Follow me on Twitter:
@GraceBurrowes
Like my Facebook page:
www.facebook.com/Grace-Burrowes-115039058572197/

TARTAN TWO-STEP
(featured in Big Sky Ever After—a Montana Romance duet)

"I'm asking a reasonable question," Bridget MacDeever muttered. "Montana State has more than fifteen thousand students, and out of all those young minds eager for knowledge, why do the ones who are also eager for a beating have to show up here on Friday night, as predictably as saddle sores and taxes?"

Bridget's brother Shamus turned and hooked his elbows on the bar, so he faced the room. "A fight means Juanita can change up the Bar None's décor. You ladies like hanging new curtains."

Bridget didn't bother kicking him, because Shamus was just being a brother. In the mirror behind the bar, she watched as Harley Simmers went nose to nose with yet another college boy.

"One of these days, Harley's going to hurt somebody who has a great big trust fund, and then our Harley will be getting all his mail delivered to Deer Lodge."

Montana State Prison, in the southwest quarter of the state, called Deer Lodge home.

"What's it to you if Harley does a little more time?" Shamus asked, taking a sip of his beer.

"He'll ask me to represent him, and I can't, though he's a good guy at heart."

Also a huge guy, and a drunk guy, and a guy with a temper when provoked. College Boy was provocation on the hoof, right down to his Ride A Cowboy T-shirt and the spankin' new Tony Lama Black Stallions on his feet.

"Pilgrims," Shamus muttered as College Boy's two friends stood up, and the other patrons drifted to the far corners of the Bar None's dance floor.

"Do something Shamus. Harley's had too much."

Bridget's brothers—half-brothers, technically—were healthy specimens, all over six feet, though Harley came closer to six foot six.

"He has too much too often," Shamus said. "This is not our fight. Let's head out the back."

Behind the bar, Preacher Martin was polishing a clean glass with a white towel. Bridget knew a loaded sawed-off shotgun sat out of sight within reach of his left hand. Preacher looked like the circuit parsons of the old west—full beard, weathered features, slate gray eyes—and he'd had been settling fights by virtue of buckshot sermons since Bridget had sat her first pony.

"We can't let Harley just get in trouble," she said, "or let that idiot jeopardize what few brain cells he hasn't already pickled."

"Bridget, do I have to toss you over my shoulder?"

"Try it, Shamus, and Harley will come after the part of you still standing when I've finished putting you in your place."

Bridget hadn't the family height, so she made sure to punch above her weight in muscle and mouth. Three older brothers had taught her to never back down and never make empty threats.

The musicians—a pair of fiddlers—packed up their instruments and nodded to Preacher. A few patrons took their drinks outside.

Bridget was off her stool and wrestling free of the hand Shamus had clamped around her elbow when Harley snarled, "Step off, little man," at the college boy.

A stranger strolled up to Harley's left. "Might I ask a question?"

"Who the hell is that fool?" Shamus murmured.

"Never seen him before," Preacher said, towel squeaking against the glass. "Bet we won't see him again either."

The stranger was on the tall side, rangy, and dressed in blue jeans and a Black Watch flannel shirt. His belt buckle was some sort of Celtic knot, and his hair was dark and longish. Bridget put his age about thirty and his common sense at nearly invisible.

He was good looking though, even if he talked a little funny.

"A shame to see such a fine nose needlessly broken." Bridget took noses seriously, hers being one of her most valuable assets.

Shamus shot her a "women are nuts" look.

Harley swung around to glower at the stranger. "What did you say?"

"It's the accent," the guy said, patting Harley's arm. "I know. Makes me hard to understand. I wanted to ask what it means when you tell somebody to step off. I haven't heard that colloquialism before, and being far from home, I don't want to offend anybody if I should be told to step off. Does it mean to turn and count my steps like an old-fashioned duel, or move away, or has it to do with taking back rash words?"

The stranger clearly expected Harley to answer.

"He's either damned brave or a fool rushing in," Shamus said.

"He's just standing there," Bridget replied, because a brother in error should never go uncorrected. "He sounds Scottish."

"He sounds like he has a death wish."

"You don't know what step off means?" Harley sneered.

"Haven't a clue," the stranger said. "I'm a fancier of whisky, and I'm sipping my way through my first American holiday. Don't suppose I could buy either of you a drink, if that's the done thing? I wouldn't want to offend. My name is Magnus, and this is my first trip to Montana."

He stuck out a hand, and Harley was just drunk enough to reflexively stick out his own.

"That was brilliant," Bridget said. In the next instant, College Boy was shaking hands too and introducing himself, then shaking with a puzzled Harley.

"Never seen anything like that," Preacher commented. "Harley Gummo ambushed by his mama's manners."

There had also been a mention of whisky, which recommended the Scotsman to Bridget more highly than his willingness to intervene between a pair of fools. *Somebody* should have intervened. For a stranger to do so was risky.

Bridget should have intervened.

Harley and College Boy let their new friend escort them to the drink station a yard to Bridget's left at the bar. She overhead earnest explanations of the rivalry between Cowboys and the 49ers, which then degenerated into an explanation of American football.

Man talk. Safe, simple man talk. Thank God.

"I do believe I see Martina Matlock all by her lonesome over by the fiddles," Shamus said. "If you'll excuse me, Bridget."

He wasn't asking. Martina was all curves and smiles, and Shamus was ever a man willing to smile back on a Friday night. He embodied a work hard/play harder approach to life, and of all Bridget's brothers, he was the one most likely to miss breakfast at the ranch house on Saturday morning.

"Find your own way home, Shamus," Bridget said.

Harley and his recently acquired buddies had found a table, and College Boy's companions took the two remaining free seats. The musicians unpacked their instruments, and Preacher left off washing glasses to help Juanita with the line forming at the drink station.

Magnus—was that a first name or a last name?—ordered a round of Logan Bar twelve-year-old single malt for table, the first such order Bridget had heard anybody place all night.

As Preacher got down the bottle, Bridget approached the stranger. "May I ask why you drink Logan Bar?"

"Because it's the best single-malt I've found thus far. Would you care to join us?"

His answer could not have pleased Bridget more. "You're on your own with that bunch of prodigies, but if you want to dance later, come find me."

"The lady doesn't dance with just anybody," Preacher said, setting tasting glass shots on a tray and passing over a menu. "Get some food into Harley, and this round will be on the house."

Magnus took the tray. "My thanks, and my compliments on a fine whisky inventory."

His voice sounded like a well-aged whisky, smooth, sophisticated, and complex but forthright too. A touch smoky, a hint of weathered wood and winter breezes.

He leaned a few inches in Bridget's direction as the fiddles warmed up on the stage. "I'll take you up on that dance, miss, just as soon as I instruct my friends regarding the fine points of an excellent single malt."

The finest single malt in the country. "You do that."

Bridget didn't wink and didn't smile, and neither did Magnus. He appreciated her whisky and was about to teach others to do likewise. If he made a habit out of advertising her single malt, Mr. Magnus could be her new best friend.

Or the Logan Bar Distillery's new best friend, which amounted to the same thing.

Order your copy of **Tartan Two-Step** in the **Big Sky Ever After** duet!

TO TEMPT A DUCHESS

EMILY GREENWOOD

CHAPTER ONE

"I had not planned on being a damsel in distress today," Olivia remarked to her friend Mary Alice from the doorway of their overturned coach. "And I'm sure you did not either. Though Francesca, as usual, is making the whole business look stylish, even in this weather." She swiped at a trickle of melting sleet making its way down her cheek.

The cold, early spring rain and sleet that had been falling all day had made the roads muddy, and their coach had taken a curve a little too hastily, with the result that it was now lying on its side on a road at some miles from the spa town that was their destination. Poor Mary Alice had bumped her head when the coach overturned, though she'd assured her friends it was nothing. Their coachman had left a groom to see to the horses and gone in search of assistance, but fortuitously, three gentlemen had just happened upon the scene and offered the ladies shelter at a nearby estate called Rose Heath.

The third member of their party, their friend Francesca, had already been helped onto the mount of Sir Greyville Trenton, one of their rescuers, and the pair was now riding away. Olivia and Mary Alice had not yet met the other gentlemen.

Olivia began to get down from the coach.

"And look, here's your very own knight in shining armor," Mary Alice said as a dark-haired man on a gray horse approached them. "Perhaps you will regret that we all agreed to travel incognito. He is handsome."

"I thought the plan was to avoid gentlemen, handsome or otherwise," Olivia said, but Mary Alice had no chance to reply because the man was now in earshot. He inclined his head and introduced himself as Mr. Christopher Stirling. The name did not initially mean anything to Olivia, but then he swept her a bow with a slant to his mouth that was unmistakably mocking, and a thought niggled. Stirling...

She just had time to gather the details of his height—rather tall—and his dark brown hair and chocolate eyes when he extended a hand from atop his horse with the bored expectancy of a lord waiting for a servant to produce some requested object. He had not even paused to hear her name!

Being that she was in fact the dowager Duchess of Coldbrook and that her two friends were also duchesses, she suspected he might have offered her a far different greeting if he'd known her identity. Ever since becoming a duchess when she'd married her beloved Harold years before, she had discovered for herself how very differently a duchess was treated than the plain fourth daughter of a baronet.

But while she appreciated the frequent kindness she was shown because of her title, sometimes she missed being simply Miss Thorpe. That her friends also yearned for a holiday from the duties of rank was one of the reasons the three of them had decided on this jaunt into the hidden corners of Yorkshire, during which they planned to pass themselves off as mere ladies. Though they had not, of course, foreseen the coach accident, which looked as though it was going to seriously delay their holiday plans.

Olivia gave an inward sigh of resignation. She had been so looking forward to the spa town, and to being with Francesca and Mary Alice, just the three of them again, as they hadn't been for quite some time. Mary Alice and Francesca had been friends since finishing school, and Olivia had first met them some years before when they were all staying at Lyme Regis.

Francesca and Olivia had envisioned that this holiday to the spa town would be a welcome escape from the London Season and its fortune-hunting gentlemen, though Mary Alice had taken some convincing. Now, instead of it being just the three of them, they were to be cast on the mercy, however temporary, of these gentlemen.

"Pleased to make your acquaintance, sir," Olivia said, ignoring his proffered arm. "I am Miss Olivia Thorpe. It's kind of you and your friends to come to our aid with an offer of shelter."

"Shan't be able to aid you if you don't take hold of my hand and mount up, ma'am," he said in a tone that suggested he had little interest in whether she did. "You may set your foot atop mine in the stirrup."

Olivia hesitated, wishing none of this was necessary. She disliked relying on others for help. And after nearly four years as a widow, she was accustomed to being independent and doing for herself.

But Francesca was already departing with Sir Greyville, and the third gentleman was making his way toward Mary Alice. Olivia did not have much choice. She took hold of Mr. Stirling's outstretched hand and was pulled neatly, and with some force, to sit before him. His arm came around her, and he pressed her firmly against him with apparent unconcern for propriety. He promptly urged his horse into a walk.

"Sir." She attempted to lean away and put some decorous space between herself and this stranger, though the chill and damp of the day had long since penetrated to her bones, and his body was exuding a welcome warmth.

"Yes?" he inquired.

Exasperating man! Any gentleman ought to intuit that a lady who was a stranger to him would not wish to be clutched tightly against his body. And that was the moment when she finally absorbed who he was: Christopher *Kit* Stirling, the Wastrel of White Horse Street, one of the most notorious rakes of the *ton*.

She knew the man only by reputation. They hardly moved in the same circles, and in any case, Olivia and Harold had spent the least amount of time possible in London each season—fulfilling the sorts of duties a duke and duchess could not evade—before returning gratefully to their country estate at the first opportunity.

Mr. Kit Stirling was the heir to the Earl of Roswell, from whom he was estranged, Olivia knew from *ton* gossip. Apparently, Mr. Stirling kept company with actresses and drunkards. He'd been involved in a notorious duel with Lord Candleford a few months before and had injured the man. It was rumored that he paid all his bills by gambling.

It was this last bit she knew the most about, because the nephew of her friend Lydia Woodson had recently lost his entire year's allowance to Mr. Stirling at cards. Mr. Stirling held frequent high-stakes games in his home, Lydia had told Olivia. She had also whispered that the man was known to change one mistress for another with dizzying regularity.

Which thought made Olivia hide a secret smile. However long she would be required to be in Mr. Stirling's company, she was unlikely to be of any interest to such a handsome, fast fellow. She had never been of interest to rakes and rogues, nor did she wish to be.

"There is no need for you to hold me in this manner," she told him. "I will be quite stable without your assistance." This was not entirely true, but as their pace on the wet road was necessarily sedate, she did not think she would fall.

"As you wish." He removed his arm.

"Does Rose Heath estate belong to Sir Greyville?" she asked.

"No, to Colonel Stratton."

"Colonel Nathaniel Stratton?"

"Yes."

Interesting. So Colonel Stratton was the third gentleman. Olivia had met him once or twice before, but Mary Alice knew the colonel and had something of an opinion about him. Things might prove interesting for her at least.

They proceeded in silence for some minutes, following along after Sir Greyville and Francesca. Olivia supposed she and her friends would have quite a laugh at some point about their rescue by three single gentlemen when their purpose in leaving London had been to *avoid* single gentlemen, and, in particular, fortune hunters. Though these men were unlikely to be seeking wealthy brides, ensconced as they were deep in the Yorkshire countryside while the Season— and the marriage mart—played out in London.

"What did you say your name was again, ma'am?"

"Miss Olivia Thorpe."

"Of?"

She was tempted to call on the haughtiness that was a duchess's privilege and deliver a stinging set-down, but alas, there was the matter of being in disguise.

"Fair Middling," she said, giving the name of her childhood home, a rustic and wonderfully unimportant place that the Wastrel of White Horse Street was unlikely to know.

He snorted dismissively. Fortunately, as a plain, sensible woman, she'd long ago discovered how much more satisfying it was to please herself rather than trying to impress men.

"And where are you from, sir?"

"My home is in London, though I foolishly agreed to rusticate here with Trenton and Stratton. But what can one do when old friends press?"

"I value old friends more than anything, sir, and never consider their invitations a burden."

"Then you are a better fellow than I."

"Quite easy when I'm not a fellow at all." What a ridiculous conversation she was having, riding a horse in far too close proximity to a stranger, who was taking her to the home of yet another stranger. Lydia had told her that Mr. Stirling was no longer welcome in certain respectable homes because of the low company he kept. Olivia had barely listened at the time, not being overly fond of gossip. But now she wished she had.

"Do you scorn the male sex, then, Miss Thorpe?"

His use of her maiden name jarred her. She had not been Miss Thorpe for ten years. For the first time, it struck her how eagerly, when Harold had proposed to her, she had abandoned her maiden name, along with everything else about herself that had felt old, dull, or just plain wrong. She had been twenty-four, a woman beginning to wonder if life would ever offer her a partner to complete her, and then she'd met Harold. He'd been her new beginning, her farewell to a life that had looked as though it would be very limited.

"Not at all. I have three brothers who are extremely dear to me, and I am very fond of the husbands of my friends."

"But not too fond for the sake of propriety, one assumes?"

Honestly! Was it his goal to be as coarse as possible?

"I won't dignify that with an answer, Mr. Stirling. Perhaps it would be better if we did not converse."

Mocking laughter greeted her words, but at least he said nothing further as they made their way to Rose Heath estate.

* * *

She smelled like nothing. No hint of floral soap wafted around her, no perfume lingered on the air, warmed by her skin. There was not even a whiff of lavender from her clothes, which Kit thought remarkable, considering that it seemed to be the goal of every laundress in the country to infuse all clothing with the scent of lavender. He did not care for lavender; it smelled sharp and reminded him of anise, which he detested.

He and Miss Thorpe arrived just in time to see Grey and the first lady disappearing inside. Stratton and the third lady seemed to have disappeared, as there was no sign of them. It was as if he and his friends had already been paired off with the three women, a thought that annoyed Kit. He gestured for Miss Thorpe to precede him up the front steps and introduced her to Stratton's housekeeper.

"She is another of the ladies who were stranded on the road," he told the housekeeper, "of whom I believe you have already met one. I believe Stratton is bringing the last of them. At least, I think she was the last of them, as no more ladies emerged from the coach."

"There were just the three of us," Miss Thorpe supplied with that prim crinkling at the corner of her lips that was already becoming familiar.

He could envision Miss Thorpe at home in her doubtless tidy, properly run household, with perhaps three or four cats in residence, and a neat sewing basket in every room. No poetry or wine-drinking for her, he thought with an inward smirk as he observed the set line of her mouth.

With her neatly cut dark frock of good cloth and her simply styled, average brown hair (it reminded him of the color of autumn leaves once they'd lost their vivid reds and yellows) and her face that could only be called average as well, she was not the sort of woman who tempted him, never mind the stiffness he'd felt seize her when she'd come against him on the horse. She seemed to be entirely predictable and... average.

"We are indebted to Colonel Stratton and his household for offering us shelter," Miss Thorpe said politely. Of course; she was a polite, well-brought-up spinster. There were certainly enough of them in the country.

Stratton's housekeeper, an unflappable specimen of the sort generally found at country homes, nodded and said that hot baths and dinner trays had already been ordered for the ladies. As Kit took himself off upstairs, leaving the consummately dull Miss Thorpe to the housekeeper's care, he could feel the lady's eyes boring into the back of his coat, no doubt a reproach for so obviously abandoning her.

He cursed quietly under his breath, wishing not for the first time that he hadn't allowed Grey and Stratton to twist his arm into coming to the country. He'd regretted it from the first moments of arrival a few days before. It was too damned quiet in the country, which was why he rarely came.

This was the trouble with friendship, particularly when it was very old friends: Affection clouded judgment. Theirs, in thinking he would be a good companion for them and that he would benefit from time in the country (he suspected they'd wished to spirit him away from "low company," though they'd insisted they simply didn't care for the Season). And his, in allowing himself to part from the noise and light and chatter of London, with its kissable women and tempting card tables, its overflowing cups of wine and its theaters and actresses and writers. He'd give anything for the arrival of even one greasy, moderately talented poet at Stratton's too-quiet house.

Though there was in truth a very compelling reason he had wished to leave London. His uncle, the Earl of Roswell, and his aunt Caroline and cousin Kate were coming to Town to celebrate Kate's engagement to Viscount Overbee with a grand party. Kit knew this because, despite a decade and a half of estrangement between them, Kate had written to invite him to the party. He hadn't heard from Kate, or indeed anyone in his uncle's family, since he'd left years before. He preferred it that way.

And now he and his friends were to play host to three proper-looking ladies, Miss Thorpe being the most proper-looking of all. There would be little chance of escaping the woman's company entirely, since the miserable weather would make it a trial even to venture out to the pathetic cluster of buildings masquerading as the local village.

He closed his bedchamber door with a clatter and stood briefly with his arms crossed, then rang for a dinner tray. When the maid arrived with the meal, she brought word that, due to some mishap, Stratton and his damsel would be stopping elsewhere on his estate for the night. Kit was not accustomed to dining alone—he preferred to have company at all times, if possible—but as Grey preferred to dine alone and work alone, clearly he would have no choice.

With no conversation to share, Kit completed his meal in seven minutes, and he found himself at nine o'clock with not a blessed thing to do.

He plucked a book from the desk and flipped idly through its pages, then tossed it down. When he realized that his fingers had begun picking at the wax that had dripped down a candlestick, he made a sound of exasperation and left his room to prowl around the manor, where he encountered not a single person.

Within twenty minutes, he found himself in the library, pulling books off the shelves and wondering if everyone else in the manor had already gone to sleep at this ridiculously early hour. Despite the addition of two ladies to the manor, it was as tomblike as ever in Stratton's accursed house.

CHAPTER TWO

By ten o'clock that night, Olivia had had a hot bath and put on the same gown she'd been wearing that afternoon, which had been put by the fire to dry, because the ladies' trunks had not yet arrived. She'd also eaten a delicious meal, which had been delivered to her bedchamber.

Word had been sent that poor Mary Alice had been injured more than they'd thought when their coach had pitched into the ditch, and she would rest for the night at the home of one of Stratton's tenants. Their damaged carriage would undoubtedly need significant attention.

When she'd planned this holiday with Francesca and Mary Alice, Olivia had naturally assumed that the three of them would be spending most of the time together. But thanks to fate, she was now alone in a lovely room with every comfort and nothing expected of her for the foreseeable future, which would likely be several days.

Olivia already suspected that Mary Alice and Francesca were going to be otherwise occupied while they were at Rose Heath. She didn't need much imagination to guess that her friends might find this detour on their holiday rather interesting, what with the presence of Sir Greyville and Colonel Stratton. Her own rescuer, though, was a different story. Not that she felt it was the responsibility of others to entertain her.

"Ohh," she growled aloud. How she disliked being idle. "This is ridiculous."

She looked out the window of her bedchamber for the tenth time and for the tenth time saw nothing but darkness. She'd written two letters and made a small, rather pathetic sketch of the chamber (she had never been good at drawing), and now she was sitting before the looking glass and experimenting with a pot of blush that Francesca had pulled from her reticule in the coach and pressed on her, insisting she looked a bit pale.

"There's no harm in enhancing nature," Francesca had said with a mischievous smile.

Olivia had laughed. "If you enhanced the excessive beauty with which nature has already endowed you, it would surely cause some sort of earth-shaking natural calamity to occur. Birds falling from trees, a reverse in the tides—at the very least, every man within a hundred miles would be struck dumb."

"Pish," Francesca had said. "And why talk this way, as if you are not lovely, when you are?"

Dear Francesca, whose affection endowed her with generously impaired vision where her friends were concerned.

"I'm perfectly happy not to be a pretty woman, since I've had years of observing what trouble it is for beauties to always have to discourage unwanted attention, and I hate to hurt people's feelings."

"You are a duchess, Olivia! When will you cease thinking of yourself as the plain fourth daughter of a baronet?"

"I've never minded being plain," Olivia said. Which was true. She felt that what she lacked in looks, she made up for in intelligence.

Francesca had made a sound of exasperation. "But you never *were* plain. And I think you know as well as I do that a woman is beautiful when she likes the way she is. Face paint is simply… fun. And maybe it helps you catch the eye of an interesting gentleman."

Olivia dabbed a smudge of the rouge on her cheeks, peered at the looking glass, and laughed at the idea of catching any man's eye, an undertaking that would never be her strong suit, no matter what Francesca said.

A woman is beautiful when she likes the way she is. Harold had made her feel loved and cherished and wanted. In a way, he had rescued her, because as the overlooked, plain, and aging fourth daughter in a family of eight children and two frequently feuding parents, she had spent years getting to know what life looked like from the edges of the dance floor.

When the Duke of Coldbrook had chosen her, a near nobody, for his bride, it had been a minor sensation. True, he'd been nearly fifty and quite bald, and he was considered something of recluse, so it had been a very minor sensation. But Olivia hadn't cared what anyone thought, because she had thought him wonderful. They'd been so happy together for those wonderful six years, until he died of a fever.

Losing him had been terribly sad, but Olivia felt grateful to have known more of love than most people ever did. Yes, it was a lingering sorrow that they had not been blessed with children, but she had made peace with that.

She swiped a fingertip of rouge across her lips, cocked her head, then frowned and reached for a handkerchief. What she looked like was a child's painted doll, not a pleasing effect for a woman of thirty-four. Clearly, she was in need of distraction. She decided to go down to the library for a book before she did something truly silly, such as going up and down the corridors knocking on doors until she found Francesca's room. Her friend was probably happily resting.

The manor was remarkably quiet as she made her way along the corridor, though it was cheerfully aglow with a nearly profligate amount of lit sconces. Once downstairs, she opened the door to the library and was soon happily lost among the volumes.

Some minutes later, she came to the end of a bookcase dedicated to volumes of history and gave a little gasp. Someone—some *gentleman*—was stretched out on the window seat with a book spread open over his face, as if to block the candlelight. Though she could not see his face, she nonetheless knew who he was, and she nearly groaned aloud in dismay. She'd had quite enough already of the thin pleasures of Mr. Kit Stirling's company.

She turned to leave, soundlessly she thought, but a voice arrested her.

"Well, Miss Thorpe. Come to relieve the boredom of this tomb of a house, have you?"

* * *

Thorpe. Was there a duller, less elegant name? Snodgrass, Kit supposed, as he regarded her from where he reclined on the window seat, propped on his elbows. Still, Thorpe, with its *orp* sound reminiscent of belches, inspired no thoughts of lazy afternoon trysts of the sort he preferred. It seemed fitting, as Miss Thorpe wasn't pretty anyway.

She had nice eyes, he would allow, of a hazel shade, but her eyebrows were much too thick and dark. Someone ought to have shown her how to do something about them by now. She was surely well into her thirties.

He crossed his legs lazily and was treated to a flicker of one of those fierce eyebrows. That house full of cats he'd imagined for her came to mind, and he mentally added yet another feline. She had five cats, he decided, and she liked a single plain boiled egg in the morning with no salt, and very scantly buttered toast. She lived alone with one old servant woman and passed her time figuring economies for her household and doing charitable works in the neighborhood. He was undecided yet on whether she permitted herself to gossip, but he was leaning toward not.

The vision of her as a solitary spinster did not exactly align with the fact that she'd been traveling with two female friends, but he decided this was her once-a-year holiday with old friends. A trip for which she—

"I find that boredom speaks more of the person than his or her environment," she said in reply to his greeting.

He was well aware that he was very lucky to still be able to count on the good will of Grey and Stratton, his two oldest friends, but that did not mean he was taking this enforced country holiday with good grace. He was rather a lost cause, though they could not seem to accept that.

He chuckled. He generally had a great deal of success with chuckling, where women were concerned, though Miss Thorpe looked immune. Of course, from the first, he'd not set out to charm her.

"Perfectly calibrated to put me in my place, Miss Thorpe. Tell me, ma'am, do you like cats?"

Those remarkable eyebrows drew together. "Cats? Yes, certainly. I find them charming." She glanced around. "Is there a cat about in the library?"

"Not that I've noticed. I was just thinking about cats. And how they make fine companions."

A few seconds of silence passed. And then one of those inky caterpillars above her eyes arched, slowly, a movement that spoke of... arrogance? Surely not. What could this plain, spinsterish woman have to be arrogant about?

"Do you wish to imply that a single woman of my age must particularly value the company of cats?"

He swung his legs to the floor and stood. "That would be most ill-mannered of me."

"Would that stop you?"

"Probably not."

She nodded, clearly prepared to think the worst of him. "I am not unacquainted with your existence, Mr. Stirling. I read the London papers. And more significantly, my friend Lydia Woodson has told me of her nephew losing his year's allowance to you in a card game at your home."

"It is no secret that I earn my keep through cards. No one made him come to the card table."

"No," she agreed. "But a gentleman would decline to fleece such a young man. He's but seventeen."

"Then I hope for his sake that he learned his lesson."

"On that we are agreed."

He propped one shoulder against the wall behind him. "And that he ought to avoid my company in the future?"

"It is you who has said it."

"But you agree?"

Her eyes traveled over his face and briefly flicked toward his shoulders and chest. Not a sexual appraisal, which he'd certainly experienced many times before. No, it was more in the nature of a general dismissal.

"I think it is wise to choose one's companions with thought and care," she said. "If you'll excuse me, Mr. Stirling, it's late and I must return to my bedchamber."

She was about to go, and he ought to be glad, as she clearly did not like him. He didn't like her either, but that was irrelevant. She would be someone to talk to, and in his experience, any companion was better than none.

"Without your book?" he asked.

"My book?"

"Didn't you come to the library in search of something to read?"

Was she blushing? It was hard to tell in the dim light offered by the fire and the sconces.

"I didn't find anything I wanted," she said.

"Or you no longer wish to browse the shelves because I am here."

He could tell by the crimping of both caterpillars that he'd annoyed her. "Good evening, Mr. Stirling."

She turned again to go.

"I'm going down to the kitchen to see if there's any treacle tart lying about," he said. "Stratton's cook makes a fine one. Why don't you join me?"

Her motion was arrested. He'd surprised her. He'd surprised himself. Apparently, he was prepared to go to odd lengths to avoid boredom.

"I... er, no." After a pause, she added with doubtless reflexive politeness, "Thank you."

"Aren't you hungry?"

"No. A substantial meal was sent to my chamber."

"Did you find it substantial? My tray had fish, and whenever I eat fish, I'm always hungry an hour later."

She paused, and in that moment, her stomach gave her away, rumbling audibly in the silence. "There," he said, "you can't say you're not hungry."

"I prefer not to eat sweets right before bedtime. They keep me awake."

"Then come have some of Stratton's excellent cheddar."

He knew he had her when her stomach rumbled once more. "Oh, very well," she said with ill grace. "I suppose a bit of cheddar would be welcome."

CHAPTER THREE

They brought a candelabrum with them to the kitchen, where a low fire was still burning in the hearth. Olivia supposed that the kitchen staff had finished their labors not long before, and she hoped no one else would be about. It was hardly appropriate for the two of them to be there alone together late at night.

He seemed to know his way about the place, going directly to an area of the kitchen where several covered dishes sat on a shelf.

"You've done this before," she said as he lifted a lid and peered at the contents and grinned.

"I'm accustomed to eating late at night." He moved the dish, which contained treacle tart, to the large worktable that took up much of the kitchen.

"The card tables?"

"Of course. The best play develops as the night goes on, when people have been at the tables for hours." A look of vague disgust passed over his face. "I suppose you prefer to rise early each day."

"I do."

He wasn't someone she'd ever have chosen to spend any time with, and she couldn't understand a person of their age who seemed not to have matured past the sorts of choices that would appeal to an eighteen-year-old. Yes, he was a handsome man, and tall, and his dark brown hair and chocolate eyes lent him an appealing air of depth, though she knew it was little deserved. He had a strong jaw, a set of manly shoulders, and a broad chest—all those attributes that made a man different from a woman and therefore interesting.

He had wit as well, and she could imagine him being quite charming if he wished. But she didn't like people who turned their charm on and off, using it like a talent. Charm reminded her of the sorts of women to whom her father had been susceptible.

It had been Olivia's mother's signal grief that her husband could not resist a charming woman, whether he encountered her at a ball or behind the counter in a shop. Olivia supposed married life would have been easier for her parents if they hadn't actually loved each other. Or, of course, if her father hadn't been weak.

But none of that mattered anymore, she thought, surprised to find herself thinking of such things. Her parents were both dead, and Olivia had gone on to experience for herself the happiness that a good marriage to a man like Harold could bring.

Kit Stirling was in every way *not* the sort of man that a sensible woman should marry, though why she should be weighing such matters when she had no interest in marrying again, and certainly no interest in Mr. Stirling, she could not have said. Such wayward thoughts must have had something to do with the lateness of the hour.

She just wanted some cheese, and then she was going to bed.

He uncovered another dish, revealing the cheddar, and gestured for her to bring a knife. She cut a chunk for herself while he helped himself to a slice of the treacle tart, and they stood together, quietly eating in the silent house. After a few minutes, she realized that standing there with him was surprisingly companionable, and with a pang, she was reminded of many such quiet moments she'd shared with Harold.

Even though Harold had been more than two dozen years older than she, Olivia had felt from the first that the two of them were as suited as two peas in a pod. They had both loved to lose themselves in piles of books, to pass companionable dinners with friends, to take brisk walks in the dusk of a late winter afternoon. They had both loved the life of the mind and valued their health and the contentment of their lives together.

Standing in that quiet kitchen eating with this man she didn't know, she felt lonely as she hadn't in months. Years. Maybe it was simply the effect of being with Kit Stirling, who she doubted cultivated the kind of genuine friendships she valued. Certainly, if he wasn't received in the homes of high sticklers despite being the heir to an earldom, he must have few enough friends. Although he was here at the invitation of Colonel Stratton, Mr. Stirling was hardly a considerate guest, speaking of how bored he was.

"You engaged in a duel with Lord Candleford several months ago and wounded him," she blurted. "There were rumors about you and his wife."

He was chewing, and his jaw stilled for a moment before he resumed. He finished his bit of tart while she wondered what had prompted her to be so rude.

"I'm surprised you've even heard of it, all the way out in Fair Middling."

"I have friends. Besides, it was hardly a secret. You wounded Candleford."

"Yes," he said dryly, "I am aware."

"You might have killed him."

"Always a possibility when dueling."

"And that didn't concern you? That a good man such as Candleford might be harmed by such an affair?"

He stared at her, then gave a little shrug, his dark brown eyes glittering with a light she could not read.

"Candleford is not a good man," was all he said.

"I've never heard anything so preposterous. Lord Candleford is unfailingly kind to all he meets. I happen to know that he's contributed a great deal of money to establish a new hospital near London."

"A man may be outwardly estimable but still beat his wife cruelly."

She gasped. "That is a strong charge. If you have knowledge of such treatment, why would you not say so?"

"Perhaps because then it might be wondered how I came by intimate proof?"

Her lips tightened. "I see."

He laughed. "If you could see your face, you would have the perfect example of outraged propriety."

"I am more concerned by the thought that Lady Candleford is being harmed by her husband."

"As to that, you need not worry. I believe he has been convinced of the benefit to his life of never again living in the same house with his wife. Or, for that matter, the same town."

She frowned and put the cover back on the cheese. His reason for dueling with Candleford, if it was true, was the defense of a vulnerable person at great risk to himself. Not what she would have expected of such a man.

But he had also apparently had an affair with a married woman, and that was something she could never excuse.

It was time to say good night and go to her bedchamber, where she should already have been, instead of lingering in the company of the Wastrel of White Horse Street.

"There's a plunge pool down here," he said.

"A what?"

"A plunge pool. Stratton's father had it built some time ago. He was much consumed with inventions for healthfulness."

"Oh." Why was he telling her this? She was beginning to get the sense he was prolonging their encounter, for what purpose she could not have said.

He put his plate down. "Shall we go look at it?"

"Now?"

"Why not?"

For so many reasons, starting with the unsuitability of even being alone here with him. And she had other reasons for not wanting to visit a plunge pool. But she didn't owe him an explanation.

"It's nearly midnight, and I wish to retire."

"Midnight is the best time to see such things. You don't want to come down here during the day, when it's full of servants bustling about."

"I don't particularly wish to be down here at all." Which was not exactly true. Being in the quiet, darkened kitchen was pleasant. The place was cozy, with that cheery air of purpose in repose. But his company made her feel unsettled.

If she were being honest, she would admit that some of this unease had to do with her awareness of the warmth emanating from his body as they stood next to each other in the circle of candlelight. They weren't touching, but she felt the presence of his bulk and warmth. His brown eyes had an intelligent light.

And there was something lawless about him that she found interesting. Not appealing, she told herself, but interesting, like unexplored terrain.

"Just come and see the plunge pool with me, then you can go up to your chamber. It will only take a minute."

She would feel churlish refusing such a simple request. But this had already been a strange evening, and she felt the pull of curiosity, not—definitely not—about the pool, but about something she could not have articulated.

"Very well."

* * *

The room was redolent of the mineral smell of wet stone. Kit supposed that the water would be quite cool, but that would have been part of the reason Stratton's father had commissioned it, as there had been a mania at the time for the health benefits of cool-water bathing. There were several sconces around the room, which Kit lit despite Miss Thorpe's protestations that it wasn't necessary.

The pool was made of neatly cut, pale stone blocks, and its water shimmered softly in the candlelight. Like everything else on the property, it was well maintained, so it looked fresh and, to Kit's eyes, like some ancient water nymph's secret grotto.

He moved closer to the edge of the pool. "Care for a dip? No one need ever know."

"Certainly not."

He laughed. Of course he had not really thought she would agree. Everything about her bespoke respectability and self-control, and she knew enough of his reputation to know he had not, for a very long time, been on the list of men that mamas wished their daughters to know.

"You really are utterly respectable, aren't you, Miss Thorpe? It must be vexing to be down here, alone, with the Wastrel of White Horse Street. I wonder that you've indulged me."

"Why? Because you think I live in a spinster's house full of cats and enjoy a very small life hemmed in on all sides by propriety?"

"Do you?"

"Just because I don't spend all my time in pursuit of vice, in bilking young people and participating in duels, it doesn't therefore follow that my life is an empty waste of dullness."

She had spirit, average though she was. Although his prolonged presence in her company was causing him to rethink the word *average*, because of those thick, strong eyebrows. Average suggested a woman with no distinguishing aspect to her face, but Miss Thorpe's face, now that he had taken a second and third look, was not unremarkable. It was distinctive. Memorable.

Her body might be interesting too, though it was hard to say because of that dark frock she wore. It was nicely tailored, but not designed to give a man ideas. He could see she was neither stout nor scrawny, neither tall nor short. Average.

"You wound me," he said dryly.

"Is that possible?"

He cocked his head. "There's something bracingly forthright about you, Miss Thorpe. In fact, for a spinster, you are remarkably devoid of the fainting airs and feeble graces of the women left behind in others' rush to marry. You seem quite at ease with the male sex. I wonder why that is."

He expected her to draw herself up in outrage at his words, but she made no immediate reply. After a moment, she said, "Cold all the way down to the depths, I suppose."

She had turned her gaze to the pool, but for a moment, he felt she was speaking of him. He was becoming as fanciful as a poet, but perhaps that was to be expected when he spent so much time with drunken verse-scribblers and actors and the like. "Sure to be. That is the point, for it to be cold and thus especially healthful."

"It's quite lovely with the light shimmering on it." She sounded surprised, as though the sight really was a wonder to her. Was it his imagination, or did she seem inclined not to draw too close to the water?

"Many things look better by candlelight," he said.

A pause. "Ah," she said. "Like plain women."

It was true, and he said, "Yes." An appallingly ungentlemanly thing to say, but how long had it been since being gentlemanly was his first consideration? Oh, he knew how to charm, how to employ the finesse of the gentleman, even though it had been a great many years since he'd concerned himself with the constraints of the gentleman's ways.

She gave a little nod, and her calm acceptance penetrated him in a way that outrage or scolding would not have and touched an unfamiliar region within him. He ignored the sensation and moved to a bench behind her, causing her to step quickly out of his way, as if she meant to avoid being close to him, an attitude as irresistible to him as a red flag before a bull. He sat down and lifted one foot to the opposite knee.

"I'm going to dangle my feet in the water," he said, tugging successfully at his boot. "Why don't you join me?"

"No, thank you," she said frostily, averting her eyes as he removed his other boot. "I'll be going now. Thank you for showing me the pool."

She turned briskly to go, no doubt wishing him to know how little she desired any further time in his company, but she must not have realized how close to the edge of the pool she had moved. In the next moment, she was stumbling.

He sprang up and reached for her, but he couldn't catch hold as she cried out and dropped down. She landed on the stairs, luckily, and not all the way in the water. But she immediately began shrieking, and she remained huddled on the steps on all fours, as if frozen, even as he reached out to help her up.

"Miss Thorpe," he said sharply when she ignored his outstretched hand. She stopped shrieking then, but instead began keening. She did not look up, as though in the grips of something that would not allow her to lift her gaze from the steps. He grasped her shoulder, but it seemed to make no impression on her. She remained on all fours, her breathing ragged in between the keening.

He stepped onto the stairs—the water was indeed quite cold on his stocking-clad feet—and said, "You must get out of the water, ma'am."

"Can't move," she said, her voice muffled, as though she'd spoken through clenched teeth.

"Are you hurt?"

A breath, two. "Can't," was all she said.

There was nothing for it. He stepped farther down into the water and bent and began to slide an arm around her back, preparatory to guiding her out. Instantly, her arms clamped around his neck with astonishing force, so that she nearly pulled him down. He steadied himself and, by dint of some awkward maneuvering, was able to gain his balance and bring them both out of the pool.

He set her down at a distance from the edge of the water, near the doorway and directly in the light of one of the sconces. He let his arms fall, but her arms remained tightly around his neck, as if this was the safest purchase she could find on him. Her face was buried against the crook of his neck, and her warm forehead pressed against the bare skin under his jaw.

"Are you hurt, ma'am?" he asked again, gently.

"No," she said into his neck.

He waited for her to unclench her arms. With her head just under his chin, he noticed now that she did smell like something after all, though it was very faint. An evanescent whiff of a clean soap scent teased him intermittently. Her grip around his neck was rather uncomfortable, but he could not complain about the feeling of her body pressed snugly against his. Her arms and a good portion of her lower half were wet, and there was the awareness of cold fabric against warm flesh, both his and hers.

After a moment, he said, "You are no longer near the pool, ma'am. If you step backward even five steps, you will not fall in. You are quite safe now."

"Too close," she said hoarsely.

He lifted her again and carried her out of the room and set her down in the kitchen, near the dying fire. She did not let go of him.

CHAPTER FOUR

Olivia's heart was still racing, though the panic that had consumed her was slowly receding. Only Mr. Stirling's presence, the solidity, warmth, and sheer bodily bulk of him, was enabling her not to be hysterical. Her eyes were squeezed shut, though she knew she must now be in the kitchen, because she could smell a lingering burnt odor, and there was a little welcome warmth from the fire.

Oh, how could she have been so stupid, so careless? She had long ago learned the wisdom of simply avoiding proximity to bodies of water however small, for the very reason that it was all too easy to fall in.

This man had stirred a sort of hubris in her tonight that had made her agree to see the pool. What was it about Kit Stirling that had brought out this desire to go against what she knew was sensible and familiar? She supposed it must have been a reaction to his arrogance and his refusal to behave as a gentleman ought.

She forced herself to loosen her arms and step away from him. It felt, absurdly, like abandoning something that she needed. *What nonsense*, she scolded herself. It was only that he was appealingly warm and she was now cold, with the unwelcome sensation of chilly wet sleeves and skirts.

Her teeth began chattering, and she clenched them in a futile attempt to stop them. "Thank you, sir, for your assistance. Please accept my apologies for behaving in such an absurd manner."

"You are freezing." He took off his coat and held it out to her. How she wanted to accept it, and the warmth it would offer, and the return to smelling his intoxicating scent. And, not least, the feeling of being looked after. She shook her head, declining his offer.

"I don't know what came over me. I... was startled. I certainly had not been expecting a plunge in the pool."

"It is not absurd to be terrified of falling in the water when one cannot swim."

He was right, but she couldn't accept his words, as if doing so would let him define her.

She lifted her chin. "I was not terrified."

He tossed his coat on the table, and she wondered that he was not chilled in his shirt-sleeves. "You weren't? Why was it then that you were clinging so tightly to me? Perhaps because you were unable to resist me?"

The blush swept over her quickly. "Only a man like you would say such an ungentlemanly thing."

Her words were not polite either, but when he replied, his tone suggested he'd not taken any offense. "Perhaps, or perhaps I am less inclined than the average fellow to speak in silky platitudes and gracious phrases. I prefer to be direct. And you were terrified."

Why was she resisting the truth? Not only had she been terrified, but some craven part of her had wanted terribly to continue holding on to a man who'd evidently had an affair with a married woman and purposefully shot her husband, even if there were perhaps extenuating circumstances.

"Very well, I was," she said. "I have been afraid of water all my life, ever since I fell in a pond as a child and nearly drowned."

"A not uncommon fear, Miss Thorpe. Why did you feel the need to hide it?"

"Because it is a weakness I do not care for in myself."

He laughed. "You are the most interesting and confident spinster I have ever met."

The arrogance! As if a woman who'd never married could not be interesting or confident. As if she'd been waiting for his approval. She fixed him with a steady gaze. "I am, in truth, not a miss. I have told you a lie."

His eyebrows rose slowly, as though she'd just revealed a piece of delicious gossip. "You are married? Should I expect a dawn appointment from an angry husband furious that I have spent the evening alone with his wife?" he drawled. "If so, I might have to prevail on you to explain that, for once, I am quite innocent."

"There will be no angry husband pursuing you, sir. I was once Miss Thorpe, as I told you. That was before I married the Duke of Coldbrook. I have been widowed these four years."

She had the satisfaction of seeing that she'd surprised him as the customary mask of boredom slipped for a moment from his face.

"The Duchess of Coldbrook. I've heard of you, though not often. Society threw up its hands over the pair of you after you married and retreated, for the most part, to the country. It all sounded terribly dull, the old duke and his shy virgin. I suppose it was months of quiet days and nights in some rambling old ancestral place?"

Her temper flared. "What a poor view you have of married life. I suppose the life Harold and I shared would sound very dull to someone such as you. We had six wonderful years before he died. And our time in the country never felt like a retreat. It was a fulfillment. We were very happy together."

"How nice for you."

His tone was mocking. Of course. What should she expect from a man who cared so little about all the things that meant so much to her? And yet, he'd rescued her, and been kind in her moments of terror. She thought again of her suspicion that he simply had not wanted to be alone.

"It *was* nice. And wonderful in every sense of the word, and many other things." She believed in love and in goodness, and if he did not, then she was a little sorry for him. But only a very little, because that was his choice.

"Still, you, a duchess. I confess I did not guess."

"That I was of the same station as the heir to an earldom?"

He grabbed the poker and stirred up the dying fire. "Oh, a duchess would trump the disgraced heir of an earl any day."

He was the heir to the Earl of Roswell, with all the duties and benefits that entailed, but he clearly had only scorn for the very thing that made him special in the eyes of the *ton*. Having come into the role of duchess, she could not understand his cavalier attitude toward what he owed the title, but he was hardly the only such wastrel—London was full of young bucks living dissipated lives. Still, he was surely near her age, and a man of thirty or more ought not to behave like a youth.

"Why didn't you say who you were to begin with?" he asked.

"I had decided to have a sort of holiday from being a duchess."

"Ah, playing at commoner, then. Thus the reason you are not currently partaking of the Season in London, where you would doubtless be popular with the fortune hunters."

She inclined her head, not disposed in the least to discuss such things with him. "Well, thank you again, Mr. Stirling, for pulling me out of the pool. If you had not been here to help me, I cannot imagine what might have become of me. Though if you had not been here," she managed a small, insincere smile, determined to banish the strange mood that had come over her this evening, "I should not have visited the pool at all."

"You should learn to swim," he said in that careless tone of his.

"Oh, well, it's a bit late for that. I assure you that I shall in future be very good at avoiding plunge pools, in addition to ponds and streams and the like. You will not be required to rescue me again."

"Why would you want to go through life avoiding something so essential to us as water, and so potentially delightful?"

How did he manage to ask a question while making it seem that he was only slightly interested in the answer?

"Because it's also incredibly dangerous?" she said with bright sarcasm. "I assure you, Mr. Stirling, I have not been missing out on swimming my entire life. I have never yearned to do it, nor, in fact, ever even given it a thought."

"How do you know?"

"How do I know what?"

"That you have not been missing out on swimming? You've never experienced it, so how can you know what you're missing?"

"In the same way I know that I should not like to step into a fire just to see what it's like, or sample the flavor of a poison."

"Water isn't like fire and poison. It's innately harmless, and with a little guidance, you would be able to swim. I could even teach you."

Could this night grow any more absurd? The Wastrel of White Horse Street was offering his services as a swimming tutor. She spared a thought for how she might recount all of this to Francesca and Mary Alice, but immediately knew that she would not. None of this was as easily explainable as it should have been, especially the part where she had clung to him. That had been from terror, but not only terror in the end.

"Kind of you, sir," she said, though she doubted his offer had anything to do with kindness. Boredom was surely the reason. "But no, thank you. I really have no wish or need to learn to swim."

His dark eyes glittered at her. "What will happen the next time you fall into some pool or pond, Duchess, and no one is there to save you? Oh, that's right, you're never going to come close again."

"Why should you wish to teach me anyway?"

"Why?" he said lazily. "It will give me something do, of course, in this godforsaken quiet place. And then, of course, there is this."

He was standing perhaps three feet from her, and when she blinked, he'd moved closer. She ought to have felt that he was invading the space that anyone would expect two people who knew each other so little to keep between them—he was—but she had already been much, much closer to him, and she remembered. Her body remembered.

"I liked having you in my arms."

His body was strong and large, and even in the midst of her terror, she had liked clinging to him, had felt the inexpressible satisfaction of a need for those things that only a man could offer her.

He lifted a hand and, with a fingertip, traced lightly along her jawline. "I want to touch you more. May I kiss you?"

She did not even think. His touch was what she wanted, though the craving was senseless. She did not know this man, and what little she did know of him, she didn't like. But she had forgotten this part of herself. She had put it away after Harold died, and now Kit Stirling was making her remember. And making her imagine that there was more, still, that she had yet to experience.

"Yes."

His head dipped toward her, and then his warm lips were on hers. He teasingly but insistently nudged her lips apart, then his mouth plundered hers with a sureness she'd never experienced. Harold had not been like this; he'd been tender and reserved. Always considerate. But Kit Stirling was completely different from Harold in every way, starting with his lack of reserve.

She responded to him with an eagerness that shocked her, barely pausing to wonder how it was possible to shock herself.

He broke the kiss to murmur next to her ear, "Let me warm you." His mouth trailed along her jaw and down her neck, stirring a response deep and low in her body. She wrapped her arms around the breadth of his chest and surrendered to the sensations he was stirring in her, heedless of alarm bells of propriety. What he was doing felt too good.

That's because he's a practiced seducer! part of her mind shouted at her. But she could not make herself care that she was merely the next woman in line for him, that she was just a body to him. Because he was just a body to her, and she wanted what they were doing, wanted it with a fierceness she hadn't felt about anything in a very long time.

From the experience of her marriage, she knew she was likely barren. This would simply be a free experience, devoid of any strings or complications, and she meant to have it.

She pushed her hand under his coat, reveling in the feel of his firm, muscled flesh under the thin barrier of his shirt. He began undoing the buttons on the front of her dress, his lips following the work of his fingers. When her dress gaped open over her breasts, his tongue came hot and wet against the tender swell of her right breast. And then he moved lower and took her nipple in his mouth and dragged his teeth rudely against the swollen tip. She loved it and moaned aloud in pleasure, something she'd never done in her life.

Pressed firmly against him as she was, she could be in no doubt of his desire for her, the evidence of which prodded her belly. He began to urge her backward, until her backside came up against the empty worktable next to the hearth, and with a sweep of his arms, he lifted her onto it. Pushing her skirts upward, he stepped between her legs.

"Let me warm you," he said again, though she had completely forgotten her cold, wet sleeves and skirts. Wishing he would not speak, she reached for the fall of his trousers. She unfastened the buttons, but she did not look. Instead, she tugged him closer to bury her mouth against the hot skin of his neck. He pushed her skirts farther back and touched her softly where she ached, and his knowing fingers made her need expand its already unwieldy dimensions.

And then he was at her entrance and pushing inside her. She pulled him hard against her, needing to wring everything she could out of this moment. He moved in her, and she moved against him, her body responding in a rhythm she had missed desperately without even knowing it.

"Good God, woman," he said hoarsely, as if the words had been torn out of him. He worked into her, and it felt unbearably good.

She cried out when she found her release and pressed her mouth to his cloth-covered shoulder to muffle the sound. He pushed into her again, then with a deep groan, shifted away from her. She knew that he was spending himself outside her body, and she kept her face against his shoulder.

"Well," he said in a quiet voice some moments later, "you are warm now. Quite warm."

Yes, she was warm now, inside and out, warmed and softened in the way only a good loving could accomplish. But almost as soon as she'd become aware of how very relaxed and languid she felt, how boneless and how, in that moment, there was nothing on earth that she lacked, the sting of remorse began to steal her warmth. This wasn't loving, what they had done together.

She shifted, urging him off her, and pulled her dress back into place on her shoulders. He handed her a handkerchief, which she accepted without looking at him.

The hearth now held nothing but smoldering ashes, and the room had grown cold and cheerless. Without speaking, they made their way upstairs. As she opened the door to her bedchamber, he quietly whispered a good night. She said nothing and closed the door.

CHAPTER FIVE

The next morning, Kit sent a note to the duchess, inviting her to come for a ride. There was no reply, so he went alone. When he returned, he was informed by Stratton's butler that the duchess's friend, the one who'd been injured in the coach accident, had arrived at the manor. As he passed one of the bedchambers on his way to his room, he heard feminine laughter.

He bathed and went to the dining room for lunch, thinking the others might join him, but no one appeared.

Kit was eager to see the Duchess of Coldbrook again. Their sexual encounter had been spectacular. And completely unexpected. When he had brought her to the kitchen, he had thought only to entertain himself with her company. He could not have guessed, from her tidy, plain looks, that she was in fact a woman of remarkable sexual appetite.

Of course, he had also not known that that average-looking spinster was the Duchess of Coldbrook. Not that it mattered to him that she was a duchess. If he cared about such things, he would certainly not let anything stand between himself and the earldom that currently belonged to his uncle. Kit was meant to be the earl's heir, and he had been brought up to know all the duties and expectations of the title that would one day be his. But that was his old life, and Kit had made a new one for himself, one that centered on all the best entertainments—of which the duchess was currently, and most unexpectedly, the most interesting one.

He finally found her in the greenhouse.

"Your Grace," he greeted her as he moved past a tall, exotic-looking plant and drew near where she stood examining an orange-colored bloom, doubtless something Grey had brought back from one of his travels and presented to Stratton, who was well known for his interest in nature and science.

She was wearing a different gown, this one of chocolate brown; apparently the ladies' trunks had arrived. Now that he knew she was a duchess, he could see that it was made of extremely fine, if very understated, fabric. Her hair was pulled back in a knot, unadorned by any plaits or ribbons. The plain style suited her. Her eyebrows were already such a distinctive and strong aspect of her face that busy hairstyles and elaborate decorations would have looked silly on her. He gave her credit for good taste.

Her lips were a nice color, he noticed for the first time. Ashes of roses, he believed they would be called. Though they were really a more rosy color than that, he decided as he considered them further. He supposed his friend Arthur, a perpetually impoverished painter who was always going into raptures about shades of color, would have had a name for the exact shade of the Duchess of Coldbrook's lips.

She looked up only briefly before returning her gaze to the orange flower. "Mr. Stirling." She leaned closer to the plant and sniffed delicately.

"I trust you are well, ma'am." His eyes were inescapably drawn to the curve of her bosom. He wanted to see her breasts in the daylight. He'd hardly been able to determine their contours the night before, had seen only erotically teasing portions. They were of an average size—there was that word again that he had associated with her from the first—but his feelings toward them now bordered on deep interest. He meant to see them again, all of them. And all of her.

"As you see," she said, addressing her words to the plant.

When she did not abandon her inspection of the flower, he said, "Might I ask what is so fascinating about this particular bloom, ma'am?"

She finally looked up properly, and he saw it: The confidence that had surprised him when he thought she was a spinster belonged to a duchess. But her air of self-command also seemed so clearly a part of her that he guessed it would not matter whether she was dressed in fine silks, plain gowns, or rags.

"I was thinking of acquiring one of these plants for Brookleigh."

He noticed a piece of foolscap near the pot, and a piece of lead. She'd apparently been making notes.

"That is the family seat?"

"Yes."

"And that's where you and your husband spent so much happy time together?"

"Yes. It's a beautiful place, and I've always loved it there."

"I suppose your husband was a paragon? The dead always are, to those they leave behind."

Her eyes grew hooded with hauteur. "He was a tremendously good man with a very big heart. We loved traveling together, and we loved staying in of an evening together. We were companions who were happiest in each other's company. But he was a real person, just as I am, and he had flaws, just as everyone does. I have not turned him into a saint in my memories of him, if that is what you wish to imply. I simply loved him as he was."

"Very admirable."

"I don't need your approval, Mr. Stirling."

His mouth twisted in a smirk. "Nor would you wish it, I believe I'm meant to understand."

She inclined her head. Apparently, she did not wish to continue their conversation, because she shifted her attention to the pale blue flower that was neighbor to the orange one. From all signs, she'd been doing nothing more exciting than making a study of flower blooms for the last hour and had been entirely contented in doing so. Her serenity irked him.

"When did the duke die?"

"Four years ago."

"Leaving you all alone, all this time."

The suggestiveness behind his words did not escape her. Her eyes flicked to his face and color came into her cheeks. "Do you go out of your way to be coarse in the hopes of getting a rise out of me? I cannot imagine why I am to be the recipient of such attention. Or perhaps this is the way you treat everyone, even your friends."

"You have to admit that you were very agreeable last night to my attentions."

"I don't believe I was, actually. Agreeable, that is. I reluctantly came with you to the kitchen when pressed, reluctantly came to the pool. I will acknowledge, however, that I was a willing participant in what happened afterward. But you are making an assumption if you think it was because I found your attentions particularly agreeable. I think we were both simply inclined towards physical contact in that moment."

He threw back his head and laughed. "Inclined towards physical contact, I like that. Surely the most bloodless description ever given of lovemaking."

"I would not call it lovemaking where there is no love, Mr. Stirling."

"Kit, please. After all, we have been intimate—we can agree on that term, I believe, at least—and need not be formal with one another."

"On the contrary, I would prefer that we remain formal with each other. We are here at Rose Heath with our friends, and there is no reason for them to be aware that there has been anything between us."

"Our friends seem to be quite taken up with each other and would likely think it a fine thing were they to discover we fancied each other." Or at least, his friends would probably be delighted if, despite his plummeting status, he were to be connected with a woman such as the Duchess of Coldbrook.

"But I don't fancy you, Mr. Stirling. And I doubt my friends would think it a good thing if they knew I had spent an evening with the Wastrel of White Horse Street."

She wanted no doubt to tell herself she did not care for his company, but her response the night before was not the response of a woman who found him unappealing. Clearly, he would have to be more circuitous in his pursuit of her, for he did mean to pursue her. He meant to taste again the explosiveness that had surged between them when they touched.

"As you wish," he said. "I can certainly be discreet."

"There will be no need for discretion," she said tartly, "because there will be nothing between us."

He traced a fingertip along the glossy curve of one of the almond-shaped leaves growing on a plant near his hand. It was quite pretty, actually. He had not, until he came in search of the duchess, spent a single moment in Stratton's conservatory. Grey, with his passion for plants, probably spent a good portion of time here when he visited Stratton. Though this was doubtless infrequently, as Grey was usually away from England, traveling the world to further enrich his studies and his collections.

It was because Grey and Stratton cared so little about Society that they had pressed Kit to join them at Rose Heath. Kit was unwelcome in more than a few drawing rooms among the *ton*, a matter in which he generally took amused satisfaction. He certainly wasn't feeling any more concerned about his status in Society just now because he wanted the Duchess of Coldbrook to be agreeable to him. He was simply realizing that—well, he was dashed lucky to have Grey and Stratton as friends.

"Have you given any more thought to swimming lessons, Your Grace?"

"I believe I made my wishes plain, sir, when I thanked you for your offer and declined it." She moved farther along the display of plants, taking her notes with her.

He moved to stand opposite her. "Ah, but I thought you might perhaps have changed your mind after what happened after your dunking."

She closed her eyes briefly, as if having to call on the heavens to deliver great forbearance. "We all have lapses in judgment sometimes, Mr. Stirling. I think you as well as anyone could agree with that. I have said all I care to on the subject and do not wish to discuss it further."

"But how can I understand such a thing as a single lapse, Your Grace, when my entire existence is surely one continuous lapse in judgment?"

"If it is, that is your own choice, as you are an adult."

He laughed. "Come, let down your hair and let me teach you to swim, ma'am."

Color flared anew in her cheeks. "You'd like that, wouldn't you? The seduction couched as swimming lesson. The sensual education of a deprived and lonely widow. But I'm not deprived or lonely, Mr. Stirling, and I've already been very happily married. Nor am I the least bit interested in spending time with a man who's little better than a youth."

"A youth?" he drawled. "You may be well into your fourth decade, ma'am, but I assure you that I am as well. I was thirty-five on my last birthday."

"And you've made no strides to do anything in life but pursue your own pleasure, have you? You seek my company here only because you are bored. I would think the country is the last place you would like, with its out-of-date fashions and its lack of Society and diversion."

She was so direct. Blisteringly so. "I wasn't bored last night. You were quite an accomplished lover. Indeed, the best I have known in some time."

"Do you think to entice me with this sort of coarse and boring nonsense? Perhaps we behaved like animals last night. I am hardly unaware that our bodies offer us all temptation. But I am not a beast, to be led only by my desires."

Boring? She found his compliments boring? True, they were coarse, he supposed with an unaccustomed prickle. He hadn't guarded his tongue in so long that he'd lost his awareness of the borders of propriety. But boring?

He picked up a trowel near him on the high table and stabbed halfheartedly at the soil in a pot of dirt in front of him, loosening it. "And I am a beast who is led by my desires, is that it?"

"I cannot say what your motivations are, sir. You must make your own choices."

"And I choose you, here, now, Your Grace. Come, why should we not get to know one another better while we are here? There is little else to do."

Her eyes flicked to the pot of dirt. He glanced down and noticed for the first time that there were a few wisps of green in the pot he was stabbing, seedlings that he'd slashed with the trowel. He felt unaccountably annoyed.

"Why are you here, at Rose Heath, Mr. Stirling? Why are you not in London?"

"I was invited here, of course. Sir Greyville and the colonel and I are old friends."

"But they are busy now, apparently, entertaining new friends. Surely you need not feel that they would be bereft of company should you leave. Why not go back to London, where there is so much diversion to be had?"

He shrugged.

"Or is there something you're avoiding in Town? Perhaps a gambling debt?"

"No. I always pay my debts. I simply do not wish to be in Town."

She cocked her head. "A few weeks ago, I received an invitation to an engagement party for the Earl of Roswell's daughter. He is your uncle, if I am not mistaken?"

He inclined his head.

"But you do not mean to be present at the celebration of your cousin's engagement? It was to be tonight, I believe."

"We are not a close family."

"Then I am sorry to hear it. Family can be one of life's chief joys. I would be quite sorry to miss sharing in my own family's happiness at such a time."

She *would* keep turning the conversation toward such dry avenues. "I think we have already established that you are a much better person than I am. And clearly a moralist as well."

She was, in a word, vexing, and it was a testament to how little else was available to Kit that he found her to be like a challenge thrown down before him. Though that wasn't exactly true either. He found talk of love and family harmony insipid, but her conversation was not insipid. *She* was not insipid. And he could not forget how she'd touched him the night before, how direct and fiery had been her passion.

"Come," he began, but at that moment, the housekeeper appeared to announce that tea was being served in the drawing room.

"Oh, thank goodness," the duchess said, heading for the door briskly. "I'm sure I have been wanting nothing so much as tea."

"Is that so?" he muttered, going after her.

She had a spirit of great passion, but not the courage to give it rein. He should have guessed, given the way she had handled her fear of water by resolving to avoid it her whole life. She likely kept her emotions under tight control; it was what he'd observed about her from the first, that she was controlled and tasteful. He must simply give her a taste for something new.

He caught up with her and spoke in a low voice, though the housekeeper had left. "If you change your mind, Your Grace, I shall be by the pool at midnight, ready to afford you the unique opportunity to gain a skill you are lacking. A skill, I might add, that could one day save your life, never mind what you've been missing through your fear of pretty little ponds and gentle rivers."

"The plunge pool is a basin of frigid water, Mr. Stirling, not some once-in-a-lifetime treat. But you may of course wish to sample its delights yourself. I wish you joy of it. Good day, sir."

She swept out of the greenhouse with her chin in the air, behaving for all the world as if there'd been nothing between them but plant talk. He watched her walk away, her hips barely swaying, the proud line of her neck giving no hint of the sensuous nature hiding within her.

He wanted her.

CHAPTER SIX

Through an unexpected, circuitous, and rather amusing set of circumstances, Olivia found herself the following day standing before a small group of local children and teaching them a song. The adventure had all begun when she had slipped out of the manor after breakfast, at which meal she had not, she thanked heaven, seen Mr. Stirling.

And to think he'd meant for her to allow him to teach her to swim! No doubt with the idea that he would be allowed all sorts of liberties with her body as she struggled in the water in little but a wet chemise. His nerve and his sordid intentions clearly knew no bounds.

Except, if she were being honest with herself, calling his intentions sordid, even in her mind, was not entirely fair. At least as far as what had happened in the kitchen, because she'd been just as eager as he for what they had done. The difference was that, for her, the interlude had been a one-time lapse, while for him, interludes were clearly a way of life.

When she found herself pacing in her room after breakfast in a vain attempt to banish thoughts of Mr. Stirling, she had set out for a bracing walk in the cool spring air, taking the path that led into the village.

She arrived there to discover that it was market day, and as she walked among the stalls selling new potatoes and pots of every size, her attention was drawn to a woman's voice that teased her with its familiarity. Seeking its owner, she discovered, amid all the strangers bustling about, someone she knew.

"Martha Sharp!" she exclaimed, rushing over to where the woman stood in an open space just beyond the pie seller's stall, amid a circle of young children.

"Olivia Thorpe!" Martha exclaimed, and then they were laughing and embracing, and recalling the times when they'd last been together, at Miss Lockhart's School.

Despite the passage of more than a dozen years, Martha looked almost the same, small and spry, with a pert nose and gentle blue eyes. She was Martha Tompkins now—she'd married the local vicar. And she was leading the children in practicing a song that was to be sung on a special occasion.

"Well, we are trying to sing together, anyway," Martha said. "But I was never very accomplished at music, and I can't seem to get this one part right with them. The music master at Miss Lockhart's did say I would never amount to anything musically." She laughed, shaking her head.

"He was not a kind music master, Martha."

"I know, but he was right, Olivia," Martha said, but then her hand flew to her mouth. "Oh, I do beg your pardon, Your Grace. Here I have been calling you by your Christian name and chattering away at you, and I had forgotten all about you marrying the duke. Pray excuse my familiarity. I shall certainly call you Your Grace from now."

"You will do nothing of the sort, Martha. I think we would both collapse in giggles if you were to attempt to establish such needless formality between us. Why, we have made suppositions together about Mrs. Brown's underlinen." Mrs. Brown had been their headmistress, a slim, hard woman with an improbably ample bosom that the girls of the school had whispered must be enhanced with rolled-up stockings. "We cannot pretend to be entirely proper now."

Martha's face softened with mirth. "Oh, Your Gr—" At a mock-stern look from Olivia, she laughed and corrected herself. "Olivia."

"And if you would not mind keeping the Duchess of Coldbrook's presence in the neighborhood quiet, I should be obliged. I'm here on a sort of quiet holiday."

"Oh—of course. I quite understand." And there was that kind smile that had so cheered Olivia when she had first arrived at Miss Lockhart's.

Olivia squeezed Martha's arm. "I shall never forget how you befriended me. I would have been alone in those first months had it not been for you."

Olivia had been grateful, at fifteen, to be sent to school. She had asked her parents for this favor, because she had understood that school would mean a chance to study and the opportunity to eventually seek employment as a governess. Her overwhelmed parents had pounced with relief on the idea that they might no longer need to concern themselves with her future.

"Nonsense," Martha said, "you would have made friends soon enough." Martha's eyes lit up. "And you had such a lovely voice too, and were so accomplished at music."

She glanced at the children, who'd been watching the exchange between the women with a great deal of interest. "Would you perhaps sing the song a time or two with the children, just to help them along? They're to perform the song at their teacher's wedding celebration. We thought it would be a marvelous surprise for her."

Which was how Olivia found herself standing in the market square with a dozen lively children, singing *Love Will Find Out the Way.*

* * *

Kit had only just managed to persuade Grey to come into town with him. His friend seemed unwilling to part from the manor, and it didn't take a genius to guess that he wished to spend not a moment away from the enchanting Mrs. Francesca Pomponio.

"A pint or two will do you good, Grey," Kit was saying as they strode through the streets toward the public house. "Isn't it fine to get out and see something different?"

Kit might as well have been speaking about himself, so constantly had he been thinking of the Duchess of Coldbrook. Her persistence in his thoughts had put him in a dark mood. Why should he be thinking about such an uncooperative woman when he knew scores of females who were willing, friendly, and far prettier too?

"There are often very fine things to see right under one's own nose, you know, Kit."

Kit grunted. The Duchess of Coldbrook was right under his nose at Rose Heath, or as good as. He was constantly plagued with insipidly romantic thoughts prompting him to consider such things as the fact that she was sleeping under the same roof as he or, when he saw water being carried up, that she was bathing. She was like a disease he'd caught that he could not shake.

They were passing the pie stall at the edge of the market area when what sounded like an entire school of little voices broke into song.

"What the devil?" he muttered.

Grey pulled his sleeve to draw his attention. "Say, isn't that our very own Miss Thorpe?" he asked, indicating a lady standing amid a group of children. Kit had, as the duchess had requested, kept her identity a secret. He quite liked that he was the only one at Rose Heath who knew she was a duchess. In a way, she was his discovery.

Though now she was, for some incomprehensible reason, standing in this piddling little market square, leading a group of children in song. In a love song, he perceived, as the words floated to him over the oinking of several excited pigs.

"So it would seem," Kit said. "What I cannot imagine is why."

"She seems to be leading children in song," Grey pointed out needlessly as they drew close.

Kit shot him a disgusted look. "Evidently." They watched for several minutes as she sang along with them in a very pleasing voice, pausing twice to go over portions of the song with individual children. The whole scene was revoltingly wholesome, and Kit felt uncomfortable watching such an open display of earnest goodness.

He whistled loudly several times, then called out, "Love will find out the way, will it? Then what will it do?" Which prompted laughter from some passersby.

The duchess turned, and when her eyes lighted on Kit, a dark look came over her face.

"Come, admit it's sentimental claptrap," he called with a grin, trying to coax a smile from her and knowing he was failing even as he spoke. Her inky eyebrows drew down.

"Who is that?" one of the children asked. "*Is* this sentimental claptrap?"

"He is no one, and he can have nothing to say to us," the Duchess of Coldbrook said, and turned away from him.

Her disdain, which he had so well earned, was like a punch to his stomach.

"If you admire her, man," Grey muttered, "this is no way to go about courting her."

"Admire her?" Kit snarled. He could not remember ever being more annoyed with himself. Grey wisely said no more.

Furious with himself, Kit drank deeply at the pub, staying long after Grey returned to Rose Heath without him. When night fell, Kit made his way to the manor, whistling, his mood having been lifted by quantities of brandy. After bribing a stable boy to find out where the duchess's room would be, he stood under her window and serenaded her—with *Love Will Find Out the Way*, of course.

He was halfway through the refrain when she opened her window. The briefest glimpse of white sleeves appeared before a cascade of cold water dowsed him.

He awoke the next morning in damp clothes, with a thick head, a roiling stomach, and a profound—and profoundly unaccustomed—feeling of self-disgust.

* * *

Colonel Stratton had reported to the ladies that the extensive repairs needed to their coach would likely require a good two weeks to fix, and Francesca in particular seemed happy about the ladies' prolonged stay at Rose Heath. Mary Alice was, thankfully, recovering from her injury. The estate was beautiful, and it was peaceful to be there in the guise of Olivia Thorpe—as long as she could avoid Kit Stirling. Fortunately, the manor was large enough that only sensible precautions were required. The morning of the fifth day, for instance, found her enjoying a tray in her room, then productively writing letters to both the housekeeper at Brookleigh and one of her aunts.

She hadn't even thought of him once that morning, she told herself smugly as she stood after addressing the second letter and shook out her cramping hands. And why should she be thinking of him? The man was nothing to her, beyond being an annoyance. She had far better things with which to occupy her time than thinking of Kit Stirling.

Eventually, she became aware that she was pacing rather vigorously on the pretty blue carpet that stretched between the two windows in her bedchamber and, with a groan of exasperation, forced herself to stop. She was failing miserably at not thinking. She didn't *want* to think back on those moments in the kitchen—she had in fact decided that they must be scrubbed from her memory. But memory was famous for not being cooperative when given such orders. And she could not forget how she'd urged him on.

Let me warm you, he'd said. He'd been referring to her wet, cold state, and she hadn't wanted him to talk, hadn't wanted reality to intrude in the form of words spoken between them. But then afterward, he'd continued, *Well, you are warm now. Quite warm.* And she had felt pierced by unwanted tenderness.

How could one be pierced by tenderness? The notion was nonsense. And certainly, to think of the Wastrel of White Horse Street being tender was foolish. He was a gambler and a rake, a man accustomed to taking his pleasure with actresses and mistresses aplenty. Of course he was adept at bringing pleasure to a woman, part of which surely involved speaking soft words at the right moment.

She had offered him what he liked to have that night, and he had taken it and enjoyed it and then wanted more. Such was the force that was male desire; she'd been married to a healthy man, and she was well acquainted with male desire. And her own. She and Harold had enjoyed satisfying marital relations.

And she had, for that one encounter with Mr. Stirling, wanted the same physical thing as he did.

But she wanted no more. She was sated. Whatever had been lurking in her that had wanted to touch him and be touched by him must be finished. Of course it must; she valued serenity and quiet walks and books and good friends. She valued the life of the mind. Such things as she and Kit Stirling had done were not to be thought of.

He was not to be thought of.

And *she* needed to get out of this room if she was to avoid making herself into a lunatic.

The rain had stopped for the moment, so she put on her sturdiest shoes and collected a hat and a thick woolen shawl. Checking outside her door (while feeling that she was becoming a little ridiculous), she found the hallway deserted save for two maids polishing the woodwork.

Despite the chill and damp of the gray afternoon, stretching her legs in the fresh air felt wonderful. She set out on the path that she'd taken the second day, which wound around the property before passing, at the farther reaches of the circuit, through a pretty wooded area that stood a good half mile from the manor. The woods opened up onto a pond, with a little wooden boathouse, that she'd seen from a distance while walking a few days before.

She made her way there now, barely sparing a glance for the little boathouse as she passed it. Keeping a good distance between herself and the edge of the pond, she stood quietly, and soon the sunlight dappling the water and the peaceful sound of the tiny waves gently lapping the shore began to work some magic on her. What need had she of swimming or even going right up to the water when she gained such pleasure from standing close enough? Mr. Stirling was wrong.

Thinking of him, though, set her teeth on edge with contrariness, and she recalled how he'd mocked her cautiousness around water and her lack of interest in learning to swim. She was not a coward. She was not! Why, she could go as close to the water as she liked, she told herself, and inched a little nearer. There. She was quite close.

And closer still, she moved, even as she felt a corresponding rise in the rate of her heartbeat. But she wasn't a coward. She was a woman, and a duchess, and by God, she was not *afraid* to stand at the edge of a peaceful little pond.

She succeeded ultimately in challenging herself to move so close that the tips of her black half boots were kissed by the water. Only the very tips, and her heart was hammering. But she was there. She was there! She was standing right at the edge of a pond, and she was not crumpling in fear or shrieking, and she was perspiring only a very little bit.

She could not have said how long she had stood there when she heard it: the sound of a throat being cleared. She started in surprise and stepped forward with a splash and a cry, only just catching herself from tumbling into the water.

"You'll say that's my fault, I'll wager," came a voice from behind her. Mr. Stirling's voice. She gasped and wheeled around in outrage, wetting her skirts further before she stepped out of the few inches of water in which she was standing, sloshing it clumsily over her shoes.

"You! How dare you startle me like that?"

He was sitting on the wooden floor of the little covered verandah of the house, which was odd since there was a chair right next to him. One of his legs was bent, the other straight, and he slouched carelessly against the wall behind him, his pose just as insolent as she would have expected.

"I suppose it was your intent for me to fall all the way in," she said. "And then you could rescue me."

"I assure you it was not my intention to turn you into a damsel in distress today. I do beg your pardon most earnestly." He did not rise, as any gentleman would normally have done, but why should she be surprised?

"I sincerely doubt that."

She gave her skirts a vigorous shake in a vain attempt to relieve them of the bits of debris now sticking to them.

"You went right up to the water of your own accord. Bravo."

As if she desired his praise!

"Now perhaps you will wish to reconsider the swimming lessons."

She did not even deign to make a scoffing sound. Instead, she lifted her chin and marched toward the side of the little house, intent on returning immediately to the peace of her walk. Though already he had spoiled her solitude and peace. *Why* did he have to be there? And why, she thought, with a sinking of something inside her, did he have to be so handsome?

Even though he was a scoundrel, he was a very handsome scoundrel, and one to whom she had already—there was no other better light to put on it—succumbed. It was as if there was a vein of wickedness in her, a wee little vein whose existence she'd been able to overlook for her entire life, and then in one strange evening, she'd let it rule her.

Fortunately for her self-respect, she now recognized this weakness in herself. Wasn't there some saying about knowing your enemy being half the battle? Though she wasn't certain if the enemy was that little vein of wickedness, or if it was simply Kit Stirling, who seemed to have brought it to the fore. Probably both.

"I suppose you were not particularly wishing for my company just now." He spoke as she was nearly past him.

Despite her wish not to engage with him, she could not resist a tart reply, and she paused to deliver it properly. "No, I was not."

He nodded. For the first time, she noticed that his face looked pale, as if he was in pain or ill. And was that a note of strain in his voice?

"Is there something the matter with you?" This was a rude thing to say, especially to someone who might not be feeling well, but she did not trust that he wasn't playing some game to gain her sympathy.

"I seem to have injured my ankle rather spectacularly." He jerked his chin toward the leg that was stretched out. "Stepped into some animal's hole just around the back of this house and twisted it. It was, er, a bit ghastly."

"Oh." He must have sprained it badly, if indeed that was all he'd done to it. "I'm sorry." She moved close and dropped to her haunches, her eyes going to his lower leg. He was wearing a pair of smart Hessians. "I'm surprised your foot was able to turn in those."

"I managed to do so by losing my balance and falling while my foot was stuck in the hole."

She winced. "That sounds painful."

"It was." He attempted one of those arrogant grins that she found so annoying, but just now it looked more like a grimace. Clearly, he was in pain, and she would be the last person he would want to see him vulnerable.

"I shall go back to the manor straightaway and get someone to help you."

"Actually, I've been sitting here since late morning, wondering what I was going to do, until you showed up. If you wouldn't mind assisting me," he said, "I will attempt to return to the manor now."

"Me, help you all the way back to the manor? I'm not sure how much help I could possibly be."

"Nonsense," he said, pushing himself more upright even as his mouth drew into a tight line, "you'll do fine. If you could position that chair so it's braced against the wall, I can use it to pull myself up."

Olivia was not at all convinced this was a good idea, but he seemed insistent, so she pushed the chair into position as he had asked.

He managed to raise himself above the seat, and then he put the bent knee of the uninjured leg on the seat and, with a heavy grunt, pulled himself upright. He leaned against the wall of the cabin, clearly trying not to put much weight on his ankle, and attempted another grin.

"I'm afraid you're not going to like this part," he told her. "I should like to use you as a crutch."

She gave him a look. "I suspected that was to be my role. I don't think I should be very good at it."

"I'm sure you are successful at whatever you put your mind to, Your Grace."

She was not one to give up easily, though she would not have expected him to know this about her.

"Now, if you would come around to my side, like so."

She came to stand where he directed her, aware that she would be allowing him to touch her as she had not meant for him to do again, but this was different. And he *seemed* different. Despite her initial fury at finding him there and her suspicion that he'd delighted in her accidental entry into the pond, he had not in fact said or done a single coarse thing since she arrived. He'd been, actually, fairly polite.

He put his arm across her shoulders and leaned a little on her, though only a little, and she imagined it must be costing him something not to lean more heavily on her.

"And we're off," he said. Only because they were so close did she hear his indrawn breath as his foot touched the ground.

"Aren't you worried that you might injure yourself further by walking back to the manor like this?" she asked as he took a step and she moved to keep pace with him.

"I don't much care for worrying."

"Perhaps you ought to." They passed the enormous trunk of an ancient elm tree. "Then you might not be injured."

"You're right, of course. I might instead be sitting safely in my room, reading a book."

She couldn't imagine him sitting quietly with a book, though she had already seen him thus in the library a few days before. She had supposed at the time that he was there only out of boredom, had in fact doubted that such a man could have any real interest in books and ideas at all.

She experienced a twinge of remorse. She did not like to think of herself as judgmental. Of course, she had heard many bad things about him. And he had lived up to his reputation for being a rake; he had certainly been very forward with her that night in the kitchen.

But then, her own behavior that night would have to be judged as well, and she would be in danger of being a hypocrite.

"Do you even *like* to read?" she asked.

"Sometimes," he said, with the barest trace of a smile in his words. "I am fully capable of it, despite my reputation. I rather think you imagine that I'm never not doing something wicked. I do have to eat sometimes, and there's nothing very wicked about drinking tea or buying an umbrella. Or walking alone down the street on a beautiful summer night."

Olivia liked to walk in the garden at Brookleigh late at night sometimes. She loved the way the darkness did away with distraction and heightened her senses, making her fully aware of the scent of lilac that she noticed only fleetingly during the day, or of the sound of her shoes on the grass. An image of Kit Stirling strolling alone by moonlight came to her. She glanced at him out of the corner of her eye and almost shared her thoughts.

Such poetic musings would sound silly spoken aloud.

"Also," he said, the words slightly labored, "I am always unfailingly considerate toward dogs, and cats quite adore me."

"And that is all the proof I am to require that you are not pure evil?"

"*I* think so."

Another stolen glance revealed perspiration beading on his brow. Had she been in such discomfort, she would have wanted to shut out the world and curl up in a ball. But he seemed to want to distract himself by talking.

"Convincing people that you aren't wicked would be far easier if you simply did not do wicked things."

"And what would be the fun in that?" he said lightly.

"Well, it might be quite fun not to be the subject of gossip. Unless, of course, you like having people speak ill of you."

"What I like, Your Grace, is doing just as I please. As, I imagine, do you."

"We are hardly speaking of the same sorts of things."

"Perhaps."

Much to her surprise, and irritation too, she was enjoying his company. At the same time, she felt quite frustrated with him. He was not so purely bad as she had thought, or at least, he had some redeeming qualities. So why did he cultivate a reputation as a rake?

She could only be grateful when their arrival at the manor cut off further thought.

CHAPTER SEVEN

Kit hobbled into the library with the assistance of Stratton's butler and sank gratefully onto the settee, having ignored the duchess's suggestion that he have a pair of footmen carry him to his room immediately. She clearly thought he was being foolish in not taking to his bed, but she simply gave an abrupt nod and, with the ease of a woman accustomed to being obeyed, asked the butler to see that a doctor be sent for. Then she ordered tea.

His leg was on fire. Not only the ankle, which had burst into agony the moment he twisted it, making a revolting popping sound, but his whole leg. He did, however, feel fairly certain that it was not broken since it could bear his weight, if painfully. At least, he profoundly hoped that it was not.

To his surprise, though the duchess might now in all conscience have left him—she'd certainly made no secret of her wish to avoid his company before—she lingered, fussing over his ankle. She brought over a footstool and gently lifted his leg onto it.

"The doctor may be some time," she said. "It would perhaps be best to remove your boot now. It could be that further damage is being done to your foot, or perhaps even to your circulation."

"You look sturdy enough, ma'am, but I don't think you will be able to assist me in removing my boot. And I'm sure I'm not capable of pulling it off myself just now."

"I don't propose to pull it off, sir." A maid was just arriving with the tea tray, and the duchess dispatched her to fetch a pair of shears.

"You propose to destroy my boot?" It was his favorite pair, and while it had occurred to him that it might be necessary to cut off the boot, he had not reconciled himself to the loss of it.

"Yes."

His foot was throbbing painfully, but talking to her distracted him wonderfully. "I believe you are enjoying the idea of ruining my boot."

"It's only a shoe," she said as the maid returned with the shears. The duchess took them, dismissed the girl, and came to stand by his leg, holding the scissors up as she considered his boot.

"You look diabolical. I begin to think your true purpose is to seek revenge on me."

"Revenge? Why should I want revenge on you, sir?"

He was accustomed to merry widows, to giddy actresses and willing mistresses— women who did not regret their sexual adventures. But the Duchess of Coldbrook wasn't a merry widow. He would have said she was a prude, but that didn't seem right either.

"Because you regret succumbing to your carnal desires, and I was the one you succumbed with. People always dislike those they associate with their own weakness."

"I expect that's something about which you know a great deal." She paused, the shears raised, and lifted her eyes to him with directness. "And who said it was weakness?"

With that, she nudged his leg a little to the side, positioned the shears at the seam on the back of his boot, and snipped, leaving him temporarily speechless on more than one account.

"And here I offered you the perfect opportunity to deal me a blistering set-down, and you didn't take it."

Was she softening toward him? He wanted her again, quite badly, even now. He had in fact had the thought, when they were walking together toward the manor, that being able to put his arm around her shoulders had made injuring his foot worth the pain. He had not stopped wanting her since that night in the kitchen. But she had so far been adamant that she would not have him again, and he could not read her expression now.

"I think I hear my valet weeping," he said as she advanced the scissors farther down his boot. She might have been irritated with him, as she generally was— and he expected that she now was, though he was finding her maddeningly difficult to read—but she was not proceeding roughly, as she might have done, careless of paining him further.

She ignored him and gently but determinedly snipped. Each inch of progress at first generated intense pressure in his swollen ankle and then relief as the tightness of the boot eased.

Her attention on her efforts allowed him to watch her unobserved. *Average,* that had been his first impression of her. Average hair color and height, average face, except for those too-strong eyebrows. Average figure too, he'd supposed.

He had been an idiot.

* * *

Who said it was weakness?

Had she really said that to him? Immediately after that first night, she had certainly felt terribly weak and foolish. She had told herself that she should never have allowed herself to do such a thing, and with this man, of all people. But now—and perhaps this had something to do with what she'd managed to do at the pond today—her initial regret had faded, to be replaced with something far different: amazement. In allowing herself to do what she'd done with Kit Stirling, she had done something deeply impulsive and out of character. Just as she'd done by putting her toes in the water of the pond.

All her life, she'd done the sensible thing. Growing up in a house as chaotic as her own, she'd learned early to look out for herself. Learned that if she wanted good things for herself, it would be up to her to choose them and pursue them.

Sensible. Measured. Thoughtful. That was how her friends thought of her, and how she strived to be. What she'd done in the kitchen with Kit Stirling had been wild and impulsive, and yes, brilliantly exciting.

She had not known she was capable of being like that.

She'd reached his ankle, and she went very slowly now. He had gone quiet, and she supposed he was in pain, though he made no complaint. She snipped, he gave a grunt, and the boot drooped loose enough that she could slip it off.

"Your ankle does look quite swollen," she observed, regarding the thickened area showing through his white stocking. "It must be painful."

"It is. Do you know what would make it less painful?"

She glanced at him. "A glass of brandy?"

"I had a different sort of distraction in mind."

A blush warmed her cheeks as the meaning of his words penetrated. Nobody said such things to the Duchess of Coldbrook. But then, the men with whom she was generally in company were gentlemen, and Kit Stirling had made no secret of his intention not to be gentlemanly. He seemed, rather, to go out of his way to not be gentlemanly.

"It's one of your main entertainments, isn't it?" she said. "Trying to shock people with your wickedness."

"I can be a beast sometimes, Your Grace. Forgive me."

His words surprised her, but his tone affected her more, with its hint of vulnerability. Was this a sign that he wished to be other than a beast? Something in her leaped at the idea. But looking at his handsome features and carefree smile, she immediately crushed it. No good would come of trusting such a man.

The doctor arrived then, saving her from the necessity of a reply. She had every intention of leaving now that Mr. Stirling would be in capable hands, but Dr. Hannibal, whose vigorous smile and upstanding tufts of thick white hair gave him the appearance of an imp, apparently assumed she was a concerned friend of his patient and folded her into the conversation.

"I was told, sir, that this happened while you were out walking and that Miss

Thorpe was obliged to rescue you?" The doctor winked at Olivia as he set his bag down and drew close to Kit.

"Oh—" she began.

"Most fortunate for me, Hannibal," Mr. Stirling said. "It's not every day a fellow is rescued by a lady."

"I merely happened upon him while out walking and assisted him in making his way back to the manor," Olivia said. "Hardly a dramatic rescue."

"But much appreciated by me," Kit said.

"Quite right," Dr. Hannibal agreed. "A very convenient thing, having a friend who's such a practical lady."

Kit smirked at her. "It certainly is."

She gave him a withering glance. But before she could excuse herself and leave, the doctor had whipped out a small pair of scissors and removed Kit's stocking. No Town doctor would have done that in a lady's presence out of respect for her sensibilities, but Olivia had a feeling Dr. Hannibal did not much concern himself with such niceties.

"A most impressive sprain, sir," he said with a cluck of his tongue. "Fortunately for you, sir, you've got friends around to visit you and see that you're properly cared for, because you'll need to keep off that foot for at least three days."

Kit looked so dismayed by this statement that Olivia almost laughed. "Can't you just wrap it up and send me on my way, Hannibal?"

"Certainly, sir, if you wish for the sprain to worsen and for your ligaments to become feeble. You will then risk making the entire ankle unstable and weak."

"I can't just sit around for three days! What nonsense."

Olivia could easily imagine that the ever-restless Kit was utterly maddened by the idea of being confined to a room for days. As her eyes skimmed over muscled thighs that were clearly used to exercise, she could not resist saying, "Mr. Stirling, I'm sure you don't mean to suggest that Dr. Hannibal has given you poor advice."

"Quite right, ma'am," the doctor agreed. "Why, any sensible fellow would be delighted to rest and recuperate in the company of such friends as Miss Thorpe."

A sly look came over Kit's face. "You're right, of course, Doctor. I shall look on my recuperation as an opportunity to enjoy Miss Thorpe's company."

She gave him a falsely sweet smile for the benefit of Dr. Hannibal and stood patiently by while the doctor applied a liniment and wrapped a bandage around the injured ankle.

No sooner had the doctor left than Kit said, "I hope very much that you're planning to read to the invalid now, Your Grace."

"I'm planning to go to my room and rest there for several hours. This has been a most trying day."

"But you heard the doctor on the importance of my friends aiding in my recuperation. Surely you're not going to abandon me here, a poor, incapacitated fellow?"

She plucked a book off a nearby table, scanning the title as she handed it to him, and smiling when she saw that it was a treatise on land management. "Here. You like to read, remember?"

She swept out of the room wearing a completely inappropriate grin and retreated to her bedchamber quite happily with a book and a tea tray.

That evening, she joined Sir Greyville, Francesca, and Kit for dinner. Mary Alice and Stratton were dining elsewhere on the estate. A burly footman helped Kit hobble into the dining room amid much teasing from his friend and expressions of concern from Francesca. The dinner conversation was remarkably pleasant, and Olivia began to see the bond between Kit and his old friend. They teased each other affectionately about travels and ideas, and they laughed easily.

They lingered only briefly afterward in the drawing room because Sir Greyville had to leave to take up some pressing work with which Francesca was helping him.

Which left Olivia alone in the drawing room with Kit as his presumptive companion. He was reclining on a settee, his leg stretched out on a stool.

"You really ought to retire to your bedchamber," she said. "Surely you will wish to rest."

"The hour is but a quarter to ten, Your Grace. I should find myself staring mutely at the walls in my chamber were I to retire so early." He was wearing a black coat and a fresh cravat and neat buff trousers. And a single shoe, on his uninjured foot, per Dr. Hannibal's instructions. She entertained unwelcome musings as to how Kit had managed to change out of his earlier attire, whether his valet had simply brought clothes down to the library, rather than having Kit helped up the stairs.

"Well, I do not find it early to retire," she said, meaning to seek her chamber. Though she had not spent the afternoon with him, still her thoughts had strayed to him again and again, and at dinner, her eyes had been drawn to him often. He was funny, and clever, and whether she approved of him or not, he made her heart beat faster. She was hardly the first woman to be attracted to a man she could not respect, but ignoring his appeal had been easier when she didn't like him.

And she did like him.

"But what about your promise to Dr. Hannibal that, as my friend, you would keep me entertained while I am incapacitated?"

"I made no such promise." She laughed. "And I don't know how you can call us friends with a straight face."

"Come now, Duchess, surely we can be friends of a sort? Or at least not enemies."

It was so easy to see how countless women must have fallen into his arms. He was an utterly charming rogue.

When she didn't reply, he said, "I know that I've behaved badly toward you in any number of ways. I... have grown accustomed to behaving thus, I'm afraid."

His unexpected admission of fault surprised her. But words were easy to say, and he was doubtless very good at saying what he thought others wanted to hear.

"So it would seem," she said.

He frowned, as though he hadn't expected she would simply agree with him. "Well, according to the good doctor, I'm supposed to recuperate in your company, Your Grace. And how will I get better if I'm stuck here alone? Why, I might become frantic from inactivity and begin pacing the room out of desperation and do myself further injury. Or perhaps even swoon from boredom."

"I would like to see a man swoon from boredom. I suspect there are many ladies who've done so, when forced to stand about listening to some man drone on about his prowess at the hunt or his latest acquisition of horseflesh."

"I assure you, swooning would be preferable to accounts of recently purchased draperies and the glories of the latest coiffure." He grinned boyishly, and a little corner of her heart melted. "Come, isn't there some improving volume you'd like to read to a rake such as myself? You have before you a helpless invalid unable to flee even should you read a book of sermons to me."

"Why would you wish me to read to you when you can do it yourself?"

"Because it will be nicer if you do it."

It was on the tip of her tongue to ask why, to provoke him into one of those coarse things he said and thus give her a pretext for leaving, but she didn't do it. The truth was, she was enjoying his company. What was the harm in that? He could hardly seduce her with his leg injured and propped on a stool. And she did want to linger there with him. It was fun.

Fun was not something she thought much about. Oh, her life was fulfilling. As the hostess for Harold's nephew, the current Duke of Coldbrook, Olivia retained many of the duties she'd always had in regards to the estates and the running of the manors. And she was happy to do so until he found a bride, which he seemed in no rush to do. Seeing to practical matters was immensely satisfying.

But is that all you really want? a traitorous voice now whispered.

Her gaze dropped to a stack of books someone had placed on the table by the settee—Gothic novels, along with a few books of philosophy and poetry.

"Very well, but I'm indulging you only because you're injured. And only for half an hour."

He inclined his head. "You are all kindness, Duchess."

"I don't credit meekness in you for a moment." She plucked one of the Gothic novels off the table.

"What, no sermons?"

"I'm not foolish enough to think they would do any good."

CHAPTER EIGHT

The duchess closed the book, her hand coming to rest on top of it with finality. "Well, I'll bid you good evening, sir."

She was about to leave. Kit couldn't let her go, and this no longer had anything to do with avoiding boredom. Somewhere between her fear and stiff pride after falling in the pool and the way she'd brought her toes to the very edge of the pond that morning, he'd started looking at her differently. Those strong eyebrows had become like old friends, her lips and cheeks and eyes no longer average but hers alone. He ached to touch her.

"Don't go yet," he said.

Her brows drew together. "Are you in pain? Would you like a pillow for your foot?" She reached for a pillow at the other end of the settee. He didn't want a pillow and in fact had forgotten the throbbing in his ankle as he'd listened to her read.

"I don't need a pillow."

"It's no trouble," she insisted in a calm, considerate voice, moving closer to his foot.

She was a good woman, a woman who'd been raised to roles that she'd accepted and fulfilled, who'd not made grand stumbles and indulged in endless vices as he had done, but had done worthwhile things with her life so far. He did not deserve to even be thinking about her.

He let her lift his foot and place the pillow under it, then set his foot down, which she did with remarkable gentleness. "Is there anything else you need before I go?"

He cursed that he must sit, that he couldn't simply sweep her into his arms. Though he was not so foolish as to believe that he would be at any greater advantage if he could physically take her into his arms, because she did not want to be there. Or rather, she did not believe she ought to be there, however much she might want to be. He should not even think of wishing for her to be there.

But he did.

"Yes."

"What is it?" Her face was in shadow, and he couldn't see her eyes. "Is your bandage uncomfortable?"

"It's fine, thank you. But if you wouldn't mind, a pillow behind my back would be most comfortable." He didn't need another pillow.

"Of course."

He imagined her making the rounds on her estates, offering kindness and hospitality to her tenants. Bringing baskets to homes with new babies, placing a cool compress on a feverish child's head, listening to a neighbor's troubles with real attention.

She found another pillow and touched his shoulder. "Lean forward." He did, and she pushed it behind his back.

"If there is nothing else?"

Just you, he wanted to say, but he could not. How could he say such a thing when he was a wastrel and she was a good woman? She didn't respect him, and with good reason. But he couldn't let this go.

He took her hand.

Her gaze snapped to his. "What is it?"

"Come here," he said softly.

She said nothing for a moment. "Why?"

How could he answer? He could not tell her that he burned for her—he'd done so already, crassly, and she'd rightfully rejected him. She had no reason to believe anything had changed in his intentions, or in him. But something had. And he did burn for her, body and rotten, ruined soul.

"Just come here," he said, and tugged gently. She allowed him to draw her closer. He reached up and curled his hand behind her neck and gently drew her downward. She acquiesced, letting her hip come to rest near him on the settee. He wasn't going to question it if she would let him pull her close, and he tugged her nearer still, toward his mouth.

She came. Her lips, soft and unbearably sweet, met his with no protest. He brushed his lips against her mouth, willing her to understand his change of heart, his hope. Her lips parted and let him in, and he poured affection into his kiss and took heart at the quickening of her breath as the kiss deepened.

After a few moments, she pulled back and looked at him, her expression unreadable. It took everything he had not to tug her close again by the hand he still held. She wanted him, he knew this, but she did not want to want him. Yet. So he had to tread carefully. He let her hand fall, and confusion warred with vexation on her face.

"Why did you kiss me?" she asked.

"Because I could not resist you."

She made an impatient sound. "And you don't believe in resisting your impulses, do you?"

"Where you are concerned, it seems that I don't."

She pressed her lips together, and he told himself that her frustration was about more than simply thinking him unworthy. She made for the door without another word.

"Good night, Your Grace," he called softly after her.

* * *

Olivia marched punishingly up the stairs, furious with herself. Kit Stirling was a rake, and a scoundrel, and completely adept at getting women to fall into his arms. Why had she allowed herself to be one of their number just now?

Because she was weak. Because she loved being with him. Because he was handsome and charming and funny. Because she was *weak*.

She felt things for him that she did not want to examine. She liked making him laugh, and she loved the way he kissed. He was temptation personified.

She knew about the wrong turns into which temptation could lead a person. She'd had frequent examples throughout her childhood, in the loud rows that would ensue whenever her father strayed with a new woman.

Olivia was no innocent—she knew it was common for gentlemen to have mistresses. But her father could have chosen to be faithful despite temptation. Marriage to Harold had taught Olivia not to believe all men were as weak as her father. She had chosen well when she'd married him, and there had been trust between them, along with love.

But to care for a man like Kit Stirling? She would be a fool.

* * *

The following morning, as she was on her way downstairs, Colonel Stratton waved to her from the bottom of the steps, where he was speaking with his butler. As she drew near, he dismissed the man and greeted her.

"Might I ask a favor, ma'am?" he asked.

"Of course, sir, anything. Particularly if what you request might repay you in some small way for your generous hospitality."

He waved away her words. "Please, do not think anything of such a trifle as playing host to you and your charming companions. Indeed, I consider the accident that brought the three of you to Rose Heath to be nothing short of providence." He smiled ruefully. "But if it would not be an inconvenience to you, ma'am, might I ask you to visit a little with my friend Mr. Stirling, since he must still rest his ankle?"

He took out a watch and glanced down at it, and she suspected him of avoiding meeting her eyes. "As his host, I would do so myself, of course, but I'm quite taken up with something that must be seen to. I hate to think that the poor man might be alone for hours on end today. And likely tomorrow as well."

Surely Colonel Stratton was not playing matchmaker? But whether he was or not, as his guest, she could hardly refuse such a simple request, no matter how much she wished to avoid Kit Stirling.

"Of course, sir. I will be happy to do so."

Which was how she found herself entering the library that afternoon, despite her awareness that repeated exposure to Temptation Personified was not a good idea.

He was sitting on the divan by the window, a book open on his lap but his gaze directed out over the garden behind the manor.

"I've been sent by our host to entertain you," she said.

He smiled at her. "Then I must thank him for the pleasure of your company."

A polite and gentlemanly thing to say, and his smile was warm but lacking any hint of wickedness. For a moment, she was taken off guard, as if he'd changed overnight into a completely different man. But that wasn't quite right; ever since his accident, there'd been something different in his behavior. He did not seem like the same coarse man she'd first met.

He was adept at charm, she reminded herself. For some reason, he'd decided it suited him to be gentlemanly at the moment.

She didn't feel entirely comfortable with this judgment of him, but it was better for her if she forgot that he had the capacity to be tender and noble.

A handsome chess set stood nearby, and she proposed a game. He agreed, and she arranged the board in easy reach of where he sat and prepared, with a little private glee, to best him. She was quite good at chess and had played often with Harold.

Fifteen minutes later, Kit had taken her queen, and she was forced to surrender.

"You are too hasty in your decisions, Your Grace," he told her, a smile teasing the corners of his mouth. "You would do better if you allowed yourself more time to consider all your options before making your move."

"I am well aware of how to play chess."

His eyes danced with mirth. "Yes, I expect you are and that you're accustomed to winning often. I also suspect that you didn't think I'd be particularly good at the game, because it requires patience and persistence and intelligence, and you think I have little to recommend me beyond a pretty face."

She scoffed, though she was also struggling not to laugh. "If I do"—she turned her attention to collecting the chess pieces—"perhaps that's because I know little else about you than how you look and what the London gossip has told me."

"That's not entirely true, Your Grace. You've had a chance to form your own opinion of me."

That was true. She knew what it was like to be with him now, which was something no one could have told her. She knew how to make him laugh, and that he bore suffering cheerfully. And she knew that he had come to Rose Heath to avoid his cousin's engagement party.

"Well," she said, taking her time putting a pawn in its own velvet-lined recess in the chess box, "I know nothing of your family, or where you come from, or why you prefer to live in such a way that people call you the Wastrel of White Horse Street."

She didn't expect him to answer, but he surprised her.

"I was the happy, only child of two very good people, who died of consumption when I was twelve," he said, handing her several knights to stow away. "My uncle, the Earl of Roswell as you know, had no heir, only a baby daughter born after years of barrenness. He became my guardian when my parents died and welcomed me into his household."

She put the last of the pieces in the box and latched the lid. "And you have repaid him by living as a wastrel?"

He remained silent for several long moments. "I was, in fact, a very dutiful nephew to the earl for half a dozen years, and I was deeply grateful to learn all he had to teach me about the responsibilities that would one day be mine. He was good to me, as was my aunt, and I was fond of them both and of my cousin Kate.

"All might have gone on that way had I not discovered a packet of letters to the earl, written to him by my father, his younger brother, begging for help. My uncle liked for people to see to their own affairs, to do the right thing, and to take the narrow path of righteousness. Uncle was unforgiving about mistakes."

All trace of the laughing rogue she knew was gone, replaced by a man who spoke respectfully of duty and gratitude. "Your father had made mistakes," she guessed.

He had turned his head toward the hearth, but she didn't think he was seeing the fire. "My father was not careful or sensible with money, and he'd borrowed large amounts from my uncle with the expectation that the money would be for repairs to our home. But my father used the money for more immediate purposes, for dinner parties and horses and clothes. He loved poetry and art and music, and he loved to entertain.

"I believe he always meant to pay the money back out of his yearly income, but when both he and my mother became sick with consumption, he still had not repaid the loans, and his letters to my uncle, begging for funds to help us, went unanswered."

"Oh," she said. "It's hard to believe anyone could be so unforgiving and hard-hearted."

Bleakness darkened his eyes when he finally returned her gaze. "I had benefited from my uncle's largesse, while my parents had been left to die."

"But you didn't know at the time, did you, about the dealings between your father and your uncle?"

"No. But at eighteen, when I found out, I believed that I should have known. There had been such a lack of warmth between them, and my father had frequently referred to his brother as 'the old skinflint.' My Uncle had been nothing but kind to me, and I had dismissed what my father said about him." His voice developed a hard edge. "I had disbelieved my own father."

She began to see. She envisioned Kit as he must have been, a decent and good young man who'd loved and lost his parents and benefitted from advantages he wished they could have had. "You confronted your uncle."

"Yes. He said, 'Your father was useless. Be grateful fate offered you a better life than you would have had with him.'"

"What a thing to say! Surely he didn't mean it."

"I assure you he did. We had a fantastic row, and I left that same day, determined to rely no further on my uncle. I sought out my father's old friends, who welcomed me. And I discovered that there is more than one way to live one's life."

"But your uncle spoke out of anger. People say terrible things out of anger, things they don't truly mean."

She had closed the chess box, but now he toyed with the latch, lifting it and pressing it closed again a few times before abandoning it with a shrug. "It was a long time ago. It makes no difference now."

"I doubt that."

"Well," he said, and rubbed his hands together, "where's that book of sermons?"

She blinked. "That was an abrupt change of topic."

He chuckled, all traces of seriousness banished. "Agreed. But that was ancient history. Surely you have something to read to me that will have my ears burning, a sermon on forgiveness, or perhaps something about temperance?"

He wanted to keep things light. She suspected he'd become very good at that in recent years. But she'd glimpsed the vulnerability behind his easy charm, and she no longer believed that was all there was to him. "I don't particularly wish to read from a book of sermons," she said.

"But you will read something to me? I should consider myself fortunate if you would."

He sounded as though he sincerely wished her to read to him. She wasn't certain she was prepared to contend with a sincere Kit.

"Very well." She plucked a volume off the table near the settee. "Poetry, then. Alexander Pope. And no complaining, as you have brought this on yourself."

He sat serenely with his leg propped on the stool, his hands folded in his lap and, for all she could tell, listened. When she closed the book half an hour later and announced that she must repair to her chamber to write a letter, he thanked her for visiting with him and made no move to press her to stay or to touch her.

He behaved, in short, like a perfect gentleman.

As she left the room, she admitted to herself that she was disappointed he'd not tried to steal a kiss. Very disappointed.

It was all most disconcerting.

CHAPTER NINE

The following morning, Olivia decided that she would visit Kit briefly, in accordance with Stratton's request, and then she would take herself off somewhere out of the vicinity of Temptation Personified. But when Olivia entered the library, Kit was not sitting on the settee with his leg propped up as he had been for the last day and a half.

She experienced a stab of worry as she looked around the empty room. What if he'd gotten up and fallen somewhere? Or perhaps he'd fallen in his chamber and was in need of help, she thought with rising concern, before she reminded herself that he was a grown man and not in need of her ministrations. Even if he were lying somewhere on the floor in terrible pain, he could still call out for help.

Unless he'd hit his head.

As she was having these thoughts in the library doorway, the butler appeared and told her that Mr. Stirling awaited her outside.

"He does?" she asked, but the butler merely replied, "Indeed," and escorted her to the front door.

Two horses stood in the drive. Kit was atop one of them, the handsome gray she remembered from the first day. He was attired smartly in a dark blue riding coat and looking not at all like a man who'd recently suffered a very bad sprain. The other horse, a chestnut mare, was improbably bedecked with a lovely garland of large white flowers around her neck.

Olivia descended the steps. "What on earth are you doing? You are supposed to be resting your leg."

"I have, despite your gracious ministrations, reached the limit of my capacity to sit in a room for hours on end. So I am going for a ride, which, as I'm sure you will allow, will not much strain my ankle. I was hoping you would join me."

Something fluttered in her chest at his words, but she paid it no attention.

"Where did you get all these flowers?"

"I did not steal them," he said dryly, "if that's what you are wondering."

She hadn't exactly framed it that way in her mind, but still.

His expression turned gleeful. "You think I've committed some horrible crime in the greenhouse, don't you?"

"Well, you did kill that poor infant plant the other day, poking away at it with the trowel. You have not so far shown yourself to be very solicitous of the welfare of plants."

His horse took a few nervous steps, and he effortlessly calmed the animal. "I cannot argue with the suggestion that I have not always been solicitous of the welfare of plants, but in this case I am innocent. Stratton said I could help myself."

The mare looked remarkably pretty with the garland of flowers around her neck, and a ripple of pleasure ran through Olivia because Kit had arranged this for her. "Well, that is good news, I suppose. At least there will not have to be a great drama between you and Stratton."

"Indeed. Will you come for a ride, then?"

"Er—" she began, thinking of all the reasons she ought not to go for a ride with Kit, starting with the fact that she liked the sound of his voice and the way he made jokes at his own expense, never mind the way his jacket stretched across his shoulders.

"Surely you don't want Buttercup to feel that she's gotten all dressed up for nothing," he said.

Buttercup tossed her mane, as if to punctuate his words. The morning was sparkling with sunlight and not too cool, the early spring air fresh on Olivia's cheeks. It would be a fine morning for a ride, she told herself, ignoring the fading voice of her conscience.

"I'm not dressed to ride," she pointed out.

"It will only take you a few minutes to change. I can have the groom walk her in the meantime."

"Very well, thank you. A ride sounds appealing." She smiled. "I'll go put on my habit."

She was doing that too much, she told herself a short time later as they walked the horses to the path at the west of the manor. Smiling at Kit. Laughing with him. Enjoying his company. He was the Wastrel of White Horse Street.

Yet, she had ceased to look on him that way. He was a man, as full of complexities as any person, and he could not be dismissed with a summation of a few words.

He had become appealing to her—terribly appealing—this man who gambled frequently and fought questionable duels and surrounded himself with low company. Yet, none of those statements was as simple as it sounded. Still, had she been looking for male companionship, she would never have chosen such a man.

And did it really matter anyway if she now liked him? If the day seemed sunnier because she was with him? She would be staying only a few more days at Rose Heath, and then she and her friends would leave, and she'd be unlikely ever to see Kit Stirling again. They hardly moved in the same circles, and even if she went to Town, she was unlikely to attend the sorts of events he would like.

Being with him was almost safe, she told herself, because nothing, ultimately, could come of it. So what did it matter if she liked talking to him? This time was just a holiday.

They cantered in silence for some time, and she did not at first notice that they hadn't spoken until it occurred to her that the silence was pleasant. It was, in fact, quite companionable.

* * *

"You ride well," he called out to her as they passed over a meadow. "But then, what should one expect from a duchess?"

She shot him a scolding look. "You're not meant to give me away by shouting out my title, sir!" The wind had tugged a few long strands of her brown hair loose, and they rippled on the wind and swirled around her head, giving her the enchanting look of a slightly feral forest nymph. Had he once told himself her hair was the color of dead leaves? He'd been wrong. Her hair was rich molasses, and it glinted with gold in the sunshine.

"There's no one to hear," he shouted back. "We can say anything."

She rode on a moment, then threw back her head and shouted, "I hate salmon!"

"What?"

"Darkest secrets!" she shouted. "I hate salmon. When people serve it, I say my doctor forbids me to eat it!"

He laughed, catching on. "Old people bore me!"

"You're terrible!" she called out, but she was laughing. "I told my cousin Harriett that I wasn't free for her to come for a visit, but I was!"

"Shocking woman!" he shouted into the wind. "I taught a friend's child a rude word! Mostly an accident!"

She was still laughing as they approached the little woods that led to the pond, though they were coming from a different direction than she had taken the day she'd found him, and perhaps she didn't recognize where they were.

They walked the horses along a pretty path lined with little blue flowers and the bright green shoots of early spring grass. The day was a little cool, but not so chilly as it had been, and it was easy to feel in the softening of the wind that warm days were just around the bend. They emerged from the shelter of the trees, and he saw the moment when she realized where they were.

"Oh, it's the pond." Her eyes held the gleam of suspicion. "Did you know the path led here?"

"You needn't look as though I mean to throw you in. I thought you liked it before, when you came. You went right to the edge and dipped your toes, I believe."

"So I did," she said slowly. "It took about all the courage I had to approach the water. And then you startled me."

"But you didn't fall in. Or at least, only a little."

"Very well, I admit that I came near a pond and nothing truly disastrous happened. A small victory of sorts."

"I feel I deserve most of the credit for that victory," he teased. "After all, I brought you to the plunge pool to begin with."

Her eyelids lowered in ducal haughtiness that was somewhat diminished by a quiver of her lips. "I should not wish to take credit for someone's near-drowning, if I were you."

"I would never have let you drown, Duchess." Their horses were moving very slowly now as they approached the boathouse. "I take it that what happened when you were a girl was quite serious?"

"Terrifying. But do you know what the most awful part was? That no one noticed. Several of my sisters were there, along with my parents, who were squabbling. I sank under the water with the sky bright blue above me and the muted voices and laughter of my family mingling with the panicked pounding of my heart. They had forgotten me, and I was going to die alone."

She laughed a little. "Or so I believed until one of the stable boys dove in and rescued me. He'd noticed I was missing, though I never knew why."

"Perhaps because he liked you. I imagine you were kind to him. You are unfailingly considerate, as I have had proof when you visited me, though you little wished to."

"Only because Stratton asked me to. Though perhaps the visiting was not *entirely* onerous for me. Perhaps I found you somewhat diverting."

"I can die a happy man now. I've reached the heights of being termed 'diverting' by the Duchess of Coldbrook. Life can have nothing further to offer me."

But though he kept his words light, she'd shared something of herself with him just now in the story of her near drowning, and that meant a great deal to him.

They arrived at the boathouse, and they stopped and dismounted, tying the horses near a sunny patch behind the boathouse where the animals could graze.

"Are you sure it's a good idea to walk on your ankle?" she asked.

"It feels steady and quite a bit better. A little walking won't do it any harm."

Kit took the basket he'd brought, and they walked by unspoken agreement to the front of the little house, where the pond was.

"I was my parents' only child," he said. "And then when the earl took me in, I became that most precious thing he'd been denied for so long: an heir. I often wished I had come from a large and boisterous family, because I wished not only for playmates, but for something to dilute the attention focused on me. But of course, there are disadvantages to being one of many. A child might feel lost in a crowd."

"I might have shouted that out when we were galloping earlier: My parents forgot about me. For much of my childhood, I felt like one in a huge parcel of children, and a very average child at that."

"You, average? Never. No one who's spent ten minutes in your company would believe such a thing."

They paused to choose a good spot for the blanket, and her eyes sparkled at him, pulling him further under her spell. "Are you certain?" she asked. "I seem to recall a conversation about dull, predictable spinsters and their inevitable cats a few days ago."

"I like cats," he said, and only just barely managed to stop himself from kissing her. He wanted this to be perfect. "And, what is even more admirable in me, I have brought a packet from Cook full of cakes and shortbread."

"A great deal can be forgiven judgmental fellows who remember cakes."

He grinned. "A fellow can hope."

He took the blanket out of the picnic basket and spread it out to the side of the boathouse in a patch of gentle sunlight that was shielded from the path, though he was confident no one would disturb them. His friends were well occupied with their ladies, and no one else would have any reason to be near the pond, which was at some distance from the manor.

They nibbled the cakes as they sat gazing out over the tranquil water.

"What do you like best about your home at Brookleigh?"

She was reclining, propped on her bent elbows, and though she had already seen much of the world, she looked young and innocent—but not timid. Despite her fear of water, he'd never once thought her timid. She had a confidence that was beyond anything to do with being a duchess and had everything to do, he suspected, with all the individual paths she'd chosen in her life so far. Choices to apply herself toward studies, to learn how to be a good duchess, to learn how to love the man her late husband had been.

"The gardens are my favorite spot," she said. "They're quite large, and sometimes I'll walk out along the paths and not come back for hours. It's sheer bliss."

"And a way to avoid being a duchess for a time?"

"Yes." She sighed. "Being a duchess is a great privilege, but I am by nature a private person, and I don't have a great deal of wants. I shall be relieved when Harold's nephew, the current duke, finds a wife."

"And what will you do then?"

She closed her eyes and tipped her face toward the sky. "Travel the world with a friend or two. Go live in a cottage by the sea all covered in climbing roses." She smiled without opening her eyes. "Acquire some cats."

His heart was beating so loudly that he felt she must hear it. "Your Grace," he said quietly, drinking in the sight of her face. "Olivia."

She opened her eyes, her expression puzzled.

"You are very beautiful."

She made a face. "You know that I'm not. Why say such a thing?"

"You are beautiful," he said firmly. "Beautiful and good. Beautiful because you are good."

A few seconds passed, and he dared to hope that she'd accepted the sincerity behind his words. But then she rolled her eyes and let her head drop back and closed her eyes again. "You sound like a fool. Are you thinking to take up poetry writing? I recommend against it in your case."

Her hand was spread palm down on the blanket, and he touched the soft back of her hand with one fingertip. Her eyes opened again, and she frowned, those dark brows drawing together into a sharp line. "What's got into you?"

"You have." He leaned closer, slowly, in case she would move away. She lifted her head, as if waiting to see what he would do.

He kissed her neck at the juncture with her collarbone. Her skin was unendurably sweet. He breathed deeply of her scent-that-was-barely-a-scent, warm, sweet, and earthy.

She let him kiss up her neck and didn't protest or move away when he pressed his lips in a path along her jawline. His guide was the sound of her breath quickening. When he kissed her mouth, she opened to him.

CHAPTER TEN

Olivia had been aware that Kit might try to kiss her at some point during their outing. She could imagine—well, she *had* imagined—that maybe they would dismount to take in a view, or stroll briefly if his ankle allowed, and that he would try to kiss her. And she had known that she would let him. Something had shifted for her, and she didn't want to deny herself the pleasure of his company anymore.

She had promised herself that if he did kiss her, she would simply keep her wits about her.

But now his lips were on hers, and they felt wonderful, and she had not the smallest wish to be sensible.

She was going to allow herself to enjoy whatever Kit was offering. Another encounter would make no difference to either of them in the long run, she told herself, even as a niggling feeling insisted this was not really true, that it hadn't been true for some time. She didn't care.

His hands explored her gently but with purpose, bringing warmth and shivers of excitement as they moved over her arms and the swell of her bosom.

She lifted a hand to his shoulder and discovered the hardness of muscles that flexed as he leaned over her.

"I can't stop thinking about you," he murmured.

"You can't?" she whispered, almost breathless.

"You don't have to sound so pleased," he growled, making her smile. He began undoing the buttons on the front of her habit.

Cool spring air floated against her skin as her garment loosened, but she hardly noticed. His arms warmed her as they slid around her, and every touch of his hands made desire heat her more. He kissed along her neck and groaned as his mouth explored the exposed tops of her breasts. When his hand moved to cup her breast, she turned liquid inside.

"Olivia," he said, and she loved the sound of her name on his lips. "I want to touch all of you. I don't think I could ever get enough."

His words spoke to a longing deep inside her. She abandoned conscious thought as desire rushed through her.

"Kit."

He urged her back onto the blanket and lay down beside her and kissed her. Gathering the heavy, voluminous skirts of her riding habit, he drew it to her knees. She whimpered as his fingers traced the tender skin on the inside of her knee.

"You want this as much as I do, don't you?" he asked. Once, she would have thought this an arrogant claim from a man who knew exactly how to get what he wanted from a woman. But his words were a question, and she believed in the incertitude behind them. That Kit Stirling might be so vulnerable she found astonishing.

"Yes."

He took his time, dallying near her knee, tracing shiver-making swirls here and there on a slow journey upward, to where she ached for him to touch her. Instead of satisfying her need, he moved between her legs and pressed himself against her through the many fabric layers, a tease and a promise. She gasped and shifted her hips against him, needing all of him.

"Open your eyes, Olivia."

She had not realized they were closed, so consumed was she with what he was doing to her, but now she obeyed. He was looking at her, his eyes dark, his face flushed. "I want you," he said. She wanted him too, was burning for him more each moment.

He fixed his eyes on hers. "God knows I don't deserve you, but I want all of you."

He was so different today. She felt different as well. And he seemed to guess this and to want her to acknowledge it.

* * *

The flush in Olivia's cheeks deepened, and Kit dared to hope that she understood how special she had become to him. How was it possible that in such a short amount of time, he could come to know this woman and care so much for her?

Sweet, sweet Olivia, with her bone-deep decency and her sensible ways and her hidden depths. Ah, those depths, how they called to him. He wanted to know everything about her—and he wanted the pleasure of discovering everything about her to be his and his alone.

"I want this too," she said.

He unfastened his breeches and worked to push aside the bulky skirts of her habit. "Never wear a riding habit again," he growled as he tussled with them.

"You should have invited me for a drive instead," she teased, but then, with a triumphant grunt, he gained access. He wanted promises from her, and he wanted to give her promises, but he must wait for what she would freely offer. She was offering him her body now, and her desire, and he believed that it might be the beginning of so much more.

He kissed her, willing his love to flow through him to her.

He touched her, found her ready for him, and entered her.

The moment was pure pleasure, and joy, like a benediction washing away the stain of his recent life.

He moved slowly in her, needing her to understand what he felt, even as he knew that she might never be his.

But he had hope. He held her eyes with his as their pleasure climbed and they found their release, their hearts beating as one.

* * *

Olivia opened her eyes to the blue of the sky and the awareness that the air was really quite cool. She hadn't noticed when Kit had been making her so warm.

She sat up and reached behind herself to set her riding habit to rights. Next to her, she could sense Kit arranging himself too.

"I hadn't expected that to happen." What she had just shared with Kit had been wonderful, an indulgence of all the sleeping yearnings he had awakened. But now that the beating of her heart had slowed, rational thought was returning. When she was with Kit, she did things that were entirely out of character for her. What more sign did she need that she must stop?

His laugh was a deep rumble. "I hadn't *expected* anything either. Though I won't say I didn't hope."

She frowned. "This isn't like me, doing things like this."

He moved to face her. "And I am like this, is that what you mean? I'm the sort of fellow who seduces women who thought they were only going out for a ride?"

He sounded serious, and she didn't know what to do with a serious Kit. Her shoulders sagged. She didn't know what to think anymore, either, and that wasn't a good feeling. He wasn't utterly frivolous. She liked him a great deal. But a man could be completely likable and even entirely kind, and also be unreliable, unpredictable, and selfish.

"I am not saying there's anything wrong with two people doing such things if they both wish to do so and no one is harmed by their actions," she said. "Only that I am not accustomed to doing such things. And that I must not do them again."

"Why? Just because you haven't done them before? You had never willingly approached a pond before, and now here you are, sitting relaxed right beside one."

"It's not the same!"

Silence fell between them, and she thought about getting up and leaving, but she couldn't make herself go. She stared at the pond, trying to understand how she'd left for a holiday with two friends and ended up in this muddled whatever-it-was that she had become embroiled in with Kit Stirling.

"I love you, Olivia."

His voice was calm and steady, his words hardly an incitement to riot, but they were the last thing she'd expected him to say, and they made her angry. She didn't like to be angry, and she didn't like that, somehow in recent days, she'd wandered into this foreign realm of unwanted emotion and entanglement. She didn't look at him. "No."

He put a finger on her chin and tipped her head toward his. "No?" A dangerous note had come into his voice. "What do you mean 'no'?"

"I mean you don't love me," she said, and the firmness she forced into her voice was just as much for herself as it was for him. They'd both forgotten who they were. "You can't possibly."

"What makes you think you can tell me how I feel?"

Nothing. She had no business saying such a thing to another person, even a man who'd lived a life of dissipation. Her words had been arrogant and hardly kind. But she didn't know how else to be, because she couldn't let this thing that had sprung up between them grow any further.

"Very well," she said, "it's your business what you wish to say. But what's happened between us can't go any further. I never meant—I don't want—I—oh!" she growled in frustration. Apparently, in addition to becoming a loose woman, she had turned into a ninny unable to express herself.

"You liked what we did," Kit said. His tone was reasonable, but his jaw was hard. "And you like me, against your better judgment."

"What if I do? That's not enough to build anything of substance on."

"Olivia, I've done many things I'm not proud of in my life, but I am more than the sum of those actions."

He was right, but he was also making it harder for her to hold fast to what she knew she needed to do. "I know that you are. You are capable of being very good."

"So why can't you want this? Why can't you want me?"

She threw up her hands, frustrated beyond words. How could he not know that everything she'd ever learned told her he was the worst risk she could ever take? "Because you scare me! How I can trust a man like you?"

"What if I've changed?" She didn't miss the frustration that laced his voice as well, and she wished he'd just acknowledge that it was impossible for there to be anything solid and reliable between them, instead of pushing for something that could never work.

"People always say they've changed. My father said it countless times to my mother whenever she discovered yet another mistress."

"Ah," he said slowly. "I see now. I see why you are afraid."

She experienced an astonishing urge to scream. "I didn't say I was afraid," she said through clenched teeth. "I meant that you scare me because I can't trust you."

"I understand why you feel that way." She should have been grateful for his reasonable tone, especially when she now felt overtaken by a jumble of conflicting emotions, but she didn't.

"I wish I could tell you that I haven't made many mistakes," he continued, "but you know that I have. A good portion of what I've done in recent years was done to thumb my nose at my uncle and all he stands for. And that's not in the least admirable."

"No, it isn't." He was giving her good reasons to refuse him, and she could only be grateful. So why did she feel like weeping?

"Olivia, I know that I look like the same man you met days ago, but I *feel* totally different."

In truth, he looked different too. No hint of mockery teased the edges of his mouth, and his eyes were clear, his gaze direct. She forced herself to meet it. "Feelings are temporary things."

He shook his head. "How I feel isn't temporary. Life looks different to me now. I love you as I've never loved anyone, and I want to marry you and be with only you all the days of my life."

He wanted to *marry* her? His words made her gasp, but "Oh!" was all she had a chance to splutter before he put a finger to her lips.

"I know." He had the nerve to smile a little. "You weren't expecting that. And you still have no reason to trust me. But don't say anything just yet."

He stood and held a hand out to help her up. "It must be very nearly tea time."

Now he was talking of tea? Feeling as if she was nearly ready for Bedlam, Olivia followed him to where the horses stood. He'd just said he wanted to marry her, then told her not to say anything! Which she should be glad about, because she didn't want to marry him.

Of course she didn't! How could she possibly?

Except, the idea of marrying Kit— there was something terribly, terribly tempting about it.

What was wrong with her that she was even *considering* what he'd said?

In a daze, she allowed him to help her onto her horse. The only sign he gave of what he'd spoken of was when he briefly kissed her hand just before relinquishing it.

He mounted his own horse, and they made their way along the path in silence. When they reached the manor, a stable boy came out to meet them. Though Olivia half expected Kit to help her dismount and try to speak with her further, he allowed the stable boy to assist her and merely gave her a wave of his hand as he lingered to speak with the fellow.

She marched up to her bedchamber and rang for a piping hot bath.

* * *

When Olivia went down for dinner that night, determined to tell Kit in no uncertain terms that what was between them was now at an end, Colonel Stratton informed his guests that Kit had had to leave suddenly but was expected back within a few days.

"He left this for you," Stratton said, pressing a note in her hand.

There's something I need to do, but please don't leave Rose Heath yet. Just give me a little time.

Kit

She folded the noted into a very tiny square and pushed it into her pocket. How could he have just left? And before she had had a chance to speak to him? And why did she care?

It was better that he was gone!

Their coach was still being repaired, but maybe they could borrow Stratton's coach. She could try to persuade her friends to leave the following day, and then she wouldn't be here when, or if, Kit returned, and she need not see him again.

Looking at her friends as they talked with Colonel Stratton and Sir Greyville, though, she could see that neither Francesca nor Mary Alice was ready to cut short the two weeks they had agreed to stay at Rose Heath. Of course, Olivia might ask for Stratton's carriage for herself, or hire one in town, and return to Brookleigh.

But she wouldn't, she decided. She would finish out her holiday and enjoy the company of her friends and the two other gentlemen. Spring was breaking out, and she was staying at a beautiful estate where no one cared whether she was a duchess, and no one needed a single thing from her. Rose Heath offered her the kind of utterly relaxing holiday she'd dreamed about when she'd been up to her ears in the business of being the Duchess of Coldbrook, and she'd be a fool not to enjoy it.

And she would not spend a single moment more thinking about Kit Stirling.

CHAPTER ELEVEN

Was there a slower, more sedate coach driver in all England than this fellow of the earl's, Kit wondered for the hundredth time that hour. Surely the man drove as though the carriage was filled with eggs instead of four healthy adults. Had he been alone, Kit would have dispensed with a coach and been back at Rose Heath already. But he was not alone—he was accompanied by his uncle, the Earl of Roswell, and his aunt, and his cousin Kate. And for that he was deeply glad, no matter that their progress was at a snail's pace.

"Do you still love to read?" Aunt Caroline asked him. Ever since they'd left London, his aunt had been speaking of the things he'd liked and said and done when he was younger. These were the topics that might preoccupy a mother, and the awareness gave him a renewed pang. Aunt Caroline had been like a mother to him when he was a motherless boy. She had loved him as well as she had been able, and he had cut her out of his life because of his feud with his uncle.

"I do, Aunt," he said, and smiled at her.

"We kept all your books," his uncle said gruffly. But then, he said everything gruffly. He was a blunt man, a decisive man, as befitted an earl. A man not used to reconsidering his decisions.

Kit's aunt and uncle had been standing by the hearth when Kit entered their London drawing room three days before. Their expressions had, at first sight of him, given nothing away, but Kit had been prepared for a difficult reception. He need not have been. Hardly had he advanced a dozen steps when his aunt rushed over with tears in her eyes and embraced him. His uncle's eyes had looked suspiciously misty as well.

Kit had hastened to offer the apology he should not have withheld for so long. "I blamed you for my parents' fate because that was easier than accepting that the people I loved could simply be taken from me by chance. I'm sorry."

"And I was a damned judgmental prig who should have put aside my rules and helped my brother," the earl had told Kit in a voice grown more raspy in the years they'd been apart. "I judged your parents and smugly told myself that I could raise you better than they would have done. I was wrong not to help them, and it took years of you being gone to make me see that."

Cousin Kate had come in then, and there had been a great deal of embracing and expressing of hopes that they might all put the past behind them and look to the future. And that was when Kit had explained what, or rather who, had inspired him to come to them, and how he needed their help. They had agreed right away. Kate, whose fiancé had left Town for a family christening, had declared herself glad to abandon London for a brief respite.

When, after another hour of their snail's pace, the familiar shape of Rose Heath manor finally came into view, Kit uttered a silent hope that Olivia would still be there. And that he could matter to her.

* * *

Kit was not coming back. It had all been some sort of joke to him, some lark. Perhaps he had simply been too weak to tell Olivia he did not wish to see her anymore and so had concocted the proposal to scare her away.

Which thoughts made absolutely no sense, Olivia told herself as she tossed a stick across the garden for one of Stratton's dogs, a black and brown fellow called Bounder. His was the only company she could tolerate at the moment, as she had awoken quite cross that morning, and she had not wanted to admit that the crossness might have something to do with a dream she'd had about Kit. He was gone, and she would be leaving Rose Heath the following day, and she was going to forget all about him. She just hadn't figured out how to make herself do that yet. But she would. She was a determined person.

Forgetting him was going to be hard. He had come to fill her thoughts.

She had always been ruthless in admitting what was true, and she did so now as she tossed the stick out across the garden with unladylike force. He had become special to her. She cared about him a great deal.

She loved him.

Oh, she was a fool.

She had just accepted the stick anew from Bounder, who showed no signs of wishing to abandon this diverting game, when she heard voices. Kit was walking toward her, in the company of three other people. The Earl and Countess of Roswell and their daughter, she realized. Something in the region of her heart gave a squeeze.

"Your Grace," Kit greeted her, there being no sense, obviously, in maintaining her charade in front of other members of the *ton*. "I believe you are a little acquainted with my uncle, the Earl of Roswell, and my aunt, the countess, and my cousin Lady Katherine?"

The earl was a man of perhaps sixty, with a craggy, hard face, and his smile

152 | EMILY GREENWOOD

had a rusty, unused quality, but it was a smile nonetheless. The countess was a small woman with cornflower blue eyes, and Kit's cousin looked like a taller, younger version of her mother.

Olivia greeted them warmly, trying to hide her puzzlement as to why they had come.

"Kit insists that you are the most fabulous duchess in all England, Your Grace," Lady Katherine said. "Which sounds as though there is some sort of duchess competition afoot of which I've not heard." Her eyes crinkled merrily. "But Kit was always my favorite cousin, so if he says you're the most fabulous duchess in England, I'm ready to agree."

Kit was avoiding Olivia's eyes.

"I can't think what your cousin is up to," Olivia told her.

Kit's only remark was to propose a stroll so that the travelers could stretch their legs.

They set off on the path that led through the garden and meandered behind the manor amid a rose garden not yet in bloom. Olivia found herself paired with the earl and suspected he had maneuvered it to be so.

"I think you must know that Kit has been estranged from my family for some years."

"Yes, he has spoken to me about that."

"We quarreled about the way I behaved towards my brother and his wife. Kit was justified in questioning me, but I had not been accustomed to being questioned."

"Perhaps the manner of his questioning was not respectful."

"Perhaps it was not, but he was young and impassioned by a matter to do with his parents, and I should have allowed for disrespectful behavior. Instead, I was harsh and dismissive, and he chose to leave the family home."

His lordship seemed to want to put Kit in a good light for her, and she was having a great deal of trouble not simply accepting his words. She forced herself not to give in.

"But Kit might have returned at any time," she said, "might he not have, and apologized? Instead, he seems to have been determined to make as bad a name for himself as possible."

Bounder, who had been running in circles, cavorted into the earl's path, causing the older gentleman to stop. The earl's craggy features were tinged with sadness as he leaned down to ruffle the dog's fur. "Have you never remarked, Your Grace, that there is no one so determined on dissipation as a disappointed idealist? When Kit lived in our home, he behaved as only the best and most loyal of sons would have done. Above all, he was a sensitive young man, and I believe those qualities were the heart of the troubles between us. He could not betray the parents he loved by accepting an uncle who'd been cruel to them. I can't fault him for that."

She thought of that duel Kit had fought to protect a woman who'd been harmed by her husband, and of his tenderness with her, and of all the other things that told her he was a good man, and something in her chest cracked open.

Ahead of them, Kit and his aunt and cousin paused to look at a statue of a dog. Perhaps he felt her eyes on him, because his gaze met hers, and her heart rose up in reply.

Her heart knew him, knew that he was a good man. Only her mind, with its caution and deliberation and plans, resisted him now. Would she let timidity rule her, just as she'd accepted the reins of fear that had kept her away from ponds and lakes her whole life?

And then Kit was by her side. "Can I persuade you to stroll into the maze with me, Your Grace?"

He offered her his arm, and she rested her hand on it. The interior of the maze was softly shadowed and hushed, and they walked for a few minutes without speaking.

"I was very glad that my uncle and aunt and cousin consented to come here to be presented to you."

She gave him a skeptical look. "Wasn't it your design to bring them here to show me that you are reconciled with your family?"

"Can I not have had a dual purpose, Olivia?"

He stopped and took her hands. "I have been a fool for far too long. But I would be a fool forever if I did not awaken to what is good and what is possible. I did hope that reconciling with my uncle would show you that I have put the past behind me, but I also truly wished to reconcile with him. I think I had wished to do that for a very long time, but I had become accustomed to things as they were, and I did not see how to change them. Until I met you."

His words touched Olivia deeply. She had thought that she was done with love, that she had tasted its lovely fruits and been sated. But she had been putting limits on love, just as Kit had, in his own way.

Love never ends.

She had forgotten that, and it was Kit, the most surprising of men, who had reminded her and shown her that there was so much still to discover about love.

Yet, still she clung to the need for absolute truth. "And I am such a paragon that you were inspired to do the right thing?"

He smiled. "No, you are not a paragon, my dearest Olivia, though you are very good. What you are is lovable. Loving you has made me want more love, in every part of my life."

His eyes, his words, the touch of his hands on hers—everything told her that she could trust this man.

"I love you," he said.

"Oh, Kit," she breathed. "I love you too."

Their eyes locked, speaking of love as no words ever could. "Will you marry me, my darling? Will you make me the happiest of men?"

She was smiling as widely as a fool, and she did not care. "How could I say no to you?" She stroked the side of his face. "Though I could not see it at first, you are in fact the finest, dearest man I know, and you have shown me so much that I did not even realize I was missing."

He gave a whoop and pulled her into his arms. Everything fell away, the maze and the sky and the faint murmur of voices beyond the tall hedges, and it was only the two of them. They held each other and kissed and savored the wonder of what life held for them.

"You do realize that I shall teach you to swim, my love?" he said some minutes later. "For our honeymoon, I think we must get a house by a lake and swim there every day."

"You just want to get your hands on my body."

"I do." He kissed the tip of her nose. "And I always shall."

They lingered together in the maze for a little longer before making their way out to share their good news.

"And to think that if you hadn't come here as a duchess in disguise, we might never have found our way to each other," he said as they walked out of the maze. The earl and his family were standing by the rose bushes and looking at them with discreetly hopeful smiles.

"An awful thought," Olivia said.

"And not to be contemplated," Kit said. "Did I mention that I love you?"

"Perhaps once or twice, but say it again, as I shall never tire of hearing it"— she leaned her head against his arm—"or of loving you."

–THE END–

Dear Readers,

I hope you enjoyed our duchesses' adventures during their unexpected visit to Rose Heath. It has been an absolute joy working with Grace Burrowes and Susanna Ives, who are not only fabulous writers, but tremendously kind and generous people.

Duchesses in Disguise is not my first foray into the topic of Regency courtships between unlikely parties ruralizing for unlikely reasons. One of my favorite stories is **The Beautiful One**, which features Miss Anna Black, who flees to the countryside to avoid scandal. Her path crosses that of Will Halifax, Viscount Grandville, who flees anything resembling messy displays of emotion. I've included an excerpt below. You can find more information at: emilygreenwood.net/books/the-beautiful-one/

You can keep up with all my releases and author events, and also sign up for my newsletter, on my website at http://emilygreenwood.net/. I only send out newsletters two or three times a year, and I will never share your email. Happy reading!

Emily Greenwood

THE BEAUTIFUL ONE

Anna Black gave a silent cheer as the carriage she was riding in lurched and came to an abrupt stop at an angle that suggested they'd hit a deep ditch.

Perhaps, she thought hopefully from the edge of her seat, where she'd been tossed, they'd be stuck on the road for hours, which would delay their arrival at the estate of Viscount Grandville. She had reason to be worried about what might happen at Lord Grandville's estate, and she dreaded reaching it.

It was also possible she was being pursued.

Or not.

Perhaps nothing would happen at all. But the whole situation was nerve-wracking enough that she had more than once considered simply running off to live in the woods and survive on berries. However, several considerations discouraged her from this course:

1. She had exactly three shillings to her name. Though admittedly money would be of no use in the woods, she would at some point need more than berries.

2. She had agreed to escort her traveling companion, Miss Elizabeth Tarryton, to the home of Viscount Grandville, who was the girl's guardian.

3. If Anna abandoned her duty, along with being a wicked person, she wouldn't be able to return to the Rosewood School for Young Ladies of Quality, her employer.

Anna was nothing if not practical, and she was highly skeptical of the success of the life-in-the-woods plan, but the dramatic occurrences in her life of late were starting to lend it appeal.

"Hell!" said the lovely Miss Elizabeth Tarryton from her sprawled position on the opposite coach seat. Her apricot silk bonnet had fallen across her face during the coach-lurching, and she pushed it aside. "What's happened?"

"We're in a ditch, evidently," Anna replied. Their situation was obvious, but

Miss Tarryton had not so far proven herself to be particularly sensible for her sixteen years. She was also apparently not averse to cursing.

Surrendering to the inevitable, Anna said, "I'll go see how things look."

She had to push upward to open the door to the tilted coach, and before stepping down, she paused to tug her faded blue bonnet over her black curls, a reflex of concealment that had become second nature in the last month. The rain that had followed them since they left the school that morning had stopped, but the dark sky promised more.

The coachman was already seeing to the horses. "Had to go off the road to avoid a vast puddle, and now we're in a ditch," he called. "'Tis fortunate that we're but half a mile from his lordship's estate."

So they would soon be at Stillwell, Viscount Grandville's estate. *Damn*, Anna thought, taking a page from Miss Tarryton's book. Would he be a threat to her?

After a month in a state of nearly constant anxiety, of waiting to be exposed, she sometimes felt mutinously that she didn't care anymore. She'd done nothing of which she ought to be ashamed—yet it would never appear that way. And so she felt like a victim, and hated feeling that way, and hated the accursed book that had given two wicked men such power over her.

She gathered up the limp skirts of her faded old blue frock and jumped off the last step, intending to see how badly they were stuck. The coachman was seeing to the horses, and as she moved to inspect the back of the carriage, she became aware of hoofbeats and turned to see a rider cantering toward them. A farmer, she thought, taking in his dusty, floppy hat and dull coat and breeches.

He drew even.

"You are trespassing," he said from atop his horse, his tone as blunt as his words. The sagging brim of his hat hid the upper part of his face, but from the hard set of his jaw, she could guess it did not bear a warm expression. His shadowed gaze passed over her, not lingering for more time than it might have taken to observe a pile of dirty breakfast dishes.

"We had no intention of doing so, I assure you," she began, wondering that the stranger hadn't even offered a greeting. "The road was impassible and our coachman tried to go around, but now we are stuck. Perhaps, though, if you might—"

"You cannot tarry here," he said, ignoring her attempt to ask for help. "A storm is coming. Your coach will be stranded if you don't make haste."

His speech was clipped, but it sounded surprisingly refined. *Ha.* That was surely the only refined thing about him. Aside from his lack of manners and the shabbiness of his clothes, there was an L-shaped rip in his breeches that gave a window onto pale skin and thigh muscles pressed taut, and underneath his coat, his shirt hung loose at the neck. She supposed it was his broad shoulders that made him seem especially imposing atop his dark horse.

A stormy surge of wind blew his hat brim off his face, and she realized that severe though his expression might be, he was very handsome. The lines of his cheekbones and hard jaw ran in perfect complement to each other. His well-formed brows arched in graceful if harsh angles over dark eyes surrounded by crowded black lashes.

But those eyes. They were as devoid of life as one of her father's near-death patients.

Several fat raindrops pelted her bonnet. "We shall be away momentarily," she said briskly, turning away from him to consider the plight of the coach and assuming he would leave now that he'd delivered his warning.

The rain began to fall faster, soaking through the thin fabric of her worn-out frock. She called out to the coachman, who was doing something with the harness straps. "Better take off the young lady's trunk before you try to advance."

"No. That's a waste of time," said the stranger from atop his horse behind her.

She turned around, deeply annoyed. "Your opinion is not wanted."

The ill-mannered man watched her, a muscle ticking in his stubbled jaw. A cold rivulet trickled through her bonnet to her scalp and continued down her neck, and his empty gaze seemed to follow the little stream's journey to the collar of her dampening frock. His eyes flicked lower, and she thought they lingered at her breasts.

She crossed her arms in front of her and tipped her chin higher. Not for nothing had she sparred with her older brother all those years in a home that had been more than anything else a man's domain. Her father had been a doctor and had valued reason and scientific process and frowned on softness, and she'd been raised to speak her mind. Life as a servant at Rosewood School was already testing her ability to hold her tongue, but this man deserved no such consideration.

"Is not your presence required elsewhere?"

"Where are you going?" he demanded, ignoring her.

"I couldn't be more delighted that such things do not concern you."

The stranger's lips thinned. "Who comes to this neighborhood concerns me."

"If you would move along," she said exasperatedly, blinking droplets from her lashes, "we might focus on freeing the coach."

His gaze flicked away from her. "Drive on," he called to the coachman.

John, apparently responding to the note of command in the stranger's voice, disregarded Anna's sound of outrage and addressed himself to the horses. With a creaking of harness straps, they struggled forward. The wheels squelched as they found purchase amid the mud, and the carriage miraculously righted itself.

She sucked her teeth in irritation.

"See that you do not linger here," the man said.

"We are on our way to Stillwell Hall," she replied, thinking to make him regret his poor conduct. He might even work for the viscount.

He looked down at her, his face shadowed so that his rain-beaded whiskers and hard mouth were all she could see. "That's not possible. No one is welcomed there."

From inside the carriage, Miss Tarryton called, "Can we not proceed, Miss Whatever?"

Anna ignored her. "It certainly is possible."

"The viscount might not be in residence."

His words would have given her pause, except that when Miss Brickle had sent Anna off with her charge and a note for the viscount, she'd said that he was certain to be at Stillwell, because according to gossip among the mothers of Rosewood's students, he'd been in residence there constantly over the last year. Though why this man should be so set on discouraging them from seeing the viscount, she couldn't imagine.

"I have it on good authority that he is. Evidently, sir," she said, "you have been raised by wild animals and so one must overlook your lack of interest in people, but I assure you Lord Grandville will wish to welcome us."

Something flickered in his eyes for the barest moment at her tart words, but his hard expression didn't change. "No," he rasped. "He won't. Do not go there."

He turned his horse away and spurred it into a gallop across the field next to the road.

Order your copy of **The Beautiful One**!

THE LOVE OF HIS LIFE

SUSANNA IVES

CHAPTER ONE

Hyde Park—one month before the notorious carriage mishap

"How delicious," Colonel Nathaniel Stratton's sister, Deirdre, Countess of Fentleigh remarked. "I understand Sir Harry has had yet another of his embarrassing marriage proposals rejected."

Her throaty laughter brimmed with malice. The sound rankled her brother's frayed nerves. He scanned the manicured grounds of Hyde Park while taking several deep breaths to keep an impolite set-down from escaping his lips.

Deirdre prattled on, "I think it should be noted in *Creighton's London Guide* that young ladies possessing some degree of wealth should expect a proposal from Sir Harry when traveling to the metropolis."

Her gaggle of townish friends howled with laughter as they strolled lazily along the crowded footpath. Deirdre's lips trembled as she tried not to chuckle at her own witticism. She was famous for her waspish, but amusing, tongue. Her utterances delighted the exclusive circle of Society that buzzed about her, drinking in her droll vitriol.

She had begged Stratton to join their old friends for the fashionable hour at the park, claiming he wasn't himself anymore. She had been saying as much since he'd returned from the war. She refused to believe that her once dashing, roguish brother had turned into a reticent man who preferred attending a dry lecture on the freezing points of various liquids to going to a gaming hell, and would rather finance an inventor than a scandalous mistress. He spurned London Society's adoration, choosing to spend his time in the country with his daughter and dull scientist guests.

"You're becoming a regular bumpkin," Deirdre had complained not two hours after he arrived in London. "Do indulge in one delicious scandal with a married woman while you are here, for old time's sake—and my amusement."

Amusement.

Stratton had once ambled about London thinking its inhabitants existed for his amusement—beautiful women to pleasure his body and everyone else to envy him and desire to bask in his bright, youthful light. Witnessing five thousand dead men on a field in Spain had destroyed that haughty arrogance, as well as most of his faith.

Not getting the rise from her brother that she desired, Deirdre returned to mocking Sir Harry. "The *on-dit* is that Sir Harry actually wept when the homely miss rejected his proposal. I'm sure his display of sentiment had less to do with a broken heart and more to do with the knowledge that he has run out of young ladies to propose to. Now he must wait another Season for a new crop of unsuspecting ladies to arrive from the country."

Her clever cruelty elicited more laughter.

Weeping Sir Harry must be this Season's object of ridicule. Every Season, Deirdre had different prey. This was not a conscious selection on her part, but rather someone who made himself or herself a ready object of ridicule—a foppish effeminate gentleman, a country-mannered boorish baron, a garish matron, or a chubby chit with too many freckles. Stratton had happily played along in the vicious game until the Season his heart got tangled up in it.

"We really must tell Sir Harry that no one wants his awkward, loose-lipped courting," his sister continued, puffed up on the attention she garnered. "It's the kindest thing to do, is it not, Nathaniel?" She was throwing Stratton a line, like an actor in a play. She waited for his response, her eyes glittering, hoping the sardonic Stratton of old would make an appearance.

"The kindest thing you could do is give the poor man respect," Stratton answered flatly, refusing the bait.

Deirdre laughed. "Listen to you! You might as well be a Methodist. Your newfound respectability ill fits your roguish frame. It pulls at the seams and hangs poorly across your broad shoulders. I know your cynical heart still beats beneath the surface. A tiger can't change his stripes."

Stratton couldn't hold back the tide of his anger. "I don't—"

A child's terrified shriek pierced the air, arresting Stratton mid-sentence. The frightening sound cut straight to his heart. He knew it wasn't his daughter's wail—she remained in the country—but he instinctively broke into a sprint in the direction of the child's cries. He had recently learned that he was a parent and had taken his illegitimate daughter into his home. He hadn't expected the dramatic change a small girl would make to every aspect of his life. Now every hurt child's cry alarmed him like the cracking sound of a firing rifle had in the war.

He rounded the trees and shrubs bordering the water. A girl in a white frock, her hair a brilliant red, darted toward the water, her arms waving wildly in the air. Her ribbons streamed loose from her braids. Mary Alice, Dowager Duchess of Pymworth and her liveried footman raced after the errant child. The duchess was a curvaceous woman, possessing a heavy bosom and voluptuous hips, but she moved with athletic agility.

"Anna, no!" Her Grace cried as the girl splashed into the river.

The child began to flail, even though the shallow water rose just above her chest. Her screams grew sharper and more frantic. Her Grace, clad in a lavender gown of half mourning, didn't hesitate to wade into the dirty water.

She reached out to the girl, but stopped just short of touching her. "Anna, shhh. It's Mama."

The screaming child only pushed into deeper waters, her mind in such a wild state as not to perceive danger.

Stratton and several nearby gentlemen had sprinted to the river's edge and were ready to dive in.

"Your Grace," one called.

Keeping her eye on her daughter, the duchess held her palm to the men. "Please stop," she said in a controlled, calm voice. "She'll only come to me."

Stratton, frustrated like the other would-be saviors, could do nothing but clench and unclench his hands.

Her Grace edged closer to the girl. "Anna, hush. It's just Mama. See? Mama."

Anna paused in her tantrum. She gazed at her mother, her shiny, unfocused eyes seeming not to recognize her. In that small second, the duchess zoomed across the water and seized the girl.

Anna shrieked and beat the air with her small fists, knocking away her mother's bonnet. The duchess's long auburn curls fell loose and gleamed a rich amber color in the sunlight. Her Grace hugged her hysterical daughter close to her chest, issuing soothing sounds. Her expression remained composed, not registering the blows and kicks she suffered as she hauled the dripping child from the water.

More gentlemen now lined the bank, eager to be heroes. Stratton remembered when the would-be duchess hadn't a friend in Society, when her desperate overtures had been met with taunts and ridicule. Now, most of Society—especially ambitious bachelors—waited at her beck and call. Stratton stepped back, concealing himself behind the others so that the duchess wouldn't see him. Now that he was no longer needed to save a child from drowning, his presence would only make the traumatic situation worse for Her Grace.

With an attentive footman in her wake, the duchess carried the wailing child to the willow tree where her two other children waited, each holding a nurse's hand. They stared at their out-of-control sibling with solemn, worried eyes. The eldest was a girl of about eight or nine years—Stratton's daughter's age. The boy appeared to be a year or so younger. Their slim build, sharp features, and black hair resembled that of their late father's, the Duke of Pymworth.

The duchess sat by the tree trunk, clutching her hysterical daughter, who squirmed and screamed as if her skin were on fire. Though Her Grace kept her face calm and composed, tears slipped down her cheeks. Stratton sensed there was something very different about this child. She acted like an inhabitant at Bedlam.

More people began to crowd the bank, feigning concern to hide their voyeuristic curiosity. The duchess scooted herself and her child closer to the tree, trying to hide under the protection of its drooping branches.

Deirdre and her friends caught up with Stratton.

"What is Her Grace doing?" his sister demanded, her voice oozing with disgust. "Why is her nurse just standing about uselessly? I would relieve my nurse on the spot, with no letter of recommendation, if my child embarrassed me in public. Oh Lord, Her Grace is sitting in the dirt and grass in her gown."

"Maybe she cares more about her child than her bloody clothes," Stratton barked. He had had enough with being polite. He couldn't take another minute with his vicious sister and his old set.

Anna finally quieted. She curled into a stiff ball in her mother's tight embrace. The duchess awkwardly tried to rise to her feet, still holding her rigid child. Stratton stepped forward, instinctively wanting to assist. However, her footman was closer and rushed to take her elbow. Her Grace's face possessed that hollowed, haunted quality Stratton had seen on his soldiers' faces in Spain and Portugal.

She motioned to the nurse that they were leaving. The young duke ran to his mother's side.

"Stop staring," he spat at the crowd as his mother and siblings progressed toward the park gates.

The young lad's fierce protection of his mother reminded Stratton of Her Grace's late husband. The duke had despised Stratton for how he, his sister, and their circle of vicious friends had maliciously treated his bride. Though Stratton didn't possess a title, he and his sister were not to be trifled with in Society. Their father heralded from an ancient line of powerful, wealthy brewers, and their mother was an earl's daughter. However, this had meant little to the serious-minded duke, who didn't suffer fools. Not fearing Society's disapproval, the duke had cut Stratton cold and wouldn't allow him within a few feet of his beloved wife.

The new young duke would have made his father proud.

As Her Grace passed, Stratton sank deeper into the crowd to avoid detection. The duchess kept her head high and gazed straight ahead.

Up close, Stratton realized the child she clutched must have been five or six—too old for such a tantrum. He could see that the duchess visibly strained under the child's weight but kept her gripped tightly, refusing to relinquish Anna to the footman and nurse following closely in her wake.

"I wouldn't allow my child in public if she was so rude and unruly," Deirdre said in an overly loud voice.

Dammit!

"You are only encouraging her atrocious behavior," Deirdre told the duchess in a smugly knowing manner—such rich advice from a woman who spent as little time as possible with her darlings.

"Quiet!" Stratton hissed.

"I'm just being honest," Deirdre protested, as if her so-called honesty justified her cruelty.

The duchess stopped. She slowly turned and raised one finely shaped brow. Her large, amber-colored eyes zeroed in on Stratton and his sister. He cursed under his breath as she approached with a menacing swing to her hips. When he had first met her, she was a round, freckled ball of a girl, fresh out of the schoolroom for her first Season. Over time, her body had taken on more womanly dimensions—heavy breasts, flared hips, and a tapered waist. Her child whimpered in her protective arms. Water dripped from the hem of the duchess's now-filthy gown. Yet she held her head high, her long curls sparkling in fiery shades of amber and sienna in the sunlight. Her wide, generous mouth and high cheekbones lent her a majestic air. Other ladies her age were beginning to lose their fresh bud of beauty, but Her Grace was just beginning to grow into her splendor. She possessed a mature beauty perfected from a loveliness of body, heart, and mind.

"Your Grace." He bowed. An electrical storm crackled in his insides at her proximity. "I'm sorry if—"

"Good day, Mr. Stratton and Lady Fentleigh." The duchess's voice possessed a low, dusky quality as she addressed his sister. "If you believe my child should stay at home because she is rude and unruly, then I would suggest the same to you and your brother. For no one's behavior is more atrocious than yours. I know that I speak for more than myself when I say your petty meanness is transparent. No one finds you nearly as clever as you think yourselves."

The duchess turned and walked to her servants and other daughter. Her son took her arm and glanced over his shoulder at Stratton, casting him a nasty look.

Dull, heavy pain weighed in Stratton's chest as he watched her retreat. He deserved her harsh cut.

The Season before Stratton had left for the war, when the duchess was just a young merchant's daughter named Miss Mary Alice Ward, she had been the object of his and his sister's ridicule. Her numerous sins had been heinous, indeed. Aside from a round face peppered with freckles, a fleshy body, and a fervent desire to be accepted into Society, she had displayed a painfully obvious *tendre* for Stratton. Whenever they were in the same company, her enormous, lovely eyes had tracked his every movement. It had become a game among his friends to whisper, "Moo," whenever she was about.

One evening he had spied her ogling him in a loose-lipped, spoony way across the ballroom. "I don't know if my ardent bovine admirer desires to flirt or serve me up," he had said loudly enough to be heard by his friends and other people milling nearby. "Perhaps both." The infamous insult had blazed through Society. Soon, people desperate to be included in Stratton's fashionable circles began quietly mooing when she was around and referring to her as "the bovine admirer."

Stratton had committed many sins in his life, and he shouldered numerous regrets. But the two that weighed most heavily on his conscience were how he had hurt his daughter and the Duchess of Pymworth.

The duchess disappeared around a hedge. The bystanders switched their curiosity from Her Grace to Stratton and his sister. Another woman might feel the slightest sting of embarrassment or censure. Not Deirdre. Whenever crossed, she slapped back, swift and hard.

"What would the Duchess of Pymworth know about cleverness?" Deirdre mused to her followers. "Does she think her station hides the stench of shop that still lingers about her?"

"I will not listen to another word spoken against Her Grace," Stratton barked in his military voice.

Deirdre blinked, nonplussed. Then she narrowed her eyes as an amused smile snaked over her mouth. "I believe you possess a softness for our bovine duchess," she purred. "How very delicious! I am thrilled because you were beginning to bore me. You know how I detest boredom. You are redeemed, Brother."

Stratton considered denying his feelings for Her Grace. But hadn't his cowardice and immaturity caused enough pain in the lives of the females he cared about?

"Of course, I have a softness for Her Grace," he replied. "She is the kindest and cleverest lady in Society."

Deirdre broke into derisive laughter. Her friends joined in like a chorus coming behind the soloist.

What was he doing here? Why was he wasting his time with shallow, malicious people who sought to alleviate the tedium of their privileged lives by making a game of casually tormenting others?

"I'm leaving directly for the country," he muttered, turning on his heel "I've been away from my daughter for too long."

He stalked across the grass. No doubt, Deirdre had another witticism on the subject of his admiration for the duchess, but he wouldn't be around to hear it. He broke into a jog. He had to get the hell away from London, which was packed with memories of the horrible man he used to be.

* * *

Don't think about Lady Fentleigh, Stratton, or the park, Mary Alice scolded herself as she sat in the nursery, still in her wet clothes and quaking with residual anger. *Be thankful that Anna is calm and well. That's all that matters. Stratton is nothing—just a horrid, vile, and arrogant blackguard.*

She had never hit anyone in her life—well, perhaps her sister when Mary Alice was four and didn't know better—but when Lady *Fentleigh* had spat her honeyed venom as Stratton smirked, Mary Alice almost smacked their self-satisfied faces.

Lady Fentleigh, Stratton, and their cruel circle had been Mary Alice's antagonists since her first Season. She had learned to swallow their clever little barbs, both veiled and otherwise, and pretend not to care, while inside she cringed with hurt. But today they'd turned their maliciousness on her child—her special, defenseless Anna. Mary Alice felt no cringing hurt, only white-hot, violent rage. But she congratulated herself on remaining calm and delivering a sharp set-down with aplomb. Her husband would have been proud. He had been the cool and measured one in their marriage, contrasting with Mary Alice's more excitable nature.

Now, Anna calmly sketched on a piece of stationery, as though the afternoon's episode hadn't happened. Usually, she loved the park. If left undisturbed, she could stare for hours and hours at bugs and leaves. But Mary Alice had made a mistake taking her to the park too close to the fashionable hour. The loud, bustling crowds had chafed Anna's nerves like flint on steel, setting the girl alight. Anna had two states: calm and hysterical. Once hysterical, only Mary Alice could successfully calm her. Anyone else only drove her hysterics higher.

She leaned close and kissed the air above her child's head because Anna didn't like being touched. "I love you, Anna," she whispered. Anna glanced up and gave her mother a rare gift—a smile. Mary Alice thought she would break down in tears again. She turned away, discreetly wiped her eyes, and then embraced her other children—Caroline, her eldest, and Little Jonas, named for his father.

"Mama loves you all so very, very much," Mary Alice said.

"Tell us more about the evil bog lord," Little Jonas begged. "You promised, remember?" The children adored Mary Alice's fantastical stories and would keep her for hours in the nursery, imploring her to tell just a little more, and then a little more, of her tales. Currently, they were deep into the ongoing epic of the evil bog lord and his vast army of ogres and trolls in Bogland that threatened to take over the civilized land from King Foradora.

Mary Alice desired only to change out of her wet clothes, put on a clean shift, and curl up under the covers. There she could drift into her own made-up, adult story, in which her shining knight—her husband—was still alive, and they dwelled happily together in a magical kingdom that resembled their London home, while the cruel people of the world, like Stratton and his sister, sank into the muddy, boggy Thames.

But Jonas and Caroline deserved her special attention for behaving so bravely in the park. Mary Alice was very proud of her older children, who seemed much more mature than their young years. No doubt the death of their father hastened their maturity. And Mary Alice felt guilty for those months when the death of her husband had paralyzed her with sorrow, and she couldn't be a proper mother. It had been hard for Jonas and Caroline to watch her grieve. She remembered Caroline asking, "Mama, how can I make your tears stop?" Those words, delivered by a confused, upset child, had broken Mary Alice's heart all over again.

"Perhaps Her Grace can tell the story another time," their perceptive nurse suggested.

"Please, please, please," Caroline and Little Jonas pleaded, their hands clenched at their chests as they bounced on their tiptoes. "We'll do geography without complaining," Little Jonas said, sweetening the deal.

"Well, maybe just a little more," Mary Alice conceded. "Where did we leave off last night?"

"Caro was captured with Fiery Boy by the bog lord," Caroline supplied. She opened the hat box that imprisoned her doll Caro, Mary Alice's doll Marcela Misslemay, and Little Jonas's wooden dragon, Fiery Boy, which had bandages wound around its wings.

"And the bog lord hurt my dragon's wings," Little Jonas reminded her. "So, he can't fly."

Anna set down her pencil and turned to listen.

"Ah yes," Mary Alice said, diving into the story.

* * *

An hour later, Mary Alice released a long sigh and combed her fingers through her hair as she left the nursery. Her tresses had all but escaped their pins, and her skirt had dried into stiff, muddy wrinkles.

The butler found her in the corridor and informed her of visitors. She sucked in her breath. As much as she loved callers, she didn't think herself capable of polite conversation when she'd rather be hurling insults at Stratton and his followers. And on top of it all, she appeared as though she had been dragged through a filthy ditch.

The butler bowed. "The Duchess of San Mercato has called."

Mary Alice spirits immediately lifted.

"Perfect!" Mary Alice exclaimed. Her dear friend wouldn't blink an eye at a vitriol-laced rant against Stratton and his sister. "Please direct her to my dressing chamber."

Francesca, the Duchess of San Mercato, ambled into the chamber as the lady's maid unpinned Mary Alice's gown.

"I know wet gowns are *à la mode*," Francesca remarked and kissed Mary Alice's cheeks in the continental manner. "But this is rather extreme. Do tell me that you intended to fluster some wildly eligible gentleman out of his wits."

Mary Alice blushed. She wasn't comfortable with the idea of flirting with another man or thinking of one in intimate terms. She had told her husband on his deathbed that she would never marry again. She couldn't imagine loving another man as she had Jonas. Though he had been a wealthy duke from an ancient line, theirs had been a true love match. She would never betray that sacred love.

"Anna and I enjoyed a refreshing little plunge in Hyde Park," Mary Alice said, putting the conversation on its correct course as her maid changed her shift.

Francesca's laughter died. "Oh, I'm sorry."

Mary Alice hadn't meant to douse her friend's lively mood and quickly moved to restore it. "Why? I'm thinking of making a new fashion. Why journey all the way to Bath and clamber into one of those dreadful machines, when I'm sure the Serpentine is equally curative."

Mary Alice kindly dismissed her servant. She picked up her silk dressing robe and slid her arms through the sleeves. "The worst part was that the little episode was witnessed by Lady Fentleigh and her brother, Mr. Stratton—or is it Colonel Stratton? Well, whatever he calls himself now. I prefer to be Russian about it and give him the title of 'terrible.' Stratton the Terrible."

"Oh dear. What happened?"

Mary Alice shook her head, further loosening her hair, and began plucking out her remaining hairpins. "You know I try to be a compassionate person."

"You are the kindest person I know, when you're not vexed, that is. All your charity work makes me exhausted just thinking of it. See, now that I'm thinking about it, I shall have to lie upon your settee." Francesca reclined on the cushions, her hands cradling the back of her head, her legs crossed at the ankles.

"Well, Stratton undoes all my best intentions by his mere presence. Just looking at his handsome face fills me with loathing. He has a poisonous beauty." Mary Alice sat at her vanity table, facing away from the mirror. She picked up her hairbrush and violently detangled her curls as she relayed the details of her encounter with Stratton, including Anna's episode and his sister's syrupy viciousness.

"Why is it that Stratton seems to loom about in the worst moments of my life?" Mary Alice pondered when she had finished. "Well, not the *worst* moment, which was when my dearest died."

"They say he is much changed since the war." Her friend's voice grew somber at the mention of war. "Quieter, reserved. I understand he has become quite the generous patron of the arts and sciences. And, of course, fatherhood may have further hastened his reformation, for is there nothing more revolting than a lascivious rake who possesses a young, impressionable daughter?"

"Stratton? The father of a daughter?"

Francesca leaned forward, eyes shining with dark knowledge. "Did you not know?"

"Not when it's gossip involving Stratton. I hear his name and cease to further listen for fear of picking up objects and hurling them."

"Well, it seems Colonel Stratton had a liaison with Lady Radley shortly before leaving for the war."

"Oh yes, I recall that time well. It was when he compared me to a cow and wondered if I planned to eat him."

"Lady Radley became *enceinte* shortly thereafter, and it was rumored that the child was Stratton's. Once born, no one saw the child. Most people assumed it died shortly after birth."

"How sad." Nothing made Mary Alice more heartsick than learning of an ill, seriously hurt, or dying child whom she couldn't help. Most of her charity work was directed at vulnerable children and poor mothers.

"Ah, but upon Lady Radley's death last year, her husband publicly washed his hands of his late wife's, quote, little bastard. It would seem Colonel Stratton hadn't known of the child's existence. He located the little girl and brought her to his estates, by all accounts immediately accepting her as his own and showering her with gifts."

Mary Alice gazed at her friend askance. "No, no, I . . . I can't conceive of this. Stratton can't spare a thought for anyone but himself."

However, she knew from her own experience that parenthood changed a person. She hadn't spoken to Stratton since he'd returned from the war. Nor had she heard of any insults emitting from his mouth concerning her. And if she really thought upon the matter at the park, she realized that all the hateful words had spewed forth from his sister. Had she been unfair to him? She liked to think she was mature and capable of forgiveness, but Stratton still summoned black rage in her heart even after all these years.

"Well, if that is true," Mary Alice said, "then I'm glad he has turned over a new leaf. For the girl's sake. Now if he would just go about his new life without bumping into my old one, we should get along quite well."

"As you say." Francesca sat up and withdrew a letter from her valise. "Now the reason for my visit. My man of business has secured the perfect holiday estate for us. It's located in an excessively rural town in the north of England. And to make certain of our anonymity and peace, I've concocted a darling little game. You will adore it. We shall go in disguise and under assumed names." The duchess's eyes glittered, she was so pleased with herself. "With no titles or wealth, what would anyone want from us?"

Mary Alice groaned inwardly. The holiday had seemed like such a good idea a month ago, but now the situation with Anna left her nervous. Aside from the episode in the park, last week Anna had simply walked out of the house and wandered about Mayfair, pretty as you please. Had a servant returning from Covent Garden market not spotted her, who knows what might have happened?

"Perhaps I shouldn't," Mary Alice began, as she mentally composed a polite decline.

Francesca shot to her feet and wagged her finger at her friend. "Don't you dare back out of our lovely holiday! You require one. I say this as your true friend."

"But—"

"I'm going to pretend that I didn't hear you utter a 'but.' You have an army of servants, your children's uncle is currently residing next door, your parents live a mile away, and your sisters and brothers are so very, very far away in the remote regions of Hampstead Heath. I think you can slip away for a few weeks of rest and serenity, and the world will not come crashing down. Everyone will remain safe and happy, including you."

"You're not going to let me wiggle out of this holiday, are you?"

"I'm prepared to abduct you, should it be required." She embraced Mary Alice and whispered, "Come away, my dear. All will be well. Stop worrying. You've worn yourself ragged with anxious thoughts."

"Mama."

Mary Alice turned. Anna stood at the door, clutching a piece of paper to her chest, her features composed into their usual blank expression.

Mary Alice adopted the musical voice she used for talking to children. "Anna, my love, you remember my dear friend the Duchess of San Mercato." Anna didn't curtsey or even flick her eyes in Francesca's direction, even after she commented on how much Anna had grown.

"I know how to escape the bog lord," Anna said, and turned the paper around to show her a stunning map.

"My goodness," Francesca exclaimed. "That's . . . that's simply brilliant."

Anna's brow creased. She didn't understand compliments. They made no sense to her.

Mary Alice reached out, letting her hand hover just over her daughter's shoulder. Then she slowly lowered it, letting it rest lightly on the girl. For once, Anna didn't flinch and try to escape.

Mary Alice pleaded with her friend silently with her eyes.

"I'll just run along," Francesca whispered and hurried out, leaving the mother and daughter alone.

Still touching her daughter, Mary Alice asked her to explain the picture and listened to Anna's explanation, amazed at the detail and creativity. She was grateful to be allowed into her daughter's wondrous imagination. It had taken years for Mary Alice to coax Anna to talk. Now the girl was opening her elusive world to her mother, just when Mary Alice had agreed to go on a ridiculous holiday.

What if Anna became hysterical while Mary Alice was away, and no one could calm her? What if she wandered away, and no one could find her? Mary Alice shivered to think of her odd, fragile daughter lost on the dangerous streets of London. No one knew her as well or loved her as fiercely as Mary Alice did. No one else would keep a vigilant guard on her.

"My dear, would you mind if Mama went away?"

"Will you come back?" Anna said with no inflection.

"Of course, I just promised my dear friends that I would go away with them for a few weeks. I don't want to, but I feel I should."

Anna shook her head. "Why?"

"Because it's important to my friends. And my friends are important to me."

Anna only stared, unable to comprehend her mother's meaning. She didn't have the faintest clue about friendship or interactions between people. In fact, she rarely noticed others. She wasn't cruel. She simply didn't react to other people. They might as well be inanimate paintings on the wall.

"I'm going to miss you," Mary Alice said. "May I hug you? A small hug."

Anna stepped stiffly forward, allowing her mother to embrace her. Even though her daughter kept her arms straight at her sides, her head up, and her eyes open, Mary Alice savored the rare experience. How fiercely she loved this special child. And how fiercely she feared for her too.

"Oh, Anna," she whispered. "I would rather stay safely here with you and Caroline and Little Jonas. I'm going to miss you all terribly." Mary Alice couldn't conceive how leaving everyone she loved could be construed as a holiday.

CHAPTER TWO

Some Godforsaken place in the north of England

Rain drenched Mary Alice as she watched her friends ride off with their designated heroes. Even as water slid down her face and dripped into her mouth, she forced her lips into a wide, painful smile to keep herself from screaming, *Why did I ever agree to this holiday insanity?* and then bursting into frustrated tears.

She didn't think that would help matters.

Her supposed savior, atop a stunning chestnut mare, approached. Something about him made her very uneasy. Perhaps the way he kept his head down and wore his hat low like a highwayman. *He's just protecting himself from the rain,* she assured herself. Yet, given how this outing had turned into the holiday from hell, she wouldn't be surprised if he were a criminal wanted for murdering women stranded on the roadside.

Help me, Jonas, she prayed to her late husband. *Help me get back safe and sound to our children.*

When the carriage had tumbled, her head had smashed against the window, shattering the glass. Her foot had become wedged at an awkward angle between a portmanteau, which must have carried several bricks, and the sharp edge of a sewing box. She hadn't felt any pain in the first moments after the accident. Just shocked surprise. In fact, she had laughed and joked about the hardness of her head to ease the others' concern for her well-being. But now, the left side of her skull felt as though it had been pummeled by Gentleman Jackson, and her left ankle throbbed and swelled against the ribbons of her slippers.

She gallantly kept a smile stretched over her gritted teeth as the third horseman dismounted, held out his hand, and raised his head. His familiar pale gray-silver eyes pierced through the rain. Heat rushed to her head.

"Stratton," she whispered, and then, "Stratton," again as shock transformed to disbelief and then converted to plain anger.

"You can just . . . just . . ." Her head hurt too much to find words that articulated her fury at the gods in the heavens. So, she just emitted a frustrated scream.

Stratton probably thought she was mad— in the Bedlam sense of the word, of course.

But she had long since stopped caring what he thought of her.

"Ride on," she hissed. "I don't require your help. I shall walk to Lesser Puddlebridge . . . bury . . . borough—whatever the nearest hanged town is called—rather than accept your assistance." She raised her head, turned, and made a defiant step away from him. But when her foot struck the earth, pain shot up her leg, and her ankle gave way. She reached for the overturned carriage to steady herself as a wave of black, nauseating dizziness rushed through her.

Stratton's hand clamped around her elbow. She yanked away. "D-do not pretend to b-be civil. I wouldn't accept your help even if you were trying to save me . . . from . . . from stampeding elephants."

She attempted another step, swallowing down the pain just to prove her point. Her husband's words echoed in her memory. *You can be the most stubborn woman in all England at times.* She would always pretend to be offended and would retort, *Just England? No, no, I'm the most stubborn woman in all Europe and parts of the Americas.*

"Your Grace," Stratton began. She expected him to say something insulting, along the lines of, *You foolish bovine chit, you don't know what's good for you, as I do. Get on my horse immediately.* Instead, he surprised her by gently cupping her elbow and saying in soothing tones through the roar of the downpour, "I know that you do not approve of me, and I cannot blame you. My past behavior to you has been inexcusable. A thousand apologies could not suffice. But it is obvious that you are in great pain. Please forgive me enough to allow me to assist you. If it helps you, pretend I'm someone else."

Mary Alice doubted she could muster the mental energy for such a feat of imagination while her skull felt as though it were being repeatedly whacked with a red-hot anvil and a hundred invisible knives jabbed her ankle. She couldn't walk another two feet, much less to the neighboring village. And every layer of her clothing was drenched.

She closed her eyes and murmured the two hardest, most humiliating words she had ever uttered in her life. "Thank you."

He kept a firm grip on her elbow as she inelegantly hobbled to his horse. Between the rain and the black splotches crowding her vision, she blindly reached for a stirrup. His large hands went around her waist and lifted her into the saddle. She heard him grunt and felt his arms shaking.

Just capital. Now her sworn enemy, who'd inspired others to *moo* around her, knew how much she weighed. Could she suffer any worse indignity?

As she settled onto the saddle, a vivid pain burst in her temple. She sucked her breath, squeezed her eyes shut, and clung to the pommel.

She felt him mount behind her. He placed a strong arm around her, forming a shelter with his chest and arms. He used the brim of his hat to protect her from the rain. She was vaguely aware that this was the most intimate she had ever been with a man other than her husband. But she was in too much pain to care that his arm rested just under the weight of her breasts. She wished only that she could press her ailing head against his hard chest to relieve the black throb.

She shoved her fingers beneath her bonnet and dug into her aching temple. Warm fluid oozed onto her fingertips. "Am I . . . am I bleeding?"

He didn't answer but muttered, "Dear God," and urged his horse.

The motion of the beast jarred her skull. "H-how far is your home?"

"Just beyond the fields." His hoarse voice reverberated in her head.

A heavy weariness descended upon her. Remaining upright proved too difficult. She leaned over, desiring to curl up on the horse's neck. "I'm so very tired."

He tightened his hold, forcing her upright again. "I need you to talk to me, Your Grace."

"Please, please, I want to rest."

He shifted his arm until it slanted painfully across her chest. "Why were you traveling this way? Tell me."

"W-we were to go on holiday." The words were ponderous, heavy things on her tongue. "My friends wanted to get away from . . . They said I needed a holiday, but I didn't want... to leave my children. I shouldn't have c-come." She turned, pressing her cheek against his chest, seeking sleep. She hadn't known a man's body for two years. She had forgotten such reassuring strength and comfort.

"I understand, indeed." His voice reminded her of Jonas's. Even when he spoke quietly, it resonated like quiet thunder.

"I miss them so . . . so much already. When I kissed them good-bye several days ago, I was crying. I . . . I haven't been away from them for more than a year." Something she said wasn't correct. "No . . . A year is too long. A week. I've never left them for more than a week. I worry for Anna. She's . . . different . . ." She shook her head, and black pain flared in her head. She scrunched her eyes closed and whimpered.

"You are an ideal mother."

"The physicians . . . They told my husband and me that we should put Anna away. But... we wouldn't let them. They would require a thousand . . . a thousand armies to take my..."

"Your child is safest with you."

She blindly tugged at her bonnet, trying to get it away from where it pressed into her temples and forehead. His hand touched hers as he gently peeled her bonnet away. A swell of cold rain rushed onto her face. His large hand cupped her cheek and drew her against his warm neck.

"I'm so tired, Jonas," she whispered. "Can . . . can we sleep?"

"The house is just ahead." She could feel his body trembling, like that first night they made love.

She opened her eyes. All she saw was a flash of green grass and gray, drenched skies before the black spots filled her vision and she had to shut her lids. "I can't make it. Let's sleep here."

"You need to stay awake for me."

"No."

Her muscles turned limp, as though she could slip from Jonas's hold and onto the grass, letting the rain lull her aching head. She remembered when she and Jonas had picnicked on a grassy cliff by the Lyme coast. She had fallen asleep against his warm body while listening to the comforting sound of waves. "The ocean is so . . . The ocean is . . ." She couldn't finish speaking. The pain paralyzed her.

She could hear Jonas call her name as if he were far, far away. All she could do was grip his hand to assure him she was well. Poor Jonas always worried about her. But it was just a headache. The housekeeper would make a draught for her, and then she could curl up beside him.

She could see light behind her closed lids. There was the sound of a slamming door and alarmed female voices. Jonas was shouting. What was wrong? Jonas never raised his voice.

Mary Alice couldn't feel the heat of his chest anymore. "Jon-Jonas!" His warm hands were on her again, pulling her toward him. Her stomach heaved. She needed to lie down, but his arm held her up. She tried to cry, "Let me sleep," but instead, hot vomit filled her mouth and poured over her chin. Then she slipped into blackness.

* * *

The roaring fire and flickering candles turned the small bedchamber in the home of Stratton's tenant into a sweltering night. Stratton had stripped down to his pantaloons, boots, and shirt and now paced, restless with worry. His tenant, Mrs. Fillmore and her girl servant, who fortuitously had postponed returning to her home in the village because of the downpour, had undressed Her Grace and clad her in a wool nightdress. He hadn't informed his tenants of their visitor's true identity. They had assumed they wound muslin bandages around the head and foot of a genteel acquaintance of his. Her Grace remained unconscious during it all. Now her head was sunk into a goose down pillow, the candle on the side table illuminating her peaceful face in gold and turning her hair the color of autumn leaves.

He was in hell. He raked his hands through his hair and strode to the small window. Rain pinged the glass. The downpour concealed the moon and trees. Just wet blackness. He felt as helpless as he had in the war when he'd walked among the fatally wounded, unable to nurse them back to health. He had noted how easy it was to kill a man but how hard it was to keep a man from dying. All things seemed to lean into death.

He heard a soft rustling of bedcovers and rushed to Her Grace's side. She hadn't moved. What had he heard? Maybe he was losing his mind. "Your Grace?" he whispered.

She didn't respond.

He reached under the quilts, found her hand, and squeezed it. "Your Grace?"

Her eyes remained shut. Her breath was as even as ever.

He sat in the chair he had pulled beside the bed.

"Please, lady," he prayed. He couldn't bear the idea that this woman, whom he had emotionally hurt so badly, should die in his care. She needed to live, to be far from him and with her children and friends who adored her. Her vivacity and kindness could not end in this dingy room, on a dismal night, and with him. She deserved better.

"You will be well," he growled, as if by his own sheer will he could alter fate. He hung his head, still clinging to her hand. Outside, the wind picked up, rushing the rain against the window. His mind flowed with horrible memories—the hurt in Her Grace's eyes all those years ago, the stillness of his soldiers as they drifted into death, the filthy rat-infested hospital where he found his daughter.

He thought it was a trick of his mind when it first happened. The small pressure of her fingers. Then it happened again. He slowly raised his head. Her Grace's eyes were open, unfocused and blank.

"Your Grace," he said quietly.

She turned and gazed at him. Her pupils seemed to sharpen as recognition dawned.

"You?" she whispered. "Stratton?"

The disgust and disbelief coloring her voice brought him only relief. The accident had not rendered her witless. She knew him and remembered that she hated him. He couldn't stop laughter from breaking over him, as all the hours of tension bubbled up and burst away.

"Yes," he cried. "It's me! Stratton! You're old enemy. Oh, thank God."

She attempted to sit up. "Ah!" She reached for her temple as pain crumpled her features.

"No!" He clasped her shoulders. "Lie still, please. Don't hurt yourself. There was an accident." He gently pressed her back onto the pillow.

Her brows furrowed. "What? Where am I?"

"Your carriage overturned." He gingerly touched her bandage, careful not to get near the wound. "You have a concussion. And, I fear, you've injured your ankle."

He studied her face, watching for any signs of permanent mental damage. Her features scrunched as she dug into her memory. "I remember being in the carriage," she said. "But…"

"It turned over, and you hit your head. At first the wound wasn't apparent, for it was concealed beneath your bonnet. You probably were in shock. My acquaintances whisked your friends to my home, but as I escorted you, your health rapidly worsened. Fearing for your life, I stopped at a nearby tenant's home."

Her brow furrowed. "I don't recall any of—my friends!" She tried to bolt up again, but he gently kept her safe against the pillow. "Are they well?"

"They were quite well when last I saw them," he said reassuringly, letting his thumbs massage her shoulders. "I shall take you to them in the morning. Please don't distress yourself."

She let his words sink in. "What of the carriage?"

"I shall ask that it be repaired. It is not my most pressing concern at present. You are."

He hadn't intended the intimate tone in his voice. Her alarmed eyes locked onto his. A strange current passed from their depths, crackling through his body. She glanced away. "Please . . . please remove your hands from me."

"Of course." He withdrew them, but still hovered close. Her profound dislike for him would not stop him from worrying over her and seeing to her wounds.

"I-I must hire a carriage tomorrow to return me to London," she said.

"That is not advisable."

She arched her brow. "Thank you for your kindness, but I refuse to s-stay in your home or your tenant's. I will not be beholden to you any further."

"I cannot in good conscience allow you to leave my estates until you are well recovered. You've suffered a head injury. I've been witness to many soldiers dying . . ." He trailed off. What the hell was he saying? He would terrify her. "It is not advisable," he repeated.

"I will not stay!" She attempted to rise to her elbows.

"No!" He reached for her shoulders again, but stopped and held up his palms mere inches from her body. "Please," he implored. "Please rest."

She released a frustrated cry. A single tear slid down the side of her face and onto her pillow. "This is so very vexing. I should have never left my children—Anna."

He drew the chair closer and sat. "I'm sorry this has happened on your holiday. And I'm sorry for my behavior all those years ago."

She studied him and then began fingering the edge of the top quilt. Her silence unnerved him. He continued to speak. All the eloquent words in the letters he had written to her over the years, but had never sent, were reduced to a halting stammer. "Every day I regret the pain that I caused you and wish I could rescind those cruel words. I loathe myself for the pain I've caused you . . . and others."

He knew better than to expect forgiveness, but he needed some word or sign that she believed him sincere. For several long seconds, she remained silent, focused on the frayed quilt. He wondered if she'd even heard him when she finally whispered, "Why did you say it? I was just a lowly merchant's daughter who fancied herself in love with the Season's crown prince. I was harmless to you."

She was hardly harmless to him. And that was the trouble. "Perhaps we should continue this conversation when you are recovered."

"I may never get another chance to know. And your words have haunted me all these years. Why? Why did you want to hurt me?"

He gently banged his balled hand on the wooden armrest of the chair. "I fear the reason may cause you to further despise me."

"Is that possible?" Whatever expression passed over his face softened her countenance. "That was cruel of me to say. Please forgive me. But I would like to know the truth."

The truth wouldn't make their situation better, but worse, sending her recklessly back to London to get away from him.

"Tell me," she urged.

He couldn't deny her, not when her eyes were so large and vulnerable beneath her bandaged forehead. They remained as powerful as they had been years before, heating his skin and charging his body.

"I knew that you possessed affections for me, and I . . ." He rubbed his chin and mouth. "I greatly esteemed you as well."

"W-what?"

"I harbored affections for you."

She stared at him, her lips parted in disbelief. "So, you insulted me?"

"Yes."

"What? And you were rumored to be intimately involved with several married ladies at the time. I know this now. Did you harbor affections for them as well? Did they receive the gift of your cruel tongue too? Are you so shameless?"

He came to his feet. "I warned that you would despise me more. Yes, I *was* shameless. The other ladies, including the mother of my daughter"—the truth burned his throat like swallowing strong spirits—"were affairs of fevered, forbidden passion. They proved my masculine prowess, but my desire for them was not the stuff of honest affection. You were different."

She blinked. "Why? Because you, the golden one, were disgusted with yourself for admiring someone so homely, so awkward, so reeking of her father's hosiery business?"

"Because what I feel for you is true!" The booming words reverberated around him before he realized what he said. "I mean, *was* true," he corrected quietly.

He paced to the chimneypiece. "I was scared. And don't ever say you are homely or awkward. You are beautiful. Every aspect of your being and spirit is lovely. I couldn't admit that then because I was immature, full of arrogance, and a coward. In my misguided mind, I must have thought that if I cut you, I would somehow sever my attachment to you."

"Did that work, Colonel Stratton? Did watching my humiliation and hurt, born of your insults, cure you of your feelings for me?"

He stirred the fire with a poker. Flames leaped from the exposed coals. "Of course, not. It made them stronger."

"How surprising," she shot back. "But I assure you that your slurs forever destroyed my affections and good opinion of you."

Her words hit like stones. He'd known he was forever lost from her graces, but hearing her say as much destroyed him. "I know I can never make up for the pain I've caused you," he choked. "Sorry is a mere word, but it's all I have." He returned to her bedside. "I can only take comfort in the knowledge that you married a better man."

"I did. He loved me very much, and I returned that love. I still do."

Her face appeared tired and ashen. Blood stained the left side of her bandage. He felt ashamed. "I have distressed you, and you've already suffered too much today."

"No," she said softly. "I asked you for the truth, and then I abused you for your honesty. I am sorry. Thank you for satisfying my curiosity by explaining why you said those horrid words years ago."

She hadn't looked at him with any degree of kindness since that first Season. He remained still, fearful of doing something that would take away that coveted tender light again. But then the silence stretched on too long, turning uncomfortable.

"You should rest," he said.

"I fear I must ask you to leave."

"Of course." He headed to the door. "But you shouldn't be left alone with such an injury. I shall see if my tenant is awake. Her servant girl comes back in the morning."

"Wait, please," she said, stopping his progress. "You needn't bother your tenant any further on my account. Just . . . stay." She gave a light, wry chuckle. "It's not as though anyone would believe we spent the night together if word were to circulate. They would sooner believe I joined Astley's Circus as a lion tamer."

He joined in her chuckle. He returned to the chair and began sliding it into the corner. "I'll just hide here in the shadows, and you can pretend I'm not here."

"That's not necessary. I'm well aware of your presence."

Instead, she turned in the bed, giving him her back. Her lustrous locks spilled off the pillow's edge. He watched her as the rain continued to fall and the tallow candle burned down. He thought she had drifted into sleep when she softly spoke. "Thank you for tending to my injuries, Colonel Stratton."

"Always, Your Grace. Always."

* * *

Jonas waited at the foot of Mary Alice's bed in her chamber in London. His cravat hung loose, and black strands of hair fell over his forehead. His dark eyes glowed with tender desire as he gazed down at her. "My love," she said, beckoning him to join her so that they might make love. But he edged away, a mysterious smile on his face.

"Jonas?" She laughed, rising from the bed. Jonas turned and dashed into the corridor. In her bare feet, she hurried after him, as if they were playing a silly lovers' game. She almost caught his hand when he vanished before her eyes. "What? Jonas, where are you?"

She whipped around at the sound of a footfall to see Jonas turning the corner at the end of the corridor. She rushed to catch up, but the faster she ran, the farther away he seemed. She saw only the flutter of his shirt as he turned another corner or exited through another door. She became panicked, running from room to room, shouting his name. "Where are you, my love? Come to me."

In her frantic chase, she bumped into a side table, knocking it over. Dozens of bottles, all Jonas's medicine, shattered on the floor. Their brown, liquid contents flowed by her feet. "What have I done?" she cried. "I've ruined his medicine. Jonas, I'm sorry. I'm sorry."

"It's well," she heard a reassuring male voice say. It wasn't Jonas's, but it was as rich and soothing as his and elicited a calming, peace in her body. A man's comforting hand rested upon her arm. "You're merely having a dream. You can go back to sleep. I'm here." She turned, drawing the strong hand closer, and sank again into deep sleep.

* * *

When Mary Alice opened her eyes, the rain and darkness were gone. Morning light peeked through embroidered ivory curtains. Sweet lavender scented the air. Last night, Mary Alice had perceived the chamber as squat and dingy, but in the light, it was airy and feminine.

Across the room, a woman in a black dress and plain muslin collar and cap stood by the commode. She turned as Mary Alice attempted to sit up. Her face was tanned and weathered, but her eyes were a vivid blue that complemented the lavender in the vase she held.

"Aye, you're blessed, ma'am." Her voice was coarsened with age. "The angels must be watching over you."

She crossed the room and set the vase on the bedside table. "My brother fell out of a tree onto his head when he was seven." She arranged the flowers. "He didn't utter a word of sense for the rest of his short life. Stayed in a bed in the stable and had to be clouted like a baby."

"Are you Mrs. Fillmore?"

"I am."

"Thank you for allowing me to stay in your home."

"Aye, I feared the worst for you, ma'am. You were a pitiful sight, you were."

That was the second time Mrs. Fillmore had called Mary Alice *ma'am*. Stratton must have kept her identity a secret, and Mary Alice was thankful. She resented the fuss made over her simply because of her title. At times it was more bothersome than helpful.

"I didn't want to tell the colonel my fears," Mrs. Fillmore continued. "Never seen a man so scared. A colonel, mind you. I thought he would have seen it all in the war."

As Mary Alice pondered how to introduce herself, the door opened, and Stratton entered holding a picnic basket with a tray atop its lid. "I bring a grand feast, Mrs. Fillmore." He had donned a fresh, stiff shirt, a pair of flesh-colored pantaloons, and a vivid blue coat.

"Let me fetch some plates so we can eat grandly like you do up at Rose Heath," Mrs. Fillmore said.

"No need to trouble yourself. My servants must have packed the entire china chest in this basket." He grunted, making a show of straining to lower it onto the floor beside the bed. "I merely require a little hot water, and to that end, I have set Fiona and Betsy to the task in your kitchen."

"What?" Mrs. Fillmore cried. "You've set those two silly girls loose in my kitchen? Not a single wit between the likes of them. And I better not find that you have stocked my pantry with honey and jam again."

"Oh no, I learned my lesson after the scolding I received the last time I committed such a heinous atrocity," he called after her. The merriment tugging the corners of his mouth suggested that the disapproving Mrs. Fillmore would find her kitchen overflowing with such goods.

He laid the tray on Mary Alice's lap. He smelled of cologne, and his cheeks shone from a fresh barbering. Still, his handsome face bore the tired traces of a sleepless night. His proximity solicited a wife-like instinct in her. She almost reached out to cup his cheek and say that he should rest and that she worried about him, as she would have done to Jonas. Why did she want to do that? Stratton didn't remind her of Jonas in any aspect. They were quite different men.

Stratton didn't notice her small, embarrassing lapse. He continued setting out silver utensils, a china plate, and jars filled with golden honey, butter, and various berry jams. "We didn't know how you prefer your scones," he explained. "So, I brought every possible option."

"You are very kind, especially to Mrs. Fillmore. I didn't expect . . ." She stopped. It would have been most impolite to say that she'd never imagined that he was so generous and humble. "I didn't expect you to bring breakfast," she finished weakly.

"Your friends, *Mrs. Pomponio* and *Miss Thorpe*, send their regards." He removed a scone from the basket, broke off the end, and dabbed it with butter. "They were highly worried, but I assured them of your recovery and pending move to my estate this morning." He held out the buttered pastry. "Do try this."

She smiled at the mention of her friends. "So, they are still playing at their little masquerade. It's rather foolish now." She took a dainty bite of the scone that waited before her lips. The flaky, airy bread and butter did magical things on her tongue. She took another, bigger bite and unthinkingly spoke with her mouth full—something she always admonished her children for doing. "Oh, oh, this scone is heavenly."

"I laugh at many of the follies of fashionable Society now, but a French chef is a bare necessity. Should my fields burn, my estate crumble, and the market collapse? All I require to live are proper boots, good books, a dependable horse, and my French chef."

She noticed how her chuckle brightened his face.

"And I don't find your and your friends' masquerade silly by any shade," he reassured her. "I wish I could pretend to be someone else every time I set foot in London. What is your pretend name?"

"Mrs. Marcela Misslemay. She's actually a character in an epic story that my children and I tell each other. It includes courageous maidens, knights, evil bog lords, vicious trolls, ugly ogres, and heroic dragons. Homer would be envious. "

"You are a wonderful mother. You are . . ." He gazed down at her for a long second and then shook his head as if waking from a daydream. "If I were to make up another existence, I should be Mr. Archibald Higgins-Carstairs." He straightened his cravat and assumed the stiff-rumped countenance of a disapproving man by comically drawing down his mouth and scrunching his nose. The effect ruined his handsome face but displayed another side to Stratton that she hadn't known existed. He was playful.

"Perfect," she cried.

"Mr. Archibald Higgins-Carstairs is a fusty, disapproving fellow who wanders about in museums or science exhibitions wearing such a sour expression that everyone leaves him blessedly alone."

He gave her a sample of this contemptuous expression, which caused her to giggle.

"What's so amusing?" he croaked. He approached her, closed one eye, and pretended to hold a quizzing-glass before the other. "Science is for serious, humorless people. I will not suffer any merriment or mirth. Frivolity is out of the question. Don't even consider glee."

That was an invitation for more giggles. "I wager your daughter adores you."

His face tensed. All of his playfulness vanished.

What had happened? What had she said that was so terribly wrong?

He strode to the chimneypiece. There, he picked up a small wooden box from the mantel and turned it in his hand, rubbing its carvings with his thumb. "My daughter doesn't adore me at all."

"I'm sorry."

"As am I."

His head was bowed as if in defeat. She desired to comfort him as she would her upset child. But what would she say? *Don't worry, it will get better?* Because sometimes it wouldn't. Sometimes cancer would take your young husband. Or your daughter would be born with a mysterious affliction and would never enjoy a normal life.

He looked at her in a way that made her think he wanted to say something more but held back his words.

She leaned in and extended her arm across the quilt, a gesture of reaching out to him. "Colonel Stratton, I would love to meet your daughter. Above all things."

"She's a bastard child," he said brusquely, as though issuing some sort of challenge. "Other genteel ladies would—"

"I'm not other ladies."

"No, you're not." His tone softened again as his eyes held her gaze. "I would like very much for you to meet her. I saw how you handled your daughter in the park, and, well, perhaps you can help me . . . us. You see, Eleanor is different. Fragile. She hides in her own safe world."

The vulnerable, imploring expression on his face seemed at odds with his powerful frame. This wasn't the man she had been spoony over all those years ago in London. This man was different. In the vivid light, she could see the premature lines etched under his eyes and around his mouth. She didn't know what horrors he'd witnessed in the war, but she well understood the pain of being unable to reach your child. Those first years with Anna had been hard, when she hadn't known if her daughter would ever talk to her but would always just gaze off, endlessly fascinated by a shaft of light on the wall or some such thing.

"I can only love your child," Mary Alice said. "It's all I really know how to do."

"Thank you," he whispered.

He suddenly appeared restless, as if the conversation had cut a little too close to the bone, and now he was uncomfortable. "I shall send in Fiona and Betsy to help you dress. When you reach my home later, you may write your children, if it pleases you. I shall send the message with an express."

"That would please me very much." Her voice cracked. "I miss them so terribly. Thank you for your kindness."

* * *

Mary Alice discovered that Stratton's servants, Fiona and Betsy, were hardly witless, as Mrs. Fillmore claimed, but clever, bright-eyed, and properly mannered young women. Sometime in the early morning, Stratton had had the overturned carriage hauled away for repairs and requested that the ladies' trunks be taken to Rose Heath. By some miracle, Mary Alice's clothes had remained dry. Fiona and Betsy had brought one of her gowns and helped dress her in it. They laughed when Mary Alice, despairing of her unfashionable bandage, adorned her head with a sprig of lavender held in place with a pin.

"I call my coiffure *L'accident*," she replied when Stratton teasingly complimented her as he helped her wobble to his carriage, for she flatly refused to let him carry her as he wanted. Her swollen ankle didn't hurt much except when she put the tiniest bit of pressure on her foot. Then it felt akin to having nails hammered into her.

Once the female servants were installed in their seats, Stratton asked the groom to drive slowly and take care to avoid any potholes. As a result, slugs could have made better time. She jokingly asked if they would require a postilion change as they inched down a long, oak-lined drive. He chuckled, an easy sound, and the light reflected in his eyes, turning their gray to a lovely polished silver color.

The carriage passed through a tall gate made of brick and iron, and the vista of Rose Heath emerged. It was the opposite of the Pymworth ancestral fortress, which was an intimidating edifice, more castle-like than stately. When she and her husband had spoken of spending time there, they had used words like *exiled* and *banished*. But Stratton's Rose Heath was a welcoming home, appearing both elegant and cozy. It wasn't a massive affair, but rather smallish for a manor home and adorned with gracefully arched windows. Trailing vines grew up the brick. Beyond the domicile, the landscape was lush and gleaming from its rain bath. It all appeared as a sentimental painting of pleasant rural life.

The front door opened, and the domestic staff flooded out. They readily smiled and formed a neat line to receive the carriage's passengers. Stratton clearly didn't browbeat and demoralize his staff, as she had witnessed at other grand homes. The staff appeared as happy and neat as the home they inhabited. This was the work of a good master who knew how to surround himself with the proper people and treat them well. After years of despising Stratton and imagining all manner of poor things about him, she was surprised at how much there was to esteem. Of course, she had always admired his handsome visage, but such surface things mattered less to her now that she was older.

Stratton gripped her across her shoulder, threatening to carry her against her wishes, and helped her from the carriage. He gently assisted her to a lovely set of chambers on the ground floor. A large, gold-painted, canopied bed dominated the room. The surrounding walls were painted a muted shade of turquoise. Once installed upon the bed, Mary Alice could look out two facing windows to a lovely labyrinth garden adorned with sparkling fountains and aviaries.

To her left, double doors were open, revealing a cozy feminine study. A rose-colored sofa and matching chair sat near a Dutch blue tiled grate.

"I combed my library for books you might enjoy." Stratton tapped a stack of volumes resting on her bedside table. "I thought you would like the works of a Miss Jane Austen. Have you read her?"

"No, I have not."

"Well, I stayed up one night burning candle after candle and turning the pages of *Pride and Prejudice*. I won't give away the plot, but let me just say the characters are like fine wine. You need to give them a little time."

She wanted to say, *Just like you*, but kept the words to herself.

He gestured to the sitting room. "We have placed your sewing box and a portable writing desk in the study. A servant will gladly fetch them. Just ring the bell." He pointed to the bell cord, which had been lengthened and threaded along picture-frame hooks until it reached her bedside table.

She smiled at his cleverness. "I shall want for nothing. Well, except for my children."

"And I shall restore you to them as soon as can be. I know they miss you."

Her throat began to burn, almost preventing her from murmuring a simple, "Thank you."

She heard a muted tap by the window and turned to see a dull female peacock pecking the ground by the glass, ignoring the male peacock beside her, who fervently shook his open plumage to get her attention. "I think she has an ardent admirer," Mary Alice said, happy to move the conversation away from personal matters.

"That's Oscar." Stratton gestured to the preening male. "He's in violent love, but alas she prefers Pedro, a vain rogue if you ask me. Ah, the romantic intrigues of Rose Heath."

"Heartless female," Mary Alice replied. "See how hard poor Oscar tries. She should take pity. If there is one thing I've learned, it's always best to take care and love who loves you rather than foolishly give your heart to some peacock that will surely break it."

Stratton's head jerked. Her skin heated with embarrassment. Oh Lord! Did he think she was making a reference to him? How she had once adored him before he smashed her heart?

"I was merely making a . . . a general comment with regards to mating peacocks. Not... That is . . .." She shook her head. "I didn't mean . . .."

Oh goodness, her verbal clumsiness was not improving the situation but making matters worse. She should just be quiet before she did any further damage. So, they lingered in an embarrassed lull for several painful seconds. Even lovesick Oscar felt the awkward silence and drooped his feathers.

One of life's chief delights was having friends who come to one's aid, even unwittingly, as in this situation.

"Thank heavens," Francesca cried, bursting into the room with a flutter of skirts.

"Don't ever frighten us like that again!" Olivia admonished. "No smiling and saying you aren't hurt when you are! Do you understand?"

"I *am* well now." Mary Alice tried to deflect the fuss. She didn't enjoy being the center of attention, even as a semi-invalid. "I was so singularly determined to rest on my holiday that I found a way to be conveniently bed-bound for its duration."

"Don't you dare joke!" Francesca cried. "Look at your head. Dear Lord, must you decorate your bandage with a pin and flowers? Can you not be serious?"

"Never!" Mary Alice exclaimed.

"If you will pardon me, ladies," Stratton piped up from where he'd waited quietly in the corner. "I shall attend to some estate details while you catch up." He bowed and strolled away, turning at the door to glance at Mary Alice again and then disappearing.

Mary Alice's friends gazed at the empty threshold that he had filled just moments before. "What have you done to that man, Mary Alice?" Olivia said slowly. "He is quite smitten."

"*E'molto innamorato*," Francesca supplied in Italian.

Mary Alice had to quickly nip this line of thought in the bud. "He is only behaving as a gentleman, given the inconvenience I have caused. He kindly tended to my wounds. That is all." She glanced up at her friends with what she hoped were innocent, guileless eyes.

They would have none of it.

"Well, I'm certain he would enjoy tending to more of you, should you let him," Francesca purred.

Mary Alice usually enjoyed her friends' delightfully wicked talent of making the lurid sound innocent, except when their game was directed at her.

"He was merely being kind," she said.

"Of course," Francesca agreed with a straight face and gleaming eyes. "I wouldn't have thought otherwise from that look he gave you. How would you describe it, Olivia?"

"Smoldering," Olivia replied.

"With perhaps a smattering of soulful desire," Francesca added.

"There will only ever be Jonas in my heart!" Mary Alice barked, and then bit her lower lip, surprised at her passionate outburst. "Please stop talking that way," she pleaded. "It's not funny. Do you not recall that Stratton and I have been enemies for years? Do you not recall all the pain he once caused me? Yes, he is sorry now. He told me as much. But our newfound friendship is a fragile, scary terrain for us and could crack at any moment. Our history is too horrid."

Her friends exchanged glances.

"Mary Alice, my dear, you are young," Francesca said. "People change, including you. Consider the possibility that you may fall in love again."

Mary Alice shook her head. "I loved Jonas so much that I cannot conceive of it. Please speak no more on the matter. Please."

"I'm sorry," Francesca conceded after a long moment. Mary Alice had the unnerving feeling that her friends thought they knew more than she did, but they were choosing to remain smugly silent.

Francesca's wicked smile returned as she focused her attention on Olivia. "So, tell me of your white knight. I must say, you are sporting a rather satisfied smile this morning. I do hope you have been delightfully naughty."

Olivia didn't answer but flung the conversation back at Francesca. "Ah, but you must tell me of this handsome scientist you've sequestered yourself with. Are you going to help him with his, hmm, *studies*? Perhaps a few exciting chemistry experiments?"

And so, the ladies dived back into their usual banter. But Francesca's somber words continued to echo in Mary Alice's head. *Consider the possibility that you may fall in love again.*

Never!

CHAPTER THREE

Stratton spoke with his man of business and to his steward, and then saw to a few pressing correspondences and authorized several cheques. Afterward, he walked to the nursery to visit his daughter, but the nurse informed him that Eleanor had finished her lessons and the garden walk that Stratton had instructed she must take every day, then fled again to the solitude of her chamber. Stratton swallowed his sigh, not wanting to show his disappointment to the nurse. Everyone in the house tried, but no one seemed to reach Eleanor. She preferred to spend her days alone in the safe shell of her chamber in the companionship of her doll—an ugly toy with leaking stuffing and a cracked, hairless head. Eleanor had been clutching the doll, Helandria, like a shield when she first laid eyes on her true father. Neither Stratton nor anyone else in his household could break or even loosen the fierce bond Eleanor had with her ugly bundle of cotton and porcelain.

He quietly turned the knob to Eleanor's chamber, cracking the door. His daughter—small for her age—lay beneath the table that held her dollhouse. He'd had the enormous dollhouse constructed for her, realistic to the minutest detail and large enough for regular-sized dolls, not the miniature ones. It was a marvel to look at. But Eleanor insisted on playing on the floor, using thimbles and boxes for furniture.

Currently, she had all the new dolls he had gifted her arranged in a semicircle around herself. She kept Helandria nestled protectively beside her and held up another doll, as if it were a barrister addressing a jury of dolls.

"Eleanor and Helandria broke the water bowl," Eleanor said in a harsh, admonishing tone. "How should we punish them?"

His daughter altered her voice, taking on another character. "Spank her with a switch and lock her in the cellar with the rats for the night."

Then Helandria spoke in soothing tones. "Don't worry, Eleanor. I know how to find the secret passage in the cellar that the fairies made."

Stratton closed his eyes. What had happened to his daughter before he managed to rescue her? He would never dream of punishing Eleanor, or any child, in such a way. Sometimes, he despaired that he could undo the damage inflicted on his daughter before he'd found her, and that Eleanor would forever remain trapped in a shell of terror.

The plank under Stratton's foot creaked. Eleanor bolted from under the table and came to her feet. "Yes, sir." Her features took on their usual guarded expression. She smoothed her cornflower blue dress. Her vivid attire contrasted with her enormous somber eyes—the same gray as her father's—and pale face.

Stratton knelt, putting himself at her level. "Good morning, Eleanor," he said, adopting a kind tone.

She scooted back, clutching Helandria to her chest. "Good morning," she answered. Her voice contained fearful suspicion whenever she spoke with adults, as if every word directed at her was a lure to some horrid trap.

"A very nice lady is staying with us. She has children your age. Would you like to meet her?"

"Yes, sir," she said, her somber expression unaltered. Eleanor always obeyed but never showed any enthusiasm.

"You know you can call me Papa." He told her this almost every day. "I love you. I hope you know that."

Her brows furrowed as though he were speaking a foreign language.

He offered his hand. She stared at it for a moment before slowly volunteering hers. It always amazed him how the touch of his daughter blasted joy through his body. A younger version of Stratton, whose shallow cynicism was a product of arrogance and immaturity, would have never believed he could be so humbled and, at times, broken by a small child.

* * *

Just writing her children's names in her letter made Mary Alice homesick. She didn't dare tell them of the accident because it would worry them. Since the death of their beloved father, her children were overly concerned with the well-being of Mary Alice and their nursery servants, who formed their extended family. So, Mary Alice wrote of the beautiful place where she was staying that was filled with gurgling fountains and lovesick peacocks. It was how she might imagine King Foradora's estates. She concluded her letter with, *Please, ask Nurse to kiss each of you for me. I miss you dearly. Your affectionate mother.*

She heard someone clear his throat and glanced up.

Stratton waited at the door, holding the hand of a young girl who peered at Mary Alice with large gray eyes. Mary Alice sensed fear in their depths and in the way the girl clutched her doll tightly to her chest.

Stratton's smile appeared pained. He spoke with the soothing, slightly higher-pitched voice that adults often use with scared children. "Eleanor, dearest, this is my friend, er . . ." He paused, his eyes searching her face.

Mary Alice immediately perceived the problem—that silly game of disguise. "Mrs. Mary Alice," she finished. "You may call me that." She smiled encouragingly, but the girl's dour expression didn't budge.

"Dearest," Stratton said. "Can you curtsey for Mrs. Mary Alice?"

Panic crossed the girl's features. "I'm sorry!" she cried. "I'm forgetful." She executed a bob-like curtsey and then another.

Stratton caught Mary Alice's gaze. Mary Alice knew that look. She had cast it at enough strangers, pleading for understanding about Anna's behavior.

"I apologize that I can't return your lovely curtsey, for I've hurt my ankle." Mary Alice pointed to the comically huge bandage wound around her ankle. "And my head. Don't I look like a quiz?" She smiled again.

The girl scooted back as if Mary Alice might eat her. *Oh dear!*

Mary Alice tried another tactic. She held up her letter. "I was just writing to my children. I have a daughter your age. She loves dolls too. What is your doll's name?"

"Helandria." She spoke so quietly that she could barely be heard.

"Helandria," her father restated.

"That's a beautiful name," Mary Alice exclaimed. "Did you make it up?"

"Yes, ma'am."

"You have a wonderful imagination. You and my children would get along very well. Would you like to hear a secret?" Mary Alice beckoned with her finger.

Eleanor didn't move until Stratton knelt and whispered something to her. Mary Alice noticed how tenderly he touched his daughter.

Eleanor edged forward nervously, still wary.

"I have a doll too," Mary Alice whispered to her.

"G-grownups don't have dolls," Eleanor said.

"Well, I do. Her name is Marcela Misslemay, and she joins my children's dolls in our alliance against the evil bog lord."

Eleanor's brows drew down.

Mary Alice scooted closer to the mattress edge, as though importing a great secret to the girl. "You don't know about the evil bog lord?"

"No, ma'am."

"Well, he is a vile sort of gentleman, the kind you can imagine being exiled to a bog by good King Foradora. The evil bog lord's kingdom is filled with muddy, murky dungeons, vicious dragonflies, hideous trolls and ogres, poisonous flower fields, and mysterious castles hidden in a dark forest. When my children and I play, we take up the entire nursery. Would you care to play with me? For, you see, I'm rather lonely with no one to play with."

"You w-want to play with me?" the girl stammered.

"And Helandria, if she cares to join us?"

The girl's hand tightened on her old doll. Mary Alice realized she was drawing strength from it. "Yes, ma'am."

"Oh wonderful, but first I need one thing. One very, very important thing. Do you have another doll that you may lend me?"

"Can you think of a kind doll that would enjoy being Mrs. Mary Alice's friend?" Stratton brushed behind his daughter's ear a wisp of hair that had escaped her braid.

"And a doll for your papa? Perhaps a prince doll or even a dragon. My son pretends to be a kindhearted dragon who recently had his wings hurt by the evil bog lord."

Eleanor stared at her for a long time, eyes a little narrowed, as if waiting for Mary Alice to disappear or transform into a child-eating witch. "I have a prince doll," she began slowly. "I-I have a prince and many other dolls that my father gave me." She ran from the room, but then reappeared at the threshold a second later, her nervous expression back in place. "But . . . but . . . you really are going to tell the story to me, truly? I mean, you wouldn't say you would and then not?"

Why did the girl think Mary Alice would lie to her? "Of course, I will, my dearest. I'm delighted to play with you and Helandria."

Eleanor began backing away, like a skittish animal, before breaking into a run.

Mary Alice didn't know how to begin talking about what she had witnessed. She feared being presumptuous, having listened to too many people tell her what they thought was wrong with Anna and how to "fix" her. Her dear Anna appeared to have been born with her unique and magical mind; but Eleanor seemed like a normal child who had endured trauma that had stunted her childhood and destroyed her trust. From the way Stratton gently held his daughter and quietly encouraged her, Mary Alice knew whatever had happened occurred before the girl arrived here. Her heart hurt for Stratton as she watched him pace. She could see him working through his emotions. She would let him start the conversation when he was ready.

"How are your injuries?" he finally asked, his voice clipped and nervous.

"I believe the swelling on my ankle is down, although you would never know it from my bulbous bandage. And, sad to say, the old nob is as hard as ever." She tapped her head and chuckled, hoping to relax him a little.

"I'm glad," he said, and then turned quiet until his gaze came upon her correspondence. "May I send your letter?"

"Yes, please, but after you play dolls with us."

He slipped into the chair by the bed. "You have been very generous, but you don't have to play—"

"Good heavens, it's my holiday, and I desire to enjoy myself."

"I appreciate your kindness towards Eleanor. She . . ." He gazed down, again lapsing into a pained silence for several seconds.

Mary Alice wanted to embrace him, but all she could do was reach out and rest her fingers on his arm. "I can see that she has a sensitive and kind heart. And I can also see that you love her very, very much."

He nodded. "M-may I tell you something both painful and embarrassing?"

"You can tell me anything," she whispered.

"You can see that something is . . . *different* about Eleanor."

"And something is different about my dear Anna."

He began to tap his foot and then rose, visibly restless. "It's no secret of my affair with Eleanor's mother, Lady Radley, nor of the child allegedly conceived from our liaison. Eleanor was born when I was at war. I learned of her birth as a casual aside in a conversation with Wellington." While he spoke, he paced about, straightening a picture that hung from the molding and then rearranging the bottles and brushes on the commode, not looking at her all the while. "I doubted the child was mine, and even if she were, it would be hard to prove. I blamed her mother and assumed she and her husband would see after the child. After all, he was an earl and supported two known bastards of his own. I gave no further thought to the matter of my supposed daughter. You know the type of man I was."

"But you've changed."

He turned. "Have I?"

"Yes." She nodded. "Very much."

"Thank you." This appeared to please Stratton for a moment. Then he combed his fingers through his hair, and several errant strands fell onto his forehead. "A year ago, I received a curious bill shortly after the passing of my former lover. It was from a place called the Sowell Hospital. The proprietor, a Mr. Sowell, said that Lord Radley had requested that all further bills for the keep of Eleanor Stratton—yes, my name—be given to me, her true father."

He crossed to the window. Oscar had returned, his feathers folded up. He pecked dejectedly about the ground where the object of his desire had been that morning.

"The hospital was not more than four hours away, so I visited to clear up the matter," Stratton said. "As you can see, there is little doubt about the paternity of Eleanor. Same eyes, hair, face. And the institute . . . It was nothing more than a baby farm. Children treated like cattle, two to a cot. Babies were in boxes, flies buzzing about one that had died that morning."

Mary Alice swallowed her gasp. She had heard about these types of places in her charity work but, thank heavens, had never witnessed the horror. "Oh God, Stratton."

"Mr. Sowell defended his hospital's cruel treatment by saying that these were children of unholy unions, thus they were the devil's offspring. Their deaths meant nothing."

"He's the devil! He is!"

"I don't want to imagine Eleanor's prior existence. She doesn't respond to me or anyone except Helandria." He chuckled bitterly. "Now even I am perceiving the doll as real. Helandria was probably all Eleanor ever had." His voice cracked. He rubbed his mouth with shaking fingers. "And it's my fault. I did this out of my—"

"No!" Mary Alice wished she could rise from the bed and hold him. "You saved her. You have years to teach her to trust and love you."

"I don't know how. Nothing I do penetrates this protective wall she's built. And can you blame her?"

"Give her time and love."

He gave a bitter laugh. "I wish I had your faith. Every day is frustrating. I shouldn't say that. I—"

"I understand." She held his gaze, silently acknowledging his fears and trials that she knew too well. "Love is hard," she said. "Inside its wonder are many failings, moments you could have lived better, pain, and regret. Yet . . . it's all worth it."

He gripped the bedpost, still looking at her, his eyes vulnerable. She was struck by his handsomeness. But it wasn't his lovely face that caused her dizzying rush, but his lovely heart she was just coming to know.

Her entire face flushed. She fingered her letter and diverted the conversation. "Those poor children in that hospital."

He returned to the window and stared out. "The Sowell Hospital has since been taken over by a charity, and significant improvements have been made."

She studied his back. Stratton was gifted with broad shoulders. She remembered how handsome he'd appeared in his clothes before he left for the war—a trim, athletic Adonis. Now his shoulders were even more powerful, but slightly drooped and rounded, seeming to strain under an invisible weight.

"You," she whispered. "You are that charity." Her eyes watered, and she gazed heavenward.

God, save me from this man.

Eleanor appeared at the door. She clasped Helandria and two other dolls.

"This is Karianna." Eleanor came to Mary Alice's bedside and held up an auburn-haired doll in an indigo ball gown. "Do you like her? Or . . . or should I get another?" Eleanor studied the floor, not looking up for Mary Alice's reply.

"She's beautiful."

Mary Alice let her fingers linger reassuringly on Eleanor's arm as she accepted the doll. The girl lifted her head, and Mary Alice gave her an encouraging smile. Kindness had a paralyzing effect on Eleanor.

"Is that handsome gentleman doll for your father?" Mary Alice asked. "He will make a wonderful King Foradora."

"It's a prince doll," Eleanora said. "But I . . . I thought we could pretend."

"Excellent!" Stratton said. Mary Alice was happy to see him take his doll without hesitation or a patronizing smirk.

"Wise kings are much handier than mere princes at stamping out evil in the land and protecting the people," he assured his daughter. "And King Foradora adores Helandria and Karianna and will fight to the death to save them."

"Ah, but how will he find Helandria and Karianna?" Mary Alice asked. "For they are imprisoned in a dank, wet prison formed of impenetrable roots and guarded by a retinue of vicious trolls." She plumped a pillow and rested it on the edge of the mattress. "Let's pretend this is King Foradora's palace. It's a—"

"It's a cloud!" Eleanor burst out.

Stratton and Mary Alice exchanged surprised glances.

"It's a ship disguised as a cloud that sails the skies." Eleanor's gaze turned hazy, seeing inward to her imagination. "His soldiers view Bogland with telescopes, but… but they can't see what's underground. We need to free a bird . . . or . . . or a butterfly. Because the king doesn't know that the evil bog lord has built a secret army of enormous dragonflies, bees, and wasps to defeat him. Helandria and Karianna must get to him and tell him."

Mary Alice flashed Stratton a furtive smile, but he didn't see it. The man stared at his daughter, his lips parted in amazement.

Eleanor leaned Helandria toward Mary Alice's doll and feigned a whisper. "Don't cry, Karianna. I know a way out."

Karianna's doll hugged Helandria. "Oh, you are so smart and clever. You are my dearest friend."

Meanwhile, King Foradora hopped about on his cloud ship. "I love no others above Karianna and Helandria. I cannot rest until they are safe. I'm out of my wits with worry."

In the realm of fantasy, a different child emerged—the real Eleanor. She was intelligent, sensitive, and imaginative. And Stratton encouraged her in this safe, pretend world, showering Helandria with praise. The king promised to never lose his precious Helandria again, but keep her safe and love her. Mary Alice hoped that in some small way Eleanor understood that he was talking about her and not a fictional character.

Never in a hundred years would Mary Alice have expected Stratton to be an excellent father. But his eyes and manners were all tenderness around Eleanor as he played by her side.

Mary Alice's husband had loved his children fiercely, but had kept them at a distance, as he had been brought up. Mary Alice grew up in a smaller home with four siblings, two grandparents, and an aunt. No one had had any privacy, and they had constantly tripped over each other. But they hadn't imagined another way to live. Whenever she and her brothers and sisters had played, their mother or another loving relative had always been nearby, intervening in arguments or telling wondrous stories to calm overly excited children.

Mary Alice's mothering style had flummoxed Jonas. As a boy, he had been presented to his mother in the mornings and before dinner for inspection. His mother had rarely visited the nursery. Mary Alice, however, spent most of her time on the nursery floor, playing blocks or reading stories.

Stratton didn't fiddle with his watch or sigh with boredom at the childish play but kept his gaze trained on his daughter, invested in her world, as a small smile curved his lips. Once Eleanor shrieked with laughter, and Mary Alice detected unshed tears in Stratton's eyes. She knew those tears. They were the same she'd cried when Anna said her first word at age four: mama.

They played for an hour, and Mary Alice desperately wanted to continue, because Stratton and Eleanor were happy, but drowsiness rested like a heavy blanket on her mind. She struggled to keep her eyes open. At last, she had to recline against King Foradora's pillow.

"Helandria, I think Karianna must rest," Stratton said.

"But the butterfly hasn't come back!" Eleanor protested.

"I mean, Mrs. Mary Alice is tired," he clarified.

The animation drained from Eleanor's face as she emerged from her fantasy world. "Are you going to . . . Are you going to die?" she solemnly asked Mary Alice.

"No, love," Stratton assured her.

"It's just when you hit your head very, very hard, you may be tired for a few days," Mary Alice explained. "Do you mind terribly if I keep Karianna tonight, in case I get lonely? Can we play again in the morning? Please, oh, please."

Eleanor's brow furrowed. "You really want to play with me again?"

"Very much," Mary Alice assured her, but Eleanor appeared unconvinced.

"Come, love." Stratton whispered to his daughter. He scooped up Mary Alice's letter. "I'll send this to your children by an express." He walked to the door beside his daughter, carrying King Foradora and the missive.

Eleanor suddenly wheeled around. "Are your children . . . Are they very nice? They're not cruel to each other or . . . or hit?"

"They are wonderful, gentle children, like you," Mary Alice replied. "They would love to meet you. You must visit us. Perhaps spend a fortnight if your papa would kindly allow it. Would you like that?"

Eleanor bit the edge of her lip and drew Helandria closer. Then she surprised Mary Alice by taking a bold step forward and loudly saying, "Yes, ma'am."

"Then we shall plan on it." Stratton's smile lit his face.

As he guided his daughter away, he glanced over his shoulder and mouthed, "Thank you," to Mary Alice.

"You are very welcome," she whispered after he was gone. Now that her bed was empty, all the joy that had rung in the room evaporated. She laid back and rested her hand on the empty side of the bed and suddenly felt overwhelmingly lonely.

CHAPTER FOUR

Stratton watched as Eleanor returned King Foradora to his home on the shelf. His daughter had a designated space for every doll, except Helandria, after she finished playing with it. Stratton had been unkempt and indolent as a child, relying on the staff to keep his young life in order. In contrast, Eleanor maintained strict routines that the servants had learned not to correct else Eleanor would become fearful and withdraw even further. She woke up when light broke, washed her face, brushed her hair and teeth, made up her bed, and then sat quietly, whispering to Helandria as she waited for the nurse to arrive. Stratton loathed to think of the harsh discipline that had exacted such militaristic behavior.

His daughter set Helandria in her prized place on the bed. Eleanor's brows were furrowed in worried concentration as she straightened the doll's dress.

"What's the matter?" he asked gently, kneeling beside her. "You know you can tell your papa anything. Please look at me."

She obediently lifted her somber eyes to his face.

"You don't have to be afraid anymore," he said. "Do you understand? This"—he gestured around him—"is King Foradora's cloud ship. You'll always be safe here."

"Do . . . do you think . . . ." she began, clearly struggling with some internal battle. "Do you think Mrs. Mary Alice's children will like me?"

Her plaintive voice hurt his heart. "I assure you that they will adore you as I do."

"But . . . but how?" she cried.

He gently touched her cheek. She surprised him by not flinching, but she remained rigid. "Why would you say such a thing?"

"Because I'm naughty, dull-witted, and forget what I'm supposed to do." She said the words quickly, as if repeating something often said to her.

His immediate reaction was rage. Who had told her this? He wanted to beat them witless. But didn't he have himself to blame as well? After all, she had been left at the miserable Sowell Hospital all those years because he had never inquired about her welfare—until he received a bill for her keep. He would never forgive himself for that. "You are a brilliant, imaginative, sensitive, and kind-hearted girl," he said. "I don't care what anyone told you before. It was all lies. I'm a thousand-fold wiser and more powerful than they were. I love you and will never hurt you. Ever."

"Helandria said . . . She said . . ." Eleanor swayed nervously on her feet.

"What did she say, love?"

"She said that you were nice. She said I shouldn't be afraid of you."

He gazed at the ragged, cracked doll—his daughter's steadfast companion. At that moment, Helandria was as alive in his mind as in his daughter's. "I think Helandria is very wise."

He slowly edged closer until his arms lightly enfolded Eleanor. Then she surprised him by flinging her arms around his neck—a fumbling, awkward hug, as if trying something new and not knowing how it was done. He carefully drew her closer, until his body formed a protective shell over her smaller one.

"I will not leave you scared and alone in some bog land ever again," he whispered. "I promise."

* * *

Stratton desired to rush to Mary Alice and tell her the happy news of his breakthrough with Eleanor. Yet twice he passed her chamber to find the door closed, and he could hear no activity beyond the wood. Then he got waylaid by dinner. He had given up hope that he would speak to Mary Alice again that night when he passed her chamber on the way to his study and found her door was cracked, sending a shaft of gold light into the dark hall. He peeked through the opening and found her propped up on pillows. On the side table, rested Karianna, a plate of scones, a cup of tea, and a tallow candle that lit the volume of *Pride and Prejudice* open in her lap.

"What a conceited, arrogant man . . ." she murmured, and rather violently turned the page.

Stratton cleared his throat. "And you said I had improved today."

She glanced up with surprise. Then a welcoming smile curved her lips, which were powdered with crumbs from the scones. It set off an electric maelstrom inside him.

"No, no, I heartily approve of you," she said, "but certainly not this Darcy gent. What a haughty man. Nonetheless, I'm wildly intrigued by him. Surely he cannot remain so insufferable."

He crossed the room and drew up the chair beside the bed. "I thought you would enjoy the book."

She arched a playful brow and wiped the crumbs from her lips. "You know me so well?"

"No, I just thought to myself, 'What would a brilliant, amusing, witty, and beautiful lady enjoy reading?'"

"Of course, you did." She possessed a musical laugh. "And speaking of compliments—in this case, earnest and true ones—please give mine to your chef. Would you mind terribly if I stole him away from you?"

"Not at all. Just allow me to fetch my dueling pistols."

Again, that laugh. It did more to mollify his soul than any fine brandy.

He turned serious. "Thank you for playing with Eleanor this afternoon."

"Oh, Stratton." She reached over and squeezed his hand. "She's a kind, sensitive child, and you are an excellent father for her—patient, gentle, and protective. You will break this sad fortress she had to erect around herself."

He slid closer, the happy news bursting forth. "She let me hug her."

"That dear child!" Mary Alice interlaced her fingers through his. "I'm so very happy for you. She realizes she can trust you."

He nodded, unable to talk for the emotion pouring in.

Mary Alice read perfectly his silence. "I know how you feel. I've experienced it with my Anna."

He gazed down where her hand held his. In that moment, he could see them together with their children, forming a family. A perfect picture. This compassionate woman could sate his every desire as a wife, lover, and mother for their children. Without thinking, he drew her hand to his cheek and whispered, "Oh, Mary Alice."

She closed her eyes, releasing a low rush of breath. Slowly, he moved her fingers over his mouth, kissing them. She released a high whimper.

"I've dreamed of you," he whispered, feeling her soft skin against his lips. "I—"

"I told my husband on his deathbed that I would never love another man!" Her words rushed out, harsh and blunt. She drew her hand away and bowed her head. "I'm sorry."

He studied her. Her neck and cheeks were flushed, and she bit her bottom lip. Her breasts rose and fell with her shallow breaths. She was the picture of a woman whose defenses had been weakened. She wanted him too, maybe not with the deep longing that he harbored, but she wasn't immune to desire and, he realized, it scared her.

In earlier days, he might have taken it as a challenge to bed her. In fact, there were several old, shameful bets on White's books that he would seduce *certain* unnamed beautiful matrons and widows. But he couldn't stomach the idea of Mary Alice despising him again. She meant too much to him. And Eleanor clearly adored her. He couldn't afford the risk.

"I've come to care about you, but all I can offer is my friendship," she declared.

Friendship. The word thudded in his heart even as he knew this outcome was the best he could hope for. He tried to keep the disappointment from his face, but Mary Alice must have seen something there, because she added, "Special friends."

"That would please me very much."

"Thank you," she said quietly.

Her rejection was honorable and kind. And he should have expected it. Yet, it still stung. He fumbled to change the subject. "So, I wager you have read the infamous scene between Darcy and Elizabeth at the assembly."

She glanced at the book in her lap. "Please tell me that Elizabeth humbles Darcy. What an atrocious thing to say—not handsome enough to tempt him. Indeed!"

He waved his hand. "You needn't worry, for they all die in the end."

"What? Impossible." The tension in the air began to dissipate. She had the power to captivate, destroy, and rebuild him in a matter of minutes. Being in love was akin to floating on a tumultuous sea, helpless to the buffeting waves.

"A deadly typhoon strikes England and kills all the characters," he said.

"Not another typhoon. I've become so very bored with the typhoon ending. So many books must have one these days." Her lips trembled, but otherwise her face was dead earnest.

"Or maybe it was an erupting volcano. I forget, because I read the book so long ago. I just remember the end was very unsatisfying. I thought of jumping off a cliff or some such after closing the book."

"Hmm, let us see . . ." She picked up the final volume from the table and flipped to the last page.

He tried to wrest the book from her, but she yanked it away.

"That's cheating," he declared, his body tingling from accidentally brushing against her breasts.

"I'm not wasting my holiday reading a story with a terrible ending that will sink my spirits." However, even though the last page remained open before her, she didn't glance at it. A mischievous light glittered in her eye.

"Must I read the book for you to keep you from cheating?" He feigned a weary, put-upon voice.

"Please, then I can just rest on my pillow, sip tea, and eat glorious scones while you do all the work."

With a smirking smile on his face, he took both volumes from her. He returned the third volume to the table and flipped the first volume back to the infamous assembly scene where Darcy first meets and then insults Elizabeth.

Mary Alice didn't sip her tea or nibble the scones, but settled upon the mattress, turned her head on the pillow, and watched him read. The rain came again. Its ping mingled with the lulling hiss of the fire. He hardly knew what he read but continued on, scene after scene, just to keep her gazing at him with those eyes that glowed like dark amber. She finally drifted into sleep after Elizabeth and Jane returned from Netherfield. He remained by her bedside, the book resting on his leg, and watched her.

When she was with Eleanor and him, his life felt whole, as if she gathered all the loose parts of him and put him back together. Mingled with this realization was the bittersweet knowledge that he could never keep her. She would never lie in his bed or wake in his arms. But he would take whatever she was willing to give him to keep her near. So, he resigned himself to being her devoted friend, if that was what pleased her.

He kissed her gently on her cheek. A light brush. "Good night," he whispered.

She cuddled against the pillow and drowsily murmured, "I love you too."

The words sounded automatic, as though she had spoken them a thousand times. As much as he wanted her to love him, he knew she spoke to a dead husband who remained very much alive in her dreams.

* * *

The next day, Bogland extended over the entire mattress and included Mary Alice's pillows, a jewelry box, and furniture that Eleanor had removed from her dollhouse. The sensitive, imaginative child re-emerged from her shell into the world of fantasy. Hearing her delighted laughter made Mary Alice's motherly heart ache for the girl in a greedy way. Mary Alice had always assumed she would have more children, but when Jonas fell ill, the physician advised against "intimacies known between man and wife."

She could see that Stratton loved his daughter, but Mary Alice wondered if his love was enough. He was just one man. In Mary Alice's way of thinking, Eleanor needed a mother and a huge family to adore her and soothe the horrors of her early childhood—a family like Mary Alice's.

Stop! Get those thoughts out of your head!

Yet, even as Mary Alice tried to stay focused on the game, her mind continued to wander to unsafe thoughts of Eleanor as her very own. And Stratton as her—

No, no. Stratton can only be a friend.

However, he certainly hadn't *felt* like a friend when he kissed her hand the previous night. A wild tickle rushed over her skin and then between her legs, where it transformed into a throbbing desire. She had told herself that she would never physically love another man as she had Jonas. But clearly, the drive to mate was more potent than the rational mind. And her body felt starved to be touched again.

When Jonas had been healthy, they had enjoyed their frequent intimate time together. Once comfortable with the act, she'd craved it and often brazenly initiated their lovemaking, doing the little things that aroused her husband. She'd never felt more complete than in those moments after their lovemaking, when he'd held her to his pounding chest, his hair wet with sweat, and whispered that he loved her. Those memories haunted her at night. Alone in her bed, her body futilely yearned for a man who could never return to her in this life.

"Once Helandria chanted the magic words, the ugly beetle's body began to transform into King Foradora," Stratton said, pushing forward his doll. Stratton's body lightly brushed against Mary Alice, eliciting a tiny explosion inside her. She released a choked, tight hum. His head whipped around. She watched in embarrassment as his eyes darkened with understanding. He knew she desired him. The space between them throbbed like the hot, wet pulse between her legs.

"It's the king, Karianna!" Eleanor cried in Helandria's voice. "He's come to rescue us from this dungeon."

Mary Alice gripped her doll and stammered absently, "That's wonderful."

Eleanor continued to play, oblivious to the tension between the adults. Stratton lightly rested his hand atop Mary Alice's, letting his thumb stroke her skin.

"My goodness, no one invited us to play," Francesca said from where she and Olivia stood just inside the threshold.

Oh Lord! Mary Alice hadn't heard them enter. She scooted away from Stratton. "W-would you like to play? We need an evil bog lord. You would be perfect." She hoped her small joke concealed her embarrassment at being caught.

But what exactly had they caught her doing? Nothing, truly. It was just her guilty conscience causing her body to heat with shame.

"Don't listen to her," Francesca said with a casual wave of her hand to Eleanor. The girl's shoulders slumped at the attention, and her face resumed its nervous, fearful visage.

"Perhaps we can play later," Stratton said quickly. "Come, Eleanor."

Eleanor seized Helandria and scurried from the room. Stratton followed her, shooting Mary Alice a farewell glance over his shoulder.

"I do believe we were interrupting something," Francesca said after father and daughter were out of earshot. Her voice dripped with knowing.

Mary Alice pretended not to understand her meaning. "We were merely playing a game with his daughter."

"Might I suggest sending the dear little one to her nurse before tearing each other's clothes off," Francesca said.

"Please don't say that," Mary Alice protested. "You're wrong. And it's not a laughing matter."

"But it's obvious that one of the most handsome men in England is madly in love with you," Francesca said. "And you're not impartial to him. Ah, don't look at me that way."

"It's Stratton!" Mary Alice cried. "A man I have spent years despising."

"You said he changed," Olivia reminded in a non-scolding manner.

Mary Alice retrieved the jewelry box that had been a muskrat's home, closed it, and set it on the side table. "Yes, he has. If I have any feelings for Stratton, it is because. . ." She faltered, not wanting to articulate her embarrassing thoughts.

But Francesca wouldn't let it go. "It is because why?"

"I miss being loved!" Mary Alice blurted. "I miss a man's touch. I miss holding him and . . . and . . . *things*! But I cannot and will not give in to these desires arising from my weakness."

"Weakness?" Francesca sat on the edge of the bed. "My dear, you are still very young. Your feelings are entirely natural. Why not marry again? Don't be so hard on yourself."

"And to be honest, you don't have to marry." Olivia crossed to the window and drew back a curtain, flooding the room with rich afternoon light. "You could enjoy a little holiday dalliance. You're not a blushing maiden but a widow. No one in Society would whisper a word."

Oscar strutted by the glass, his glorious feathers spread. He shook them as if to say, *Look at me! Look at me!*

"It's not honorable," Mary Alice protested. "An affair born of pure desire cheapens my love for Jonas. Don't you understand? I truly loved my husband in a profound, deep way."

Her friends exchanged annoyed glances.

"Oh dear," Mary Alice said. "I didn't mean to imply that you didn't love your husbands as much as I loved mine. I . . . I . . . You see, I simply can't take a lover. Any relations I share with a man must mean something beyond our physical intimacy. It must be honorable. And I told Jonas that I could never love another. So, you see, it's all hopeless."

"Do you think Jonas wouldn't have wanted your happiness?" Olivia used that maddeningly patronizing tone of someone trying to sound reasonable to an irrational person. As if they knew better than Mary Alice. How could her friends not understand this simple problem?

"I have three children!" Mary Alice said, her distress surfacing. "What man could love another man's children as much as his own? What if they didn't like Stratton in turn? What if he took me away from them? And once we married, what if he changed and reverted to the old Stratton? What if he . . . he died . . . I can't . . . I can't bear that pain again." She covered her face with her hands.

Francesca drew Mary Alice into her arms. "Hush now," she whispered. "Let us consider some other, more hopeful courses. What if you were very happy? What if Stratton made a wonderful father to your children? What if he outlived you?"

"Please don't talk that way." Mary Alice pulled away. "I will not marry or . . . enjoy a dalliance with another man. Say no more on the matter. I see no course but to continue our holiday as planned. We must leave as soon as may be."

"But your head!" Francesca exclaimed. "And your foot! You shouldn't leave that bed. Not for days and days."

"They are both better," Mary Alice assured her. "I can walk with some assistance."

Francesca wagged her finger. "Ah, but remember our carriage is still very badly damaged."

"We shall hire another," Mary Alice said. "I'm sure the nearest village possesses some kind of contraption that can drive the few miles to our destination."

"Why, dearest, should we hire a carriage when we have a perfectly good damaged one?" Francesca reasoned.

Mary Alice opened her mouth to protest, then stopped. Her gaze flicked suspiciously between her friends. "Oh, I see," she said slowly. It didn't take a huge mental leap, but a mere hop, to discern that gentlemen were involved in her friends' reluctance to leave.

"I, for one, find the views here spectacular." Francesca gestured to the window. Oscar was still outside in resplendent courtship form. "And the chef…"

"Ooh, yes, yes, the food!" Olivia gushed. "Simply delicious."

"And the gentlemen?" Mary Alice asked. "Are they delicious, as well?"

Francesca hiked a brow, and her lips moved into position to deliver a finishing retort. Mary Alice realized she was going to pay dearly for her little witticism.

"Why don't you take a nibble and find out for yourself?" Francesca suggested.

CHAPTER FIVE

Stratton noticed that something about Mary Alice had changed after the day her friends interrupted their playing. The shift was tiny and probably perceivable only to him. She continued to laugh and tease and come so close to him as to spark his annoying fantasies of sharing their lives together. But then she always sensed when she had wandered into emotionally dangerous territory. Her smile would remain intact but lose its glow, and she would draw her arms about herself. He knew that she was trying to protect herself, and he couldn't fault her. But the times when she was unguarded and lost in the moment, she was the easiest person he had ever known. He didn't have to work so hard around her. Their conversation and laughter effortlessly flowed forth. He hadn't considered himself in gloomy spirits, certainly not to the degree he'd felt them after coming back from the war, but being around Mary Alice energized him with joy.

He was greedy for her and her magic. In his mind, they were living as broken pieces, but together, they and their families could become whole again. Yet he had lived long enough to know that some dreams would remain elusive, and trying to catch them would only cause them to vanish into thin air.

Although she kept him at a distance, she brought Eleanor closer. Every day that they played Bogland on Mary Alice's bed, a little more of Eleanor emerged. He was beginning to see the true girl hidden beneath the fear and emotional scars. He wouldn't dare endanger that bond forming between Eleanor and Mary Alice by foolishly admitting his dreams. So, he kept his feelings tamped down as, day by day, he watched Mary Alice recover. Soon she would leave them. He could no longer keep her caged, and she would fly away from them. He positively panicked when he and Eleanor came to visit Mary Alice and found her out of bed and limping about the chamber in a lavender gown of half mourning. Her head bandage was gone, replaced with a cap. When she saw them, a joyous smile that devastated his heart stole across her lips.

"I simply couldn't spend another minute in bed." She turned her gaze to Eleanor. "Would you care to give me a tour of your lovely home? Mind you, I adore secret places and hidden passages. Do you have any of those?"

"I . . . I can show you the workrooms!" Eleanor suggested. "They aren't secret places but they have many interesting things."

"Visiting scientists and artists use the workrooms," Stratton explained. "However, you have just recovered from an accident. I wouldn't—"

"Oh, stop with that good-sense talk," Mary Alice protested. "I'm as stubborn as I am reckless. I would love to see the workrooms." She winked at Eleanor. "I've been cooped up for so very long that I would be perfectly happy to visit the stables and dairy too. Lead the way, dear Eleanor."

He told himself that he was only being gentlemanly when he held her arm as they toured the estate and cottages, but in truth he just wanted to hold her because he knew she would leave soon. He carefully watched her gait, looking for any signs of fatigue or pain as they ventured through the gardens. Eleanor clutched her doll and walked ahead, nervously glancing back to ensure that Mary Alice was well.

He requested that all the fountains be turned on in her honor. The sunlight sparkled on the arc jets of water. Colorful parakeets and canaries darted about in the aviaries.

"This is magnificent," Mary Alice said, holding out her hand to let the water splash upon her palm.

"It's actually just a large, overgrown scientific experiment. Water in its forms—liquid, solid, gas—fascinates me."

"How do you control the pressure for the water?" Mary Alice asked. "Yes, yes, I know ladies shouldn't find such matters fascinating, but I do. Especially with the exciting advancement in steam engines. I tell my father that soon a steam engine will do the work of a dozen men in his old factory. He doesn't believe me. But I am right, of course." She flashed him a devilish smile.

"Of course, you are. Without a doubt." He chuckled. "Shall I show you the future plans for my fountains for your approval?" He gestured to the first of a series of brick outbuildings at the garden's edge.

"Please." Mary Alice smiled.

He led her across the grass and then shoved open an old outbuilding door that had swollen with the rain. He let Mary Alice and Eleanor enter before him.

"Ah, we have it all to ourselves today." He left the door open, letting the sunlight pour into the otherwise dark workroom. Three rows of tables ran down the room, and shelves covered the walls. Scattered about were glass beakers, weight scales, burners, and books. The future plans of his hydraulics were open on the first table, anchored at the corners with iron weights.

"You see the extent of my foolish ambition," he quipped, gesturing to the drawings. "What did Macbeth say about ambition?"

Before he could answer his own question, Mary Alice quietly quoted, "'I have no spur to prick the sides of my intent, but only vaulting ambition, which o'er leaps itself and falls on the other.'" She ran her fingers over the plans. "Anna would adore these sketches."

"She's interested in pipes and plumbing?" he asked incredulously, without thinking.

Mary Alice didn't take offense. She shook her head. "She's interested in drawings like blueprints and plans. It's hard to explain, but she can picture very complicated things in her head."

"She sounds brilliant."

"She is, in certain ways. Not in others." Mary Alice glanced about the workroom. "And you fund all this work?"

"I try to advance the good work of scientists and scholars. People with far greater minds than mine."

She lifted a brow. "I suspect you are more clever than you give yourself credit for."

The way the light caused her eyes to glow like dark amber arrested his thoughts. He wanted to kiss her. The pull was as strong and natural as Newton's gravity.

There was a crash of glass, and Eleanor gasped. Stratton whirled around, thinking she had been hurt. "Eleanor!" He rushed to the back worktables.

The child clutched her doll to her chest. Shards of glass were strewn at her feet. "I'm sorry!" Eleanor cried. "Don't whip me! I'm sorry! I wasn't holding Helandria tight enough, and we accidentally hit it. I'm sorry. Please."

"Love, I would never whip you. Never. Look," he said, motioning to the shelves where more beakers and vials sat. "There are many, many more. This one won't be missed."

His words didn't soothe his daughter. She backed fearfully away from him, tears in her eyes. "I didn't mean for it to happen. Truly."

Mary Alice came to her side. "Eleanor, it was an accident," she said gently. "No one is upset with you."

"I'm sorry!" Eleanor cried, unconvinced. Tears rolled down her cheeks.

Stratton panicked. Things had been going so well. He grabbed a small element sample from a box containing other elements and metals and held it before her in his palm.

"What do you think this is?" he asked to distract her.

She wiped her eyes and looked at the tiny orange fragment in his hand. "A . . . a small rock?"

"Yes, but it's a very special rock. It's an element. Do you know what an element is?"

She sniffed and shook her head.

"Why don't you keep this element?" he said. "I'll tell you and Helandria all about them while we picnic. I was very sneaky and didn't tell you, but I asked that a picnic be set up at a special hiding place, in honor of Mrs. Mary Alice's love of secret passages and such. Come."

* * *

Mary Alice let Stratton lead her and Eleanor through a greenery maze of boxwoods and trees, then under an arch built of trailing vines and into a small oval glade. In the center of this private garden stood a lovely female statue with downcast eyes. Water flowed quietly from her head and down her body, forming a veil of water.

"It is my favorite fountain," he told them. "But I keep it hidden, showing it only to my favorite people."

A blanket had been laid on the grass and set with china, silver, cloth-covered baskets containing sandwiches, and corked jars of wine and lemonade. Mary Alice glanced at Stratton and smiled approvingly at the small detail of including a doll-size china plate for Helandria.

After helping Mary Alice sit, Stratton stretched out on the blanket beside her. Something about how he gazed at her, his eyes squinting in the sun, his head propped on his elbow and his long legs extended, made her self-conscious. She focused on pouring drinks and passing along baskets so she wouldn't look at how his tailored trousers fit his muscular legs or the bulge at his crotch.

He drew a biscuit from a basket and held it up. "Do you know what makes this biscuit?" he asked Eleanor.

She dutifully answered, "Flour, eggs, sugar, and milk."

He turned the biscuit, observing it. "Yes, those are the basic ingredients of a biscuit," he said. "Elements are the ingredients of the earth. If you were to break the earth apart to its smallest units—its core ingredients—you would find it's composed of elements. Some are solid, some are gas. Most are too small to see. They have names like oxygen, nitrogen, and carbon. We don't know all the ingredients yet. That's what some of my scientist guests are trying to discover in the workshops."

Stratton patiently explained basic science to Eleanor in terms a child could understand. Watching them interact, Mary Alice realized what a good papa meant to a child. Her children still had their uncle and maternal grandfather, but neither lived with them. They didn't share meals, or flow in and out of their lives in the course of a day. She wondered how Little Jonas would fare without a proper father to guide him. Was she enough for him, or did boys need a strong paternal role model?

"Have you discovered an element, Papa?" Mary Alice was pleased to hear Eleanor call Stratton Papa.

Stratton shook his head. "No, but perhaps you will someday."

"I'm not intelligent enough."

"Yes, you are!" Stratton assured her. "You are extremely intelligent. Don't ever think otherwise."

Every little thing about Stratton was weakening Mary Alice's resolve. She reflected on her friends' suggestions that Jonas would only want her happiness. And how could loving a good, honorable man disgrace her husband's memory? As one part of her ventured into the scary idea, another, stronger part held tight to Jonas's memory. She wasn't ready to give him up yet. She wished she could crawl again into the safe black crêpe of deep mourning where she didn't have to make decisions.

"Colonel Stratton! Colonel Stratton!" An alarmed liveried footman sprinted around the trees. "A letter has come by express."

Stratton's expression turned grave. He rose to receive the letter. Mary Alice watched him read the address with a furrowed brow. Her heart sped. How easily she panicked since Jonas's death. How readily she expected terrible news. Then a grin cracked Stratton's serious countenance. "Ah, 'tis a letter from your children."

Mary Alice was ashamed at how greedily she tore the missive from his hands. She broke the wax with her fingernail. Her children's handwriting, adorned with corrections from their nurse, filled the pages. Homesickness hit like a punch to her heart.

"Do you miss your children?" Eleanor asked. Mary Alice could see she was curious about her family.

"Very much. Why don't you help me read their letters? Come."

Eleanor snuggled beside her, the closest the child had ever got to her. Mary Alice put an arm around the girl, savoring her scent and soft hair. Oh, she dearly wanted this child to be her own. But then, Mary Alice also desired to love and keep all the world's abandoned and mistreated children. Jonas once remarked that she married him only so she could set up an orphanage in his ancestral home. Mary Alice had denied his claim but pointed out that it was a good idea and thanked him for suggesting it to her.

"Ah, Caroline writes that her little brother is annoying her." Mary Alice pointed to the letter. "He hid a huge, hairy spider in her bed. Oh dear!"

"Brothers are impish creatures, Eleanor." Stratton winked at his daughter.

"Ah, but see," Mary Alice continued, "Little Jonas is angry at his sister because she killed his pet spider, Ignatius, who had gotten loose and wandered, without Little Jonas's help of course, into his sister's bed. However, he seems to have emerged quickly from his arachnid mourning period because he writes that he has found hundreds of tadpole eggs at the park and brought them home in a bucket. Oh no!"

Stratton sipped his red wine. "You may find that you have a frog or toad infestation when you return to London."

"Hmm, how would you feel if I took up permanent residence in my rooms here?" Mary Alice joked to Stratton. "I'll be very quiet. You won't notice me at all."

Poor Eleanor didn't perceive the jest. "I would love if you lived with us."

Mary Alice felt horrible. She needed to explain that she had her own home and family who needed her, but that would just hurt Eleanor. She would feel further rejected.

Mary Alice was spared the pain of letting Eleanor down when Stratton cried, "Good God!"

Mary Alice glanced down. Unthinkingly, she had shifted the letters, bringing Anna's picture of Bogland to the top. She had completed the map in Mary Alice's absence. "This is Anna's work."

He drew the picture from her lap. "She is quite the artist, or cartographer. This is incredible. The detail, the precision. How old is Anna?"

"Five," Mary Alice gushed, proud of her unique daughter.

"Five!" He gave an incredulous bark of laughter. "She's brilliant."

Mary Alice's eyes wetted as she watched him study the picture with nothing but honest awe on his face. A man who sponsored England's greatest artists, scientists, and scholars admired her daughter's work!

"It's Bogland as she sees it." Mary Alice pointed to the left side of the map, where a great dragon clutched a tiny island in the sea. "This is Dragon Island. In our version, Jonas has his own dragon kingdom in the middle of the monster ocean." She moved her finger upward on the map to a hot air balloon floating above Bogland. "Caroline's doll, Caro, lived in a hot air balloon until the bog lord shot her with a rock and she tumbled from the basket. Now she's trapped with her friend Marcela Misslemay in the swampy, underworld dungeon."

"Helandria would love to play with Caro in a hot air balloon," Eleanor said wistfully. "Helandria is so much more adventuresome than I am."

"Pray, why don't you write Caroline a letter?" Mary Alice suggested. "She would adore a correspondence with a girl her own age. You see how her brother torments her by putting spiders in her bed. Tell her about Helandria."

"Will Caroline like me?"

"Of course. She's very kind, but she's been quite sad since her papa died. She needs a good friend."

Eleanor's lips trembled. Mary Alice could see the girl was nervous but also longing to have friends, like a normal child.

"Please write to her for me," Mary Alice continued to persuade the girl. "It will make her so happy. Tell her about Helandria and your papa's lovely fountains."

"I will!" Eleanor cried. "I will! Shall I do it now?"

Mary Alice smiled. "If it pleases you."

"Yes! Don't . . . don't send your letter until I'm done. Please."

"Of course not."

Eleanor edged away and then broke into a run.

"How do you do it?" Stratton asked.

Mary Alice tilted her head. "What do you mean?"

"In a matter of days, you've done more for Eleanor than my staff and I have done in months."

Mary Alice leaned closer to him. "Here's my magical secret. Deep, deep inside, I'm still a little girl. I've never truly grown up." She laughed and gazed upward, enjoying the sun and breeze on her cheeks.

He shook his head. "You're a wonder. But I want to return to the topic of Anna." He picked up Anna's map again. "I'm in great awe of her talent."

"She is a special girl. She's difficult to know, her mind is so different from mine. She can be very frustrating without meaning to be. My father always said that I was the most impatient girl in the world. But Anna taught me patience."

He studied her face. "May I ask what happened that day in the park when Anna ran into the water?"

Mary Alice shrugged. "Anna can't tolerate loud noises and people. It's all too much for her."

"I have a lot in common with Anna." He took another sip of wine. "The day I carried you from the carriage accident, you mentioned not putting Anna in an asylum."

"I did?"

"Yes, you said that you didn't want Anna to be put away."

Mary Alice didn't remember what had happened in those hours directly after the accident. What had she said? She felt too vulnerable to gaze at him as she spoke of those dark times when Anna was a toddling child. Instead, she focused on twirling a piece of grass around her fingers. "The family physician said that he had seen Anna's kind before. He said she would be an unresponsive simpleton her entire life, that there was no hope, and it would be best to put her in an asylum. But I . . . I couldn't imagine my child alone and at the mercy of strangers who didn't love her."

Stratton edged closer, resting a tentative hand on her arm. She didn't withdraw from him, letting his strength reassure her. She felt very alone at times even though an army of family, friends, and servants surrounded her. Every day she had to muster the strength to put on a strong front, to be both the mother and the father. She was so tired inside.

"But . . . I knew there was something within her," she continued. "An intelligence. I saw it in her eyes. I became highly upset with the physician. You don't want to know what I said. I have a fierce temper when someone hurts one of my children. Genghis Khan only wished he could be as barbaric."

"As you should," he approved.

"I had expected Jonas to try and calm me. He was always composed. We were quite the opposite in temperaments. But I had never seen him so upset. He growled at the physician to get out, that our family no longer required his services." She gazed at the marble woman with the watery veil but didn't see her. Jonas filled her mind. At least what she remembered of him. Every day, more of him slipped away, no matter how hard she tried to keep him. The tide of time was merciless, eroding the shore of memories. "I had always been in love with my husband—madly in love. But I fell even more in love with him that day. Again, and again, he was my hero."

"The late duke was a good man."

"He was," she choked. She had to stop speaking of Jonas, or the tears would come again. So, she changed the subject to Stratton. "What changed you? You are not the man I was spoony for all those years ago."

"The war." He didn't look at her, leaving her to study his profile. "The day I gazed out onto a single field strewn with thousands of dead men. Thousands. Until then, I had believed all the words about honor and breeding. But at that moment, I realized they were just words. Shadows, really. They weren't real. Nothing I had believed was real. I couldn't feel the victory over Napoleon. Everything became empty in my mind. It's hard to explain. It's as if all meaning broke apart, and I had nothing. Just gray oblivion. For months, I literally felt nothing." He drew up his sleeve, revealing two thin scars running parallel across his arm. "I wish I could say this was a war injury, but it's where I cut my arm with a penknife and watched the blood drip just to reassure myself that I was still capable of feeling."

"Oh, Stratton." She let her finger trail gently along his scars. "I'm sorry. I remember the numbness after Jonas died. Grief came in waves. Sometimes I felt everything. Sometimes nothing. Just numb."

His hand traveled up her arm to her face, brushing back the curls that blew across her cheek. She couldn't deny that she drank in the sensation of him and didn't resist when he drew her against his chest. He was both power and vulnerability. Hardness tempered with tenderness.

"When I returned to England," he continued quietly, "my sister and our old friends immediately tried to put me back in my old role, but I couldn't even go through the motions of my previous life. Their lives are stupid games. They care about the most preposterous, trivial matters in their tiny worlds. But they made me feel again, so I must give them credit. I felt hate. I hated who I once was. I hated how I had treated people, how I'd thought myself some god and everyone else existed for my pleasure. I was like a poison in this world. I went from feeling nothing to living in rage. The smallest thing could explode inside me. And I couldn't get away from the anger, from myself."

"Did finding Eleanor ease this anger?"

"It was gone before then."

"Time healed it?"

"No." He gently drew her chin up. "I saw you again."

"Me?"

"Yes." His voice was a low whisper. His eyes searched her face. She didn't know what he found there, but a small, wistful smile curled his lips. "I saw you again after all those years. You may not recall me lurking in the corners of the Royal Academy, hoping you didn't notice me. But I *saw* you. You were so beautiful that day, a contrast to the gray cold outside. I can't explain this, but pure love and true kindness seem to radiate from you. You are like a merciful Madonna portrait come to life. And that's probably why I . . . I had loved you all along."

"Nathaniel." The tears were back. She couldn't stop them. "Why do you want to break my heart again? Why must you make this so hard for me?"

His mouth waited mere inches from hers. She just had to lean in the smallest bit, letting gravity do its work, and their lips met. Touching, but not moving. Although he remained still, she could feel his body straining for her, enveloped in the same raw yearning that throbbed in her. He was letting her choose what happened next. A small voice in her mind screamed for her to run away as she opened her mouth, letting their tongues tentatively touch. He moaned, a sound of ecstasy and frustration that cut through her weak restraint. Her hands rose to his head, tipping off his hat and knotting in his hair as she deepened their kiss.

He didn't kiss like her husband had. It didn't shock or cause her any guilt. She felt strangely like a virgin again, exploring unknown terrain. He cradled her as he lowered her, his lips never leaving hers. His hand slowly, slowly slid down her throat and finally found her breast. He cupped it, moving his finger over the fabric covering her nipple. Her body, untouched for two years, was ravenous, charging ahead of her rational mind. He moved his thumb faster as she whimpered into his mouth.

His hardness thrust against her thigh. She instinctually reached for his hardened sex, enticing him with her hand. He ripped his mouth free and whispered her name. She undid a button on his pantaloons, reached inside, and wrapped her hand around his hot erection. His face crumpled with the acute pleasure. It didn't take her long to discover what he enjoyed. His happiness became her happiness.

Then he gently removed her hand, and his mouth claimed hers again. She felt his fingers trace up her legs to her wet, swollen sex. He stopped and waited. In his silence, he was asking her another question—one she knew she should deny, but couldn't. All that consumed her thoughts was his cock sinking deep into her, satisfying the need that kept her up at night, writhing and frustrated. She instinctively opened her legs a little wider, encouraging his touch.

His lips moved from her mouth, across her cheek to her ear. "I love you," he whispered. "Give me a chance to make up for the pain I've caused you. To show how grateful I am that you have come into my life." She couldn't answer, because his finger flicked across her mound, sending shudders over her. He didn't to try to slow the pleasure, but stoked it higher. Her pent-up climax was coming too fast, too powerful.

In a graceful motion, he slid atop her, his thighs sinking between hers. His cock pressed against her vagina. This was wrong. Quite wrong. She should stop, but instead, she arched her back as she whispered his name in welcome.

She heard a high, girlish, surprised gasp, and her eyes flew open. Stratton leaped back, pulling her with him, shielding her with his body as he tugged down her skirt.

Mary Alice gazed beyond his arm. Eleanor stood, her mouth hanging open, a piece of stationery in her hand. "I . . . I forgot Helandria."

Mary Alice sat up and tried to put on a semblance of normality as shame washed over her. Stratton discreetly buttoned his pantaloons.

Oh God, what have I done?

"Helandria was here . . . waiting for you," Mary Alice said with a nervous little laugh.

Eleanor began to sway on her feet, her lips moving as if she wanted to say something but was afraid.

"Dearest, Mrs. Mary Alice and I were . . . You see, I care for her very much . . . and . . ." Stratton faltered. He gazed at Mary Alice, desperate.

"And I care for him," she continued, but like Stratton, she found there was no fitting explanation for a child's tender ears.

"Are you going to m-marry Papa?" Eleanor stammered. "Will I have a f-f-family?"

The radiant hope in Eleanor's face pierced Mary Alice's heart. She couldn't refuse the girl, who had known so much pain and loneliness. She didn't have to look at Stratton to feel his despair. His traumatized daughter, who had just recently dared to peek out from under her shell of fear, who struggled to trust, was about to have her heart crushed again. She couldn't hurt that dear, courageous child. Mary Alice would rather maim herself.

"Yes," Mary Alice whispered. "Yes."

* * *

An hour later, Stratton walked Eleanor back to her chamber. He had offered his hand, and she'd slowly slid her small, delicate one against his palm. His heart ached for his emotionally frail daughter. Away from Mary Alice, Eleanor's face returned to its nervous visage. He wished he could reassure her of a family and Mary Alice's tender love. He wanted to believe that Mary Alice really desired to marry him, that this brilliant, sun-filled day would be the happiest one in his life. But the stiff, polite smile Mary Alice had worn for the remainder of their picnic confirmed his sad suspicions—she had consented to marry him only for Eleanor's sake. Oddly, her little deceit to please his daughter only caused him to love her more, even as he knew he had to set her free.

At the door, Eleanor stopped and tightened her clasp on Helandria. The doll's empty, glass eyes stared blankly at Stratton. "Is Mary Alice really going to marry you? Will she really be my mother?"

He hadn't the strength for the dreaded discussion yet. Nor could he lie. He knelt and drew her close, something she hadn't allowed him to do before Mary Alice had arrived.

"You're going to be very happy," he whispered. "I promise." But he didn't know how. He had been a natural rogue and competent soldier, but fatherhood confounded him. It required more strength, wisdom, and resilience than he possessed.

He left Eleanor in her chamber. As he was closing the door, he heard her talking to her dolls. "We're going to have a new family. We must be nice so they'll like us."

He wished he had the magical powers to make the world perfect for his daughter. He wished he could keep Mary Alice by his side, merging their struggling families together.

He wished many things but knew wishes were flimsy, heartbreaking things.

The door to Mary Alice's chamber was closed. He told himself to give her privacy, but he couldn't bear the torture of unknowing. He tapped the door and whispered her name. He heard footsteps approaching on the other side of the wood, and then the door swung open. Her skin was ashen, her eyes, though now dry, were glassy and red-rimmed from crying.

When he stepped inside, she reached for him, pressing her head into his chest. "I don't know what to do. I shouldn't have said yes."

He'd known this would be her answer. Yet he hadn't realized how much he had clung to the smallest hope until it shattered. His throat burned as his hand caressed her back, drawing her closer. "Hush," he whispered. "Don't trouble yourself."

"I didn't want to hurt that child. I couldn't . . . And Jonas . . . I feel so horrible." She pulled away, wiping her eyes.

"No," he whispered. He wanted to continue to hold her, even if what she said cut to the marrow of his bones.

She walked to the window. The deep hues of the coming twilight gathered around the trees. She said nothing for several long seconds, leaving him to study the line of her bowed head.

"Do you truly want to marry me?" she asked finally.

How could he answer that question? Would *yes, more than the world* make the situation worse? He gripped the bedpost. "I desire you to be my wife. But more than all this, I don't want to cause you further pain. I love you."

She released a hiccup-like sob, which she covered with her hand.

"Mary Alice, I know you didn't want to hurt Eleanor, and that is why—"

"Don't you understand?" she cried. "I'm falling in love with you!"

Stratton heard her words. He saw how her scared eyes searched his face. But he couldn't make sense of it all, like a hard blow that the mind registers before the pain floods in. Except this time, he felt no ache, only the dawning of joy.

"Mary Alice." Her name rushed on his breath. He stepped to take her into his embrace, but she gently pushed him away.

"This wasn't supposed to happen. I feel like . . . I'm unfaithful to my husband. But he's . . ." She squeezed her eyes shut. "He's dead." Tears flowed from under her lashes.

He knelt down before her and took her hands. "You still love him because you're an honorable lady. I would never hope to replace his memory. How can I? He was a fine gentleman. I will do my best to be a good father to your children. I will love them as you have come to love Eleanor."

Her body convulsed with tears. "But you're not Jonas," she choked.

"I know," he whispered. "But I'll do my best to be a good, loyal husband to you."

She lowered to her knees and rested her cheek on his shoulder. He was afraid to move, to do anything that would break this fragile, beautiful moment. She might love him, but she still wasn't his. He couldn't trap her or force her to remain. He knew that the harder he tried, the sooner she would slip from his grasp. So, he remained quiet, giving his heart's fate over to her.

She raised their intertwined hands to her lips and kissed his fingers. "Will you allow me time? My world has turned too fast. I need to think. I want . . . I want to leave with Francesca and go back to my family."

He tried to hide his disappointment, but she must have discerned it. She leaned in and brushed his lips. "Please," she murmured. The innocent kiss shot straight to his sex, where the frustration of their interrupted lovemaking lingered. He didn't want her to leave. He wanted to take her to his bed and make love through the night, and then, in the morning decide which chambers her children would occupy and how best to merge their domestic staffs. The one thing he didn't want to do was wait. He had been waiting for years.

"When can Eleanor and I see you again?" He knew mentioning Eleanor was underhanded because she wouldn't refuse his daughter. "We can come to London."

"May I have a fortnight?"

"Of course."

"Nathaniel." She held his face between her hands, forcing him to gaze into her eyes, shiny from tears. "No . . . no matter what happens, please rest assured that I would never desert Eleanor. She will always find welcome in my heart and home."

"Bless you," he whispered.

CHAPTER SIX

Mary Alice waved from the carriage window at Eleanor, Stratton, Olivia, and Mr. Stirling. Olivia appeared happier than Mary Alice had ever seen her. Despite the sadness of her own departure, she was thrilled for Olivia and her new match. Mary Alice wished her love for Stratton could be that uncomplicated and not so fraught with fear and guilt. Stratton kept his hand protectively on Eleanor's shoulder as his daughter waved at the retreating carriage—her face both sad and hopeful. Mary Alice wanted to break into sobs but restrained herself in front of Francesca and Stratton's servant, Fiona, whom he'd insisted should accompany them.

Mary Alice continued to watch Eleanor and Stratton until the carriage drove out the gate and a brick wall separated them. She rubbed the letter in her lap from Eleanor to Caroline. The missive mentioned nothing of the impending marriage because Stratton had asked his daughter not to say anything until Mary Alice had spoken with her own children.

A gloomy loneliness washed over her as soon as she lost sight of the last chimneystack of Rose Heath behind a tree. Even Francesca seemed despondent. So, the ladies traveled south in silence, each lost in her own troubled thoughts.

Francesca had decided to remain in York, so at the coaching inn near the York Minster, where they changed horses, Mary Alice kissed Francesca's cheek and whispered as a farewell, "I'm sorry." She didn't know what had happened between Francesca and Sir Greyville, but whatever it was, it had broken her friend's heart. Poor Francesca's lovely holiday had gone awry for her. Now, instead of smiles, there were tears.

Mary Alice and Fiona continued south. Mary Alice felt almost the same as she had in the months after the acute grief of Jonas's death had subsided. The world lost its vibrancy and time slowed to a trickle. She missed Stratton. She missed the strength of his presence, as well as how his touch electrified her body. This love was so different from her first time with Jonas, when all she had experienced was naïve excitement. She'd had no idea what marriage meant. Now she did. She couldn't dismiss the shame that she was betraying Jonas in the worst way, by possibly letting Stratton usurp Jonas's role as father.

Acknowledging that her husband was dead and wouldn't know only plunged her deeper into sadness. She didn't want to believe that Jonas was truly gone. She preferred to believe that he was still with her, watching over her and the children from behind an invisible curtain that divided the living from the dead. But she didn't want to hurt Eleanor either. The girl was just learning to trust. The dear child might think Mary Alice was rejecting her, not her father. Every path Mary Alice might choose involved guilt and pain.

Only when she opened the nursery door in her London home did her melancholy break. Caroline and Little Jonas rushed to embrace her as Anna walked in excited circles around them. Caroline and Little Jonas eagerly talked over each other, telling Mary Alice everything she had missed. She pieced together from their collective accounts that the butler had coerced Little Jonas into letting his tadpoles live in a bucket by the mews instead her son's chamber. Now numerous, ugly toads were hopping about. But he assured her that only one had been squished by a horse. Caroline had lost another front tooth and couldn't eat apples, and Anna had built an impressive tower from rolled pieces of newspaper.

Mary Alice told them about her accident, showing them the plastered gash on her head. They were quite impressed.

"And I have a special letter to Caroline from a wonderful girl I've met named Eleanor. She adores dolls and possesses a wonderful imagination. Sadly, she spent years and years in a dark place like the bog lord's dungeon."

"Is she well?" Caroline asked, concerned. Her eldest child worried over others, as well as homeless kittens and tired hack horses.

"A wonderful gentleman named Colonel Stratton rescued her. He is really her father, but no one knew."

"He's like a prince in a story!" Caroline exclaimed.

Mary Alice remained mum about this wonderful prince. She thought it best to settle in for a few days before she brought up the subject of her possible marriage. Normality had finally returned to her children's lives after losing their father and witnessing their mother's distraught mourning. She needed to be careful about how she brought up the issue of Stratton, especially if the children had formed the wrong impression of him after Anna's episode in the park. But Eleanor was another story. "Eleanor has agreed to visit in a fortnight. Do you think you could be Eleanor's special friends?"

"She can be my friend," Caroline assured her mother. "My dearest, dearest friend."

"Why don't we make special gifts for her?" Mary Alice suggested. "Maybe you can draw her one of your wonderful pictures, Anna. I know she would cherish it."

"I shall draw a great bridge!" Anna cried, and ran faster in her circles.

"I'll make her a sword for slaying ogres," Little Jonas announced. "I'll paint blood and innards on it and . . ." His face quickly fell. "But she's a girl."

"I think she would like a bloody ogre sword," Mary Alice assured him.

Little Jonas lit up at the idea that a real girl would be impressed with a bloody ogre sword.

"I think I'll really like Eleanor," he concluded. "She sounds much better than Caroline."

* * *

Mary Alice enjoyed tea in the nursery with the children and then changed into a comfortable robe and closed herself into Jonas's chamber. She lay on her side in his bed, drawing her knees up, studying the miniature of him that she held. She had spent so many wondrous nights in this bed, when the air was sweetly perfumed and candlelight danced on their naked bodies as they made love. Now the room was silent and felt hollow. The mattress had been changed, the invalid chair and medicine bottles removed. Otherwise, the chamber remained as Jonas had kept it when he was well.

"Help me, Jonas," she whispered to his likeness.

No portrait had captured the spirit of Jonas as she knew him. Like this miniature, they made him appear too regal and somber—that was the Jonas the world had seen. But she wanted to remember the man with the tender, dark eyes who'd held her in this bed.

"I don't know what to do. I love you, Jonas. But I love him too. And dear Eleanor. You would adore her. I could be her mother. She needs one. Tell me what I should do. Please."

Jonas just stared silently back from his frame.

* * *

Mary Alice continued to put off telling her children about Stratton. She kept finding excuses, such as *Oh, but they are so joyous making gifts*, or *But they need to concentrate on their studies*. Two weeks slipped away in this manner, until it was the day before Stratton and Eleanor's arrival. She had run out of time.

After dreading the conversation all morning, she went to the nursery after lessons. Little Jonas and his wooden dragon, Fiery Boy, were playing with the bloody ogre sword, while Caroline finished her embroidery—the name Eleanor decorated with an ivy vine. Anna sat cross-legged, drawing on paper on a portable desk.

Mary Alice fingered her wedding ring. Apprehension churned in her belly. The moment felt wrong. In fact, the entire idea of the marriage suddenly seemed wrong. Perhaps that was why she didn't want to speak of it. Deep down, she knew it wouldn't work.

Nonetheless, the words that had been swirling in her head for two weeks finally burst forth. "How would you feel if Mama remarried?"

The children stared at her with blank eyes, as if she had uttered something in Mandarin.

"But you are already married," Caroline pointed out after several seconds. "To Papa."

Mary Alice should have stopped then. She could tell they weren't receptive. But she foolishly forged on. "Papa...is...Papa is dead, so I can marry again." She tried to brighten her tone. Instead, her words came out brittle and forced. "You can have a new papa."

"What?" Little Jonas asked, confused.

"If I remarry, you can have a new papa."

The terrible realization dawned on his young face. "No!" Jonas screamed. Tears spurted from his eyes. "I already have a papa. You can't marry someone else! You can't!"

Mary Alice watched, horrified, as Jonas threw his beloved Fiery Boy at the chimneypiece. The wooden dragon shattered, and its pieces rained onto the floor. Anna, alarmed by the sound, covered her ears and started crying.

"You can't remarry because I hate him," Jonas shouted.

"You haven't even met this new gentleman," Mary Alice said, trying to remain calm. She sat by Anna, but her presence only seemed to agitate the upset girl.

"I hate him!" Jonas flung himself onto the floor before her and hid his crying face.

"Little Jonas, please look at me," Mary Alice implored him.

"No!"

"Darlings, please. I haven't agreed to marry this gentleman. I just...." How could Mary Alice explain that she hadn't meant to fall in love? Nor had she intended to hurt her children. She rubbed her hand up and down her son's back, trying to soothe him.

"Don't touch me!" he wailed and rolled away from her.

"Why would you want another husband?" Caroline demanded.

"Because when you're an adult, you get lonely for another adult," Mary Alice said. It wasn't the best explanation, but she couldn't tell her young children that she missed intimately knowing a man, that sometimes she needed someone to lean on and kiss her scrapes. "I . . . I get lonely."

"But you have us," Caroline wailed. Her eyes, so like her papa's, brimmed with tears. "How can you be lonely if you have us?"

"Of course," Mary Alice said, feeling broken. How could she explain to her children that, while she loved them more than herself, they weren't enough? She was a grown woman with needs.

She looked heavenward. Perhaps this was Jonas's reply to her question. "I'm sorry," she whispered. "I won't marry. Come, my darlings. Stop your tears. You needn't worry. You will have no new papa."

CHAPTER SEVEN

Stratton pulled the bell at Mary Alice's door. Eleanor gazed up nervously at the enormous mansion on Grosvenor Square, with its massive columns and numerous rows of windows. The building rose so high that the top windows were lost in the low London clouds.

"Does . . . does Mrs. Mary Alice live *here*?" She held Helandria to her chest, as she did whenever she was afraid. The child had been happy for the entire trip and had taken great delight in her grand hotel chamber adjacent to her father's. But his heart sank as apprehension and fear returned to her features.

He couldn't admit it, but his nerves were on edge too. He feared this visit as much as he anticipated it. Had Mary Alice changed her mind? Had her passion been the product of a holiday fever?

"Do you want to know a secret?" He bent until he could whisper in Eleanor's ear. "Mrs. Mary Alice is truly a duchess."

Eleanor's eyes widened with alarm. "They won't like me." She tried to edge away, but he kept his hand firmly on her back.

"You know Mrs. Mary Alice adores you. Remember, don't mention the marriage to her children. It's supposed to be a surprise to them." He had kept up the little lie he and Mary Alice devised to shield Eleanor from the truth that Mary Alice might not become her mother after all.

The door opened, and a regal butler peered down his nose at them. Eleanor tried to bolt, but Stratton picked her up and swung her onto his hip.

"Colonel Stratton and his daughter, Eleanor, wish to wait upon Her Grace and her family," Stratton said.

The butler studied Eleanor and then winked at her, all the while maintaining his imperious countenance. "I believe your visit has been the cause of much excitement and anticipation. Please come in." He stepped aside and let them enter.

"Eleanor!" Mary Alice hurried down the grand curving staircase.

Stratton knew he loved Mary Alice, but he hadn't been prepared for the boyish excitement that rushed through him at seeing her again. When she wrapped her arms around both him and Eleanor, it felt akin to returning home from a long journey.

"Come, the children are upstairs," Mary Alice said. "They are so glad you've come, Eleanor. They've spoken of little else since I told them you were coming." Still holding Eleanor, Stratton followed Mary Alice up the stairs. In her own home, her warm personality flowed forth. He loved how, when she glanced over her shoulder to talk to Eleanor, her smile appeared to glow like it had its own light, radiating in her eyes and throughout her whole body. At the same time, he realized that he couldn't possibly have won this amazing lady's love.

She opened the door to the nursery. "My darlings," she announced. "Eleanor is here."

Mary Alice's children didn't form a quiet line to wait and be introduced, as Stratton's nurse had posed him and his siblings when visitors called. Little Jonas ran forward without a greeting, wielding a sword with painted blood. "I made you a sword to kill ogres," he shouted excitedly at Eleanor.

The eldest, Caroline, bumped the boy out of the way. "You're scaring her," she told her brother. "She doesn't want a stupid sword." She performed an elegant curtsey. "I'm Caroline. It's so wonderful to meet you. Is that Helandria? Mama told me many wonderful things about her."

Stratton was grateful that Caroline made no note of Helandria's ragged appearance.

As all this transpired, the younger daughter, Anna, circled them, holding a picture. "I drew a bridge," she said over and over.

Stratton set Eleanor down and Caroline took her hand. "Come, let me show you and Helandria my dollhouse. I readied it for you."

Eleanor glanced nervously over her shoulder at Stratton. He smiled and nodded his encouragement.

Caroline shot her brother a nasty look when he tried to follow the girls. "We don't want to play with your ugly sword."

The boy appeared crestfallen. "But you said that she would like an ogre sword," he told his mother.

Stratton repressed his smile. Life must be trying for the only son in a house of females. "That's a fine sword, young man," Stratton declared.

Little Jonas's face lit up. "I know! I—wait!" His eyes narrowed. "Aren't you the man in the park who upset Mama?"

"It was a misunderstanding," Mary Alice quickly interceded. "I believe you and your sister have a few of those. I recall one earlier this morning concerning the outcome of a certain card game."

Little Jonas remained unconvinced.

"Why don't you show Colonel Stratton your sword?" Mary Alice used a meaningful tone that made her polite words a command.

Jonas reluctantly handed the toy weapon over. "It's not real blood," he said. "Mama wouldn't let me use pig's blood."

"Those poor, rational, put-upon mamas always spoil the fun," Stratton said with a straight face, and then winked at Mary Alice.

"It's what I wake up wondering every morning," Mary Alice quipped. "How can I spoil everyone's fun today?"

Stratton chuckled. He cleanly sliced the air with the sword, careful of Anna, who still circled, holding her picture.

"Do you know how to sword-fight?" Little Jonas asked, impressed.

"I know a few moves." Stratton executed a lunge at an invisible opponent.

Little Jonas's eyes became as big and shiny as newly minted sovereign coins.

"Colonel Stratton fought with the Duke of Wellington," his mother explained.

Clearly, this little nugget changed Little Jonas's assessment of Stratton from mere *fine fellow* to *god-like*. He ogled Stratton, his mouth dropping open in awe.

"Would you like to learn to fence?" Stratton asked.

"Uh-huh," the boy managed.

"Please say, 'Yes, sir,'" Mary Alice reminded him, and then glanced an apology at Stratton. "I'm sorry."

Stratton shook his head. "Think nothing of it."

He had been rather ashamed of his Machiavellian ambitions to win over Mary Alice's children, but to his relief, he found that he truly liked Little Jonas. He was a rough-and-tumble young fellow with a big heart. And Little Jonas clearly enjoyed the relief from the female companionship of his sisters and mother, who didn't appreciate the finer things, such as bloody ogre swords.

Mary Alice had drifted over to the dollhouse where Caroline and Eleanor were engrossed in play. He could hear Eleanor's excited voice say, "Let's pretend that King Foradora is having a ball, and a witch puts a spell on the bog lord, turning him into a lady so he can secretly attend."

"You are so very clever," Caroline exclaimed.

Mary Alice flashed Stratton a smile that said she was pleased the girls played so well together.

Stratton felt a bump on his leg and glanced down. Anna held up her picture. "I drew this," she said. "It's a bridge. And I made that tower." She pointed to a shelf where a complex tower structure stood.

He knelt and examined her drawing, which was rendered with a draftsman's precision. "You are extremely talented. Do you know that?"

Her expression didn't register the compliment. Anna only stared, not at his face, but at his cravat.

He studied the drawing a moment longer, looking at the symmetry and shapes. Then it struck him that this quaint little girl perceived the world in lines and geometry. "Why did you use arches?" he asked, although he already knew the answer.

"Watch." She pointed to the timepiece hanging on his waistcoat.

"Yes." He unfastened it from its chain and handed it to her.

She flipped the top and studied it. "Arches are stronger."

"That's right. Who taught you that?"

She furrowed her brow, her eyes focused on his watch. "Nurse only teaches me reading and writing." She abruptly turned and walked away, taking the watch with her.

"Anna, love," Mary Alice said, "that's Colonel Stratton's watch. You should give it back to him."

"Let her keep it," he said. "It's stuffed with gears and other wondrous things." He had a feeling his watch would be returned to him disassembled. This wouldn't bother him at all. In fact, he wished one day he could show Anna the mechanics of his garden hydraulics. He wagered the girl would find them fascinating.

He returned his attention to Little Jonas. "To fence, you must first put your feet like so…"

Stratton had envisioned a short first visit to Mary Alice's home, a little awkward, with stiff, polite conversation. Instead, he lost track of time as he taught his overly enthusiastic fencing student, who was intent on killing imaginary ogres whose blood spurt everywhere.

Anna did, indeed, disassemble his watch and then began drawing. She approached with her new picture, walking in front of Little Jonas as he violently swung his sword. She clearly perceived no danger. She had drawn a series of circles: the circle of his watch gears, the circle of the window on the top of their house, the spire of St. Paul's Cathedral. What fascinated him most—and there were many amazing things about this child—was her precise memory. She seemed to remember everything in minute detail. He wished he could spend a day with this child, learning more about her brilliant, unique mind.

The butler and nurse entered carrying two teapots on a silver service platter—a large china pot and a doll-sized one. "How does Miss Helandria prefer her tea?" the butler inquired.

"Cakes!" Little Jonas dropped his sword and hurried to the table, where the butler set down the tray.

As the children gathered excitedly about the confections and tea, Stratton crossed to Mary Alice. Silently, he took her hand. She glanced to where their fingers entwined and then at his face. The sadness in her eyes told him everything—she would reject him.

* * *

226 | SUSANNA IVES

Mary Alice led Stratton to her parlor, a cozy room decorated in shades of cream and sienna. Comfortable sofas and chairs, perfect for reading or sewing, were arranged by a warm hearth. The servants hadn't straightened the room from when Mary Alice had fussed about in it earlier that morning. The blanket still hung, unfolded, on the armrest, and Jonas's miniature rested atop a pin box on the side table.

She rubbed her arms, feeling self-conscious. "This is my parlor."

Stratton stepped closer and gently cupped her cheek in his large palm. As at Rose Heath, her body surged at his touch. Time and distance had done nothing to dampen her attraction.

"I've missed you," he said. He kissed her mouth, a slow, gentle kiss. She closed her eyes and released a whimper of frustration and yearning.

He trailed kisses to her ear, where he whispered, "And I know that you've decided against this marriage."

She had to turn, putting her back to him. She didn't have the strength just yet to look at him and speak the horrible words. "I dreaded telling you."

She heard him release a low breath of disappointment. "I understand."

"But I didn't expect the children to warm so readily to you today. I see how Little Jonas worships you. He requires a good gentleman to teach him how to be the man he needs to be. And I can see how Caroline adores Eleanor. I . . . I thought I was so sure that our marriage wouldn't work. And in a way, I found it a relief. But then I saw you again and . . . I love you. I love you even more now than I did at Rose Heath."

He placed his hands on her arms and slowly spun her around. "What do *you* want, Mary Alice?"

Jonas's miniature rested on the pin box, watching them with his painted eyes.

She studied Stratton's face, which was filled with concern and love. How could he be so unselfish, so patient as she toyed with his heart because of her own fears? "I'm sorry," she cried. "I know I'm hurting you. And that's the last thing that I desire to do. I'm just very confused and scared."

He kissed her cheek. Her breasts brushed against his chest, sending a hot tingle to her sex. Again, he asked, "What do you want?"

Him.

She wanted him. She wanted to love him and be loved. She was tired of the internal war of guilt and shame that consumed her. In a fast, almost violent motion, she placed her hand behind his head, drawing him to her lips. She unabashedly pressed against his body. Her aggressive overture didn't dismay him or turn him away.

What she was doing was rash, but she was tired of being caged by responsibility, sorrow, and her own rigid ideals. When she'd told Jonas she would never love another, she hadn't really known what that meant. When he had been slowly dying before her, she hadn't conceived that her broken heart would heal enough to open again. Yet, she had fallen in love again and with the same recklessness and determination of her youth. She loved Stratton and would instinctively come to him, despite any obstacle.

Stratton hungrily kissed her as he lowered her onto the sofa's cushions. He caressed her breast through her layers of clothes. His lips were still on hers as his hands drifted from her breasts and pulled up her skirts, finding her sex, wet and wanting. His fingers danced upon her as his mouth drank in her muffled moans of pleasure. In a graceful motion, he slid atop her. She released a sigh, and her body rose to welcome him inside.

"I love you," he whispered, studying her face.

"And I love you."

They paused, taking in the magnitude of the moment. She was an honorable woman who wouldn't take a lover but a husband. He was an honorable man now who wouldn't make love to a woman he didn't intend to marry. They knew that more than their bodies were meeting, they were giving their essences to one another—all their love, hopes, fears, and hurt. The complicated wonder of love. From this moment, their lives would be as entwined as their bodies.

She combed back the hair that had fallen over his forehead and then let her fingers trail down his cheekbone and the edge of his jaw. He was hers now. They belonged to each other, and there was no going back.

His mouth descended onto hers again as he began to move. She arched her back, driving him deeper. She noticed what gave him pleasure and increased it, as he did for her. Their love turned frenzied, until she cried out, her thighs trembling, grinding against him, milking him for pleasure. He threw his head back and groaned through gnashed teeth as his liquid heat spilled into her.

Then he lowered himself upon her and held her close, his head resting on her breast. For a minute, they were lulled by the sweet afterglow of love. But he felt her anxiety when it returned.

"Don't worry, my love," he whispered.

"I'll have to tell the children soon. They may get upset again."

"Should we speak to them together?"

She shook her head. "Maybe you should visit one more time so they can become more familiar with you. And then I'll tell them. Oh, Nathaniel . . ."

He raised his head. "What is it, my love?"

"We will be happy together, won't we?"

He kissed her. "I will do everything in my power to be a proper husband."

"And I will be a good . . . good wife." She bit back her tears. She certainly didn't feel like a good wife as Jonas looked on with his painted eyes.

* * *

After her lady's maid left that night, Mary Alice changed out of her shift and donned Jonas's favorite of her nightdresses. It had lain folded at the bottom of her commode for more than two years.

She opened the door to Jonas's adjoining chamber and crossed to his bed, but no lover waited for her there anymore. She sat on the edge of the mattress and held his miniature. She couldn't see his painted face in the darkness, but she caressed the glass frame. "I'm going to marry him," she whispered aloud. A tear slid down her cheek. "I love him. I didn't want to fall in love, but I did. Oh, Jonas, don't think poorly of me. He will make a wonderful father to our children. And our little boy . . . He needs a man to guide him. Please understand. Please."

She waited, hoping for a sign, as she had for many days and nights, something to let her know that Jonas was still near her somehow.

All she received was silence.

"Can you hear me where you are? Can you see me?"

Was he truly gone? Had all her beseeching and prayers to him reached no heaven? She couldn't accept that every part of him had ended when he died. It hurt too much. She wanted to believe that his beautiful soul continued on in an afterlife.

"I'm sorry, my dear. I must keep on living and loving. I hope that, wherever you are, you can forgive me."

* * *

Eleanor passed the evening at the hotel praising everything about Caroline. She was infatuated with her future stepsister. She wanted to dress like Caroline, talk like her, and play the same games.

"Caroline is a wonderful girl, but so are you, Eleanor," Stratton reminded her when he came to her bedside to say good night. "I adore you as you are. And so does Helandria." He gave her favorite doll a little pat.

Her face clouded at the idea that she didn't need to be someone else to be loved. He wished his little girl could miraculously acquire confidence overnight, but he knew that wasn't realistic. So, every day he would work to assure Eleanor of her specialness.

He knelt and kissed her cheek, savoring the smell of her skin. "Good night, my dearest," he whispered. "Your papa loves you."

He rose and removed the candle burning at the bedside table. He had almost reached the door when he heard her softly say, "Papa."

He turned to her. "Yes?"

"I . . . I love you."

He was too emotional to speak. He returned to the bed to hug this tiny, brave girl who had given his life so much meaning.

"I love you," she said again. "And Mrs. Mary Alice. And I'm going to love Caroline, Anna, and Little Jonas too."

He closed his eyes and thanked whatever forgiving god had blessed such an undeserving man with a precious child and the love of a magnificent woman. He vowed that he would live the rest of his life trying to be worthy of their love.

CHAPTER EIGHT

The next morning, Stratton strolled out of the hotel, holding both Helandria and Eleanor, as his daughter finished a cream-filled scone. Her falling crumbs attracted a metallic blue and green pigeon that began to follow them. The persistent bird delighted Eleanor. Her giggles made Stratton smile. He gazed at the bustling scene on the street. His younger self wouldn't have had the time to notice the people and places around him, too sunk in his own world and petty ambitions. Now he felt truly awake. As he strolled to Mary Alice's home to formally ask her to marry him, he experienced a profound sense of well-being he'd never felt before

However, the feeling proved to be short-lived. As he turned into Grosvenor Square, he sensed something was very wrong. The door to Mary Alice's house was flung open and household servants were scurrying in and out.

Mary Alice's distraught voice rang in the air, "Anna! Anna! Where are you? Answer me! Please!"

Oh damn, he muttered to himself. He set Eleanor down and clasped her hand. They dashed across to the square.

Mary Alice stood by the iron railing, gripping Little Jonas's and Caroline's hands. She wore a pastel violet morning dress but no cap, coat, or gloves. "I know that you've just searched the attics, but please search them again!" she cried to a servant.

Stratton touched Mary Alice's taut back, and she jumped. She released her children's hands and whipped around. Her eyes were dilated with panic.

"Nathaniel! I can't find Anna! I can't find her! She's been missing all morning. We've . . ." She pressed her trembling fingers to her mouth. "We've searched the house and streets. But . . . but . . . what if something happened to her?"

Stratton drew her into his arms. He could feel the tension crackling through her body. "What happened?"

"She just left," Mary Alice cried into his shoulder. "A servant saw her in the hall, and then later the door was open and Anna was gone. But we keep the door locked!"

He didn't think for a minute a lock could stop Anna.

He stepped back and looked Mary Alice straight in the eyes. "Listen, we are going to find her," he said in a deep, resolute way.

She shook her head. "She won't come to anyone but me. Oh, Nathaniel, what if someone hurts her? She doesn't understand people or perceive danger."

"Don't give in to those dark thoughts. We will find her," Stratton growled. He surveyed the square, taking in the chaotic situation. Female servants dashed between houses, calling for Anna. Footmen raced from the square in the direction of Hyde Park.

"We should search in pairs," he boomed in his military voice. "That way, when she is found, you can send the other to fetch Her Grace."

He knelt before the children. "I need you to stay with the duchess. You must tell her reassuring things and not to worry. Can you do that?"

"Yes, sir," Caroline said, taking her mother's hand again. But Eleanor remained silent, her features rigid with fear.

"I'm not staying here!" Little Jonas announced. "I'm going to find Anna."

"Little Jonas, please," Mary Alice begged. "Don't be difficult. Not now."

"I can find her!" Little Jonas insisted. Stratton realized that Little Jonas would only further upset his mother if he stayed. He saw himself as a brave knight, galloping out to face the danger.

"Then you're coming with me." Stratton gestured to the boy.

"Nathaniel, no!" Mary Alice protested.

"Let him go," Stratton said. "I'll keep a close watch on him."

"Please, Mama!" Little Jonas pleaded.

She studied her little boy. Stratton could see on her face the internal struggle to keep her son close and safe, or allow him to venture into manhood. She raised her eyes to Stratton's. "Very well," she quietly conceded.

The boy followed Stratton as he strode to the center of the square.

"What do we do?" Little Jonas asked.

"We think like Anna," Stratton replied. He pivoted on his heel, taking in the square, seeing it as Anna might—all shapes. He noticed the straight line the iron railings made down the left walk. It didn't break at the other corner but continued to the next row of houses.

"Come," Stratton murmured. He followed the line into the blocks of Mayfair homes, always keeping the paling to his left. About a half mile passed in this tidy fashion until they reached a busy intersection. Here, Anna would have gotten flustered.

What would she have done?

He gazed up and down the street. The railing had ended, and every storefront was different. No consistency. People crowded the walks, and coaches and wagons clogged the streets. All the clean lines were blurred.

"What do we do now?" Little Jonas asked, distressed.

"We remain calm and think. Can you do that?"

"Yes, sir." Little Jonas put on a stoic face, but his lips trembled.

Stratton headed north until they came to three streets flowing together, all the traffic merging into a knot of noise, carriages, horses, and people. No, she would not have passed this way. He swung around and headed in the opposite direction.

Now his heart thundered. She could have easily taken this road straight into the notorious St. Giles rookery. He hoped he was wrong about her direction and that she had headed to Hyde Park, and that some of Mary Alice's servants had found her there.

Stratton asked shopkeepers lounging outside their doors if they had seen a girl of Anna's description. He received negative replies until, at last, a wine merchant reported that such a girl had tripped a man delivering barrels of wine half an hour earlier. The merchant said the rude girl kept walking, not paying attention to the merchant's wife, who'd demanded an apology.

Stratton and Jonas quickened their pace to a jog. They passed the outskirts of wealthy west London and moved closer to the heart of the old city, where the neighborhood rapidly degraded. Rotting buildings and grimy gutters lined the road. The place reeked of human and animal urine and feces. Derelicts were slumped on the walks and against storefronts.

"Stay close to me, Little Jonas," he ordered.

"D-do you think Anna went in there?" Stratton could hear the fear in the boy's voice.

"God, I hope not." Stratton studied the chaotic scene. Ragmen and vendors, shouting out their filthy wares, clogged the road and walks. "No, she couldn't see the lines anymore. She wouldn't have come here."

Stratton rubbed his temples and tried to tamp down his own panic. Where was this child? "Let's turn back," he advised.

"But you said—"

"I know what I said, but I was wrong. Sometimes people are wrong."

Tears welled in Little Jonas's eyes. His brave façade was breaking apart. "Will someone hurt Anna?"

"No!" Stratton lied, because admitting that he didn't know would only further terrify the child.

Stratton turned and jogged up the street again, this time on the opposite walk. He passed a meandering lane that cut through the streets. He'd noticed the lane before but had decided the broken wheelbarrow upturned at the entrance would have discouraged Anna. This time he stopped. A cold prickle crawled up his back. He took several steps toward the alley and noticed something he had missed the first time. Between the buildings, rising on either side of the narrow footpath, he could make out the spire of St. Paul's Cathedral.

"This way!" Stratton gestured to Little Jonas. Stratton ran as fast as he could, still keeping the boy close behind him. The narrow lane curved and wound around buildings and small squares. All the while, the cathedral spire remained in sight. Stratton apologized to people he accidentally brushed against or alarmed as he hurried past.

Then he began to hear them. Screams!

"That's Anna!" Little Jonas shouted.

Stratton and Little Jonas rushed into a small crowd. The people formed a semicircle around Anna. She was curled on the ground beside a brick wall, screaming and pounding the pavers with her hands. A kindly old woman tried to comfort the flailing girl, but every time she touched the child, she only stoked Anna's hysterics.

"This is my daughter," Stratton boomed. "She becomes panic-stricken in crowds. I'm here now and will return her safely home. Please continue with your day. I will take care of matters."

He knelt beside the hysterical girl, careful not to touch her. "I assure you that she will be fine," he told the crowd, which was reluctant to leave.

"She's my sister," Little Jonas shouted. "And I'm a duke. I order you to leave us."

"Please." Stratton tried to soften the boy's foolish words. "If we give the child some quiet, she will calm down. Thank you for your concern and assistance."

Slowly, the crowd dispersed, glancing back worriedly as they ambled away.

"Anna," Little Jonas said. "It's me, your brother. Why did you run away?"

Anna screamed and struck the brick wall with her bloodied fist.

Stratton rested his finger on his lips, hushing Little Jonas.

He and the boy sat in silence, guarding Anna as her fit played out. Slowly, her internal storm subsided until she lay limp, her cheek on the ground, her small chest rising and falling with her slowing breaths. Stratton removed the pin on his cravat—a simple gold circle—and held it before Anna. He watched as her eyes focused on the pin. He slowly turned it, letting the light reflecting off the metal enthrall her.

"Anna," he said in a low, quiet voice. "You're going to follow Little Jonas and me home now. Do you understand?"

She nodded.

* * *

Mary Alice paced about Grosvenor Square. She had her servants knock on neighbors' doors and check their ground floors and mews. Caroline followed Stratton's order to hold her mama's hand and tell her not to worry, but Caroline was a sheltered girl who didn't know what evils lurked in the streets. But Eleanor knew. She had turned silent again and clutched Helandria tight. Mary Alice couldn't muster the motherly strength to tell her that all would be well, because it might not be.

A footman sprinted around the corner. Mary Alice released a cry and rushed to meet him. "Did you find her? Did you find her?"

"No, Your Grace, but a watchman in the park said . . . " The boy swallowed. "He said an unknown girl had drowned this morning and that you should see the coroner."

"What?" Mary Alice whispered, the words not making sense at first. "Please, please, no!" Tears flooded her eyes. "Jonas, help me," she cried. "It can't be her. Let it not be her. Not my child."

"Mama!"

Mary Alice wheeled around at her son's voice. He was running toward her. "We found her! We found Anna! The colonel and I found her!"

Then Anna strolled into the square, Stratton protectively behind her. Mary Alice's knees buckled under her. She grabbed the fence railing and forced herself to stay upright.

"Mama," Anna said, as if nothing were amiss.

Hot tears streamed down Mary Alice's face. "My child." With shaking legs, she hurried to Anna and embraced her, not caring that Anna tensed at her touch.

"I was so worried, darling," Mary Alice wept. "You scared Mama."

"I'm sorry," Anna said matter-of-factly. "I didn't mean to upset you."

"We decided to go on a stroll because there are so many fascinating things in London to observe," Stratton explained in calm tones. "But then we became lost. And when some kind, concerned people wanted to help us, we became scared and had to rest on the ground. That's how we became dirty."

"Oh, thank God. A child drowned in the park today and I thought . . . Oh, Nathaniel. I was so scared. I've never been more scared in my life." She pressed herself against his chest.

"There now," he whispered, trailing his hand down her back. "We are well. We are going to be a strong, happy family. We'll take special care of each other so we don't become lost ever again."

"I love you," Mary Alice cried. "I love you so much."

"Are you going to marry my mama?" Little Jonas asked Stratton. "Because you told those people that Anna is your daughter."

"Yes," Stratton said quietly. "I love your mother. I want to be with her, and with you, for the rest of my life. Would you, Caroline, and Anna accept me as your stepfather? I know I can never replace your true father. He was a great man, like you will be one day soon, Little Jonas. But I will love you as my own."

Mary Alice held her breath, fearing their reactions.

"Then you can teach me to fence!" was Little Jonas's enthusiastic response.

Caroline hugged Eleanor and jumped up and down on her tiptoes "We can share a room! Then we can play with our dolls all day!"

Mary Alice broke into laughter of relief and joy. Then an intense sensation enveloped her. She couldn't explain it, but she knew Jonas was present. She felt him like a ghost inside her heart He came with no resentment or anger, only love. "Thank you, Jonas," she whispered. "Thank you."

–THE END–

Dear Reader,

We had so much fun the first time around with *Dukes in Disguise* that we decided to do it again. This time for the duchesses. It's a joy and privilege to work with such amazing women as Grace Burrowes and Emily Greenwood. They are as supportive and thoughtful as they are wonderful writers. I hope our enthusiasm for these stories and our friendship infuses these novella pages.

If you would like to read more of my work, please check out my new Victorian romance *Frail*. I have excerpted the first scenes for your reading pleasure. Find more information about *Frail* at:
susannaives.com/wordpress/books-2/frail/

My website contains excerpts of all my works, as well as interesting historical tidbits. Please stop by!
susannaives.com

Sign up for my newsletter to receive information about my exciting upcoming releases.
http://eepurl.com/bO51hv

FRAIL

December 1860

I should have taken the first train out of London.

Music thundered in Theo's ears. His hands shook. Sweat poured down his back, drenching the shirt beneath his evening coat.

On the chalked dance floor, couples swept to a waltz being played by a chamber orchestra of violins, flutes, and a harp. The light of the gas flames in the chandeliers glistened on the silk and taffeta skirts as they swished to the lift and fall of the dance. The young ladies' cheeks were flushed from the heat, and their hair was styled into stiff waves and spirals and adorned with beads and flowers. The scent of perfumes and men's hair oils burned Theo's nose. He balled and flexed his hands, taking long breaths to slow his racing heart. The last five years tending his gardens and living like a monk in the Snowdonia mountains of North Wales hadn't managed to lessen his angst at coming back to the city.

"Pray, Theo, it's but a dance, not a parliamentary debate," Theo's stepmother Marie, the Countess of Staswick, said. She scanned the ballroom with her shiny cocoa eyes. "You are going to scare off the ladies with that glower you wear."

He forced a smile. Before him, another season's fresh crop of debutantes whirled—one of whom, his stepmother had assured him, would make a lovely bride. Marie had never surrendered her belief that the soft arms of a loving wife could "cure" Theo where quack doctors and opiates had failed.

"Much better." Marie inspected Theo's smile from under her long lashes and then glanced at her husband. "All the ladies are peeking at your son—wanting to dance with such a handsome man. He resembles his father, of course." She laughed.

"You look fine this evening." The words sounded stiff on his father's lips. It was the same compliment he had given Theo when he had entered the parlor dressed in black coat and white cravat.

Over the last year, the two men had reached a raw, uncomfortable truce. When Theo and his brothers were growing up, the earl never lavished praise on his sons. His voice boomed in the House of Lords, but, at home, he preferred to communicate with a curt word or a hard look of disapproval. Now he was nervous and awkward around his middle son, repeatedly asking him how he was feeling, about his home in Wales, or his opinion on political matters. Both flailed for the right words, inevitably choosing the wrong ones. A simple *sorry* couldn't wipe away the pain Theo had inflicted on his family after returning from Crimea. In those months, he hadn't been able to sleep for the racing of his mind, which he tried to numb with alcohol, opium, flesh, and violence. He had passed his nights stalking alone through the streets, his eyes darting from side to side, constantly watching, his muscles flexed, on a razor's edge, and ready to reach for the rifle no longer at his side.

"I know one of these pretty ladies is going to fall in love with you," the earl said, straining to sound casual. He looked at his wife as if to ask, *Did I say the right thing?*

Theo heard a burst of tingling female laughter rise above the music. Several couples quickly stepped aside for a young lady who had forgotten all rhythm of the dance and was spinning wildly under her partner's arm. Her pastel blue gown was cut so low the ruffle of lace running across her breasts and shoulders barely covered her nipples. Black spiraling curls lifted in the air around her white porcelain face. A reckless grin hiked her high cheekbones and sparkled in her arresting eyes. They weren't the dark brown or deep gray eyes he would have expected with her coloring, but a light silvery blue, matching her diamond necklace.

"Who is that?" he asked, although in his gut he already knew the answer. She fit all the descriptions he had read in the papers: exotically beautiful and wild.

"*That* is Miss Helena Gillingham," his stepmother answered, confirming his assumptions. She leaned closer until her mouth was near his ear. "If you won her, you could turn Grosvenor Square into your private garden. No need to traipse off to Wales anymore."

His throat burned. His poor parents had no inkling Helena's father, John Gillingham, was the reason he had torn himself away from Wales for the first time in five years.

"I think even Petruchio would draw the line at her," he quipped dryly. "Is her father in attendance?"

Marie shook her head. "I rarely see the man at parties. But your father converses with him at the club almost every day."

Theo replied with a terse *hmm* and edged along the wall to get a better view of the human whirlwind as she slipped from her partner's grasp and spun like a top into an aging couple. They shot her a hot glare.

"I'm so terribly, terribly sorry," she said, appearing anything but contrite as she pressed her hand to her mouth to stem the flow of giggles.

So this was the daughter of the man who was bilking hundreds of his fellow men.

She turned as if she knew he was thinking about her, her unsettlingly pale eyes locking on his. Her gaze swept over his person, returning to his face. An odd combination of heat and cold spread over his skin. He couldn't deny her allure. She had the type of sparkling gaze that trapped a man like an insect pinned to a board. She studied him a moment more, then her lips formed a *moue*, and she gave a saucy toss of her head.

Was she flirting with him? A grave error.

A number of men who had served with him in Crimea had recommended he place his savings in her father's bank. They trusted the banker with large parts of their modest savings, dependent on his five percent return. Theo first became suspicious of the banker when his neighbor, Emily, casually mentioned she had repeatedly written to her cousin Gillingham in London for help when her husband and son were first sick. She received no reply. What began as mere curiosity about the wealthy man turned into Theo's two year-long investigation into his fictional board members, dubious stock trades and holdings, and doctored financial statements. That morning, Theo had disembarked the train from Chester and met with a Scotland Yard officer named Charles Wilson who had agreed to keep Theo's name in confidence.

"Gillingham has set up a phony board of directors for his bank and is siphoning money to himself by giving loans to suspicious companies," Theo had told the officer. He pointed to Sheffield Metalworks of which Gillingham owned a majority of shares and sat on the board with several of his cronies. The machinery was outdated, and the company received perhaps one or two small railroad contracts a year. Why would Gillingham have this firm and others like it except to hide money?

"I estimate about seven hundred thousand pounds has been intentionally taken from his bank's capital," Theo had continued. "He is stealing. He is going to run and leave his customers—my soldiers—with the full extent of his liability."

And now Gillingham's daughter flirted and twirled in a shining silk gown financed by the same men who were sent to war in ridiculous uniforms, and made to contend with flimsy tents and no food. Theo may have left the army when he stepped onto the London docks after two years in Crimea, insisting on being called a plain *mister* again, no longer Colonel Mallory, but that primal need to take care of his men remained.

"She's a beauty, isn't she?" a voice said, jerking him from his thoughts.

Theo turned. Beside him stood a young man with bristle-like, blonde whiskers and a squared dimpled chin. "Eliot," Theo whispered.

"Pardon?" The man blinked.

Damn. Eliot was dead. One of a dozen that day who were still reeking of dysentery when he was lined in a ditch beside his dead comrades and covered with dirt.

"I'm sorry," Theo muttered. "I'm confused."

The gentleman laughed. "Miss Gillingham does that to a fellow."

Theo made no response and continued along the edge of the dance floor. He knew he should square away a partner for the next set to appease Marie. Instead, he motioned to a servant to bring him some wine. He lingered in a corner, sipped from his glass, and observed Miss Gillingham.

She had traipsed back to her partner. Her lips curved in a childish pout that, no doubt, her admirers found adorable. As she lifted and fell in the 1-2-3 rhythm, her gaze kept drifting in Theo's direction. When the song at last ended, she clasped her partner's arm, allowing him to escort her from the floor, then peeked over her shoulder at Theo—with an invitation in her eyes.

But he had seen enough to satisfy his curiosity about the woman. She was a spoiled, oblivious child, and he wasn't going to let her sit on his conscience. And yet he continued to study the graceful curve of her back as she crossed the threshold into the parlor where the refreshments were laid out. Again, she tossed her curls, casting him a beckoning glance before disappearing into the room.

He finished his wine and signaled for another glass, which he gulped down. He knew he shouldn't drink so much so quickly, but the people and noise were crowding his senses. He sleeked his palms down his face, smoothing the bristles of his beard. His hands were rough and wrinkled, belonging to a man of sixty, not thirty. Under his nails were tiny rims of dirt he couldn't scrub away. He closed his eyes, for a moment letting his mind wander through the memory of his gardens at *Castell Bach yr Anwylyd*. When he had left, the grounds were dormant in the winter. Deep in the soil the bulbs and roots waited out the cold, and all the seeds to be planted were germinating in the green house. Against the enormous sky and vaulting mountains, the oak tree branches were still, stark bones.

* * *

People crowded Helena in the parlor. She muttered the appropriate *just darling* and *oh, how clever* to their chatter as she strained to look over the crush of shoulders, searching for *him*. Her fingers holding her champagne shook; her nerves were electrified. She waited and waited, staring at the threshold as her friends babbled on. *Who was that gentleman?*

The violins began thrumming a new song. A strong hand gripped her arm. "My turn," a voice whispered and began tugging her towards the dance floor.

"No!" she cried, ripping herself free, splashing her drink. She covered her